Cassandra
Parkin

The Winter's Child

Legend Press Ltd, 107-111 Fleet Street, London EC4A 2AB
info@legend-paperbooks.co.uk | www.legendpress.co.uk

Print ISBN 978-1-7850790-3-0
Ebook ISBN 978-1-7850790-2-3
Set in Times. Printed by Opolgraf SA.
Cover design by Anna Morrison www.annamorrison.com

Cassandra Parkin grew up in Hull, and now lives in East Yorkshire. Her debut novel *The Summer We All Ran Away* was published by Legend Press in 2013 and was shortlisted for the Amazon Rising Star Award. Her short story collection, *New World Fairy Tales* (Salt Publishing, 2011) was the winner of the 2011 Scott Prize for Short Stories. *The Beach Hut* was published in 2015 and *Lily's House* in 2016. Cassandra's work has been published in numerous magazines and anthologies.

Visit Cassandra at
cassandraparkin.wordpress.com
or follow her @cassandrajaneuk

For the woman on Scarborough seafront:
So far it's all been true

Chapter One
Saturday 14th October 2017

In the warm cigarette dimness of the caravan, the Roma woman's eyes are shrewd and bright.

"You've lost someone," she says.

We gaze watchfully at each other across a table of polished glass, etched with a cornucopia of flowers. Its bevelled edge is sharp to the sight but not to the touch. I'd imagined the inside of a traditional vardo, painted wood and bright patchworks, but instead I'm surrounded by glass and china and crystal, intermittently set ablaze by the lights of the carriages that dip and wheel above our heads. The cabinet behind my opponent is filled with china girls with arms like ballerinas, waists no wider than their necks and frothing, intricate skirts. Do all showmen live in this impossible delicate luxury? How do they take their homes from place to place without breakages?

The fortune-teller is looking right into my eyes, watching and waiting for a tell. I force myself to sit cool and blank, trying not to be distracted by the fragments of my reflection – blonde hair, blue eyes, slim figure – that appear, startlingly distorted and inverted, in the million reflective surfaces of the caravan.

If my sister Melanie finds out what I've been doing, she'll be furious. I'm supposed to have given this game up years ago. I shouldn't be here.

"A husband, maybe?" The fortune-teller shakes her head. "No, not a husband."

I keep my breathing slow and quiet, in and then out, refusing to let her see the satisfaction this gives me. In fact, I have lost a husband, or rather my ex-husband and I have lost each other, torn apart by the brutal tragedy that ripped through our life like a tornado. When we first married, I imagined that losing John would break my heart. When it finally happened, we were both too exhausted to summon more than a weary acceptance.

"Boyfriend, then." I imagine I can feel the caress of her eyes as they flick, flick, flick over my face like the smooth dry kiss of a snake's tongue, looking for the micro-expressions that will tell her if she's on the right lines. "No, not a boyfriend."

Next she'll change track completely. She'll go for an easy hit so I'll forget about the misses.

"You've come to the Fair since you were a child," she says. "You've loved it all your life. I see you in a hat and coat, holding the hand of a tall man and laughing."

I try not to snort. She'll know from my accent that I'm a local girl, and what else does she need to know to guess how deeply Hull Fair is lodged in my heart? Fair Week is the darkest and most beautiful spell our city casts, a residential street and a patch of waste ground suddenly ablaze with the showmen's last wild gathering before they disperse into a mysterious continental winter, and we all hunker down and wait for the more respectable follow-up of Christmas.

"I see you coming here as an adult, too," she continues. "There's a child with you. I see a little boy in a blue coat, riding on a train. When he gets frightened and cries, you buy him a stick of candy floss."

More easy hits. Not half an hour ago I lifted my nephew Thomas out of the ghost-train and held him tight, trying not to laugh at his wild terror of the man who jumped out at us and rocked the carriage on its tracks. "It's all right," I told him over and over. "It was just one of the guys from the ride. See? Look there and you'll see him do it again... now, shall we get some candy floss?" And three minutes later Thomas's fright is melting stickily on his tongue among the threads of spun sugar. A scene played out thousands of times each night. Perhaps she even watched me, or had one of her fellow showmen watch me, so she'd have something in her pocket to dazzle me with. Perhaps they watch all of us.

Nonetheless, her words conjure another, more tender memory: washing Joel's face in the dim light of the bathroom while John put the car back in the garage. I can still hear the high singing in our ears as they rang to the echo of the pounding music. I can still see the tracks of tears on his cheeks, the sweet pink crust around his mouth.

"A child! That's it. A child. You've lost a child."

Her words come so fast I can't prepare. Stupid Susannah, stupid stupid stupid, walking into the trap like this. She's seen the truth in my face. There's no escape from what's coming.

"A little boy." My whole body twitches with the pain, and she nods in satisfaction. "Give me your hand."

My hands are clenched into fists beneath the table. Perhaps the angle of the glass hides this from her. Perhaps not. I bring them out slowly, forcing my fingers to uncurl. The skin is sticky from the nougat, the chips, the hot dog, the brandy snap, the candy floss for Thomas, which he generously shared with me as we watched Grace twirl solemnly round in a teacup and I held onto the gluey remnants of her toffee-apple. The collective name for these foods is *fair junk*, as in, *Shall we bother with tea or shall we just get fair junk?* John's big scrubbly face and Joel's little rosy one, side by side on the sofa, already dressed in hats and coats because they're clever enough to guess my answer. I swallow tears and force myself to meet the Roma woman's gaze. These memories are sacred. She can't have them.

"He was your boy," she says, almost crooning, as if I'm a fretful child she's lulling to sleep. Her fingers creep over the table and trace out a thin path across my palm. "Your boy. And you lost him. But he hasn't left you. Not yet."

"He's still alive?"

I don't want to ask this but I can't stop myself. This is what they do, the charlatan's terrible gift. They draw you in, they make you believe, and then they cut you open and dabble in your spilled blood with their cold fingers.

"He hasn't left this world," she repeats.

"So is he still alive? Is he out there somewhere? Or is he - ?"

"He hasn't left. That's all I can say."

This is another trick I recognise. When the facts are uncertain, they'll leave themselves as much room as possible. I wrote another blog post about this just three weeks ago, prompted by the desperation of a reader and the lies of a medium in Liverpool, titled *Open letter to the mother of J.M.* I should be back at my computer, dealing with the fall-out, but Thomas begged me as only a ten-year-old can ("Please, please, please come with us, please, Auntie Suze..." and when I looked at him severely, "... annah! I was going to say it! I was!"). His delight at successfully teasing me, and the hopeful trust in Grace's blue eyes, were too much. I should be with them, not wasting time and money on rediscovering what I already know. I force myself to smile.

"If I pay you more, will you be able to say more? Is that how it works?"

She flicks her eyes over my face again, and in spite of myself I wince at the shrewd pitiless light that glitters there. Now she'll torture me by telling me about the thin veil that separates the living from the not-living, and that because the veil is transparent to her, she cannot always say on which side our loved ones are. I ready myself for the blow.

"I see him," the woman repeats, and lets go of my hand to light a cigarette. I try not to watch too greedily as she draws in a long rich lungful, holds it, then lets it go again, the frail smoke coiling seductively around my nostrils. I gave

10

up smoking years ago, in the long desperate vitamin-filled alcohol-free desert before Joel. But every now and then, I'll catch a breath of smoke and something stirs in my brain and whispers, *Go on. You know you want to. Just the one. Just one cigarette. What harm can it do now?*

"What are you doing here, love?" she asks, and takes another draw on her cigarette. "You don't believe."

"If you can really see the future and the... the dead and so on, it shouldn't matter if I believe or not. Gravity works whether or not people think it's true."

She hold the smoke a moment longer, then lets it go. "So you're one of them. Think you know how it's done."

Does she know who I am? I write under my real name, my photo is on my website, and while I'm not what anyone could call famous, *Life Without Hope* contains enough vitriol, written over a long enough period of time, to get me noticed by people in the business. Perhaps they keep lists, as scammers are said to do, so they can separate the sworn enemies from the gullible believers.

"All I've heard so far is misses and guesses," I say. "Everyone brings kids to the Fair and buys them candy floss. Just about every little boy I know has a blue coat, and if I hadn't bitten at that one you'd have said *No, wait, a green one*. You don't know anything about—"

With a sudden pounce, she grabs my hand again, pressing it hard against the cold glass table. The ash from her cigarette grows long and pale as the coal burns towards the base.

"Now you listen to me, my love," she hisses. "Here are three things that are true from your past. You were born first and grew up the richest and the prettiest, but your sister was still the lucky one. Your husband loved you and he loves you even now, but he still left you. Your son was all you ever wanted, but he still tore your heart in two."

Her grip hurts, her hands on mine hurt, and the coal of her cigarette is growing close to my skin. I try to take my hand back but she won't let go.

11

"Now, three things from your present. You haven't been here since you lost your boy, but this year you let a child... your niece? No, your nephew... talk you into it. You came with them both, a boy and a girl, and the girl pointed at my caravan and asked if she could go in. You told her no because we're all thieves and liars – oh yes, you did, my love, that's what you said – but the spirits spoke to you and told you it was time to listen. You lied to your sister and her children, and said you were afraid to ride the Ferris wheel but they should go without you, so you could come back here and see me. Did you wonder if that meant something? You're right, my love. It meant everything. You're meant to be here, in my caravan, talking to me. The world's a bigger place than you know."

"You're hurting me. Let me go."

"That's your penance for not believing. Yes, shout if you like, my love, but no one's going to hear you. Now, here are three things from your future that will come true before the year turns."

"Please. No more. I don't want to know. Don't tell me any more. I'm sorry, I shouldn't have—"

"I see three people waiting for you. I see a woman who'll hate you on sight because she's afraid she'll be just like you, then come to love you like a sister. You'll let her get close, then you'll push her away, and the pain will break her heart. I see a man who belongs to someone else, but he'll come to you anyway. You'll let him get close, then you'll push him away, and the pain will break his heart."

This is nothing, it means nothing, an empty performance from an angry show-woman. Despite this, tears come to my eyes. What if I've been wrong all these years? What if she's right? What if it really does mean something that I was drawn to her caravan? Hot flecks of ash drop onto my skin and I flinch.

"I see your boy," she says.

I forget the prickles of pain in my hands.

"I see your boy. He had many who loved him, but he

loved you best of all, you were the centre of his world. You let him get close. Then you pushed him away. You turned away from him. You listened to false advice. And the pain broke his heart."

"Stop it, please, stop it—"

"But he's coming back to you. For better or worse, your boy's coming back to you, my love, and this will be the last Christmas Eve you'll spend without him. The road won't be easy. But if you're strong enough to walk it, then when the snow falls on Christmas Eve you'll see his face again, and you'll know where he's been, and why he's been there." Her face is so close to mine I can see the tiny millimetres of silver at the roots of her lustrous black hair, scented with grease and hairspray. "And then, my love, you'll never be apart again."

She lets go of my hands, but I can't move. I feel as if she's stabbed me through my heart with a silver knife, pinning me to the chair.

"That's all, my love. You've had your fifty quid's worth." She laughs. "Was it good enough, darling? Good enough to believe in? You going to write me up on your website?"

So she does know who I am. It was all a performance. Everything she said was pieced together from the information that's available to anyone with an internet connection. She doesn't know anything about what happened to Joel. I stumble out of the caravan, her mocking words clinging to my back, my head spinning, my knees weak, my hands clumsy, and fall into the crowd, letting the tide carry me down Walton Street. If I was alone, I could simply get lost in the dubious comfort of the company of strangers, but I'm not alone, there's no time, no time, I'm expected elsewhere and I have to pretend everything is normal. So I stop and catch my breath by the greasy metallic warmth of the chip van, breathing deep draughts of fried food and diesel, wishing I had a cigarette, trying to compose myself enough to return to the Ferris wheel where Grace, Thomas and Melanie will be waiting for me.

I plunge back into the Fair, drowning my heartbreak in lights and screams and fumes and thumping music. A long rotary arm skims over the top of the Hook-a-Duck booth and the pounding Europop is overwhelmed by the shrieks of the riders. I pause to watch the Cyclone, forcing myself not to flinch as the carriage hurtles towards me through space, then shoots away again. For those in pain, the Fair is like an anaesthetic, its insistent assault on the senses wiping out all possibility of focused thought or feeling. My phone vibrates in my back pocket.

We're off the wheel but can't see you. You okay?

Sorry, massive queue for the toilets. On my way now.

It's hard to hurry but I do my best, squeezing between slow-moving families, skittering over metallic walkways. Dotted among the bright faces of the riders, watchful showmen balance effortlessly on whirling, uneven floors, their faces so blank and unaffected they might be statues. One man stands beneath the Octopus as it flings its carriages in a perilous vertical spin, so close it looks as if they'll take his head off; but he scrolls through his phone without even looking up. Another spins the cars on the Waltzer, indifferent to pleas and shrieks. His face is serene and empty, as if he's meditating in a green field.

In the puddles beneath the Ferris wheel, Melanie does her best to wrangle Thomas and Grace into standing still and waiting nicely. She's just about got them within bounds, but they won't hold out much longer. When she sees me, and before she gets her face under control, I see exasperation, swiftly suppressed. It's not her fault. I'd feel the same. Grace is telling me something, but the music's so loud I can't make it out. I kneel down so I can press my ear closer to her perfect little mouth.

"Auntie Susannah!" Grace can hardly speak for excitement. "I went all the way up there, look! All the way to the top!" As five-year-olds will, she performs each word, arms windmilling wildly. Beside her, Thomas smiles tolerantly. "And I saw you from the top, and I waved!"

"Grace, you do know you didn't actually see Auntie Susannah," Thomas tells her. Melanie looks at him sharply, but doesn't reprimand him. I suspect he's had to hear this story several times already. Grace looks hurt.

"Did you see me?"

"I think I saw someone," I say, and kiss her plump cheek. She smells of toffee-apple. "Someone waving right at the top of the wheel?"

"Yes! That's what I did! I waved!" She beams. "See, Thomas, I told you Auntie Susannah would see me."

Now it's Thomas's turn to look hurt. I pat his shoulder and give him a wink, letting him in on the deception, and he smiles at me. I'd always imagined my life would be filled with moments like this, effortlessly navigating the tricky waterways of parenting multiple children. Instead...

"Are you okay?" Melanie has always been hyper-attuned to my moods. Now she slips one arm through mine and squeezes gently.

"I'm fine."

"Not too tired yet?"

"Course not."

"Where did you really go?"

The question catches me off-guard, and because I don't have a reply ready, she instantly knows the answer. She looks at me for a long minute.

"Right," she says wearily, and gathers Grace and Thomas together, corralling them like a sheepdog. "Come on, kids. It's Auntie Susannah's turn to pick, and she wants some pictures of you on the galloping horses." Thomas points hopefully to the Mirror Maze. "No, not the Mirror Maze, you're not bashing your nose in again. Galloping horses. Go."

"What happened to your nose?" I ask Thomas, in the brief pool of relative quiet by the dartboard games ("Prize Every Time Free Giant Minion If You Lose Score Over Ten To Win").

"He walked into a glass wall," Grace begins.

"Grace, I'm telling this story. I walked into a glass wall—"

"That's what *I* said—"

"And it made my nose bleed. And it took me ages to get out."

"And when he came out he was crying," adds Grace, with satisfaction.

"Well, if you walked into a wall so hard you made your nose bleed, you'd cry too," Thomas tells her. "And besides, you're too little to go in, so you don't know what it's like, and anyway, stop trying to tell my—"

"That's enough," Melanie tells them both. "No, seriously, that's enough. Nobody's come here to listen to you squabble. Do you want to go on the same horse or separate ones?"

"Same."

"Separate."

"Oh, for God's sake. Okay, Thomas, if you'll go on a horse with Grace without complaining, you can go in the Mirror Maze again. Deal?"

"Deal." Thomas's face is one huge triumphant grin.

The carousel slows, then halts. Grace and Thomas scramble up the steps. Thomas helps Grace heave herself onto their chosen horse, Mickey, and hops up behind her. She leans confidingly back into the comfort of his jacket, and he looks at her for a moment, then drops a brief kiss on the top of her head. Melanie has a five pound note ready but I push her hand away and get to the showman first, hoping to soften her with generosity.

"Okay," says Melanie as the horses begin to twirl. "What d'you think you were playing at?"

"It was just a laugh," I say. Grace and Thomas go past, cherub faces turned outwards, starfish hands waving. I smile and wave back.

Melanie says nothing.

"I just saw the caravan and she didn't have anyone with her so I thought I'd go for it."

Melanie says nothing. Thomas and Grace reappear. I raise my phone and take a photograph.

"It'll make a good post, that's all. It was good material."

Melanie says nothing.

"Look, if I can save just one person from what I went through – if I can reach just one person – save them from believing the shit they spout to get your money—"

My voice cracks. Thomas and Grace reappear. I force myself to smile and wave. The shape of my face isn't right. The pain's showing. I hope they're too little to notice.

"It's just," I say, and I know I should keep lying, because these words will take me dangerously close to collapse, "it's just I saw the caravan. And it… it called to me. I know that's stupid, but it called to me. And I thought, *What if this one's the real deal? Maybe it means something that I'm being attracted to this one?* So I just… I just… I had the money and everything, and I couldn't help myself." Thomas and Grace reappear, but blurrily, framed by tears lit up like jewels by the glow of the lights.

Melanie turns to me then, and takes my hands in hers. I can read on her face all the love and all the exasperation, all the despair and all the longing, the complicated mix of emotions that comes when your older sister acts like an idiot for reasons you understand only too well.

"Suze," Melanie says. She's the only person in the world who's allowed to shorten my name, and even she only does it when no one else can hear. "You know they're all the same. You know that. Better than anyone."

"She told me Joel would come back to me by Christmas."

"She what?" Melanie's hands tighten on mine. "She told you what?"

"She said he'd come back to me by Christmas, and then we'd never be apart again. Why would she say that if she didn't know something? She might know something—"

"Suze, you have to stop this. It's not true. Darling Suze, I don't know where he is, none of us do, but I'm as sure as

I can be that some random Fair woman in a painted caravan can't tell you, all right? Please don't do this to yourself again, you've been doing so well recently. Look, the ride's stopping, I'll go and get the kids."

The watching circle of parents moves around the ride like clockwork, following their children scrambling down from the golden horses, wobbling on dizzy legs, ready to be lifted down while a legion of replacement riders scramble greedily up. John once told me he'd love to film the scene from above, people flowing like blood around the body of the Fair, driven by the beats of the rides as they stop and start and stop again, as lovely as the hearts he repaired on the operating table. He tried to get Joel interested too, to show him the hidden connections that drive the universe, but Joel would grow panicky and anxious and then naughty, frustrated and frightened by his inability to please his father. Thomas and Grace will be back in a moment. They'll want to see the photos. I turn away and try to get my face in order.

It's the sight of the discarded milk carton that does it, tossed carelessly into the black rubbish-sack on top of the polystyrene chip trays and the cheery paper cones. I blink just once and then I'm back in *before*, the very last time our family was together. John and Joel clashing as they so often did, Joel's face alternating between rage and terror, as John shook the plastic bag in his face, battering down Joel's *Don't I get any privacy then* and *It's not even illegal in lots of places* with *How dare you bring this crap into our house, how dare you put our family at risk like this?* Joel turning away, slamming the front door, yelling something about his friends understanding him and one day he'd live with them and never see either of us again, pausing to drain the milk carton into his mouth and fling it furiously into our front garden. I ran into the front room to watch him go, and our eyes met through the glass and in that moment I saw the little boy he still was, despite being fifteen and taller than I was. *Help me, Mum. Help me. I need you.*

And I would have gone after him. I would have run down the street and grabbed his hand, told him it was all right, it was all right, I'd call the school and say he was ill, and we'd get the bus into town, go to a café and get some breakfast and talk about it. But then John was there beside me, and when I tried to follow Joel he put his arms around me in what felt almost like a hug, and he said, "Not this time, pet. We're at the end of our tether here. We need to get tougher with him. Let him go. We'll talk about it tonight." And his embrace was so warm and solid and comforting, and I was so tired, and he seemed so sure he was right.

So I stayed in the living room with John. I did not follow Joel down the street. I did not phone the school to say Joel was ill. We did not get the bus or go to a café. Joel went to school, registered for his first and second lesson, went out at lunchtime, saying he was going to meet someone, then vanished. His official status is mysterious. Neither definitely living nor definitely dead, he is simply *missing*. One of the thousands who vanish and do not return.

The fortune-teller recognised me, that's all. She knows my story, which is also Joel's story. She was tormenting me with what she knew, and what she knew I wanted to hear, dabbling her hard nicotine fingers in the pool of my neediness, fishing with her cold clever hooks for the money in my purse and the hope in my heart. She was punishing me for making it my calling to protect others from the spiritualists and the mediums and the spirit-channellers, the cold-readers and frauds and the vultures who scour the newspapers, the deceivers, the liars, the hungry ones, the greedy ones. I know all this. I should write this up as a blog post, another warning in a long chain of warnings, and then I should forget every jaggedy hurting word.

But instead I stand still and silent in the heart of the Fair and stare at the tawdry plush creatures that dangle bright and hopeful from the booths and replay her words, locking them into place in my head. I'm a fool, and a hypocrite, and I so desperately want to believe that what she told me is true. I want this to be the last Christmas I will spend alone, waiting up until midnight in the vain and foolish belief that at last, this year, my lost boy will come home to me.

Life Without Hope:
Five more ways psychics fool us

1. They do their research

Some psychics use pre-event registration to harvest personal details. Once they have your name and your age, they can often find out if you've lost someone recently. If you, like me, have a loved one who's missing, know that we're particularly vulnerable to this because we do everything we can to get ourselves and our stories into the public eye.

2. They exploit large groups and the laws of probability

Large events open to the public are popular with psychics, because they can use the *law of probability* to quickly score lots of easy hits. They'll take a look at the people in the room and start throwing out some names. *I have a message here from someone whose name begins with D, perhaps David or Dave. Someone called Jim or James or Jamie, is anyone hoping to make contact with them?* Chances are, someone in the room will pick up on the names they're offering. They do the same for common diseases of old age. *Did she have trouble with her heart? Her heart, or maybe her joints, definitely something that affected her mobility a bit?*

3. They know how to exploit contradictions

When they describe our lost loved ones, they'll use sweeping statements and opposing descriptors to sound specific while staying very vague. *She enjoyed her own company, but she loved a good get-together when she was in the mood. He worked hard at putting other people first, but he could be a little bit self-centred from time to time. She loved to laugh, but there was more to her than that. Sometimes she was very serious.*

4. They get us to fill in the blanks

A skilled psychic makes sure their sitters do at least half

of the work. *I'm seeing a letter*, they say, or *There's a piece of jewellery that's significant.* Then they'll ask, *What could that mean, do you think?* And before we know it, we've done their job for them.

5. They blur the timelines

When they make a prediction that turns out to be a miss, they'll say it's just because it hasn't come true yet. Don't know anyone called Bob? Not yet received that letter? *Hold onto that; it will be important in the future.*

Ultimately, all of this only works because we let it. When all other hope has been taken from us, we want to believe that this might work. It's hard for us to recognise how much we collaborate in deceiving ourselves. But the truth is, that's what is happening. They thrive off our belief. We're what keep their profession alive.

Posted on 24th November 2013
Filed to: Why All Psychics Are Frauds
Tags: psychic fraud, missing people, support for families, Susannah Harper, Joel Harper

Chapter Two
Sunday 15th October 2017

In the silent darkness of my bedroom when we return from the Fair, as the showmen pack away their stalls for another year and Saturday tips over the peak of midnight and becomes Sunday, I dream that I'm standing on a wooden platform by water. Something has happened to disrupt my senses, because the world around me is dim and fuzzy and the smell of the river – brown and barren, the scent of sterile earth turned over in winter – pours off the surface and coils around me like the smoke from the fortune-teller's cigarette.

As I stand and breathe in the muddy fumes, I realise that there is someone there with me, standing just behind me and to the left, close enough that if I reached out my hand behind me it would meet theirs. I can't tell if they are a friend or an enemy.

"Help me," I say, without turning round, without knowing who I'm speaking to. "I need you to help me. Please help me. I'm lost." And when two hands clasp my waist, I can't tell if they want to embrace me or to push me into the water.

If this were a film of my life I would wake flailing and gasping, struggling from the strait-jacket of sleep into violent consciousness. Instead I wake quietly, smoothly, and sit up and fold back the duvet as stealthily as if there's still someone beside me in the bed who is exhausted and needs his sleep, someone who if I wake him will reach out and smile and draw me back beneath the covers. I've slept alone for four years, but I still sleep only on my side of the bed.

I make myself wait before reaching for my phone. This is part of the discipline I've learned to impose on myself, to keep myself sane and well. Hope is the enemy, pinning you to the past with an iron spike that will gradually corrode inside you. I have a text waiting, but I know it won't be from Joel.

The message is from Melanie. Before I open it, I make myself smile, because the actions of your body can be used to compel your brain into feeling better emotions. I've been unlucky in one terrible way, but lucky in many small ways, and since I can't get back what I've lost, I have to make the best of what I still have. I'm lucky that my sister loves me, and that her children also love me. I'm lucky that, amid the busy mundanity of getting two exhausted overexcited children to sleep, she's taken the time to text me. Perhaps it's to confirm plans for my birthday, or an invitation to join them at the local fireworks display for Bonfire Night. Perhaps there will be a picture of Thomas and Grace, fast asleep in Melanie and Richard's bed after our wild and beautiful night at the Fair. Perhaps in their sleep, they will be clutching the prizes they won on the Hook-a-Duck stall.

There is no picture, only words like tiny snakes waiting to strike:

Hey it's me. Can we have a chat about Grace and nightmares about being taken away by bad people please? She's woken up twice already. – Mx

The time-stamp is 2.15am.

My heart thumps guiltily, although I can't think why. The stolen-by-the-Fair-people story resurfaces in the school playground at the beginning of every October, passed down through the generations along with the woman who died in a fire and bit off her lip and and the boy who choked on a gob of chewing gum and the old man who keeps mad dogs in a shed at the back of the playing fields. Melanie must know this. She must know I'd never, ever do anything to frighten Grace. When she was born, a scant six months after Joel's disappearance, everyone was terrified that I would take against her, but instead she became the first small glint of light that reminded me life might still be worth living.

Still, I'll go and see them later, maybe take Grace a present. Something with Peppa Pig on perhaps, or a new stuffed toy. I allow myself to replace the picture of Grace waking in terror with one of Grace beaming with joy over a new plushy animal. Melanie says I spoil her, but I can't help myself.

That's it. No more text messages. The first part of my daily admin's completed. There are things I need to do on my blog, but those can wait until after breakfast.

I take a shower. Wash my hair. Get dressed. Go to the kitchen and make myself coffee, peel a banana and eat it. I watch the clock while I do this, making sure I don't take too long over any particular step, because even though all my deadlines are self-imposed, I need structure to my life. When I've eaten my banana and drunk my coffee, I go out into the back garden.

The ancient apple tree at the bottom of the garden is growing ugly with spotted yellow leaves, its usual preparation for winter. A few apples lie rotting in the long grass around the trunk where the lawnmower doesn't quite reach. Once the leaves have fallen and the grass has died back the tree will become beautiful again, its rough bark and twisted branches stark against the winter sky, but for now it's simply a nuisance, creating a dank mouldy carpet that will have to be raked up before it smothers the lawn. Nevertheless, I walk down to it and lay my hand against the bark. When I look up at the house next door, I see my neighbour, standing in the window of the back bedroom and looking down at me.

The man who lives next door is frail and white-haired

like an angel, and like an angel he watches over me with a tireless silent benignity. He was described to me by the people we bought the house from as *The most perfect neighbour we've ever had. He lives on his own, dead quiet, but he never complains, even when the children are shrieking the place down. God, we wish we could take him with us.* He took a tender interest in Joel, shuffling down his front path to peer into the pram and touch a thin dry finger to Joel's peach-fuzz cheek when I, proud and shaky, made my first solo voyage around the neighbourhood. When I crept out of the house on the mad, purposeless searches that consumed the emptiness of my nights when Joel first left us, I would often come home to find him standing in the front windows of his house, and when I looked at him he would raise one arm in greeting and I would know I was not alone. Once, he wrote a note that saved me.

And on the morning after John left me, beneath the apple tree was a bunch of long-stemmed white roses wrapped in a cone of paper. I went out to gather them in, turned around and saw my neighbour standing in the back bedroom, the room the local gossips had told me he had not been into for more than twenty years, since his own daughter died in there. As I stared up at him in wonder, clutching my roses, I saw there were tears on his cheeks and something passed between us and I knew I had found the first glimpse of my future. That was the day when I wrote my first blog post for *Life Without Hope*. Since that day, I wake each morning at the same time and make my pilgrimage to the apple tree.

I look up at my neighbour and he looks down at me, and we wave to each other in silent solidarity. *I've made it through another night so that I can be here and make sure you are still alive. I will be here tomorrow.*

The morning wears on. I fill the minutes with the tasks I need to do. When my cleaning is done, I go to the little office we made in the small bedroom over the porch to check my blog for activity.

There are three comments on my most recent post – a short, optimistic piece about giving ourselves permission to move forward – awaiting my approval. I open the first one.

I have read all of your blog and I must tell you that you are a DISGRACE taking away someone's only comfort is knowing that their loved one is watching over them from the other side and you are taking that away from them. I have lost my mam recently and six months after she passed I received a message from the other side telling me she was watching me it was the best comfort I could have and you are taking that away from me and people like you should be ASHAMED are you proud of what you have done you stuck up bitch? Just because you have money you think you know everything but you do NOT know everything no one can prove that there is nothing after this life all we have is faith and so many people have that faith all cultures all over the world and so there must be something we all know it by instinct. Life after death is REAL and we WILL see our loved ones again.

The first comment on anything I post – whether it's to do with mediums or not – is always something like this. While the name of the commenter varies, something about the tone and style makes me think it may be the same person each time. Sometimes I wonder if the writer has genuinely experienced loss, or if they're just a shill for the psychic community.

At least there are no death threats in this one. I approve it without comment. We all find our own ways of coping. There is nothing I can do to help her.

Thank you so much for sharing your inspirational story with the world. Like all parents I have days where I feel 'weighed down' with parenthood and get angry, lose patience etc – but reading your tragic story has reminded me of how precious our children are and that we should cherish them every second. Thank you again for making me a better parent, I have forwarded your blog to all my friends.

I take in a deep sharp breath, then let it go again. MummyOfThree has no way of knowing how much it hurts to read comments like this. What matters is the intention, and I know she meant only kindness. I take another deep breath, approve it, and even force myself to tap out a swift reply – *Thank you for your kind words, they mean a lot. S* – and click on the third comment.

Mummy please is that you it's me Joel Im sorry I ran away I need you to come and get me please help me

This is the third kind of commenter, and the worst. The ghouls who feed on the hope and pain of the vulnerable. The internet is a wild frontier where all things are possible – including the existence of people who get a thrill from tormenting the mother of a lost child. The first time this happened, I called the police station and sobbed joyfully down the phone, telling them that Joel had made contact and all we had to do was track down the IP address and go and find him. The pain of realisation was almost worse than the day Joel first disappeared.

I press the delete button. Am I sure that I want to delete this comment? Yes, I'm sure. I watch in satisfaction as the little wheel spins in the centre of my screen, taking out the rubbish and leaving my blog clean and untouched.

Just as it disappears, I glimpse the name of the commenter. *JoelMoel.*

Oh no. Please no. No no no no no. I stab frantically at my keyboard, trying to stop the deletion. As a last resort, I hold down the off-switch, chanting out loud, "Come on, come on, come on," like an incantation. *Are you sure*, my laptop asks.

Why does everything have to be confirmed? Can't any piece of technology just trust that I know what I want? I click to confirm, pace around the office, chewing on the inside of my cheek as I wait for the computer to shut down so I can turn it back on again. *Count to ten*, John used to tell Joel when he got impatient and tried to restart things too quickly. *No, come on, Joel, don't cry about it, just count to ten!* I count out loud, forcing myself to be patient. Power on. Welcome screen. Log in. Open up the browser. Back onto my blog. It all takes an unbearably long time.

It's gone. The comment from JoelMoel has disappeared. But no, I don't need to panic yet, it must be possible to get it back. I search through my admin page. There's no sign of a 'deleted comments' section. No. No. This can't be happening.

It's all right. I still don't need to panic. The internet is for ever; you can always get everything back. A quick Google search – *recover deleted comments Wordpress blog* – leads me to a user forum filled with exhortations to create database back-ups and smug reminders that we should only delete things if we're sure we don't want them. Then, a nugget of hope. Do I get email notifications of comments on my blog? Yes, I do, indeed I do. Oh, thank God, thank God. I open my email folder with trembling fingers.

PinkyBear1248 has commented on your post. MummyOfThree has commented on your post. That's it. No more. I scroll back and forth, open both notifications in case they've somehow chain-messaged into a single thread. Nothing. Nothing. Where is the notification for JoelMoel? Where is it? Where has it gone? What have I done?

"I'd like to speak to DI Armstrong," I tell the officer at the desk. "Or leave a message for him if he's not working today?"

"DI Armstrong. Okay. Can I ask what it's regarding?"

"It's to do with my son, he disappeared and I might have found some new evidence—"

"Your son, who disappeared… and maybe some new

evidence. Okay. Can I take your name please?"

"It's Susannah Harper. And my son's Joel, Joel Harper."

Does the name mean anything to her? It's impossible to say. She takes my details, and in return gives me the particular nod and half-smile that police officers must learn in training college – both open and aloof, conferring no status, creating no sense of expectation that may be awkward later, a greeting equally prepared for the possibility that I am a victim, a witness or a criminal. No matter what horrors or hilarities they're presented with, the officer on the desk will always offer the same attitude. *Okay, sir, so just to re-cap, you're saying you've been assaulted in your sleep by someone who you believe to be from another planet, and you'd like us to investigate. Can you just take a seat over there, please, sir, and an officer will be with you shortly.* Something I've learned about police officers: their public persona is a carefully cultivated air of industrious boredom. Crime as admin. The door behind the desk swings open.

Whenever I see Nick, I experience that small electric jolt as my body registers once more how good-looking he is. His skin is smooth and brown, his square jaw dusted with stubble. His nose is strong with a bump over the bridge, just imperfect enough to save him from prettiness. His hair is thick, clipped short. His eyes are large and liquid. His body is lean and strong, but not so impossibly sculpted that your first thought is *That man lives at the gym,* and he fits perfectly into his suit.

I don't want sex, not any more. The loss of my son and the ending of my marriage have sealed me tight in a little capsule of chastity. When I imagine taking my clothes off with a stranger, letting him kiss me and stroke my hair, putting his naked flesh next to mine, the only emotion I can conjure is a blank curiosity – how could I ever have wanted to do such a thing in the first place? But sometimes, when I see Nick, at our regular no-news meetings – *There's nothing new to share unfortunately, but this is what's been happening on Joel's investigation, I'm so sorry I don't have anything more productive to tell you* – or even today, when I'm electric with terror and despairing excitement, my body forgets for a moment.

"Susannah." Just for a minute, before he forces his mouth into the usual professional half-smile, I see something warmer and realer, as if he's genuinely pleased to see me. "How're you doing? I gather you've got something new that might help us find Joel?"

"Yes, yes, I have. Well, I think I have, it might be nothing but it might be important so I thought I'd better come straight away." I know I'm talking too fast but I can't help it, any more than I can help the way my breathing is growing fast and frantic or the trembling in my hands.

"Okay, no need to panic. We've got time. Calm down now. Deep breaths. No rush. Good. That's it."

"I'm sorry."

"Don't be. It's good, okay? It's really good. Come down to the meeting room and we'll have a chat."

Nick's good at calming down frantic visitors. I think he could defuse a bomb simply by talking to it in that calm, reassuring voice. I breathe deeply as we walk, get my thoughts in order. Nick opens a door, then takes a startled step back.

"Oh. I do apologise—"

In the corner of the room facing the door stands a woman, one arm wrapped around herself, chewing fiercely on a candy-pink fingernail. She's small and slim, her tight little body poured into skinny jeans and a bright pink t-shirt. Her hard, pretty, pitiless face makes me think of a weasel. She wears her make-up like armour, her gel-painted nails like weapons. She would have been the kind of girl who used to frighten me when I had to pass them on the way home from school. When she sees Nick, her expression turns dark with hope and terror.

"I don't have any news," he says instantly.

Her eyes harden into little black stones. "Well, why am I even talking to you then? And who are you?"

"I'm... my name's Susannah. Susannah Harper." Her gaze, that hard girl I-could-bray-you stare, makes me quail. What does she want from me? "I don't work for the police... I just... my son went missing five years ago and I—"

"Oh, shit. Oh no. What the hell are you doing here?"

"Mrs Nelson, there's no need to get upset." Nick steps forward to block the other woman's view of me. "I'm really sorry we disturbed you, I hadn't realised this room was occupied. Tell me who you're waiting for, and I'll go and find out what—"

Nick might as well not be in the room. The woman's eyes are fixed on me. "Go away. Get out. Get out. I don't want to talk to you."

"I'm not here to talk to you! I told you, my son's missing and I—"

"I know who you bloody are. I recognise you. You had that boy, what was he called?"

"My son, Joel, he went missing five years ago and—"

"Five years. Oh, fuck no, not five years. No, I can't do five years. I can't, I can't, I bloody can't, I'll go mad. Go away. My Ryan's not going to be gone for five fucking years, you hear me? I'm not like you. I'm not." Her face is crumpled tight with the effort of not crying, but despite her best efforts, there are tears on her cheeks. She wipes them away with a tattooed wrist. "I don't need your help because my son's coming back, all right? He's just giving me and his stepdad a scare and he's coming back. He'll be back today. I know it. Okay? I know it."

"Jackie?" The room's growing crowded. This time it's a young police officer, her face thin and tight with patience, carrying a car seat where a sturdy dough-faced baby in an elaborate pink dress screeches lustily. "There isn't any news. It's just Georgie, I think she's missing you." She holds the baby out like a talisman. Above the frilly rim of the dress, the face is puce with rage.

"Jesus Christ, why d'you let her get into this state?" Mrs

Nelson – Jackie – snatches the car seat from the officer, working furiously at the buckles. A few seconds of effort and the baby's free of the seat and draped over her mother's shoulder. "Lot of bloody use you lot are. There. It's all right. You're all right. Stop that racket now. Are you hungry? Mummy'll find your bot-bot."

I have to fight the urge to offer help, to take the baby from her while she hunts for the bottle. I used to seek out opportunities to hold other women's babies, even the angry ones, even the smelly ones, even the ones who would shriek, for no apparent reason, for hours. From the look on the younger officer's face, we're not alike in this. *I'm never having one of them*, her expression seems to say. *Sexist pigs, putting me in charge of the bloody baby.* Or maybe I'm making this all up to distract myself from the envy that still pricks me, of women who reproduce frequently and apparently without effort.

Jackie finds the bottle, drops tiredly into a chair, plugs the nipple into baby Georgie's mouth. The yells are replaced with a ravenous sucking and grunting. I wonder if the milk's warm or cold, how long it's been in her bag. I was always so careful with Joel's milk, but then he was my first. *You're more relaxed with the second*, Melanie said when Grace was born. I never had the chance to find out. Jackie glares at us as if she might stab us both. I'd thought the act of feeding her baby might soften her, but she isn't giving an inch.

"What you still doing here?"

"There's no need to get angry. Who are you waiting for? I'll find out how long they'll be."

"Not you! Her!" Her hand clutches tighter around Georgie's pale, plump thigh. "I want her out of this room right now, you hear me?"

"I'm sorry, I only came in here by accident. I'll go now."

"Well, fucking good! Cos what happened to you is not going to happen to me, all right? My son's coming back. He's coming back. He'll call me soon. And he'll come home. Now get lost and leave me alone."

I close the door on the sight of Jackie, crouched protectively over her daughter, her hand with its chewed pink nails grasping the baby's strong chubby leg. Nick is looking at me anxiously.

"I am so sorry about that."

"It's all right."

"Are you okay? You want a cup of tea or something?"

"No, I'm fine. Honestly."

"You probably gathered her son's missing. Jackie Nelson, her son's Ryan but he's Watts, Ryan Watts. Been gone just over two weeks now. It was on the news."

Something tickles in the back of my memory. A woman with black hair and a tanned face, and a man with a neck as wide as his head. A story I turned over quickly before it could sink its claws too deep.

"The baby's to a different fella," Nick adds. "She had three with Ryan's dad, Ryan's the youngest, and they split up when Ryan was two, he hasn't been in contact since. Brought them up on her own. Didn't do a bad job really, all things considered. Then she met a new bloke, and now they're married and they've got a new baby..." He sighs. "She's in the angry stage at the moment. Had a right go at us this morning. Reckons we're not doing enough to find him. Wants to know why his face isn't on the six o'clock news every night."

I think about that fierce little face, that lithe ferocious body, that heavy make-up. Her spikey nails and spikey gaze. Her tattoos. Her accent, placing her as precisely as a pin stabbed into a map, *This one's a Hull girl all the way through.* Her terror, perfectly disguised as hostility. Missing fifteen-year-old boys from tough backgrounds don't make for good television.

"Sorry you had to cop for it too," Nick adds.

"It's fine. I'm tougher than I look."

He smiles then, his real smile, not the smooth professional

mask with its cool aloof look and limited range of movement. "I know, but I don't want a civilian getting into a fight on the premises. The paperwork takes hours. I'm drowning as it is." He smiles as he says this, opens another door and ushers me in, sits me down opposite him across the table, takes out his notebook. "Now, what was it you wanted to tell me about?"

I'd almost forgotten why I'm here. I take the seat opposite him, compose my breathing.

"It was a comment on my blog. I know, I get them all the time but this was different."

"What did it say?"

"It said…" I breathe through the pain, make myself speak slowly and clearly. "I can't remember exactly, but it was something like *Mummy, this is Joel, I'm sorry I ran away; can you please come and get me.* But this one was different, it really was! The name—"

"Just one sec." Nick's notes are neat and careful, recording everything in its proper order, refusing to be hurried. Conditioned by decades of crime dramas, I'd imagined a missing-persons investigation to be frantic and panicky, all tense jaws and shouty phone calls, everyone rushing into cars and screeching off at top speed. Instead it's a careful meticulous sifting of possibilities. "Was that the whole message? Did it mention any location, for example?"

"No, no location, nothing like that."

"Did it mention a time or a date?"

"No."

"And definitely nothing about location? Not a description of where he was? Like somewhere warm, or somewhere bright, anything like that?"

What Nick is truly picturing is *somewhere cold, somewhere dark*. His careful kindness makes me want to weep.

"No. Nothing."

"Okay. That's okay." Another little pause while Nick records my answers. He has a long slender scar on the back of one hand. I first noticed it when he took the initial report on

Joel, sitting in our living room writing comprehensive notes while John talked about Joel and I sat and trembled, longing to get up and run around the neighbourhood, searching in dark corners and behind garden fences. I noticed everything that night. The smear on the frame of the mirror where I'd tripped over Joel's trainer and saved myself with a newly-lotioned hand. The dust on the top of the photographs we had taken when Joel was eighteen months old. The scar on Nick's hand. The expression on his face.

"So, tell me about the name."

"It was Joel Moel. That's M-o-e-l. It was a joke between us. When he was little he loved *Wind in the Willows*, I read it to him every night and he loved Mole because it rhymed with Joel. And he always thought it must be spelt m-o-e-l, and he was amazed when he found out that it wasn't. No one else would know about that, Nick, no one."

"So you called him Joel Moel? And it was that specific spelling?"

"Yes, and his birth year as well."

"Was it something you only called him when you were on your own? Or did you call him Joel Moel in front of John, for example? Would he have known about it?"

"Yes, of course John knew, but no one else."

"Did John ever call him that name?"

"Yes… yes. Yes, he did." And Joel sometimes accepted it, and sometimes grew angry, declaring it to be *Mummy's special name for me, you're not allowed to use it, Daddy*. John tried his hardest to find this funny, but I could see the hurt in his eyes.

"Okay, so you and John both knew the Joel Moel nickname."

"Yes, but John would never—"

"I'm just making sure we know all the people who might know the nickname. Did you call him it in front of the rest of the family? His aunt and uncle? His cousins? Close friends?"

"I… probably, I don't know. Yes, I suppose we must have."

"Okay." Another pause for note-taking. Nick is collecting facts, but it also feels as if he's talking me down from a very high place, taking everything slowly, cautiously, keeping his voice orderly and calm. Something's draining out of me, but I can't tell if it's anxiety or hope.

"Did you ever write his nickname down? Like in a birthday card, or on a form for school, anything like that?"

"Yes, I signed all his birthday cards to Joel Moel, always."

"And how about Joel himself? Would he have signed cards to other people that way?"

Joel's little face as he came into my bedroom on Mother's Day, his tray bearing a bowl of cornflakes, a mug of tea and a vase of daffodils. The card was resting against the vase, his giant exuberant handwriting sprawling all over the envelope.

"Cards to me, yes, always. Not to anyone else."

"Would other people have been able to see the cards?"

"I... yes, I suppose so. I put them on the mantelpiece."

"How about cards to his friends? Would he have signed like that to them?"

"No."

"Not even his close friends? Or notes or anything?"

"No. Definitely not. It was a private family name, he wouldn't have used it to his friends. Look, I can see what you're getting at – there are some other people who would have known his nickname and how to spell it, but they wouldn't ever – I mean, this is John you're talking about, and Richard and Melanie. They wouldn't... not ever—"

"No, I'm sure they wouldn't." Another sanitisation to save my feelings. Nick is a police officer; he's seen everything and trusts no one. "It's just that they might have mentioned to someone else that Joel had this nickname, that's all. And his friends might have read it in his card. Maybe even teased him about it. The point is, it's not impossible that someone else – even someone you've never met – might know Joel had this nickname, and they might be using it to torment you."

"Oh God. You're right. I know you are. I'm so sorry."

"Don't be sorry. And don't feel guilty. But what made you come and see me about this one?"

"It was stupid, I'm sorry, I don't mean to waste your time."

"No, Susannah, it's not a waste of time, this is my job. I promise. That's not what I mean. What I'm asking is, I know you get a lot of these. So what made this one stand out to you?"

This is the part that always takes me by surprise; that Nick is on my side. He believes in me. Despite the long silence of the years, he hasn't given up, any more than I have. He too has faith that one day Joel will be found.

"Was it definitely just the nickname? Was there something in the language, maybe? A particular phrase that stood out? Something about the time it was sent?"

At first, in the early days when they still thought John or I might have done something to Joel, I was afraid of Nick. His questions were so careful and relentless, so pointed and so unexpected. It felt like he was inside my head, slicing my brain into pieces with a scalpel. I was terrified to lie because I needed him to know everything – even the bad stuff, the hard stuff – in order to find Joel. But I was also terrified to tell him the truth, in case he thought I – or, more likely, John – had done something to Joel and would stop looking for our living son and start looking only for a body and, in stopping the search, miss something that might mean he would never be found again. Now I find comfort in knowing that if there is anything to be found, Nick will uncover it.

"No. Sorry. No."

"Take your time. Think back to when you opened the message. Remember how it made you feel. What made you think this was important?"

I close my eyes. I think back. Nick waits. He's good at dealing with silence.

"No. Nothing. There's nothing. Just the nickname. It was the nickname. That was what stood out to me. I've never – no one's ever – they've sent me some awful stuff but nothing with his nickname – I'm sorry, I shouldn't have—"

"Come on, Susannah. You know I can't help if you're not honest with me. What's the point of keeping things back from me?"

"Because I'm ashamed. It's so stupid. You're going to laugh."

"I won't laugh. When have I ever laughed? You can tell me anything. Anything at all."

"I went to see a fortune-teller," I admit. "The one at the Fair. And she told me, she told me—"

Nick waits, patient as a rock by the side of the road.

"She told me Joel was coming home. She told me he'd come back to me by Christmas. And then, the day after, I got that message, and I thought… oh, it's so stupid, isn't it? I can't believe I fell for it."

"I saw Derren Brown once," says Nick. "He got people up on stage, told them all sorts of stuff about their dead relatives. Special jokes only they knew about, clothes they used to wear, favourite foods, all sorts. And it felt so real. He said at the start of the show, and before the act, and all through the act, and right at the end of the act – *This is all an illusion, I can't see the future, I can't talk to the dead* – and still I went away thinking, *Bloody hell, what if he really can? What if it's all true?* But it's not. I know it's not."

"I know, my God, I ought to know, I blog about this the whole time, I'm so sorry."

"The point is, they make you feel like it's true. That's what they do. Even when they're telling you it's not real, it can still feel like it might be. Don't feel bad about falling for it."

"So you definitely think it was a hoax."

"We can take a look at the comment. See if we can find out anything. We won't get much but whatever there is, we can find."

"I deleted it," I confess. "Before I even called you. And once you've deleted them you can't get them back. So it was stupid even to come and tell you. And then I couldn't even find the email notification, so now I'm wondering if it... I mean, what if I just imagined it? I'm so sorry, I'm wasting your time."

"You needed someone to talk to," Nick says, with that gentle devastating kindness. "But try not to torture yourself any more, okay?"

When I dab at the skin beneath my eyes, my finger comes away smudged with watery black.

"My mascara's running."

"You look gorgeous. But my missus swears by a pair of cheap dark sunglasses. She reckons you can hide anything behind them."

"How's she... um, how she's doing?"

He looks at me shyly. The brief glimpses we've had into each other's lives have made a tender place between us where we both tread gently.

"All right. She's all right. Having a good patch at the moment. Not too up, not too down, just calm and steady. New meds seems to be doing the trick. We're making the most of it."

"That's good."

"I read your blog the other day. Actually I read your blog every time you update it. You're such a good writer."

"Oh... thank you." Now I'm the one made shy. "Thanks for talking me down."

"Any time. It's what I'm here for."

"Is there still any chance he might come home?"

"It's always a possibility."

Always a possibility. Nick's careful sidestepping of what he really thinks. I've known for a long time now that Nick believes Joel is dead, lost to drugs or alcohol or accident or malice. The case remains open as long as they don't find a body, but that's the best outcome he's expecting by now. But because he's a kind man, he never says this.

In my head, I know that Nick is right. But my heart is stubborn and treacherous, because it secretly believes Joel is still alive. Deep within my chest is a rhythm that began beating the first time Joel was put into my arms and I felt his weight, warm and heavy, saw his head turn towards me and heard his high, piercing cry. If Joel was dead, surely that pulse would stutter and come to a halt?

As I climb into my car, I wonder if Jackie has the same connection to her boy Ryan, if she still believes he will return. Or perhaps his place at the centre of her life has been taken by Georgie. Perhaps it's only possible to love one person that much at a time. When John and I were still married, during the times when we argued, this was always the dark heart of our disputes; the hierarchy of love. It was a simple and terrible truth. Even after we finally became parents, John always loved me best, but the one I loved the best was Joel.

Chapter Three
Tuesday October 15th 2002

"Look at that! What a gorgeous picture. Mummy's going to love it. Is it some flowers?"

I hear Joel's gurgling laugh. I'm spying from behind the door, but only because hearing my two boys when they think they're alone is the best and sweetest present anyone could ever give me. "No, Daddy, it's not flowers! It's Scrap-dog."

"Again? No, don't do Scrap-dog for Mummy's card, fella, let's do something else. Why don't you draw some flowers? Or a picture of you and her holding hands?"

"No, I want to do Scrap-dog. This is my very best picture ever."

"Your very best ever?" I love the smile in John's voice. I love knowing that he will be ruffling up Joel's hair as he says it. I love that he's got up early on his day off to spend this precious before-school time with our son. I love that he's let Joel get out paper and crayons, even though it will mean a rush to get him hustled into his coat and out of the door on time. Most of all I love that they're not behaving like this for me, but for themselves. This is just how they are when they're alone, and it's beautiful. "Okay, if it's your very best ever then it's good enough for Mummy's birthday card. Now, are you ready to do something really cool and new?"

"No, thank you, I just want to colour."

My hand pressed shamelessly against my heart, I mouth the words back to myself. *No, thank you. I just want to colour.* That heartbreaking combination of good manners and stubbornness. Can anything be sweeter than my sweet boy?

"Come on," John coaxes. "This is for Mummy, remember? And we love Mummy so much, don't we? So we're going to surprise her by you writing your name in her card!"

"No, Daddy, no, I don't want to."

"Don't worry, I'll help you. Just pick up the pencil and have a go. Look, I'll do it first. Down like this, a long stick straight down... and then a hook on the bottom like an umbrella. Okay? Now you try."

"*No*, Daddy, I don't *want* to."

"Come on, Joel, be sensible. Hold the pencil. No, don't drop it, hold it. Hold it! Properly, not like that. You know how to do this, you're just being stubborn."

"No! I don't want to!"

For two people who love each other so much, they're dreadful at communicating sometimes. If I went in and intervened, I could smooth all of this over in four seconds. Instead I stand behind the door and gnaw at a hangnail.

"Look." John's irritation is growing. "Hold it properly. There. That's right. See? You can do it when you want to. So why were you pretending you couldn't? Hmm? Now then. With me. We'll do it together. A long stick down... come on, Joel, a long stick down..."

"I don't know how to do it!" That note in Joel's voice that John defines as *whining* and I describe as *panic*. I'm confident that my interpretation's better, but I can't make John see things my way without going in. "Daddy, please, I don't want to do this!"

"Well, tough. Sometimes we have to do things we don't want to do. You're five years old now, Joel, you're a big boy. All the other—"

Don't compare him, don't compare him, don't compare him. Perhaps my thought transmits itself to John, because he stops himself just in time. "There's no need to worry about getting it wrong, okay? You just need to try. Together, now. Start at the top... a stick down... no, Joel, no, what do you think you're doing?"

"I did a stick down! Just like you said!"

"Yes, but not all the way onto the table! Come on, fella, make an effort, will you? Don't you want to write your name nicely in Mummy's birthday card and make her proud of you?"

As if I care about that. Joel can do me a scribble if he wants, he can sign with a blob of paint or even a jammy handprint. When I press my ear to the door, I hear a faint sniffle.

"Oh, please, Joel, don't cry. I just want you to give it a go, all right? For me. Or for Mummy, okay? Let's try for Mummy. Pick up your pencil. No. Properly. Come on, pick it up properly. For God's sake, you could at least look like you're trying."

"I'm trying, Daddy!"

"Well, not hard enough. Look. Like this."

"Ow! You're hurting me!"

"No, I'm not, don't be ridiculous. Look. Like this. Straight down."

"Ow! Let go of my hand! Ow, Daddy, you're hurting, you're hurting!"

"No, I'm not, you're just cross because I'm making you do it properly. All the way down, that's right. And then make a hook at the bottom. There you are, look? You made a J. J for Joel. Good work! Look at that! That's brilliant! You made a J for Joel! What are you crying for?"

Joel's wail cuts through me like glass. I have the door open before I know it.

"Hey, Joel Moel. What are you up to? Look at you all dressed for school, good boy."

Joel flings his arms around me and clings on tight, as if I've dragged him from a burning building, as if he's been drowning and I'm his lifeline. John looks at him with such sorrow that for a moment I consider loosening Joel's death-grip on my thighs. For a moment.

"It's all right," I croon, stroking his fluffy head. "Don't be upset. It's all right. You're fine. You're fine. What's made you so sad?"

"I was teaching him how to write his name," John says. Does he know I was listening at the door? Probably, but he's willing to play the charade with me. "He's just upset because he wouldn't hold the pencil properly, so I had to be firm with him. But he got it, didn't you, fella? You did a beautiful *J for Joel*. Come and get it to show Mummy." He holds out the paper towards Joel.

"No!" Joel buries his face mutinously between my knees.

John's face is very vulnerable. *Help me out*, his expression says. *Be on my side. Support me. I'm doing my best here.* With his little hands clutching tight to the back of my jeans, his face smothered blissfully against me, our son asks me for the same thing. Who am I going to choose? I know the answer without having to think.

"He's a bit little for all of this, isn't he?" I say, keeping my voice light and tentative.

"Of course he's not too little, he's at school!"

"But they're still such babies. Why are you trying to rush him?"

"I'm not trying to rush him, I'm trying to—" John shakes his head and sighs. "How am I supposed to help him when you keep—" I know what he wants to say, but I also know he won't say it in front of Joel. Perhaps I should send Joel to his room so we can talk like adults. Or perhaps I should do exactly what I'm doing, which is to stand here and hold onto Joel and defend him against all comers – even his dad – and let him find the comfort and security he needs above all else.

"It's all right, Joel," I repeat, stroking his head. I'm in the right, I know I'm in the right, but I don't quite dare to look at John's face. I watch his hands instead, as he tidies away the paper, the crayons, the card with its picture of Scrap-dog and its single wobbly J. I press Joel against my knees as if by doing so I can keep him safe from all the terrors of the world.

"Come on, Joel, let's kick the ball."

Joel holds Scrap-dog up to his ear.

"Scrap-dog doesn't want to play football."

"Well, I'm not asking Scrap-dog to play, am I? I'm asking you. Look, let's see who can kick it the furthest, shall we? I bet you can beat me if you try."

No, I think, standing in the shadow of the back door where I can watch without being watched. *Don't make it a competition.*

"Come on, you give it a kick. Hard as you can. See if you can hit the fence."

"I want to have a tea party for Scrap-dog."

"Maybe we'll do it later. Come on, let's try kicking the ball first, then we'll do the tea party afterwards. How about that?"

Joel's bottom lip quivers.

"Just give it a kick, fella. You can do it."

Joel takes a mutinous step towards the ball, then kicks out from over a foot away so that the tip of his toe just touches the leather.

"Not like that, like this." John grabs Joel beneath his armpits and moves him closer. Joel wails. "Don't be silly, that doesn't hurt. Now kick it, okay?"

"No, Daddy, no! I'm scared!"

"What? There's nothing to be scared of, you plonker. It's just a ball, it's not heavy or anything."

He's scared of failing you, I think. *He's scared because you wanted a tough little football nut who's good at maths and that's not who Joel is, not at all. He's scared of not living up to what you want from him.*

"Come on now, take a really big swing at it and see how far you can get it. I'll help you." He takes hold of Joel beneath his armpits again, swings him out so that his feet hit the ball. Joel screams and collapses onto the floor. John stands over him, bewildered. His hand hovers over Joel's head, about to ruffle his hair comfortingly.

Do it. Comfort him. Go on. Be soft. Be gentle. Do what I'd do.

John's arms reach down. His hands close around Joel's arms.

"Right then, fella. Get yourself up off the floor and let's have a cuddle and make friends, shall we?"

Joel, lost in despair, rolls into a tight ball and clutches tightly to Scrap-dog.

"All right. All right. Well, if you'd rather stay there than do something nice, that's up to you. You can come in and talk to us when you've finished being silly."

John's sudden return to the house takes me by surprise. I didn't want him to know I was watching him. I wanted him to think I was in the kitchen. Instead he catches me two steps from the back door.

"He's having a paddy," John says to me. "He's tired after school, that's all. Leave him to it and he'll come in when he's ready."

Joel's sobs tear into me. I can't trust myself to speak.

"Please don't look at me like that," John begs, and reaches for my hand. "I'm his dad. I love him too."

"He doesn't like football."

"How can he possibly know he doesn't like it if he doesn't even try? I don't want him to be left out at school, that's all. All the other boys are footie mad. How's he ever going to fit in if he doesn't learn the basics?"

"He doesn't have to *fit in*, he's fine as he is. He likes the stuff he likes. Not the stuff you think he ought to like."

"God almighty, I'm just trying to help him belong! Footie's a big deal for little boys."

"Not all little boys, some of them like animals and role-playing and—"

"Well, the little boys in his class, the ones he's going to be at school with for the next fourteen years, it's a big deal for them, all right? And that's who Joel's got to be friends with. The boys there actually are. What kind of a time is he going to have in the playground if he cries every time he sees a ball?"

We never used to argue like this. There was time when I thought John and I agreed on everything, and then an even sweeter time when I discovered that John would change his mind, giving in to what I wanted, just for the pleasure of making me happy. Until Joel came, I never knew John could be so stubborn. Out in the garden, Joel's sobs are a hook dragging at my heart. Resisting the pull is physically painful.

"Please don't go out there and comfort him." John's voice sounds as if he's asking me, but he puts himself between me and the door. "Just let him get it out of his system, he'll come in when he's ready."

"He's scared."

"He's not scared, what would he be scared of? He's in his own back garden with both his parents ten feet away. He's just mad because he can't have his own way."

He's scared, I think, *because he thinks you don't like him.* I push against John's strong physical bulk. He puts his arms around me. Is he holding me? Or holding me prisoner?

"Please." John's voice is warm against my scalp. "Back me on this one. Just this one. Please."

"I always back you."

"Not when you think I'm wrong. And you always think I'm wrong."

"No, I don't! Look, this isn't about who's right or who's wrong. Joel's out there crying in the garden and I want to go and comfort him, and I'm going, all right? I'm his mum. That's what I'm supposed to do."

"He's five years old. He needs to learn."

"He's little and the only thing he needs to learn is that we love him exactly how he is and we'll always be there for him.

Whether he's any good at bloody football or not. Let me go out there, please." John doesn't move. "You know I'm not strong enough to push you out of the way."

John sighs and moves aside. I know I'm right, so why do I feel as if I've done something unforgivable? When I brush against his chest and stomach, the muscles there are solid with anger. It doesn't matter. I'll worry about this later.

Joel is still curled on the grass, still clutching Scrap-dog, still sobbing. I kneel beside him and gently stroke his back. He responds with the faintest uncoiling. I keep stroking. After a minute, a little hand shoots out and grabs onto mine, pulling it into the centre where Scrap-dog nestles, warm and damp and in need of a wash. I lie down beside Joel and curl around until he's tucked beneath my chin. The sobbing stops, replaced by the small hitches in his breath that tell me he's returning to a place of calmness. I can smell the autumnal warmth of the soil and the broken grass-stems and the shampoo I use to wash Joel's hair. I forget all about the row with John and simply bask in the comfort of lying in low slanting sunshine, on the grass, with my little son. This moment is all I have ever wanted. Whatever comes next, I'll have had this.

"Shall we go inside?" I whisper.

"Daddy's cross with me," Joel whispers back.

"No, he's not cross with you, why would he be cross with you?"

"Because I wouldn't kick the ball. He wants me to be good at football but I'm not. I don't want to make Daddy cross."

Something in my chest breaks a little.

"Daddy's not cross because you're not good at football. And anyway, how do you know you're not good at it?"

"I just know."

"Well, maybe if you just tried it you might like it."

Joel turns his face towards me then. His eyes are huge and red-rimmed, brimming over with still unshed tears.

"You love me more than Daddy does," he says.

"Oh, my darling. Daddy loves you more than anyone

else in the world, okay? He'd do anything for you. He's just – he's not – he just thought you might enjoy playing football with him, that's all. But he doesn't mind that you don't want to. He's upset too, you know. He's sad because he made you sad."

"Are you sad, Mummy?"

The unexpected question pierces me. I have to take a moment before I answer.

"I'm happy when you and Daddy are happy. You're the most important people in the whole world to me. So if you and Daddy are friends again, I'll be the happiest one of all."

Joel scrambles to his feet. Scrap-dog beneath his arm, he marches towards the back door where John's figure, tall and inscrutable in the darkness of the doorway, is waiting for us both. When Joel sees him, he hesitates and turns back towards me.

"What's the matter? There's no need to be frightened. Come on, sweetie, in we go."

Joel climbs up the back step. John turns sideways to make room. Joel and I both blink as we adjust to the darkness of the inside. John's arms are folded and he's standing very straight.

Be nice, I think at John. *Be gentle. Don't crush him.*

"I love you, Daddy," Joel says at last, and holds out his arms.

"And I love you too, fella." John scoops Joel up and hugs him. Scrap-dog falls in the movement and I see Joel wince and follow his fall, but thank God, John doesn't notice. His bear hug crushes Joel's ear against his shoulder, but Joel accepts this stoically. Another fierce minute and Joel is returned to the floor and Scrap-dog is back in his arms.

"But we both love Mummy best, don't we?" Joel says, reaching for my hand.

My heart catches in my throat. Then, thank God, John laughs heartily and takes my other hand, pulling me towards him for a bear hug of my own.

"That's because Mummy *is* the best," John says.

"You don't need to pick who you love best," I say. "Love doesn't work that way. I don't love you more than Daddy or Daddy more than you. I love you both exactly the same amount. Infinity."

"Infinity means where something goes on for ever," says Joel, looking at John for confirmation.

"That's right. See, you can remember stuff when you want to, can't you? Never mind all this *I don't know* and *I can't do it* rubbish, hey?" Joel blinks and I tense in anticipation of a new conflict, but it's all right, it's not serious, John's not being serious, and the next minute he's proposing a quick trip to the park and then fish and chips for tea. The darkness was only temporary, as it always is. There's nothing to worry about. It doesn't mean anything. We're all friends again and love is infinite and nobody loves anybody better than anyone else, and the sun is shining and my family is perfect and we are all perfectly happy.

"Look at him," I say, putting my hand on John's knee as we sit on the bench and soak up the last of the day's warmth. On the roundabout, Joel sits alone and spins slowly, round and round, round and round and round, Scrap-dog tucked between his feet, dreamily staring out at the world. "He loves that roundabout."

"I asked him if he wanted to come on the swings. But he said, *No, thank you, Daddy, you can sit down, I'd rather be by myself.*"

"He's got the best manners of anyone I know."

"And then he said, *Please, may you ask Mummy to come and push my roundabout?*"

"Oh, bless him." I stand up, but John pulls me back down again.

"No, don't go to him now, he's happy enough. I need to talk to you about this morning."

"What about this morning?"

"About the way you and Joel behaved."

51

I try to stand up again. "I'm going to see to Joel, he'll be waiting for me."

"No." John pulls me back down again. "Leave Joel. You can see he's fine. Look at him, he's completely off in his own world. And I need to talk to you, I really really need to."

The tenderness in his voice hurts my heart. I make myself sit beside my husband and wait.

"All right. So. I need to say this first: I love Joel every bit as much as you do, all right? I do. You know I do. And I love him exactly the way he is, no matter what. But this is what I've noticed. When I tried to get Joel to hold a pencil this morning, he cried and said he couldn't do it. When I ask him to tidy his toys up, he cries and says he doesn't know how to. When I tell him to put his plate in the dishwasher, he cries and gets upset, and half the time he drops it on the floor. When I ask him to put some bubble bath in his bath water, he gets in a state and pours out way too much and fills half the bathroom with bubbles, and then cries when I tell him to be more careful next time."

"But he can do all of those things." I feel dizzy with relief. "He can do them all perfectly."

"I know he can. For you. Not for me. That's the thing. He's good for you, but dreadful for me. He's good for you because he wants to please you, and dreadful for me because he's trying to make me go away so he can have you there with him instead."

I stare at John in shock.

"Look, it's not his fault. He's little. He had a tough start. And he's just that kind of person, isn't he? A very exclusive person. I'm not angry about it. But we do need to help him. He can't go through life like this, wanting to be with you and only you, all of the time. You have to start letting him go a bit. Make him realise there are other people in the world who love him as well."

"But it's not that," I say, when I can finally speak. "Joel loves you. He doesn't do stuff for you because he's *afraid.*

He's scared he'll do it wrong and you won't love him, okay? That's why he wouldn't kick the ball. That's why he wouldn't hold the pencil. He thinks if he does something and gets it wrong you won't love him, so he doesn't dare try at all."

John is not used to this. He is the theoriser, the pattern-spotter who sees the system and structure at work beneath the surface. I can tell from the shape of his mouth that he's sceptical. I have just one point in my favour: he desperately wants to believe me.

"So what was all that this morning, then? About us both loving Mummy best?"

"He's trying to find some common ground with you, that's all. He wants to be like you, and he's afraid he can't. Please stop thinking he's trying to get you to go away, what an awful thing to think." I take John's hand and stroke his fingers gently. "He loves you so much."

If John was the sort of man who let his feelings show more, he would dissolve into tears at this point. Instead, he puts his arm around my shoulders and settles me into place against his chest. I feel him kiss the top of my head. We sit together in the sunshine and watch the leaves blowing, while our son twirls and twirls on the roundabout, and the sounds of other children playing drift over to us on the cool breeze.

Chapter Four
Tuesday 31st October 2017

My birthday used to be filled with small reminders that the universe considered me special. Gifts and celebrations. The faint interest of teachers and strangers. The chance to knock on the doors of people whose names I didn't know, and win myself extra handfuls of sweets as a reward for being born on 31st October. A ready-made theme for teenage parties. Then later, the slimy, seedy satisfaction of gutting and carving a pumpkin with Joel, and the pleasure John took in putting his surgeon's skills to work on his own masterpiece.

Today, it means my house will remain silent and unadorned in a street bright with pumpkins and fake cobwebs. Today, the small bright faces will turn towards my house and then away again, knowing that I'm not playing but not guessing the reason why; and behind them the shepherding adults will look towards each other and shiver at the reminder of their own darkest nightmares. It means waking to a cold silent bedroom and the first real frost of the year. In the branches of the apple tree, the birds sit with their feathers fluffed out around them, keeping utterly still to avoid wasting precious calories. Birds can't store fat. It weighs them down. When I go out to the apple tree, I scatter a handful of stale bread crusts onto the lawn.

He'll come back to you by Christmas, and then you'll

never be apart again. For a moment I'm back there in the Hull Fair caravan, while a strange woman gloats over the pain she's causing me. Joel used to have nightmares about birds sometimes. He was afraid of their strong feet and reptilian eyes. If the gypsy woman's prediction comes true, will I have to leave the birds to starve? Over the hedge there are no feeders, only a wild tangle of thorns and roses, as if a princess sleeps inside. For my sake, my neighbour's learned to force himself each morning to enter the room where his daughter died, simply so that he can look down at me each morning while I look up, and both know we're not absolutely alone. But even the kindest heart has its limits, and the garden where his daughter played remains sacred and forbidden.

I look up and my neighbour looks down. Our eyes meet. We raise our hands in greeting. This morning, there's something else. He mouths something to me through the glass. I strain to make out the words. At last it comes to me. *Someone's coming.*

I hear the click of my front gate. A moment later and someone knocks once, twice, three times. In spite of myself, my heart leaps and I scurry through the house to the front door. It's my birthday. It would be so wonderful...

When I open the door, it's the woman from the police station. The woman whose son was missing. Mrs Nelson. Jackie.

She's fiercely groomed, her make-up a pretty beige mask, her eyes shaded black, her hair ruthlessly sleek and straight. Her skinny jeans could have been painted on and her spike-heeled boots are cheap, slick and frightening. There is no sign of her baby. She looks ready for war.

"What are you doing here?" I regret the words as soon as I've said them.

Jackie looks me up and down, one quick assessing glance that's the mirror of my own. I've wrapped my woolly hooded cardigan around me as if it might shield me. My hair is wispy and morning-ish and I'm devoid of make-up. The diamond engagement ring John gave me is the only bright thing about me.

"It's a free country."

"How did you get my address?"

"By looking. That all right by you? You going to report me to the Internet Police for stalking? I've come cos I want a word with you."

"But I don't even know you."

"Well, I know you. You write that blog, don't you? All about wanting to help other people who're going through what you've been through? And all the stuff about mediums and psychics? And how they're all a bunch of con artists? Well, you're wrong. My nanna had gypsy blood in her and she saw things all the time so I know it's real. And I've got proof."

This is what Melanie has been warning me about for years. That one day, someone is going to turn up on my doorstep because of my blog, and I won't be able to get rid of them. I shouldn't have used my real name. I shouldn't have included so many personal details. "Look, you can read everything I've got to say online, it's all on the blog and I'll answer any comments you have there—"

"No way! I want to talk to you face-to-face, not hiding behind screens and that, with all your bloody keyboard warriors coming after me." She looks at me shrewdly. "Or are you scared I'm going to bray you as soon as we get in the house?"

When I was at school and missed the bus, I would have to use my pocket money and take the service bus instead. Most of the time my fellow passengers would be old people and students, but sometimes there would be a group of girls my age, twagging off for the day and out for mischief. Then I'd sit small and still in my seat, self-conscious in my school uniform, counting down the seconds until I reached my stop, trying to ignore the insistent fingers that jabbed me in the back, the small tugs on my hair, the giggles as they tried to force a reaction from me. Once, I found the back of my blazer dotted with spit-balls. Another time, there was a thick clot of chewing gum stuck in my hair. This is how I feel now, listening to Jackie pick and jab at me. I'm a physical coward. I always have been. I can cope with abuse online but not in person.

"I'm not scared of you," I lie.

"So why are you looking at me like I'm shit on your shoe?"

She's so bright, so loud. I think of parrots, of their bright feathers and sharp intelligence and fierce beaks that can crush a man's hand. In a less gentrified area, everyone would be out on their driveways by now, enjoying the show, but rubbernecking isn't something we go in for around here. Despite this thought I'm conscious of eyes peering from behind stained glass and half-drawn curtains. I wonder if my neighbour is watching too. I wonder what he would tell me to do.

"Making a show of you in front of the neighbours, am I?" Jackie asks, saccharine-sweet. "Bit short on entertainment round here? Maybe you'd better let me in before they call the coppers on us."

I'm about to refuse and shut the door and take the consequences, but then we both make the mistake of looking straight at each other for a moment – not at our clothes or hair or jewellery but straight into each other's eyes – and I see her and she sees me and I finally understand that despite the bravado, despite the rudeness and the shrillness and the aggression, we're the same, trapped in the same Hell. Jackie makes a strange little noise in her throat, somewhere between a gasp and a growl, and turns her gaze away from me, staring up at the towering trees that whisper above us like benign suburban spies, waving her hands before her eyes to try and dry the tears before they roll down her cheeks and ruin her make-up.

"Of course you can come in," I say, and hold the door open.

She follows me into the hallway, glancing dubiously at the polished wooden floorboards.

"You want me to take off my boots?"

"No, it's fine, don't worry about it."

"Don't be soft, I'll wreck your floor with these on." A long smooth tug of her lacquered fingernails, a slither of leather and Jackie is suddenly three inches shorter, her feet in Mr Grumpy socks small and vulnerable.

"They're Ryan's," she says, seeing me looking. "Daft, but—"

"It's not daft."

"I like feeling close to him. I've got his old T-shirt in bed with me an' all." Her voice wobbles.

"This way."

The room at the front looks out onto a triangle of grass where three huge willow trees shiver and shed their yellowy leaves in the chill October breeze. The duck-egg velvet of the sofa is scarcely worn, the cushions on its matching chair undented. The blue-and-copper rug with its faded shadowy pattern still has that faint new-carpet scent. When I first told John what I wanted this room to look like, he laughed and asked how I thought it would fit into our lives with a young child. 'I don't know,' I remember saying. 'We'll use it if the living room's a mess and the police come round or something.' And he instantly christened this room *The Policeman's Room*. Although when the police actually came, I was afraid that this room would make us look like a cold and unloving family, so it wasn't to the front room that I led them.

"Sit down. I'll make us a drink." I scurry off to the kitchen, realising too late that I've forgotten to ask if Jackie wants tea or coffee, milk or sugar. I'll make up a tray instead. It will take longer but I don't mind, and it will make me look like a prissy fifties housewife with too much time on my hands but I don't mind that either. I need to compose myself. I rummage in the cupboard for the cafetiere. Might as well do the thing properly. Perhaps if I take long enough, Jackie will give up and go home again.

I spin out the preparations as long as I can. When I carry the tray through, Jackie has claimed one end of the sofa, her feet neatly together on the floor and her hands in her lap, as if she's here for a job interview. She gives the overcrowded tray a shrewd assessing look and moves her handbag so I can get to the coffee table.

"I forgot to ask if you wanted tea or coffee so I—"

"I'll have tea, please." I try to pick up the teapot but my hand betrays me, giving a curious spastic jerk so that the lid rattles and the spout knocks against the mug. "It's all right, you get your coffee and I'll sort myself out."

I do better with the cafetiere, filling my mug without too much trouble. Jackie adds an inch of milk and three teaspoons of sugar to her mug and looks at me over the top of it.

"Thanks for letting me in. Wasn't sure if you would." She curls her fingers around her mug and I notice again the perfection of her nails, which are now a rich damson. She must have found time to repaint them since I saw her at the station.

"Is your little girl with your husband?"

"Georgie? She's with my mam. Lee's at work, he won't be back till lunchtime. You only had one, didn't you?"

"Just the one."

Her eyes wander to the mantelpiece where Joel, wide-eyed against a white background, stares wonderingly out at the room.

"He looks like you." She puts her mug down and fumbles in her bag. "Here's my Ry."

Ryan has his mother's colouring, dark and dramatic, and his mother's sharp features, coated with a light speckling of acne. The wide low forehead and thick neck, the roll of pudge beneath his chin, presumably come from his father. The photographer has done his best, but the boy who stares out at the camera looks tough, scrappy, working-class in all the ways we don't value any more, the kind of boy you see coming towards you and make a point not to make eye contact with, a boy who if he was with his mates you'd cross over to avoid having to pass him too closely. Ryan, in short, looks like trouble.

"He's a good-looking boy," I say.

"No, he's not. Not in that picture, anyway. But he's a good lad. He's really good to his little sister. He kisses her every time she smiles at him."

"That's sweet."

"He looks like a little thug, I know he does, but he's really not. He's my boy. He's been gone for a month now. And the coppers are winding down the search and that, because he's been gone so long they think he's—" She disguises her shudder with a mouthful of tea, tries again. "They think he's -" Her hand is shaking. "They think they're looking for a—" A slop of tea slings itself out over the side and splashes her leg and the rug beneath her feet. "Oh, shit, your lovely rug."

"It's fine."

"I didn't come here to wreck your house."

"Honestly, don't worry, it doesn't matter."

"Course it matters. Just tell me where the stuff is and I'll clean it up. I just need a minute—"

"Just forget about the rug, will you?" She looks as though she's about to cry. If she breaks down in front of me I think my heart may shatter. What can I say so she can get herself back under control? "Tell me why you came here. You said you'd got proof about something?"

"Yeah. And I have." She fumbles in her bag. "I got this email last night."

Dear Ms Nelson (Jackie),

Forgive me for contacting you out of the blue like this. My name is Marcus White and I'm a professional psychic. I believe I can help find your missing son, Ryan.

Of course, Jackie, you'll want some evidence that I can do what I promise. So here are three predictions of events that will shortly come to pass. When you've experienced the truth of these predictions, and you feel ready to reach out to me, together we can work to bring Ryan back to you.

My predictions are:

- A woman will soon come into your life in connection with Ryan's disappearance (or perhaps she already has). You will initially reject her help, but she has good intentions.

- Someone close to you will offer you reassurance and advice. However, you will soon discover that they may not be all they seem.

- Some unexpected evidence or information surrounding Ryan's disappearance will come to light within three days of you receiving this message.

Jackie, I strongly believe we are meant to work together to bring Ryan home. You'll find my contact details as well as details of my fees on my website which is listed below. Please call at any time of day or night.

May the kindly spirits watch over you, Jackie.
With love and light,
Marcus White

"Jackie," I say, as gently as I can. "I know this isn't what you want to hear. But this definitely isn't real psychic powers. It's just guesswork. I used to get emails like this all the time. It's not even a very good one."

"But look!" Jackie taps the paper with her damson fingernail. "That first bit. The woman that's going to come into my life. I thought of you straight away. When we met at the police station, and I was real angry cos I thought they'd brought you in to meet with me. I thought they were trying to set us up together, two mams with missing kids."

"No, it wasn't that, I promise, they'd never do that to either of us. I was there for... for something else. It was just a coincidence."

"Well, that makes it more believable then, doesn't it? There's no way he could have predicted it."

"But what he said could apply to hundreds of people. If you hadn't met me, you might have thought it was one of the police officers."

"He couldn't know for sure one of them was going to be a woman, how could he?"

"No, he couldn't, but it's a good bet, close to fifty-fifty. Maybe higher when you think about the kind of case yours is. That's what psychics do, you see. They play the percentages. You see how he's said *will shortly come into your life, OR perhaps she already has?* If you hadn't already met someone who fitted, you'd just assume it hadn't happened yet. And if it didn't happen, you'd forget about it, because he's got a sure bet in the list as well."

"But—"

"You see that last one, *new information within three days?* That's his banker. He's included that one because it's time-bound, and that means you'll look out for it and really remember it when it happens. And you can guarantee there'll be something new in three days at this stage of the investigation, even if it's just CCTV searches coming back or something. So the mystery woman won't matter either way, she can turn up or not, because he's proved himself, right? But it's the second one he really wants to reel you in with."

I'm almost forgetting that Jackie is here listening to me.

"This one, about someone who offers advice but they're not all they seem? That's his hook. It sounds so specific but it's actually incredibly vague. It could apply to someone in the police, or a reporter, or, God, I don't know, all the other psychics who'll start bombarding you with messages even. Neighbours who want some gossip. People you knew at school who just fancy getting involved in the drama, so they get in touch and ask if they can help. Basically anyone you've talked to recently."

"But there's got to be summat in it or people wouldn't—"

"And because he's said *they're not all they seem*, he's making you feel like he's got some special inside knowledge, and there's something he can tell you no one else can. So when you go to see him, that's the one he'll start working on. *I've been feeling very strongly that there's someone in your life now whose intentions you shouldn't trust. Who do you think that might be?* And then he'll start picking away at you. *Anyone who suddenly showed an interest? Anyone asking a lot of questions? Anyone trying to make you look bad?* And eventually he'll get a hit, and he'll start feeding stuff to you about what their motivations might be, and he'll probably even be right because people are pretty predictable really, and that'll be it, he'll have you. And you'll pay him. And that's all he wants."

Hunched against the arm of my plushy duck-egg sofa, Jackie looks very small.

"I'm sorry." I risk patting her arm.

"You used to believe though."

"I did. I wasted so much time and money and effort. God, I wanted, so much, for there to be this special magic trick I could use to find Joel. But there isn't. There really isn't. All we can do is wait and let the police get on with their jobs." She's looking at me as if she's hoping for something more, but I don't know what else to give her. "I hope they find Ryan soon."

"Yeah. Me too." She reaches for her handbag. "Thanks for the tea. I'd better go. Do you mind if I use your toilet first?"

"Course you can." I lead her out into the hall. "Up the stairs and on the right."

Jackie is a while in the bathroom. She must be freshening her make-up. That immaculate mask she puts on like armour, but that will do her no favours and win her no sympathy. People prefer the mothers of lost children to look wilder and more unkempt. How much longer will she be? I hope her son is found soon. But I doubt he will be found alive. I hear the click and scrape of the ironwork gate on the front path.

The postman has already been. Melanie is coming to see me later to bring a homemade cake and her children, but she always phones ahead. John never comes here any more. So who—?

Then I see the wavery shape outlined in the glass, the hand coming up to knock on the glass, and I'm across the hallway in a single bound. This is it, the moment I've waited and dreamed of for so many nights and days, all the pain made worth it for this one single instant of longing fulfilled, because it's happened, it's happened, it's finally happened, my love, my darling, my only boy…

But there's no one there. The garden gate is shut. The doorstep is empty. I'm alone in the hallway, just me and my shadow, and a stranger's footsteps on the stairs as Jackie comes down in a hurry.

"Are you all right? I thought I heard you scream."

"No! No, it's nothing, it was just I thought there was someone at the door."

"Someone knocked and ran away? Trick-or-treaters?"

"No, they didn't knock, I just thought I saw someone coming up the path. My mistake." I swallow my fright. I won't share what I thought. It's no one's business but mine.

I want Jackie to put her boots back on and leave but she won't. Instead she's hovering at my elbow. "It's shook you up, hasn't it? You want to sit down?"

"What? No, I'm fine, it's nothing." I can cope with anything but kindness. Why won't she go away? "I'm fine. What time's your bus?"

"Did you think it was Joel?"

"Of course I didn't think it was Joel!"

When our eyes meet, I know she knows I'm lying. And as we stare at each other defiantly, I suddenly know something else. Jackie was lying too. She knew the email she showed me was a poorly written fraud. Her grandmother did not have gypsy blood; she never made predictions. Jackie came here for something else entirely.

"That first year," I say slowly, "I used to hear him coming back home all the time. I'd wake in the night and hear him creeping into the house. I used to run down the stairs to greet him. But he was never there."

"I do that about eight times a day." Jackie wipes fiercely at her mouth. "I act like I'm coping but I'm not. I can't do this. I don't know how much longer I can stand it. I can't sleep at night, so I get up and clean. My house has never been so clean, you'd think I was trying to sell it. And ironing, I iron everything, even sheets. And when I run out of housework I do my nails. Different colour every night, just so I'll have summat to think about that's not listening for the door and praying it's Ry. I can't help it, when Lee comes home I have to get up, I can't be in the bed listening to him sleep while I lie awake and I think about all the things that might have happened. I sometimes wonder if... if...."

"For a while," I say, "the police thought that John might have hurt Joel. Or that I might have. They never managed to prove that John didn't. I know he didn't, but in the night sometimes I still used to wonder... no wonder he left me."

"Lee was supposed to be out at work," Jackie whispers. "The day Ryan went, I mean. He's a taxi driver, he normally works mornings and nights, but he was going to do the afternoon as well, and stay out and work straight through. And I was taking Georgie to my mam's. Ry knew the house was going to be empty. So he twagged off school. Only the school called me, you know the way they do – I can't believe Ry thought he'd get away with it, I was so angry – so I came home early from my mam's to catch him out. But when I got home, there was just Lee in the house. Work was dead quiet so he'd come home after all." She looks at me imploringly. "I mean, I know he didn't hurt Ry. I know he never would."

"I knew straight away something was wrong. But I didn't dare call the police until John came home. Because if I called them, that made it real. And now I wonder, if I'd called as soon as I thought there was something wrong, would they maybe have found him—"

"I knew too. But I didn't know what to do. I mean, I tried

to call his mates, but I don't even know who half of them *are*. I rang all the ones I knew but there was only about four of them, and then I went out looking in all the places they hang around, and then... but Lee said we had to wait at least twenty-four hours before we called the coppers or they'd do us for wasting their time."

"Sometimes," I say, "I dream they've found Joel's body. I get the call in the middle of the night and it's Nick's voice saying, *I'm afraid I've got some bad news*. And it breaks my heart, but it's a relief too, because it's over." Jackie's face is crumpled and ugly with pain. "Then I wake up and he's still not found. And I think, *I wish today they'd call. Even to tell me he's dead*."

"Me too," Jackie whispers. "It's only been a month and I'm already having times when I wish they'd tell me he's dead, just so I can stop wondering. I'm so ashamed—"

I put my arms around her and hold her, absorbing the sweet shock of holding a strange woman so intimately, feeling her resist and hold herself rigid at first, then give in to the comfort of my embrace. She lays her face against my shoulder and howls, her make-up coming off in smears and streaks against my T-shirt. I sit quietly on the stairs and let the grief pour out of her and watch the sunlight stream in through the stained glass and cast lozenges of light on the polished floorboards, and feel glad that no one is here to see us. We mothers of lost children are not pretty criers.

Life Without Hope:
The Monsters Among Us

On 20th January 2014, from ConcernedFriend:

I know the people who have your boy, he is being held for use as a sex worker and it will cost you $8250 to buy out his contract form the people who have him. I will be in touch by email within three days to discuss further

On 8th March 2014, from JoelIsLost:

Mum it's me Joel. I'm in San Francisco. I'm so sorry I ran away and I'm sorry it took me so long to get in touch. I guess I was embarrassed about all the fuss. I've been working in a bar to save the $$ to come home but I was just laid off and I can't make my rent so I will be evicted soon. Please please please can you wire me some money so I can come home to you mum, I miss you so much and I am so so sorry

On 17th March 2014, from SlummyYummyMummy:

You deserved to lose your son because you stole him from another woman. I am sorry to say this but it is true

On 2nd April 2014, from YourBoyJoel:

Mum its me Joel I was got by real bad peple who wont let me go until you pay them some money IDK how much it is as they wont tell me and I dont know why they havent got in touch already but please come and get me they dont let me use the computer but they left it on for just a few minuts so I can send this please come and find me quick I hae to go now cuz they will be abck soon

On 31st October 2014, from YourBoyJoel:

Mum happy birthday mum they said I cud send you a msg cuz its your birthday I miss you so much I wish you wud just pay them the £££ they want so I can come home to you I love you Joel

On 28th November 2014, from MichaelJBrown:

Mrs Harper, I am sure you will not recognise my name but I am a well-known 'fixer' in what might be termed the underworld. I have recently uncovered intel that may be of interest to you in the search for your son. If you would like me to investigate this further on your behalf then please get in touch immediately. Please note that the police will *not* be able to help you and any attempted contact by them may result in serious harm or even death to Joel.

On 15th December 2014, from MichaelJBrown:

Mrs Harper, please be advised that the intel I have for you has developed significantly since my initial contact. Your son is in danger and you need to act quickly. Get in touch with me soonest so that we can resolve the situation swiftly and with a good result

On 24th December 2014, from JoelIsLost:

Mum I guess this is it and you dont want me back it hurts so bad to know that but I guess I can understand why you dunt want me now. I think they are going to kill me soon cuz I hae not made them the money they was hoping n they dunt want to feed me or clothe me no more. I love you mum so much n I wish I cud have seen you one last time before I die love you always Joel

On 8th January 2015 from TheLostBoysCollective:

Hi there, we are the Lost Boys Collective and we work with former sex workers and victims of trafficking to help reunite them with their families. We believe we may be able to find out something about your son Joel and if you are able to fund us to complete our investigations we will gladly do all we can to help you. Please get in touch soon as we really think we can help.

On 31st January 2015 from TheLostBoysCollective:

Hi there, it's us again. We have just had a VERY good lead come to us as part of an investigation we are doing for someone else and we are now CONFIDENT that we can find Joel with just a little more work. All we need to complete this stage of our investigation is $875 which will cover fees, supplies etc, so that we can get to the answers quickly. Please email us – we want to help so much!

On 15th February 2015 from JoelHarperMissing:

Mum please it's me, I am so sorry I didn't get in touch before but I didn't know what to write because I was so ashamed of what I did. I know I hurt you so much by running away and I will do anything to make it up to you. Please please forgive me I am so sorry and all I want is to come home to you.

Mum I have been travelling for a long time trying to get home and now I have run out of money and if you could just find it in your heart to send me $1263 via Moneygram that will pay for my tickets to come home.

On 26th April 2015, from User1784253:

You are a child stealer. You got what you deserved. Social Services STEAL BABIES and you collaborated with them. How does it feel now???

On 9th May 2015 from JoelHarperMissing:

Mum I can tell how angry you are with me because you have not got in touch with me. I suppose I can't blame you really. I know how bad it was what I did and I don't blame you for not wanting me back again.

Mum I have done something really stupid I was trying to earn the money to get my ticket and I got in with these people who told me I could earn the money dealing drugs for them. I know this is wrong but it was only weed and I didnt think it was so bad. Unfortunately I got caught almost at once and was arrested and now I am in prison and will be there until I can pay my fine to get out.

Mum I know I don't deserve your help and I understand that you won't want me home after this. But if you could just pay my fine to get out of jail and then I will do my very best to go straight and not make you ashamed of me any more than you already are. I need $250 which I know is a lot but it would mean the world to me. I promise I will not get in touch with you again if you don't reply

On 15th May 2015 from ConcernedPoliceOfficer:

Dear Mrs Harper, I am an officer with the Arizona State Police and we currently have your son Joel Harper in custody. I am aware that he has already contacted you with a request that you pay his fine so that we can release him. However I do not know if you are aware of his entire situation. I have been able to get him into a half-way house where he will be able to pick up the pieces of his life and begin to rebuild. However to be released to this program he MUST pay his fine and will also require a further $185 as bond to enter the program, making a required total of $435. I am so touched by your son's condition that I am happy to pay half of this sum but cannot do more. If you can wire $220 via MoneyGram we will be able to help your son and his life can begin once more.

On 1st July 2015, from WeHaveYourSon:

We have your son Joel. We will release him to you in return for a payment of £5000. We will be in touch shortly to provide details of how you can pay this money. DO NOT attempt to involve the police or we WILL be forced to terminate your son's life.

Today, 31st October, is my birthday. My gift to myself today is to not read any of the vile, hateful, misleading and criminal messages the internet trolls have seen fit to send me.

Posted on 31st October 2015
Filed to: Miscellaneous
Tags: missing people, support for families, internet trolls, Susannah Harper, Joel Harper

Chapter Five
Thursday 9th November 2017

9th November has its claws in me before I even open my eyes. I know the only way I can get through this is to pretend it is just a day like any other, clinging to each task I've set myself like a handhold as I cross this wasteland of a day that marks *five years gone*. For some, the days on the other side of Bonfire Night signify the making of lists and the buying of tinsel, the first beginnings of the Christmas season; but not for me. It's Thursday, and in the orderly regular life I've planned for myself, Thursday means clean-sheets day.

My own bed has been stripped and changed, the white-on-white-set changed for the delicate floral blue, the silk throw rearranged across the foot. Later I will wash everything and hang it on the line to dry, then bring it in scented with the clean cold scent of autumn. Some days when the mists come in and the drizzle falls for days I have to tumble dry it, but today I'm lucky. When I went down to the apple tree this morning I had to screw my eyes up against the low orange sun that hung in the air, fat with life and promise like the yolk of an egg. Today my washing will dry quickly and by tonight, everything will be crisp and ironed and folded away, another small domestic victory against the forces of chaos. I stand at the threshold of Joel's room, my arms weighed down with clean bedding, and force myself to focus on that thought – the cleanliness of the linen, the scents in the cupboard – so that I can make myself strong enough to pretend that this is all simply routine, that the bedding I'm about to wash is musty with boy-sweat and not with disuse, and thus make myself cross the threshold to my son's bedroom.

I have to do this. It's Thursday. I always do this on a Thursday.

Joel has three sets of bed linen. A rather nasty beige-and-brown-patterned set donated by John's mother, who bought it unopened at a church bazaar and then regretted it, but was incapable of throwing anything out. A dark-blue gingham set bought just before he left us, in recognition of the fact that he was a young man now, not a little boy. And the one that's on the bed now, the Sonic the Hedgehog duvet cover from the Christmas he was nine years old.

John – as unsentimental a man as any woman could fall in love with – wanted to throw this set out when Joel was thirteen. *It's old*, he said, caught between laughter and despair. *Look, it's all faded. You're always telling me you're not a kid any more. So get rid of it and let's get your room looking like you're thirteen and not six. And tidy it up while you're at it.* And Joel, still vulnerable beneath his shell of teenage anger, turned his face towards me and gave me that single, helpless look, the one that always jabbed piercingly at my heart: *Help me, Mum. I need you to help me.*

So I waded in and told John sharply that of course Joel didn't have to throw away his Sonic bedding if he didn't want to, and what was the matter with him, shouting like that over a duvet cover? A bloody duvet cover? John retorted that it wasn't the duvet cover, it was about Joel wanting to be treated like an adult but still acting like a child. I mocked him, reminding him that he had clothes in his wardrobe that were older than Joel so he was in no position to talk, and besides, what did he think teenagers were meant to be like? The argument rumbled on throughout the day, disappearing for a while and then resurfacing in spats about what to have

73

for lunch and how to stack the dishwasher, until I was afraid the whole weekend would turn sour on us.

Then, after Joel went to bed that night, defiantly sprawled out beneath the Sonic bedset, I snuggled up to John on the sofa and nuzzled my mouth against his ear, letting my breath coil around the delicate nerve endings, my fingernails scratching gently and exquisitely at the back of his neck. I remember John's gradual capitulation as my caresses lapped like water at the hard knot of his anger, until he turned to me and put his hands on either side of my face. We were quiet and slow that night, conscious in a pleasant way that Joel was asleep above us and that he might hear us and be disturbed. I think that was what brought us back together again, even more than the sex; the reminder that we had both willingly and unquestioningly committed ourselves to a life built around Joel.

Then when the moment was over and I took the wine glasses to the kitchen and turned on the dishwasher and we went upstairs to bed hand in hand, we both paused to look in on Joel. He was five feet six inches tall when we measured him on his thirteenth birthday, but he still slept with his bedside light on. A silent reminder of childhood that never failed to tug at my heart. In the dim forgiving light of the little red lamp, a never-sleeping Sonic peered back at us from beneath one arched eyebrow.

Look at him, I whispered to John. *Our boy.*

Yes, said John, and sighed. *Look at him.* And I realised John knew that I had sex with him earlier as a sort of consolation prize, to make up for the fact that I had taken Joel's side over the duvet, and I saw a glimpse of a truth I'd been stalking for years: *John is jealous of Joel.*

This memory hurts, but I've learned you can evade pain by subjecting yourself to a lesser but still significant pain, and the hurt of this long-ago argument is enough to numb me to the hurt of stripping the bed that no longer smells of my son. I handle the duvet cover carefully. Years of washing have worn it almost into rags. I don't dare put it through the machine any more. Instead, I sink it into a rich bath of Lux suds, then drape it tenderly across my airer so the weight of water can't tear the cotton.

His room's not precisely as he left it. I've allowed myself the luxury of tidying up, making it welcoming and neat. The dirty clothes strewn across the floor have been washed, ironed and stowed away. One agonising day around the three-year mark it dawned on me that even if (when) he comes back, they won't fit him any more. But I can't bear to let his wardrobe stand empty. The Warcraft figurines that he loved and used to beg for still stand in their places along the windowsill. But their predecessors, the action figures from kids' cartoons and video games, have been tidied away into a carefully labelled carton, each one laid to rest reverently and with care. I considered wrapping them in tissue, but thought that might seem excessive. When (if) Joel comes back, I don't want him to laugh at me.

The books in the bookcase are topped with fluffy grey fronds, as if they all need a haircut. Like everything else in the room, they're years too young for him now; but he might want to re-read *The Wind in the Willows* and the *Faraway Tree* stories he adored so much, in the way adults often do. Or perhaps he'll simply want to hold onto them as souvenirs of his childhood. Surely there were some memories he would want to hold on to. Surely he can't have been so unhappy that he'd want to get rid of everything.

The gingham duvet cover is on. The bed looks welcoming and comfortable, smooth and neat. Perhaps too smooth and neat. Is there a suggestion of the shrine in the perfection of the crisply ironed duvet cover, in the neat alignment of the corners that all hang at an equal distance from the floor? Perhaps it would look better if I rumpled things up just a little. I don't want Joel to be intimidated by the cleanliness. I press in the centre of the pillow with the palm of my hand, just enough to create the faintest indentation that might suggest it's been recently slept on. That looks better. Now if (when) he comes back, he won't feel as if his room is better without him in it.

What I want desperately to do is to lie down on the bed, press my face into the pillow and cry. But if I do that, there's a chance I may never get up again. And that can't happen. I need to be strong.

I turn away from the bed and look around the rest of the room. I don't like to keep things too immaculate for the same reason that I don't like the bed to look too perfectly straight and untouched, so when it comes to dusting, I ration myself, cleaning one third of the room on the same rotation that I change the duvet covers. This week, it's the turn of the skirting boards, the bevelled edges of the wardrobe doors, and the mirror.

The skirting boards take the most time, so I do them first, enjoying the sense of accomplishment as the glossy wood emerges fresh and clean. Beneath Joel's bed, an enormous dust bunny has crept in from elsewhere in the house and is lurking on the carpet. I sweep it up into my duster and crawl out to wash it down the bathroom sink. Coming back in, I see the dent in the pillow, the crumpled place in the duvet where someone has sat down, and I feel my heart throb, momentarily deceived by my own treacherous illusion. I have to force myself not to look more closely.

The wardrobe has collected very little dust, just the faintest traces sullying the dampness of the duster. I do it anyway, taking my time, using up the minutes, allowing myself to linger. When I can't spin it out any more, I turn my attention to the mirror. Clean cloth. A careful, even spray of Pledge. Elbow grease. The mirror, clean before I started, turns misty with polish, then begins to gleam. The sunlight catches on the edge and jabs a dagger of rainbows into my eyes. When I blink them away, I see something in the mirror that should not be there.

Grief and longing cause all sorts of hallucinations. Walking through the shopping centre, I'll catch the scent of Joel's hair, sweaty from an afternoon of racing around the park. Queueing in the traffic that fills the wide crowded streets in the mornings, I see his face looking out at me from between two cars. Sometimes at night, in the silent hours when the street outside is empty and the distant buses have stopped running and the taxis have all gone home and even the clocks seem to stop ticking, I hear Joel's voice whispering to me from across the landing.

This, though. This is new. I blink several times, trying to make the illusion in the mirror disappear. It remains stubbornly visible. Scrap-dog. Joel's best beloved, his constant bedtime companion.

Scrap-dog cannot possibly be there. Scrap-dog cannot be there because Scrap-dog went everywhere with Joel, hidden in his backpack even as a teenager. The two of them vanished together. Careless of the smear I will make, I lean my forehead against the mirror and close my eyes, count to ten. It's a flaw in the glass, a strange artefact from the sunlight in my eyes. When I open my eyes again and look, Scrap-dog will be gone. I open my eyes. In the reflection, Scrap-dog's gleaming black button eye stares blandly back at me from his spot on the pillow.

"Right," I say out loud. My voice is so loud, I feel as if I might have broken something. It's a fold in the cover, a duster I've left there that's somehow fallen into an evocative shape, a simple delusion. I turn around and glare at the bed, daring Scrap-dog to still be there.

Scrap-dog's eyes still shine glossily when the light catches them. His head flops to one side as if someone has wrung his neck, and across his belly I can see the wobbly imperfection of the seam that split along the furry patches that make up his body, stitched back shut by me long ago.

This is going on too long. I don't think my heart can stand it. I make myself go towards the bed, force my hand to reach out to grasp the toy's worn body. He won't be there. I'll reach out and clutch empty air and Scrap-dog will vanish. My hands close around the stiff rigid shape of his muzzle, strange contrast to the limp floppiness of his body. Why isn't he disappearing? Why is he still here? Is he an early Christmas gift, the first harbinger of the only thing I really want? My hands clutch him tight, too tight. If I'm not careful I'll tear him in half. How can this be happening? I bring Scrap-dog slowly up to my face, press him against my mouth and nose, and take a deep breath.

The scent of mud is overwhelming. The floor tilts and sways beneath my feet like a funhouse. I reach out one hand to try and steady myself but there's nothing, nothing between me and the drop. I'm falling through empty space towards cold dark water and now I'm choking, spluttering, drowning. I try to breathe but my mouth and nose are plugged shut, all I can feel is the pain of trying to breathe and failing, and a thick clog of vomit rises in my throat but it has nowhere to go because the mud and water are overwhelming, and I can't breathe and I'm choking to death and no one will find me and help me, this is the end. Only Scrap-dog is here to watch me as I drown, only Scrap-dog with his black button eyes gazing sorrowfully down at me from some high place where an angry giant holds him by the neck and watches pitilessly as I fall and fall, down and down and down, my eyes open, my hands clenched tight.

Then my muscles turn weak and whatever I'm holding onto falls away from me, and the mud is gone and now I can throw up, a great plume of vomit that arcs across the carpet like the spume of a whale, and I fall forward onto my hands and knees and gasp and choke and whoop and retch some more, letting gravity empty the vileness from my mouth, feeling as if I'm coughing up the contents of my whole body onto the carpet, and with each heave comes a splatter of words that ring in my ears:

Mummy, where are you? Please help me. Where are you? I need you.

At last the spasms pass and I can sit back on my heels,

savouring how good it feels to breathe. Beside me on the floor, Scrap-dog lies quiet and innocent, his face turned enquiringly towards me as if he's concerned and wants to help.

What just happened? I have no idea. I only know that I'm icy cold, shivering as helplessly as if I've dragged myself from freezing water, and all I want to do is to crawl away and hide in my own bed until the warmth returns to my body. But Joel's room is a vile, disgusting mess that must be cleaned before I do anything else.

I force myself to my feet. My ears sing and soar as I stagger across the landing. The stairs look terrifyingly steep, so I sit down and shuffle slowly down on my behind, as if I've become either very young or very old. I'm glad there's no one here to see. In the kitchen I rummage clumsily beneath the sink for the old washing-up bowl, cloths, carpet cleaner and yet more cloths. A plastic bag to throw things away in when I've finished. I creep back to the stairs and crawl up them on all fours. In the bathroom, I fill the bowl with hot water. I will myself not to slop it onto the floor.

Scrap-dog is no longer on the floor. He's back on the bed, nestled against the pillow.

Scrap-dog is real, isn't he, Mummy? Joel's anxious little face, crumpled with that frown I hated to see, possessed by the worries that only came to him in that liminal space between wakefulness and sleep.

Of course he's real, silly. Look, he's right here. See? I picked Scrap-dog up, made him kiss Joel's cheek.

No, but really real. No, no, no, I don't mean real… alive. Scrap-dog is alive, isn't he?

Well, I say, slowly.

Dad said he's not really alive.

Well, Dad… um… John is concerned that Joel, aged seven by the calendar but seeming much younger by any other measure, is in danger of getting lost in a fantasy world, setting more store by the affections of his stuffed toys than the friendship of his peers. But Joel's eyes, so full of worry, make me want to tear John's head off and shove it down his stupid clumsy neck. *Well, it's like this. Scrap-dog is alive in a different way to us. He's alive in your imagination, and no one else can see Scrap-dog being alive, but it still counts. Okay? But Dad doesn't want you to only play with Scrap-dog all the time, he wants you to have –* I nearly said 'real' *– human friends as well.*

But I like Scrap-dog best, Joel protests.

You don't have to choose with friends. You can have your human friends in the day, and Scrap-dog at night. Can't you?

Scrap-dog talks to me when I'm by myself, Joel tells me, *and he jumps around and catches my feet. Look, he's watching us talking now. He's guarding me to make sure you're a nice person. But he knows you're safe. Scrap-dog won't ever hurt you.* And so convincing is the world that my son has created that, just for a minute, I imagine I see a glint of malice in Scrap-dog's eyes, as if some hidden violence lies waiting beneath his fur.

And now Scrap-dog sits on Joel's bed like a sentry and watches me.

I must have put it there myself. I don't remember doing it but that's what happened. There's no way the dog could have moved by itself. It's just a stuffed toy. Nonetheless I don't like feeling its gaze on my back as I begin the hard, unpleasant task of cleaning my own filth from the carpet. Trying not to gag, I scoop up the congealing mess and drop the cloth and its contents into the plastic bag. It's wasteful, I should rinse the cloth out and reuse it, but surely I will get away with this one small act of poor housekeeping. See, Scrap-dog? I'm not doing anything wrong. I'm being a good mother, cleaning up my son's bedroom.

I soak a new cloth in warm water and sponge carefully at what remains, beginning at the outside of the stain and working inwards, making sure not to grind it deeper into the pile of the carpet. I'm good at this, I like looking after things, even carpets. I won't turn round and check to make sure Scrap-dog hasn't moved. I'll just concentrate hard on cleaning, and distract myself with memories. When John and I were first married, people were often surprised that I did all my own housework. *You just look like the sort of person who'd have a cleaner*, a colleague of John told me once, and in her strange clumsy words I recognised the compliment to my good looks and good grooming and instead of getting upset, I smiled and said that was very kind of her. Scrap-dog's eyes bore into my back.

I'm not turning around to check. I'm just stretching my back, and reaching for another cloth. It's not my fault if my eyes happen to fall on Joel's pillow. Where is Scrap-dog? I can't see him. Has he moved? Where is he? I crane my neck. Has his head turned a little so he can keep an eye on me? Has his mouth opened in a snarl?

Scrap-dog sits exactly where I last saw him, sprawled against the pillow. His face is blank and innocent. I return to the carpet, cleaning, cleaning, working slowly backwards towards the door. No matter how closely I look, I can find no trace of mud. The whole thing must have been a hallucination. But what does it mean? What does any of it mean? Scrap-dog's face stares straight at mine, his stitched-on mouth fraying just a little at the corner, a long thread hanging down so he looks as if he's contemplating something sad but beautiful. Where did he come from? What does it mean that he's here?

Scrap-dog must mean something. He hasn't been seen since Joel disappeared, and now he's back. But where has he been all this time? Is he a threat, or a warning?

Of course I know he's neither of these things. What he is, is a piece of evidence, a link in the long slow chain that leads back to Joel. He's something Nick needs to take away in a plastic bag, to pass to the Forensics lab for inspection, analysis, perhaps even dissection. They won't hurry. Joel's been gone for so long now that the urgency has disappeared. Perhaps they won't even bother. Perhaps they'll decide Scrap-dog must have been tucked away in a corner of my linen cupboard, must have suddenly resurfaced in the way hidden possessions so often do. Nonetheless, I should call Nick, and let him come and take Scrap-dog away.

Instead, I tiptoe over to the bed, pick Scrap-dog up by one ear, and carry him gingerly over to Joel's sock drawer. One swift smooth movement, whip and drop and slam, and Scrap-dog has disappeared again. I collect my cleaning supplies and go to the bathroom to pour away the grimy water. The weakness in my legs has all but disappeared. When I go down the stairs, I don't even need the handrail. By the time I get to the bottom step, I can tell myself that it was all in my head, that I was simply feeling queasy and the smell of the Pledge turned my stomach, and that if I were to look into Joel's sock drawer, there would be no sign of Scrap-dog.

By the time the carpet dries, I may even be able to put the whole incident from my mind entirely.

Chapter Six
Friday 9th November 2012

Day One. We've entered Hell, but we don't yet know it. On the table in the dining room sits the bright yellow one-eyed Minion plushy, shaped like a pill and dressed in dungarees that Joel won for me at the Fair. It's the last thing he will ever give me. Beside it sits the fat bag of clumped-up green-brown shreds, their sweet herbal scent whispering treacherously of wholesomeness, that John discovered in Joel's room. The argument it provoked was the last conversation we'll ever have with him. This is Hell. But we don't know it yet.

I clear the table and remind myself to buy more milk later. I stack the dishwasher, finding comfort in the sound of things being made clean. I consider taking down the Christmas decorations from the attic and looking them over to see what needs replacing, but decide I can't face the dust today. I put Joel's Minion on the mantelpiece, so he can peer out at us from his single innocent eye. The bag of weed I have no idea what to do with. Am I supposed to rid of it somehow? How does one dispose of illegal drugs? I can hardly throw it in the bin. I could flush it down the toilet, but it might clog the drains. I could take it to the police station and turn it in, but that would mean telling them where I got it and Joel's already on his last chance. And what about John? What will he think if I get rid of it? Will he accuse me of covering up for Joel?

I settle for hiding the weed in the dresser. The drawer's already full and as I push it shut, the bag splits, releasing a strong sweet scent that makes me flinch. I light a scented candle to disguise it. The name of the scent is Clean Cotton; exactly the scent you'd expect someone like me to choose. Is it strong enough to mask the smell of the weed? I can't tell.

When the dining table is clear and wiped down, I make myself a cup of coffee and sit down. Normally I would be cleaning the bathroom at this time, but today I feel I've earned the right to take a break. I sit with my coffee and consider what I imagine has been a difficult morning and think about all the things I wish I didn't have to deal with.

I wish John hadn't gone through Joel's room again. I wish John was here instead of at the hospital, so he could tell me what we ought to do about the bag of weed. I wish he'd let me go after Joel this morning. I wish my life was easier. Because this is the hardest thing I've ever had to survive, I believe this is as bad as things can ever be. I've been made soft and lazy, my heart fat and tender with too many years of love.

Day One continues. Nothing happens to warn me of the events that have already begun to unfold, like a paper flower dropped into water, like a cocoon hatching a tightly-folded monster. It's Melanie's day off, so we meet for lunch and we sit in the window of a chic little bar-restaurant in the Avenues. The décor subtly encourages an early start to festive excess (*Plan your Party season with us*, murmurs the sign in the window, and the tall plant in the corner already wears its twinkly lights in token of the season). The menu, however, is composed almost entirely of food for women like me – white fish, smoked salmon, slenderly shredded chicken, roasted vegetables, seeds of various kinds – with a token dish of steak and chips for husbands. If I could know the nights and days I have ahead of me, I would forget all pretence of dainty dieting and instead choose this strong savage dish of red meat and fried carbohydrates; I would order it rare and eat it with my fingers, letting the juices run down my chin, filling me with strength. Lacking the terrible gift of foresight, I remember the dress I've bought for John's Christmas party and order the chicken salad and leave most of the dressing in its cup, allowing myself only a token drizzle across the rocket, the chard and the radicchio. I resist the temptation to order a small glass of white wine.

Melanie looks tired but blooming. She says she's bored at work and ready for something new. When she reaches for her glass of sparkling water, I glimpse a grey elasticated band two fingers below the wrist-joint. These scraps of information click together in my mind, pricking me with envy. I brace myself for Melanie to tell me her news, but she says nothing. I wonder how many more weeks I have left to practice putting on my happy face. Perhaps she and Richard will announce it over presents and fruit cake on Christmas afternoon, and John will exclaim with pleasure and insist on opening champagne. I remind myself that my fertility exists independent of Melanie's; however much it feels like it, she has stolen nothing from me. The seconds and minutes tick by.

I'm back at home, waiting for Joel. He's normally in by half-past four, and I'll steal a precious few minutes with him as he eats the snack I've made, before disappearing to his room to do homework, or else (more likely) to lose himself in a world peopled with orcs and wizards and elves. Today I've made him a crusty sandwich fat with deli meats and mayonnaise, the kind of sandwich only very young men can eat and still find room for dinner. Joel was slow to leave behind the peachy tenderness of childhood, but now he stretches up like a green sapling, seemingly growing as I watch. His top lip has become fuzzed over with downy hairs that, to John's frustration, he refuses to shave off. This is what I'm thinking about as the clock ticks towards a quarter to five, and the drip of mayonnaise on the plate begins to dry around the edges, and Joel does not come home.

John returns late, just after half past eight, hungry and exhausted. Normally he's greeted with wine, kisses, the scent of food cooking. Tonight I can serve up only my own pale frantic face, my wringing hands, the flood of words I've been holding back. Joel hasn't come home. He walked out of school just before lunch. I missed the call. He hasn't come home. Help me. Do something. Find him.

Here's what I want John to do: to be calm, to take control, to construct an orderly plan of how we are going to find Joel and bring him home immediately. Here's what John actually does: to my fright and perplexity, he flies into an immediate and terrifying rage. What the hell were the school playing at, not making sure we knew Joel was truanting? What does he think he's doing, the little shit? If he thinks disappearing for a few hours is going to get him off the hook, he's got another bloody thing coming, that's for sure. He, John, doesn't need this after the day he's had. He's spent half the day watching people die and the other half trying to protect the team from budget cuts, he had to walk out of a meeting this afternoon he was so angry, he's been driving round for hours trying to calm down. What do I think I'm doing, greeting him with this the second he walks through the door? *Why are you being like this?* I demand, my voice high and fragile like a little girl's voice, and then I know the answer; John, like me, is terrified. Something has gone terribly wrong.

I tell John I'll ring the police. I want him to tell me he'll do it. I want him to tell me we don't need to call them at all. Instead he nods wearily and sits down at the table where Joel's sandwich still waits for him. John reaches for it in a daze, eating in the thoughtless, mechanical way I've seen him do so many times before, just a body taking on fuel while the driver stares into the distance and waits for the tank to fill. I want to say, *Don't eat that, it's for Joel!* I want to say, *How can you eat when our son's missing?*

Two hours pass. I pace the house, round and round from one

room to the next, beginning and finishing beneath the clock in the hall. Joel has been missing for nine and a half hours, but I have only known about it for five. Each time I come back to rest beneath the clock, I'm astounded to find that time has yet again moved on and the nightmare continues, and that somehow I'm not yet dead of terror or exhaustion, I still have the strength to pace and wait and listen for sounds. The sound of the gate. The sound of footsteps on the path. The sound of Joel's key in the lock. One of these sounds has to happen soon.

I see the patrol car pull up outside my house. Our neighbours will see it too, watching avidly from behind closed doors. I don't care, and this frightens me, because that means I'm adapting to a terrible new reality where what the neighbours think is unimportant. I want to keep everything the same. I want to care what the neighbours will think. I want time to stop so I can catch my breath and regroup. I also want time to skip ahead to the moment of reunion, when all of this will dissolve in warmth and light and voices. Time won't stop. Time never stops. Time keeps ruthlessly ticking by, no matter how badly you want to freeze it in place. The police come to the door.

There are two of them, one older than me, one about my age. The one about my age is Nick, although it will be months before I know him by his first name. We look at each other.

For a fraction of a second, before we both remember who we are and why we're meeting in my hallway like this, time stops.

The panic has not truly begun to set in yet, but the search has begun. Everything is real and official now, as the swirl of possibility solidifies into recorded fact. Joel is missing.

The police are scarily efficient. They take the details of Joel's mobile phone (make, model, payment plan, phone number, service provider), then ask for the names of Joel's friends, and when I confess that I'm not sure, most of them are online, they take the names of the few I can produce, and casually agree between themselves that they'll get the names from the lads themselves. (Why didn't I think of this? Why didn't I drive round to their houses and demand their phones and scroll through them and call every single contact they have? Because I'm weak and useless. But I'm learning. I'll get better. I'll find my son.) They ask if we've called Joel's number, ignoring John's irritation, and then call it themselves anyway, carefully walking the house and listening for a tell-tale ring or vibration. They make no apology for doing this.

Within minutes they've split open the events of this morning, no drama or preparation, just a few quick questions and it's all spilled out onto the carpet. Yes, we argued with Joel this morning. Yes, it was to do with drugs. Yes, we've known for a while that he's been experimenting. Yes, he had drugs in the house, John found them in his room.

Where are the drugs now? I go to the drawer and take out the burst bag. Shreds of weed fall out onto the carpet and a huge gust of laughter whooshes out of me, high and hysterical. Nick absorbs all of this with no sign of shock, taking the bag as naturally as if it's a cup of tea or a bag of shopping. He makes it easy for us to share these things we think are shameful, making them routine and normal so I almost forget I'm telling a strange police officer my son is a criminal. They tell us the facts: most runaways come back of their own accord; the majority are found within forty-eight hours; the most likely explanation is that Joel is simply angry with us and is staying at a friend's place. They advise us to try and get some rest, and leave.

John and I sit side by side on the sofa. The curtains are still open and the night stares in. I don't want to move. If I move I will be changing things, accepting this new reality. Forty-eight hours. Does the clock start ticking from when he vanished, or from when I first reported him gone? Either way it's unimaginable. There's no way I can get through that amount of time without knowing where my son is.

After a minute, John reaches out and takes my hand. When I turn my face towards him, he's silently weeping.

Because the police have told us to, we go to bed. We're still secretly convinced that the key to finding Joel is to stick to the rules, follow procedures, go by the book, be the good boy and good girl we've both been all our lives. Why would we think anything else? It's worked for us up to now. In the bathroom, a pale stranger stares back at me from the mirror. She has my face, but her eyes show me a different, darker woman. I climb in beside John and lie quietly on my back with my eyes closed. We do not touch.

"Do you blame me?"

Words spoken out loud create their own sweet shock in the deep cold silence of the sleeping hours. I'm so surprised that I almost forget to answer. And in the pause between my forgetting and then my remembering, the sound of my breath as I try to shape the words I know I must speak, the sound of my silence as I fail to speak them, I feel the tender shell of our marriage crack and splinter a little.

"No," I say quickly. "No, of course I don't blame you."

At six o'clock we give up our pursuit of sleep and creep downstairs like thieves. The first night has passed and my lungs have not ceased their tireless labour of pulling down oxygen into my blood, my heart has not yet stopped its steady insistent work behind my breastbone. My son's been missing for eighteen hours now and I'm still alive. I have no idea how this could have happened.

The day crawls on. A second night. Police officers disrupt our house with their brief shocking strangeness. Nick disappears and returns, disappears and returns, his calmness a narcotic that dulls me to the pain of questions like surgical instruments. I cling to every word he speaks, every gesture he makes, more passionately attentive than if he were my lover. Accustomed all my life to getting what I want from men by charm and flirtation, I have to discipline myself to keep my behaviour within bounds. I would do anything if it would help Nick bring Joel back, I would smile shyly every time he spoke, I would bend a little lower than necessary as I passed him a mug of tea, I would rest my hand on his arm as I spoke to him. I would fuck him right here on the floor of the living room if that's what it took. I would kill John in front of him if Nick asked me to: kill him and eat his raw and bleeding heart.

But this is not what he wants. This is not what it will take. So instead I learn a new discipline. I learn to speak concisely and with accuracy, to remember times, dates and incidents, to answer the same question asked a dozen different ways with patience and without resentment. To accept that nothing I say can be taken on trust.

John's slower to learn than I am. He grows impatient at the relentless repetitive rhythms of interrogation. He doesn't understand why DI Armstrong and DC Wood are here in our home, going over and over the same information, when Joel is not here but elsewhere. He doesn't understand why they're not out looking for him. He doesn't yet realise that his job is not to dominate and criticise and sigh and demand to know what the point is since he's already answered this a dozen times, but to sit quietly, cooperate, accept there is a purpose and answer the questions. He's an alpha male who has never had his word seriously questioned before and he doesn't realise how his behaviour is making him look.

The police need access to Joel's phone bill; something we can do easily. All our bills are together in one real-time online inventory, all the numbers we've ever called and all the connections we've ever made in a slow itemised list that has caught Joel out several times before (*I know you were on your phone in class because I can see the data usage, okay? There's no point pretending with me*).

The numbers are quickly identified: me, John, the few boys Joel classes as friends. Only one number refuses to give up its secret. It belongs to an unregistered pay-as-you-go phone bought from a shop in the City Centre just over a year ago, and a call to this number always precedes one of Joel's periodic disappearances from school, including the day Joel disappeared.

This should shock me, but instead my heart bounds with unreasoning secret gladness. This is a drugs thing, after all. Joel is off taking drugs somewhere. The places where the addicts go are known to the police, who prefer them corralled into known locations. And that means that Joel can and will be found.

Another deadline passes: the completion of the forty-eight hours in which seven out of ten lost boys are found and returned. Our own lost boy remains a blank. He's not at any of his friends' houses and despite repeated reinterviewing, no one has cracked and told us where he is, where he's hiding from us. Instead, one of them drops a single treacherous truth like a small pebble dropped into a pool of dark still water, sending out ripples that will distract everyone. *Joel was scared of his dad.*

And like that, everything changes.

I am not under arrest. I am free to leave at any time. I can have a solicitor with me if I want. I do not have to answer the questions they ask me, but it may harm my defence if I do not mention when questioned something that I later rely on in court. Everything I do say may be given in evidence. I lie and say that I understand. I vow to myself that this is the last lie I will tell them. No, I don't want a solicitor present. Yes, I'm aware that I can change my mind at any time. Is John in a room next to me, having the same conversation? Has John requested legal representation? If he asks, will it count against him?

The questioning is deceptively gentle, knives wielded by a kindly assassin in velvet gloves. How was Joel's relationship with his father? When I say it was *good*, what does *good* look like? What does *doing his best* mean to me? How do I know they were happy with each other? Were there any problems in their relationship? What would I say is the *usual teenage stuff*? Did Joel ever talk to me about his relationship with his dad? How did he describe it? Was John ever violent towards Joel? How did I know John was never violent towards Joel? Were there times when John expressed disappointment with Joel? Did I know that John had said during his first interview that he was 'about ready to wallop Joel into next week when he came home, and if he didn't watch out he'd find himself with something to be really sorry about'? I can't hide the shock on my face as Nick tells me this. Is he lying? Surely he's not allowed to lie. But how would I know if he was? The spooling of the tape recorder in the corner reassures me. Nick can't lie while there's someone else listening.

I've been thinking of Nick as our friend, or at least as someone on our side. It's hard to remember that he is only here to find Joel, and that finding Joel includes the possibility that we are the enemy.

For a time, I'm included in the category of *people who might have done harm to Joel*. The precise anatomy of my own personal Day One is delicately dissected, each moment and movement recorded, accepted, abandoned and then suddenly recaptured, like a cat that lets a mouse run briefly free only to pounce on it again. When did I turn my phone off? Why did I turn my phone off? Wasn't I expecting Joel to truant from school, given his history and what had happened that morning? I cry when they ask me this, because the answer is that yes, I suspected Joel would truant, but for once, I didn't want to know. I wanted my lunch with Melanie, my precious two hours in a chic little restaurant, and I couldn't bear for Melanie to witness the school calling to tell me Joel had bolted. I couldn't bear to look like a bad, failing parent in front of my sister. They absorb this as they have everything else, pass me a box of tissues and keep going.

What time did I come home from lunch with Melanie? And then what did I do while I was at home? And can anyone verify that at all? And can I talk them through the details of exactly what housework I did? Did I watch any television? What did I watch? Read a book? Which book? How far did I get with it? What happened? I endure it because I know I must. I'm trapped in the mills of police procedure, and now it's my turn to be ground into dust.

"Please," I beg Nick, during a brief respite when the tape recorder is turned off and his companion has gone to fetch more coffee. "Please. I know you have to do this, I know you have to be sure it wasn't me. But promise me you're still looking for him *as well*?"

"This is just a chat, remember? You're not a suspect, we're just talking. You haven't been arrested. You're free to leave at any—"

"But you're still looking?"

"We're pursuing all lines of enquiry."

"Please," I repeat. "I know he's still out there. Promise me you won't stop looking."

When he looks at me, something dark and electric flows between us. If we could touch, just a moment of flesh against flesh, we would be able to understand everything about each other. My fingers creep across the table towards his. His eyes are fixed on mine. We are both holding our breath.

"All right," he whispers. In the waiting silence of the interview room, the words are like a shout. "I promise."

When DC Wood returns, she beckons Nick out of the room for a minute. Something must have happened. What have they found? And is it bad, or good? When they come back in, I find I'm clutching the edge of the table.

"There's no news about Joel," says Nick, and my spine turns to limp string. "But we've finally made contact with

Mr Palmer. Your next door neighbour," he adds, seeing my confusion.

"He spoke to you?" The thought is astounding. In all the years we've lived side-by-side, I've never heard his voice.

"He wrote us a note," says DC Wood. "It says, *I would like to confirm that on the day her son disappeared. Susannah Harper arrived home alone at around two o'clock and did not leave her house all afternoon and no one else came to the house. I am rather lonely and pass my time by watching the neighbourhood comings and goings and for this reason I am confident that I am right. I am happy to testify to this in court.* So we can probably wrap this interview up for now."

She glances sharply at Nick and then at me, as if she senses that something important might have happened in the few minutes she was out of the room. I'm unnerved by her intuition. Is she simply sensitive to the atmosphere? Or was she watching us through the mirror, to see how we might behave when we thought we were alone?

Chapter Seven
Thursday 16th November 2017

"I just hope you're being careful," Melanie says in my ear, and sighs.

Being careful used to mean *don't get pregnant*, in the days when a younger, fresher Melanie watched her older sister groom and preen before the mirror with the breathless attention of a devoted acolyte. I enjoyed showing her how to copy me, dreaming of the day when I would finally retire in a froth of tulle and orange-blossom, leaving Melanie to bask in my reflected glory, and captivate the drooping and lovesick suitors who I had chosen to leave behind. *Be careful*, she used to say to me in her best old-lady voice, when I finally turned away from the mirror. Be careful. I would always laugh and say *Okay, Mum*. But now she doesn't mean *don't get pregnant*. Now she means *don't get too close to Jackie*.

"I'm fine. What are you worried about?"

"I thought you had an online forum for people who wanted to talk to you, like a support group."

"I did. I do."

"So why does she need to come round to your house? I thought you were going to keep everything online?"

"Look, she's a friend as well, all right? I'm allowed to have friends."

"Suze." Melanie's voice is like a reproachful kiss. "You

need to protect yourself. You'll end up getting hurt."

"I know all that. You don't need to tell me. I've been blogging for years, I know how to deal with nutters."

"Then why aren't you taking your own advice?"

The skin of my ear is burning. I switch my phone to the other side and try to think of something to say. Melanie waits, waits, waits.

"We've got things in common," I say.

"You've got one thing in common and that one thing could be dangerous for you."

"How could it be dangerous?"

"Just because her son's missing doesn't make her a nice person. You don't know what she might have done, her and her husband."

"How can you say that? That's a horrible thing to say! You haven't even met her."

"I saw them on the news last night. I've heard them speak. And have you seen the husband? He must have had something to do with it. It's what everyone thinks. Even the police. You could see it in their faces at that news conference."

I made myself watch the news last night because Jackie begged me to, although I couldn't bear to hear the words and had to have the sound turned down. A manager who had stolen the money from her colleagues' Christmas savings club; a cheery piece about the switch-on date for this year's festive lights; and sandwiched between them, my friend, looking faintly unreal. Jackie's make-up was like a smooth bronze mask, with traces of her own pale skin just visible around her hairline, like a geisha. Her nails, a flawless startling teal, caught the lights of the cameras as they flashed, like baubles.

"Don't talk about her like that. You don't know her at all. Every word of this is just snobbery."

"I'm not being snobby, I'm being honest. What kind of a woman gets herself done up like that when her son's missing? I don't think you even took a shower for the first few weeks, you were such a mess—"

"Don't."

"Okay, I'm sorry. I won't. But you've got to admit it looks a bit strange. I mean, even her nails were immaculate. I haven't had nails like that since before Thomas was born."

Jackie, who put on her make-up like war paint, a way of commanding the attention of people who otherwise would never give her a second glance. Jackie, confessing that she sat up each night filing and painting her nails because she had to fill the silent hours somehow, and with the house clean and the baby asleep, what else could she do? I used to walk the streets, but I had no one at home who needed me.

"You don't know what it's like." My voice is unexpectedly hoarse.

"Suze, I'm sorry I've upset you."

"You don't know what it's like," I repeat. "But she does. She gets it. And I need to talk to someone who gets it."

"You could talk to me."

"And what would you know about my life?"

"Suze, that's not fair."

"You know what's really not fair? You get everything. You get two children without any effort and you get to see them both grow up, and you get to keep your husband and you get to live with your whole life with everyone you love, you get the perfect family Christmas to look forward to every single year, while I've got nothing and no one and when I finally find someone who understands, all you can do is go on about what colour their nails are and tell me they're not good enough for me to know!"

In the early days of telephones, there was a receiver you could slam down and storm away from. Even a clamshell allowed you the pleasure of snapping something shut, a definite final gesture of rejection. But there's no drama in ending a phone call on a touchscreen phone, just the uncertainty of *did it hang up properly? Has she gone? Yes, it's ended.* I want to throw my phone at the wall but I can't risk it. I need to keep my phone safe, just in case.

I watch the screen, waiting for it to ring. Melanie always rings me back when I throw a tantrum. She understands how hard things are for me. She's always there for me, never grudging, always generous. Although I'm older I often feel now that I'm the younger one; or rather, than I've been frozen in place while everyone else keeps growing, changing, discovering new things. Will I accept her call when she rings? Of course I will. The screen blinks and flashes. *Melanie Mobile*.

"I'm sorry," I say as soon as the call's connected.

"No, I'm sorry. I didn't mean to upset you. I'm just tired, that's all. We all had a horrible night again. Thomas was awake with a stinking cold and Grace is still having nightmares about being taken away by bad people."

"Oh, that's a shame."

"She was really upset, going on and on about how these bad people were going to take her away and she'd never see any of us again."

"We used to believe that too, do you remember? The child-catchers of Hull Fair. Can't believe it's still doing the rounds."

A deep, exasperated silence. Strange how the absence of words can express itself so differently even when the silent one is connected to you only by a phone call.

"Susannah, we both know that's not where she got it from. Look, I know things are difficult, but I've got to say this. You really frightened her that night at the Fair."

"I… I what?"

"At the Fair. You remember."

"No, wait, hang on a minute. I never told her that story about the Fair people taking kids away, why on earth would I do that? She'll have heard it in the playground just like we did."

"Not the *Fair* people, *bad* people. And she definitely got it from you, Susannah. You were watching them on the carousel, and then suddenly you were sobbing behind the bins and going on about Joel."

"No! No, I didn't, I never mention Joel to them, either of them, never *ever*, I never would. I know I was upset but I wouldn't—"

"Well, trust me, you did! You were hysterical, it was awful, you kept saying his name over and over, they were both terrified. God, I don't know how we ever got home, and now Grace is convinced someone's going to take her away and she'll never see us again. Do you honestly not remember this?"

I force myself to keep my temper. I remember every moment of that night, including that one. I was upset, I had to be comforted, but it was nothing like the apocalypse Melanie's describing.

"Of course I remember, I just didn't realise... look, I'm so, so sorry. I didn't mean to scare her. I love Grace so much, you know that. I was upset but I never meant to frighten her. Please forgive me."

Melanie sighs. "Okay. Forget it. Shit happens." In the distance, I hear a shocked and joyful shriek. "Oh, for goodness sake, Thomas, stop listening in."

"Mother! You swore! You said—" His voice is high and husky with cold.

"Oi. Enough out of you. You're supposed to be in bed sick, remember? I can still take you up to school at lunchtime if you're feeling better."

"How am I supposed to learn not to swear if you swear?"

"You're cleverer than me, you'll figure it out. Susannah, I'd better go, Thomas needs me."

I wish I could ask her to leave the call open, carry her phone in her pocket as she goes about the beautiful banality of a morning at home with her children. When I visit them, I feel the household subtly reconfiguring as it always does when a visitor comes: the television going off, the standard of everyone's manners going up a notch, sweet wrappers straight in the bin or shoved sneakily down the side of the sofa. But sometimes, if I stay long enough and sit quietly enough, they begin to forget again, like experimental subjects in a psychology project. Thomas and Grace giggling in a corner over a drawing that Grace has done and Thomas has embellished. Melanie and Richard snapping crossly at each other over the dishwasher, then giving each other a biscuit to make up again. I had all of this once too.

Instead, my Thursday morning will be spent on self-imposed household chores, in a house that stays unnaturally clean because only I live here. Thursday. Clean-sheets day. I always change the sheets on a Thursday.

Joel's room is waiting for something. It's in the breathless way the dust motes hang in the air and everything around me is frozen, waiting for time to begin again. It feels like the moment at a party when the music stops and every child freezes in place, and you stalk cautiously between them, watching out for a wavering arm or wobbly leg. I catch myself humming a tune as I move through the room. Nothing is wrong here. Everything is fine.

On the shelf beneath the mirror, the little pot of hair wax has long ago dried out and turned unusable. I lay the duvet cover carefully down on the bed, take the lid off the hair wax and breathe in. My nose fills with the greasy smell of candles, laced with the fading ghosts of chemical flowers. Joel liked to tousle his hair into thick lank waves around his face, and begged to be allowed to dye it black. I would have let him, but John's flat *no* was law. I consoled Joel by reminding him that Kurt Cobain was blond.

As I replace the pot on the shelf, I catch a glimpse of movement in the mirror. There's someone standing behind me.

"John!" My voice is shrill and shocked. "How did you get in here? Are you all right? Is there any news…"

My voice trails into silence, because there's something wrong about the way John looks. His skin is pale and unhealthy, as if he's standing under a different light to the

100

thin grey gloom that creeps through the lowering grey clouds. His head is bowed. His hands hang heavily by his side. When he takes a step towards me, there's a jerky quality to his movement, as if he's pulling hard against something that's holding him prisoner. And there's a smell about him, too, a terrible damp earthy smell, as if he's been buried alive and has dug himself up to freedom.

"Help me." His voice is slow and thick. "Help me. I need you. Are you there? Please don't leave me."

"John, what's happened? How did you get in here? I didn't think you had a key any more—"

He raises his head then, and when I see the dreadful brightness of his eyes I understand that I am in terrible danger, because John, my gentle, rational, cardiac surgeon ex-husband, has somehow become mad.

"Look at the mess you made," he says, and picks up the duvet cover. "This place is disgusting. It makes me sick. How dare you make us live like this?"

"I was just about to change the bed, that's all, I'll have it tidy in a second, I promise." John is between me and the door. "Does... does Nathalie know you're here?"

Mentioning his new wife makes John angry. He snarls and lurches closer to me, invading my space so I can feel the size and heat of him.

"We're not discussing anything until we've talked about this great big filthy fucking mess! Look at it! Look! Mud everywhere! And it's all your fault!"

"John, please, I'm sorry. Let's go downstairs and talk. Sit down and be comfortable?"

"Oh yes. I like downstairs. Let's go downstairs, and you can suck me off in the living room." His free hand fumbles at his belt. "Suck my prick, and make the daddy-monster go away for a while. I used to like that. Let's do that again."

"No! Don't do that, please don't do that. Not in here, not in Joel's room, let's go downstairs at least, we can't do that in here—" I think about ducking beneath his arm and making a run for the door, but he takes a step to the left to block me. "Come on. Let's go downstairs and have a cup of tea or something. Shall we?" I try to smile but the muscles of my face are too frozen to move properly. "John, please, I'll do whatever you want, but I don't think you're well, you're not yourself—"

"Of course I'm not myself! I'm the man you made me into. I tried to be a good father and a good husband, I really did, but you took away all my choices!" He's wrapping the duvet cover round his hand, round and round until his fist is fat like a boxing glove. "I loved you, though. That was the only thing that mattered by the end. So I've come to warn you. You'd better stop all of this shit while you still can. What the mud swallows, it holds onto for ever. But if you dig deep enough you'll find something I don't want you to find, and then I will be very, very angry!"

"John, what are you saying? What did you do?"

"What did I do? What did I do? I did what you made me do, Susannah, we all did!"

His bunched fist, wrapped in faded blue cotton, slams out with a strength I'd never imagined. It connects, not with me, but with the mirror behind my head. The sound of my scream blends with the high tinkle of the mirror shattering. I cover my head with my arms and drop to the floor. John stands over me, an angry giant. He pulls the wrapping from his fist and drops it contemptuously to the floor. Despite the protection he gave himself, his knuckles drip with blood.

"Do you see yet?" he roars. I hide my face in my hands, but he pulls them away and grabs at my face, smearing my skin, forcing me to look at him. "Do you see what you made me into? You blame me for what happened to Joel, but the truth is it was all your fault!"

"John, I'm sorry! I'm sorry! I'm sorry!"

And then, just as suddenly as he appeared, he's gone. He doesn't leave. He just vanishes. One moment he's standing over me, his tall shape blotting out the light, his blood dripping onto me, that terrible rotten-earth smell pouring off him in waves, his breath hot and loud against my cheek. And then the next moment...

"John?" My voice quavers in the calm, clean silence. The duvet cover that lies crumpled by my feet. When I pick it up, I feel a thin pain and then the warm trickle of escaping blood. "Oh, damn it. Ow. Ow." Something's tickling my forehead. I reach up to touch it. Glass. There's glass in my hair. No, not glass. A long slice of silver, like a dagger or an icicle. Joel's mirror is broken.

I don't want to wrap my bleeding hand in Joel's duvet, so I bunch my T-shirt around it and clench my fist tightly, trying not to panic at the size of the stain that leaks out into the cotton. When I stand up, five more long glittering spikes tumble to the floor. Thank God I'm wearing shoes.

In the centre of the mirror, a raggedy circle of plywood has appeared, surrounded by cracked fragments of silvered glass. It looks like a prop from a movie. I touch it wonderingly. Am I dreaming this? What's going on?

John was here. I'm as sure of that as I possibly can be. In every way, he was here; I felt him, heard him, saw him, smelled him, his hands touched my face. And then he was gone. I'm alone in the house. But what if I'm not? And what if he's still angry? Am I safe? Where's my phone? Should I call someone? And who can I call?

My fist clenched tightly in my T-shirt, I creep out of Joel's room. The door to my bedroom is half open. From a safe distance, I peer into it. Then I study the gap between the door and the door frame, trying to judge if someone's hidden in the space behind. Nothing. I push the door hard just to make sure. Nothing. There's no one under the bed. When I fling open the wardrobe, the rattle of coat-hangers makes me shriek, but there's nothing in there but my clothes. A trickle of blood crawls around the curve of my wrist, ready to drop onto the carpet. I wipe it against my stomach and keep going.

Nothing in the little office box room, so empty and sterile

now it no longer holds John's books and papers. Has the chair moved a fraction since I last looked at it? I give it a tiny push, notice the resistance as the wheels leave the grooves worn into the carpet. When I take my hand off the back of the chair, it rolls back into place.

Nothing in the bathroom, No lurking shadow behind the shower curtain, no ominous reflection in the mirror. My fingers pulse with pain. Standing over the sink, I unwrap the T-shirt and inspect the damage.

Oh God. Is that bone? Can I see bone? Tendons? I put my good hand to my mouth, press hard to muffle the scream. No, it's just the whiteness of my cut skin, that's all. It has to be. I don't want to go to hospital. I just want this to be over. I turn on the cold tap, force myself to hold my fingers underneath. The flow of blood accelerates again, turning the water pink, but at least now I can see what I'm dealing with. Once the wound is purged of the mess surrounding it, it turns out to be smaller than I'd feared. I'm going to be fine. I fumble for a towel, blot blood and water from my skin, open the medicine cabinet and clumsily rummage for dressings. It's hard to bandage your own palm and fingers, especially with your non-dominant hand, but living alone forces you to learn all sorts of unexpected skills. When I close the cabinet, I glimpse my face in its mirrored front and see that it's smeared with blood.

I look into the mirror for a long time. John smashed the mirror. His knuckles were bleeding. He touched my face. Then he was gone. I cut my hand. I came into the bathroom. I saw the damage, and I put my hand to my face. So whose prints are on my skin? Are they mine? Or my ex-husband's?

My phone is charging on the table in the hallway. Sitting on the third step from the bottom, I scroll through the list of my contacts, trying to hold myself together long enough to make the call.

My fingers are slow and clumsy as I stab at the screen. The phone rings four times, five, six. Then, a brief fumbling sound and Nick's voice, low and blurry, as if he's speaking to me from beneath deep water. I must have woken him from sleep.

"Susannah? Is everything okay?"

"Is this a good time? I'm sorry, I shouldn't have called you."

"No, please don't be sorry, it's fine. What's happening? Any news? Have you had another message from JoelMoel?"

"No. Nothing like that. Is it your day off? Have I rung you at home? I'm sorry, I'll leave you in peace."

"Shush. If I minded, I wouldn't have taken the call. Now tell me what I can do to help you."

How do I begin? I can hear Nick's breathing. I wonder what he wears to sleep in. If he's alone in the bed or if Bella lies warm and comfortable beside him, her hand on his back as a sleepy reminder that she's still there, he still belongs to her. Through the window I can see the faint muzziness in the air that tells me it's begun to rain.

"I was in Joel's room this morning," I say at last. "Changing the bedding. I know it's stupid but I do it every week, I want there to be fresh sheets on the bed just in case he—"

"It's all right, you don't have to explain. And what happened?"

"I was thinking about when he first disappeared. And I wondered... I thought... I don't know why I even thought it, but I just wondered... is there any chance that John might have..."

"John? Your husband, John?" Nick is instantly alert.

"Oh God, I know that's stupid. I know he wouldn't. I don't know why I even thought it, I shouldn't have bothered you with it. I'm wasting your time. I'm sorry."

"Susannah. It's all right. Stay on the line. It's all right. Can you hear me? Are you still there? Okay. Now, I tell you what. How about I come round later and we can have a chat about things?"

"No, you don't need to do that. I'm sorry, I shouldn't have called you."

"Not up to you. I'll be round about two, okay?"

"You don't have to do this. I don't want to ruin your day off."

"To be honest, you'll be doing me a favour. Bella's got her book group coming over. They all met in therapy, they call themselves the madwomen in the attic. They scare the shit out of me."

"If you're sure you don't mind—"

"About two, okay? Make sure you've got the kettle on. Two spoons of coffee, two spoons of sugar. And get some biscuits in as well. I'm horrible when I'm hungry."

I've just called a police officer and told him I suspect my husband, and all the evidence I have is an experience I can never discuss with anyone. I'm wasting police time and making trouble for John. I should be terrified. But all I feel is a strange weightless happiness. Happiness, and a strange cracking feeling in the skin of my face, as if I'm wearing a face mask and it's time to wash it off. I'm still smeared with blood. But whose fingers put it there?

Perhaps I should treat my body as a crime scene, preserve the evidence for when Nick arrives at my house for his mug of strong sweet coffee. Instead, I go upstairs to the bathroom and, working carefully with my one good hand, wash the blood from my skin, then apply a thin sheen of tinted moisturiser. Later I will come back and apply make-up, to make sure I at least look human. In the meantime, I have to clean up Joel's room.

The Sonic duvet cover is still bunched on the floor. I pick it up gingerly and, holding it by the edges, shake it to dislodge the scraps and shards of broken mirror. Fragments of light tumble onto the carpet. There's a long smear of blood across Sonic's face. I'll have to wash it again. I carry the cover down to the sink.

Hot water, Lux, a gentle but firm submersion. It's hard to wash anything with just one hand but I'll manage somehow. If John was here he'd tell me I was making work

106

for myself. He often said that about the things I did for Joel, not understanding that, after waiting for so long to become a mother, I did even the most mundane tasks with joy. Something scratches lightly at my palm, and I feel delicately around and pull out another huge shard of mirror, long and deadly like a dagger. I pull the plug out and lift the cover to let the water drain away. The weight of water drags at the frail fabric and I can see what's going to happen, grabbing uselessly at it with my bandaged hand, not caring about getting it wet. But it's too late. The thin fabric gives way, leaving a ragged hole right across the centre, a tear that I can already see will be impossible to repair.

Perhaps the fabric was always flawed, and this is an inevitable accident that has been waiting for years for me to handle it with just the right degree of clumsiness. Perhaps it was the broken mirror, starting with a tiny little slit that the water has stretched out into a giant hole. Perhaps it's my fault, for washing it so diligently, each round of hot water and detergent nibbling away at the fibres of the cotton until at last there was simply nothing left to hold it together. The reasons don't matter. All that matters is that it's torn. Joel's favourite duvet cover is torn. And nothing I can do will ever fix it.

Life Without Hope:
Why I Was Lucky

If we'd met and talked when we were young, you probably wouldn't have liked me very much. This won't make me sound very attractive but I'll say it anyway because it's true; I was the kind of woman other women often secretly hate, because I was born lucky and I knew it. I knew I was good-looking, I knew I was clever enough but not too clever, I knew I was good at making men like me, and making them keep liking me even after they'd got used to my prettiness. Most of all, I knew I was lucky because what I wanted (work for a few years, get married, have children and stay at home with them) was all achievable for me with what I had. If a man went shopping for the kind of wife I wanted to be, I would be the picture he'd have in his head.

And for a long time, that's how it went. I passed my exams. I got a job I quite liked but wouldn't mind quitting when the time came. At just the age I wanted to settle down, I met my lovely husband. We fell completely and sincerely in love. Our wedding was perfect. Our honeymoon was perfect. We started trying for a baby on our wedding night, and when I checked my dates before the wedding, I knew we'd be lucky again because our wedding night fell right in the middle of my fertile window.

Except I couldn't get pregnant.

I think I knew the very first month that my luck had run out and this was going to be a struggle. John, being a doctor, kept telling me not to be so silly, it took most couples around six months or so, I'd been stressed to the eyeballs with our wedding, and what with strange food and jet-lag and so on, it would have been a miracle if we *had* got pregnant.

And I knew he was right. But I also knew he was wrong. And he was wrong. Six months later, we still weren't pregnant.

So I went to see the doctor, who told me to come back

if we still weren't pregnant in a year, and six months later I *was* back, and then we started the investigations, and they found... nothing. John's sperm count was good. My tubes were open. I was ovulating. We were having plenty of sex, at the right time of the month. We were officially *unexplained*.

Of course, I had my own explanation. I'd used up all my luck. And serve me right.

So I quit smoking (not that I smoked much, but I stopped even those few at parties) and I stopped drinking (ditto) and I bought a mountain of vitamin pills, and we started IVF. And it didn't work. And it didn't work. And it still didn't work. So we took a break. And then we went back. And it still didn't work. And we went on holiday. And tried again. And it didn't work. And I quit my job. And we had another holiday. And we tried again. And still, still, still, it didn't work. I was officially out of luck.

But along the way, although it was brutal and awful and punishing, I think I might have become a slightly nicer person. Because when John suggested we look at adoption, I didn't immediately wonder if they would have the sort of child I wanted. Instead I thought, *How can I learn to be a good enough parent and give a child whatever they need?* If you'd met me then, I hope I was a bit more likeable by that time.

And then, the most amazing thing happened. It was the thing that they tell you right at the start not to even dream about, because what with better contraception and a more accepting world it basically never happens any more, but despite what they say it does still happen occasionally, and it happened to us.

A baby. There was a baby. John and I were matched with a baby.

And that baby was Joel. Our Winter's child. He came home just before Christmas. And he was perfect. And for the fifteen years we were lucky enough to have him, our lives were transformed.

Maybe no one can be as lucky as I was for a whole lifetime. Maybe that's why Joel had to leave us the way he did. But I still wouldn't change a thing. Because for those fifteen years, I was the luckiest woman alive.

Posted on 12th January 2014
Filed to: Family Life
Tags: parenting journey, family life, adoption success story, missing people, support for families, Susannah Harper, Joel Harper

Chapter Eight
Thursday 16th November 2017

Nick's been in my house many times before, but today feels different because we are alone, and because instead of the crisp shirt and suit, Nick is wearing jeans and a soft shabby T-shirt that smells faintly of fabric-softener. Or perhaps the difference is the blur in my head from the handful of painkillers I've downed, trying to drown out the nagging of my injured palm. Perhaps it's because making the coffee and laying out the biscuits with just one hand is a struggle, all my movements turned slow and clumsy in the way that's faintly reminiscent of the sweet dreamy awkwardness of being alone in the house with boys I really liked. The rain taps at the window like a visitor asking for admission. Nick has left the living room and is now standing in the doorway to the kitchen.

"I'm afraid I've ruined your reputation. The woman over the road saw me arriving."

I take my time over the biscuits. "Did she speak to you?"

"No. I just saw her nebbing through the window at your gentleman caller. Now she's out there pretending to hang up her Christmas lights."

"Already?"

"Only thirty-eight sleeps to go now. What happened to your hand?"

"I broke a mirror."

"It's bleeding through already. Sit down and let me take a look at it."

"It's fine."

"Where's the first-aid kit?"

"Really, it's fine." Nick shakes his head sternly. "Oh, look, it's upstairs in the bathroom, but honestly—"

"Right. In the dining room. Sit down at the table. Back in a minute."

I abandon the coffee-making and sit down at the table, obedient and well-behaved, a good little girl. Once it would have been John telling me to sit down and wait while he fetched the first-aid supplies. Now, instead, it's Nick. Do all men do this to women who need help? Do all women take the same pleasure in it? I can hear Nick moving around upstairs, the click of the bathroom cabinet as it opens and closes, then his feet as he comes down the stairs. The rhythm of his footsteps is different to both John and Joel.

"Okay." He takes my hand, firm and brotherly, and begins to unwind the bandage. "Let's have a look." The gauze is stuck to my skin with half-dried blood, and I try not to wince as he lifts it off. "Sorry, I know this must hurt." The last of the gauze comes away with a tearing sensation, and Nick's fingers tighten around my wrist. "Jesus wept, Susannah, that's a bad one."

"It looks worse than it feels."

"It could do with stitching. Any chance you'll let me take you to hospital?" I shake my head and he sighs. "We'll do the best we can with what we've got, then." He dives into the first-aid box, choosing Savlon cream, fresh gauze, surgical tape, another bandage. His touch against my hurt palm is unexpectedly delicate.

"You found the first-aid kit all right?" I ask, to break the tension.

His smile takes my breath. "I'm quite good at looking for things in strange houses. Some people say I should be a copper. Are you sure you don't want this stitching? Last chance before I wrap it up."

"It'll be fine."

"Tougher than you look?"

"That's me."

"I know it is." His fingers are lying against my wrist and the light catches his wedding ring. I wonder if he can feel the butterfly flutter of my pulse.

"So." He's carefully not looking at me, concentrating a little harder than he needs to on the task of dressing my hand. "Do you want to tell me what made you start wondering about John? Has he been in touch with you recently? Done something to frighten you or upset you?"

"No! God no, nothing like that. He wouldn't ever... no. He hasn't. I promise. I don't even know what made me call you. I'm so sorry."

"You know," says Nick, "we had a bloke in the other week telling us his neighbours were running a cannabis farm. Nothing dodgy-looking about the house mind you, no strange noises, no funny comings and goings, nice enough couple, both had jobs as far as he could tell. So we asked him why he thought that, and he said it came to him in a dream."

Is it all right to laugh? I'm not sure I dare. What if the end of this story is *so we charged him with wasting police time?*

"He said that in this dream, he went round to their house to water their plants because they were away. And when he opened the front door, there was a great big pit with this huge plant living in it. He said it was like the one in *Little Shop of Horrors*. And when he woke up, he knew. Well, we nearly didn't bother, in fact we told him it was an offence to waste police time, but he stuck to his story, not making a fuss, just really determined. Said he knew how it sounded and he'd understand if we didn't act on it, but he wouldn't feel right not saying anything. Anyway, we had someone in the area that day, so we dropped round for a quick recce just on the off-chance, and you know what? He was right. They'd got a trapdoor in the living room to a secret basement and they had this huge operation going on underground."

"You're kidding."

"I'm not. And my point is, information comes to people in all sorts of ways. Especially if they've been through a traumatic experience. In dreams... in flashbacks... visions..." He gives me a quick, friendly smile. "And they can be so powerful that they can compel ordinary blokes to come along to the station and risk looking like an absolute prize tit, just because they know they might be right."

"I... um..." But I can't make myself say *I had a vision of John*. "It was something that came to me suddenly. Just an idea that he might have done something bad. But you looked at him at the time, I know you did. I feel so stupid. I'm sorry. I know this isn't helping."

"How did it come to you? Was it like an image, or a sound, or what?"

"It was like someone talking to me. Someone saying—"

"Yes?"

If you dig deep enough you might find something I don't want you to find.

"Saying that John did his best to be a good father, but he didn't always manage it. Something like that."

"Was there anything else? Did you see anything, maybe?"

"I got a sort of picture as well. It was John. And he was angry. More angry than I've ever seen him. I didn't even know a person could look like that. He looked—"

"It's okay. You can tell me."

"He looked angry enough to kill someone. And I thought, what if he did? So I called you."

"And you know what? When you told me that – as soon as you said his name – I felt I had to come round here straight away."

I catch my breath. "Does that mean anything?"

"It means we both thought it might be important. So I want you to promise me something."

114

"All right."

"If anything else comes to you – by any means at all, I don't care how irrational you might think it is – I want you to call me. All right? Will you do that?"

"So you don't think I'm going mad?"

"I think you're really brave and you've been through a dreadful experience and it's left you with some scars."

"Is that a nice way of saying yes, you think I'm going mad?"

"Hey, it's all right if you are. I'm good with mad women, remember? Got married to one and everything. That's better, I like it when you smile." The table judders with a sudden vibration. "Is that your phone or mine?"

"Mine. It's all right, I'll let it ring out."

"Jackie *Nelson*?" Nick's looking at the screen. "Do you mind me asking? Is that the Jackie Nelson whose son's missing?"

"Yes. She came to see me, we've been chatting, that's all."

The phone falls silent. Nick looks at the screen thoughtfully.

"Is that all right? Are we allowed?"

"Yes, of course you are."

"So why are you looking like that? As if I've done something wrong? I didn't mean to cause problems for you."

"You haven't caused any problems for me."

"But?"

Nick reaches out as if to take my hand again. Hesitates. Lets his hand fall. "If I tell you something, do you promise to keep it secret?"

"I promise."

"It has to be completely off the record."

"I won't say anything. Not to anyone."

"Not even to Jackie? In fact, especially not to Jackie?"

This time, the tingle in my scalp is not because of his nearness.

"Why? What is it? What do you know about her?"

"It's not anything I know, it's just a precaution. I want you to be careful around her. Don't tell her anything too personal, nothing you might regret later if… well, just nothing too personal. Don't let her get inside your head. All those boundaries… you make sure you keep them up nice and high where she's concerned. Just in case anything happens in the future that might make you wish you hadn't been close to her."

I don't dare tell him that Jackie already crawled into my heart and found a safe haven there.

"You think she…" I don't even want to say the word. "You don't think Ryan's alive any more?"

"I don't think anything for sure, not yet. I'm not saying she's done anything wrong at all, not her or her husband. Okay? I'm absolutely not saying that. We're still investigating Ryan's disappearance as if he's a runaway."

"But you can't possibly think she—"

Nick raises his finger and puts it to my lips. His flesh against my mouth feels sharp and tender, all my nerve endings exposed. I can feel the rough calluses of his fingers, the dryness in his skin, the warmth of him. I can smell the Savlon he's been putting on my injured hand, mingled with soap. *He's married*, I think to myself, as I've thought a million times before, *he's married and he's the investigating officer for your son's disappearance. This can never ever happen not ever, he doesn't see you that way and he never will so don't even think about it.* But none of it matters, because Nick is touching me – my hand, my wrist, my mouth – and even though the touch is meaningless to him, it is the most intimacy my skin has known for what feels like a lifetime.

"Just be careful," he repeats.

He's hardly left the house before the phone rings again. When I answer, Jackie's voice sounds very lost and forlorn.

"Susannah? It's me. Jackie, I mean."

"How are you? Any news?"

"No. You?"

"No."

"So how are you doing?"

My hand throbs treacherously. I bite my lip against the pain and hide it behind my back so I won't have to look at it.

"Not bad," I say carefully. "How about you?"

"Honestly? Terrible. I'm sorry, I didn't mean to ring you up just to be miserable—"

"It's okay, you can tell me."

"I realised this morning, it's starting to feel normal. It was bad enough when we was all just running round in a panic thinking we'd get him back in a couple of days, but getting used to it, that's just... you know what I mean? Well, course you do, I'm sorry, I wasn't thinking."

"That's okay."

"I thought I heard him come back last night. I was sat up in Georgie's room, I heard the front door go and everything. Heard his feet on the stairs. I jumped out the chair and ran to look and then he just... There was nobody there."

"That used to happen to me too."

"Does it ever stop?"

"You have it less as time goes on."

"God, I can't afford to start howling again. Georgie'll start too, she always does when I cry. I just wondered, is there any chance you can come round to mine for a bit? Maybe stop for tea?"

I hesitate. I'm still high and floaty with shared secrets and painkillers and the touch of Nick's fingers on my hand and wrist and mouth. I want to sit quietly and absorb the sweetness into my skin. If I open the window and lean out, will I see the ghost of his car disappearing into the rain?

"Please." Jackie's voice is urgent. "Lee's working straight through and my mam's busy with a GP appointment for my dad. I really need someone to talk to. This awful thing happened at the police station this morning and I need you, I'm sorry to beg but I do. Please come. Don't drive, you'll not find us. Just get off the bus at the hospital and I'll come and meet you and walk you down."

This is what Nick means by *boundaries*; the brutal ruthless process of protecting the time you need to serve your own wants, against the brutal sucking pit of others' needs. I'm not used to being begged so shamelessly, so guiltlessly. The feeling of being needed is intoxicating.

"Okay," I say. "Give me about half an hour."

The diesel thrumming of the bus shivers through my body and I'm grateful for the warmth of my fellow passengers. They said on the radio this morning that this winter would be the coldest for forty years and already the chill is creeping into the bones of the city. Perhaps we'll even have a white Christmas. I hope Jackie and Georgie won't get chilled waiting for me at the bus stop. The bus windows are steamy with breath and the wheels hiss as they skim over the slick wet surface of the road. My feet are cold, but my belly is hot with anxiety and guilt. This is the very opposite of what Nick told me to do.

Jackie's face turns bright with relief when she sees me, waving frantically up at the window like a little child, turning the pram and seizing Georgie's pudgy fist and making her wave too. Her hair sparkles with droplets of water and I can see from the puffiness around her eyes that she's been crying again. When I stumble off the bus, she grabs me with sharp fingers and hugs me tight. I can smell the chemical strawberry of her shampoo, and I think how far we've come since I first saw her at the police station, how quickly we've opened up to each other.

"Thanks," she whispers into my hair. "This way."

The walk takes us down the kind of street I would dislike being alone on. We take a narrow iron walkway over a wide railway line, stride quickly past grey pebble-dash houses with high railings and barred windows, and aging cars with bright yellow locks on the steering wheels and wheelie bins with the house numbers of their owners painted in high wavering numerals. Georgie's scarlet buggy, darkened with rain, rolls onwards like a tank, clearing pigeons and pedestrians from the narrow footpath and onto the mown verge beside. We turn through a narrow entrance, squeeze the buggy through iron barriers built to stop bicycles. Down another path, and we're in front of a terrace of three dark-brown houses with small windows and paved gardens. Georgie waves her arms in recognition as Jackie opens the creosoted gate of the centre house and takes out a bunch of keys, jamming them into the front door. I'm in Jackie's home for the first time and, as she dangles Georgie from one arm while folding up the buggy with the other, she's watching my face to see what I'll do, what I'll say.

The dominant feature of the hall is a large canvas print of a family photograph. Jackie, radiant and trashy, holds a smaller Georgie in her arms, bald and beribboned and tufted with fuzz, looking like Alice's Wonderland pig in her christening gown, a bonnet crammed onto her overheated head. Jackie's surrounded by her menfolk. Her two older sons, one too thin for his suit, one too fat. Their little brother, Ryan, despite the suit, might as well have the word 'trouble' tattooed on his forehead. And a man a few years older than Jackie, thick-necked with a shaved head. I turn back to Jackie to say something nice about the photograph and see the same man coming towards me through the doorway that leads to the kitchen. I find myself flinching in anticipation of a blow.

"I thought you were working." The sudden hope in Jackie's face makes me want to put my arms around her. "Is there any news?"

"No, nowt. I just come home for a—" he glances at me and grins. "—to use the facilities. You must be Susannah. Did I scare you just now?"

"You just made me jump." Did he like seeing my fear? Does he like seeing that simply by asking that question, he's made me more frightened? If this man pulled up outside my house driving a taxi, I would hide behind my curtains until he drove away again. I'm glad Jackie is here in the house with me. I wouldn't want to spend time with Lee on my own. When he smiles, I see his yellow teeth.

"Bonnie lass, your new mate, eh?" He gives me a wink, then chucks Jackie under the chin. "Wouldn't swap you, though. Right, I'm off back to it. I'll see you at teatime." He pushes his bristly face into Georgie's and gobbles at her skin until she shrieks, then kisses roughly at Jackie's mouth. When he passes me in the narrow hallway, his body presses hard against mine.

It doesn't matter. I'm here for Jackie, not for Lee, and Jackie, I can see, is crumbling. I take Georgie wordlessly from her arms and jiggle her gently around, murmuring nonsense into her ear, pointing at whatever I can see to catch her attention – *look at that mirror, look at that pretty girl in the mirror, look at that glass in the door, can we see through it, no we can't can we because it's all wiggly* – so that Jackie can turn her face away from her daughter and hide the silent howl that contorts her face, stretching her mouth wide and ugly and scrunching up her eyes, as she once again buries the hope that has been treacherously raised within her heart.

"Give her here," Jackie says at last, reaching out rude impetuous arms for her daughter. I pass Georgie silently over, knowing that the roughness, the rudeness, are part of the process of pulling herself back together. Jackie sniffs hard at the top of Georgie's head, smiles at me over the top of it. "Thanks. That's better. Go in there and I'll make a cuppa."

I follow her pointing finger into the lounge. The suite is black leather. The chair with the prime view of the television has today's *Daily Mail* resting on the arm. I choose the sofa instead, taking off my coat and gloves and laying them neatly down. The tinny sound of next door's daytime television choice comes through the wall. Over the mantelpiece is a photograph of Jackie and Lee on their wedding day. The tightly-corseted strapless dress, beaded and boned and unforgiving, clings like a crust to Jackie's tiny bronzed shape.

A Tinkerbell tattoo peeks out between the satiny laces. Jackie comes back into the living room, expertly dangling Georgie from one hip and with a bottle of formula in her hand.

"Need to get this one her milk or she'll not give us any peace," she explains. "D'you mind feeding her while I make us a drink?"

I take Georgie into my arms and cradle her against me. Her mouth opens wide and champs vigorously onto the bottle. One sturdy fist thwacks me hard in the breast. I ignore the pain and focus on the satisfaction of seeing the bulging greed in her eyes melt into a blissful milky haze. She's not a conventionally pretty baby, but she's strong and powerful, she knows what she wants, and what could be better for a girl than that?

"Make sure you burp her halfway or she'll whinge all afternoon." Jackie's back in the room again, quick and sudden in the way you can only be when you live somewhere small. I can hear the low rumble of the kettle as it comes to the boil. "And grab that muslin there, she pukes a bit sometimes."

I sit Georgie up and rub her back. A giant bubble of milky air escapes. When she lies back down, the frantic gulping is replaced with long, lazy pulls. Her eyelids flutter shut.

"Did you see the appeal on the news the other night?" Jackie asks.

"Yes. Did it do any good? Did they get anything?"

"Yeah. They got summat all right. That's why I wanted to see you so bad."

For a moment, I'm engulfed by a black clot of envy.

"But that's great," I make myself say. "What did they find out? Who came forward?"

"It's not great at all. It's awful. I can't even tell you how awful."

"My God, what happened?"

"They rang us up this morning, the coppers I mean. You know the way they do. *Can you both just come in for a chat, just a few questions we want to ask you.* Well, Lee wasn't

121

very happy cos he was supposed to be working this morning, but I put my foot down, so we both went down together. Took us into separate rooms, just like always, and they started off going through all the details of what happened when I realised Ry was missing, just like always. You know how it is, going over the same stuff you've been through a million times already? But I didn't mind cos I thought this is obviously just what they have to do, maybe they didn't remember what I said last time. I was almost bored, you know? Maybe that's what they wanted. To get me off my guard and that. Because then it all suddenly started to change." She wipes the end of her nose with her hand, and reaches for Georgie. "Come here, I'll take her. She's due for a nap anyway. Aren't you, little monkey? Hey? Who's Mummy's little monkey? Little horror, aren't you? Yes. But I love you anyway. Yes, I do."

On the other side of the wall, the neighbour's programme has come to an end. We hear the bright blare of the theme music, followed by a loud advertisement for kitchen cleaner.

"So anyway. They suddenly started going on and on about my phone. *When you went out to look for Ryan, did you have your phone with you? And can you remember if you made any calls while you were out? And did anyone call you that you can remember?* So I said, yes, I had my phone, and I'd called Ry a couple of times, and he didn't answer and no one called me, because that's what I could remember. And then they asked me if I knew about location services, where your phone tracks where you go, and I said, yes of course I knew, everyone knows about that. And they said... they said... oh, God—"

She takes a deep breath. A new programme starts. Rapturous applause, and then a man berating another man, his voice angry and hectoring.

"They'd had our phones off us. That was almost the first thing they did," she says. "They just asked for them and we handed them over I'm sure they said what they wanted them for but I wasn't listening. And they got out this file, and in it they had details showing where our phones had been. They showed me Lee's first, and it showed him going into town, driving round a bit, hanging round at the office, then coming back to ours about three, all what he'd said he did. I was acting interested, trying to be polite and that. And then... and then they showed me what mine showed. And according to my phone, I came home from my mam's like I said, and I dropped Georgie with a friend down the road, and then I came back home, just to check if Ry had come back while I was gone. And then I didn't go out again."

"But that doesn't mean anything. Does it? Just that you forgot your phone."

"Well, that's what I said! I must have forgotten my phone. And then just imagined that I'd called Ry while I was out looking. I mean, I'd been that mithered with trying to sort out someone to have Georgie for me, get her bag sorted out and that, and even then I was starting to worry about where Ry was, it's not really a surprise I forgot it. It doesn't look good though, does it? *Do you often forget to take your phone with you? Why would you forget your phone when your son was potentially missing and your daughter was being looked after by someone else? It's just a bit strange that you wouldn't check you had it with you, isn't it?* On and on and on."

In Jackie's arms, Georgie has fallen asleep. Her arms hang limp and a fat dribble of milk sits at the corner of her mouth.

"And then," Jackie continues, "they started in on this other thing. Had I been to East Park while I was out looking? And I was dead confused, because of course I hadn't been to East Park. I mean, apart from anything else, it would have taken me about an hour each way to walk! And then they told me someone had come forward after the appeal."

This must be what was in Nick's mind this morning. I refuse to let myself shiver. "So what did they say?"

Jackie's hand tightens for a moment around Georgie's plump white thigh.

"It was some woman, I think. I don't know who but I

don't suppose it matters really. Anyway. This woman. She said she'd remembered that on the day Ry went missing, she was at East Park. Out for a run, I think she said. And she saw a lad who looks like him getting into a car. She remembered cos he was crying and she thought it was funny to see a lad his age crying in public. And there was someone who looked like me – a woman, she said, slim with long dark hair – making him do it. A dark blue saloon car. That's what she saw. And that's what Lee's taxi is. A dark blue saloon."

In the silence of the living room, we hear the sound of applause like a sudden shower of rain.

"But that doesn't make any sense," I say at last. "They can't have it both ways. You can't have been at home in your house waiting for Ryan, *and also* at East Park making him get in a car."

"No, you don't get it," says Jackie. "That's not what they're saying. They're saying I might have left my phone at home on purpose, so it wouldn't give me away. And then found where Ryan was somehow. And took Lee's taxi to East Park. Maybe with Lee, maybe without him, I don't know. Please, you can't tell anyone about this. Not anyone."

"Of course I won't."

"And you know what the worst bit was? They must have known about my phone for weeks. All this time they've been sat on that little bit of information, letting me tell them over and over, yes, *I took it with me when I went out so I could keep calling Ry while I was looking, yes I'm sure*, and the whole time they knew it was wrong. And they never said a word! Not until it suited them. I thought they were on my side, you know? And instead they've been biding their time and trying to catch me out."

I fumble for something to say. "Did they talk to Lee as well?"

"Yeah, all morning, he had to miss work and everything. He was fuming with them. That's why he's working this afternoon. Trying to make up."

"How does he feel about it?"

"He wasn't bothered really. He says he doesn't care what they think cos he knows he didn't do owt and I should stop worrying, they'll cotton on it wasn't me or him in the end."

"And he's right," I say, making my voice as firm and brisk as I can. "Forgetting what you did with your phone doesn't mean anything. Nobody ever remembers everything exactly how it happened, nobody. And the woman at East Park made a mistake, that's all. They'll realise you didn't have anything to do with it."

"But what if they don't? What happens then? What if he's still out there somewhere and they've not found him?"

"It'll be all right," I tell her, because what else can I say?

"But it won't be all right, will it?" Jackie's face is very hard and set. "It won't ever be all right, not for either of us. Nothing's ever going to be right for us ever again. This is how it is from now on, isn't it? Not right ever again."

We sit in the tiny living room and watch Georgie twitch and snore on Jackie's lap, and listen to the sounds of the television coming through the wall.

Chapter Nine
Wednesday 16th November 2011

For all of us, there are certain details that infallibly recall the sensation of being young and powerless. For me, it's the particular cluster of stimuli hovering in the corridor by the headmaster's office. The scent of rubber-soled shoes, of dust and ink and paper. The sunlight creeping thinly in through too-short curtains that are never closed, and glinting gently off the trophy cabinet, where a wooden shield, nailed over with smaller metal shields, proclaims the annual winners of the House Championship, has not been updated since 1996. The single twist of tinsel twined across the cabinet, that may be a relic from last Christmas or may be all they can be bothered to put up for this one. The hum and chatter of office staff in the background. The scrape of chair legs against well-worn parquet flooring. The taste of fearful anticipation in my mouth. Does John feel this too? I can't tell. He's better at hiding his feelings than I am. Without looking, he reaches for my hand and gives it a brief reassuring squeeze.

"Joel? Sweetie?"

Joel's a huddled lump beneath the duvet, even his head invisible beneath the covers. He acknowledges me not by emerging but by creeping further inside his cocoon, pulling the ends underneath to seal himself completely away. I sit down on the bed and pat gently at the place where I guess his back must be.

"You'll be late for school."

From within the duvet cover, I hear a faint whimper of protest, like a small hurt animal.

"What's the matter? You can tell me."

No reply. I put my arms around the bundle of boy-child hidden away beneath the folds. Patting and stroking, I begin to feel my way into his shape. He's turned himself right around in the bed and is lying on his right side, long arms and legs folded into the core of himself like a chick waiting to hatch. I can feel his tense misery even through the duvet.

"Won't you feel better if you tell me?" A faint movement as he shakes his head. "All right. I guess we're just going to be here for a while, then, hey?"

The room smells fusty and boyish, the scent of teenage years that is supposed to be repulsive but that I can't bring myself to dislike. I like the reminder that my son, despite everything, continues to grow and thrive, the processes of his body unlocking and unfolding even as his head buzzes and chatters with mysterious rages and unfounded fears. Nonetheless, I open the curtains and then the window, letting in the breeze from the garden and the faint sound of morning traffic from the distant dual carriageway. Then I climb onto the bed and fit myself around Joel's bundled form.

Time passes. It's peaceful in this room. My breathing begins to synchronise with Joel's. When he was small we'd lie like this for hours, drifting between sleeping and waking, doing nothing together in the sunshine. I'm not falling asleep exactly, but I'm reaching the place where reality begins to blend with my mind's creations to turn the room fantastical. An apple tree sprouts in the doorway, and its scent breathes over us both. A bird perches beside us and tugs speculatively at the cover. As the bird becomes my own hand, the top of Joel's head emerges and I smile in triumph.

"So what's the matter?" I whisper.

"I'm scared," Joel whispers back. His eyes are shut. He can never tell me his problems with his eyes open.

"What of? What's happening that's scary?"

"Other kids." Another thing about Joel in distress; he'll only release the smallest fragments of truth at a time. To understand the whole picture I must become a combination of artist and detective, trying out solutions to complete the parts he cannot bear to tell me.

"Other kids. Which ones? In your tutor group?" Silence. "In some of your classes?" A faint quiver. "The classes you have today?" I close my eyes and try to recall Joel's timetable, pinned on the corkboard in the kitchen. "Maths? Science? PE? English? PSE?"

"All," Joel whispers, and takes my hand.

My heart hurts. His body is thirteen but he remains so childish. Five years from now he'll be an adult, free to choose his own truths and consequences. I will protect him for as long as I can.

"And what are they doing? Are they hurting you? Taking your stuff? Calling you names?"

"Weird," Joel mutters.

"They call you weird? Oh, sweetie." I kiss the hand that clutches tightly to mine, the greasy blond hair that I long to wash and then brush smooth and soft. "But you don't have to listen to them, do you? Can't the teachers help?"

"Hit," Joel says, and ducks back beneath the duvet cover.

"They hit you?"

"Mr and Mrs Harper." Mr Elliott's smile is carefully calibrated to build rapport but not friendship, allowing for the possibility that we may end up not on the same side. John responds in kind, taking the offered hand and shaking it firmly, letting Mr Elliott know that they are equals. My own instinct is to ingratiate myself. To use my smile to make this man want to impress me, and then to subtly let him know that he can achieve this by making school an easier, gentler place for Joel.

This has worked well enough in the past, but I don't dare do it in front of John. John thinks Joel needs a firm hand, not the treatment I call 'being understanding' and he despairingly calls 'smothering'. The same argument we've been having since Joel first went to playgroup. They say the secret of successful parenting is to be united, but what are you supposed to do when you know in your bones that your partner is wrong?

"Okay, fella." John arrives like a tornado, slamming the window shut, whirling up the duvet cover into the air and down into a corner, tearing Joel from my arms. "Enough of this. Come on. Out of bed." Joel's skinny teenage body is exposed. John grabs him beneath his armpits and heaves briskly.

"Stop it, you're hurting him."

"He's fine, aren't you, fella? That's it. Enough of this nonsense. On your feet. Now into the shower." Joel looks up at John with huge frightened eyes. "What's that dying-rabbit look for?"

"I'm not going in," Joel says. John shakes his head.

"No, we're not playing that game today. In the shower now. Go on."

Joel looks at me despairingly.

"John."

"We're not going to start with the not-going-in lark. Are we, fella?" John is trying to keep his tone light, but I can hear the worry in his voice. This is what breaks my will every time. What John does can sometimes look rough and unloving, and I'm almost certain it's the opposite of what Joel needs, but he does it because he loves our son.

"You can't make me go." It sounds like defiance but I can see it's terror. Something at school has frightened Joel so badly he would rather cower under his duvet than go in to face it.

"Afraid I can, fella." The strained lightness is disappearing,

129

replaced by something simpler and darker. "Get in the shower. Now." Joel hesitates, looks at me. "Never mind trying to get round your mother. Just because she's soft doesn't mean I am. Shower. Now."

And because we all know John is the strongest of all of us, Joel squares his shoulders and creeps, step by reluctant step, towards the bathroom.

"See? That's all he needed." John, unbelievably, looks satisfied, as if he's solved a problem instead of making everything much worse. "You're too soft with him, love."

"John, he said he's scared. You've got to listen when he says something like that."

"He's just swinging the lead."

"No, he's not. He was really, really—"

"Christ, is that the time? I've got to go." He kisses me quickly on the mouth, and it's only because I know him so well that I can taste the anger concealed behind his briskness. "Joel! If you don't get in on time there'll be trouble at mill later, you hear me? Right, see you both."

And he whirls out again, leaving me to pick up the pieces.

The shutting of the front door is Joel's cue to leave the shower. On the landing, wrapped tightly in his towel, he puts his arms around me for a moment. Stroking his stringy hair and damp back feels like a rebellion.

"I'm sorry I'm so useless," he says.

"You're not useless."

"Yes, I am. Dad hates me. I don't blame him. I hate me too. I'm a waste of space. I can't get anything right."

"Don't say that, don't ever say that, do you hear me? You're my darling wonderful son and I wouldn't change anything about you." I stroke his hair.

"Dad wants to change everything about me. He wants me to be great at Maths and Biology and football and I'm not, I'm just not! I wish I was but I'm not."

"Joel Moel, stop being so silly. Dad loves you just how you are."

When Joel lets go of me and looks me in the face, I can't meet his eyes.

"So what do you think's going on with Joel?" Mr Elliott's face is a careful neutral blank, like his words, like the sheet of paper that lies on the desk beside the fat closed file that is presumably some administrative summary of my son.

"Well, I think the problem is that he's—"

"Why don't you tell us what you're thinking first," says John, taking my hand as compensation for shutting me down. Mr Elliott raises his eyebrows a fraction.

"Okay, so here's where we are. In the last two terms, we've had six unauthorised absences from Joel, all following the same pattern. Joel leaves home as expected and on time to come to school. But then he either fails to appear at registration, or he leaves the premises at the first break. And these unauthorised absences were followed the next day by a phone call from yourselves—" He's pretending to talk to both of us, but he's looking at me, he means me. "—to say that Joel's unwell and won't be in that day. Is that a fair summary?"

"Hang on," says John. "Go through that again."

My face burns. Mr Elliott looks as if some crucial piece of evidence has just fallen into place.

"Six unauthorised absences in two terms," he repeats. "As you can see, they're getting more frequent." The blank sheet with all its possibilities is brushed aside to make room for the important papers, the ones that document what's already happened. This makes me irrationally angry. Why not the blank sheet of paper? Why can't we talk about the future instead? Why not put aside the file of evidence and say, *What can we create together to help Joel be happy?*

"No," says John. "The authorised absences. That's not right, there's a mistake somewhere. We would never—"

"There's no mistake." I'm so determined not to whisper that the words come out as a shout. "I made those phone calls. I authorised the absences."

John's face is vulnerable with shock. Mr Elliott carefully squares off the edges of his paperwork.

"So Joel's missed twice as much school as I thought? You let our son miss twice as many days?"

I hold my face very still and keep my breathing very steady. I will not let myself feel like a naughty child who's been caught out. I won't cry in front of these men. I will be strong.

The days when Joel doesn't go to school are radiant days, stolen days. He wakes at the normal time and gets dressed as usual, but as soon as John leaves the house he goes upstairs and changes into his own clothes, and with the shedding of his school uniform I see the weight of expectation tumble from his shoulders and he becomes sweet and easy, joyful and spontaneous, the boy I know he truly is. While I bustle around the house, he sits at the dining room table and draws, impossible curving fantasies of horses and elves and dragons and warriors. He reads, laughs, plays music, surprises me with spontaneous hugs. He's like a convalescent from a serious illness. That's how I think of these days, as convalescence. He needs this time to build the strength to carry him through until the next crisis.

"Obviously the most important thing is the future," says Mr Elliott. Fine for him to say that now. "School refusal can blight a young person's life. So we really need to nip this in the bud."

I don't dare look at John.

"However, we also need to talk about Joel's behaviour while he's in school." A different piece of paper comes out of the file. "As you both know, there have been repeated incidents of Joel hitting or punching other pupils." He pauses a moment to check that we do, in fact, both know about this. I steel myself once more for John's shock, but he's ready this time. He doesn't admit this is news to him. Instead he nods grimly and takes my hand once more. His loyalty to me, in the face of my betrayal, makes me want to weep.

"It's worth remembering that Joel's well over the age of criminal responsibility. If the parents chose to go to the police, we'd have no choice but to support them."

I can judge the quality of Joel's day from the sound of the gate. When it drags slowly across the concrete and does not close again, I ready myself to meet the child who will greet me in the hall. White-faced, slump-shouldered, short of words, oozing despair.

The worst part is that I can see what makes Joel such a victim. His silence. His unconcealed passion for pastimes and pursuits they consider pointless and lame. His open contempt for the more conventional subjects that absorb them. His refusal to join in, to conform, to meet them even remotely halfway. Most of all, the way he reacts to their needling; by turning away, hiding his face in his arms, making small animal noises when touched, until at last the rage within him explodes out into violence. He's like a game I had as a child, where a plastic shark opened a wide red mouth to reveal an assortment of tokens – a bone, an anchor, a rubber tyre – that players removed one by one. There was an insistent pleasure in the gradual slow removal, a spasm of terrified delight when the mouth finally snapped shut. Their teasing is despicable. But I can see why they do it.

"But the teasing," I say. "We've talked about it, they torment him, they have him in tears sometimes."

"And there are strategies in place to deal with that. Joel knows that if he's unhappy he needs to talk to one of the staff. We *will* listen to him, we *want* to help him, but he needs to tell us."

"But they start it, they provoke him. If they just left him alone—" This is the central point, the one thing I need them to grasp. "It's making him so unhappy."

"That doesn't justify Joel being violent."

"I agree," says John.

"But he's so unhappy," I repeat.

The look they turn on me is identical.

"Joel, we need to have a chat about your report."

Joel remains stubbornly slouched in the dubious safety of his bean bag, earphones jammed over his ears. His on-screen avatar duels a gigantic scorpion.

"Joel, turn that off right now."

Joel stares unflinchingly ahead. John might as well not be there. His determination to escape the real world is total, almost frightening.

"Joel, this is your last warning."

Joel's eyes are glassy and frightened. His fingers flicker over the controller. The scorpion's sting jams into the warrior's muscle-packed leg. The warrior grimaces, but recovers. His swords blazes with light.

In one smooth move, John tears the headphones from Joel's head, the controller from his hands. I see the powerful muscles in his back move and flex as he gives one quick sharp tug and the wire rips free from the back of the controller. The headphones tremble in his hands and I can see how badly he wants to snap them in two and I want to say, *Don't, don't break his headphones, please,* but I'm afraid of making Joel even more distraught than he already is.

"Joel," John repeats, his voice carefully still and controlled, "we're going to talk about your report. Stop staring at that game and pay attention to me. No, look at me. At me! For God's sake, will you at least look at me while I'm talking to you!"

From beneath the curtain of his hair, Joel glances sideways at me. A quick frantic plea for help.

"John, please. Don't shout. He's listening. You need to be gentler, you're frightening him."

If John would get angry with me, I would know what to do. If he shouted at me, I could shout back at him, and in the blaze of our rage we might burn down the barriers between us and reach some mutual understanding. But instead he just looks at me in silent despair, his expression telling me that when I undermine him like this I'm letting all of us down. I stop myself in my tracks, because sometimes I'm afraid he's right.

"I'm sorry, I'm sorry, I'm sorry. Joel, your dad's right. We need to talk about your report."

Now it's Joel's turn to look betrayed. He and I have already talked about it. He wept on my shoulder and told me he was useless and he hated himself. I promised I'd help make it right with his father.

"This comment from your Maths teacher. *Joel has unfortunately chosen not to apply himself this term and is in danger of not meeting his year-end target, ultimately risking his opportunity to gain a C grade at GCSE.* Anything you want to say about that?"

Joel picks up the ruined controller and examines the broken wires.

"And this from your English teacher. *Joel has the capability to succeed, but his attitude this term means he is not making the most of his abilities and is in danger of missing his year-end target. This makes it more challenging for Joel to achieve the GCSE B or C grade he should be easily capable of gaining.* At least give me a sign that you're listening."

Joel shrugs his shoulders.

"So you can hear me. Look, what's going on? The teachers aren't saying *Joel's not clever enough*, they're saying *Joel's not putting in the work*. So why not? This is serious stuff, fella, this is your future you're messing up. If you don't get at least Maths and English then what chance have you got?"

It's because he's afraid of failing! I want to scream out the words. *He told me himself, this afternoon! He's afraid of letting you down and then he gets so frightened he can't even make himself try! Why can't you see that when you go on at him like this, it just makes everything worse?*

Joel slumps down inside his shirt collar.

"Joel, talk to us. Tell us what the matter is. Something's not right. You're a bright lad. You could have a great life if you put your mind to it. So why are all your teachers – I mean, it's not just English and Maths, it's Science, Languages, History, Geography – even the bloody Art teacher says you're not putting the effort in, for Christ's sake. Don't you care?"

"Of course he cares. We talked about it this afternoon—"

John holds up a hand. "From Joel. Let him speak for himself."

I should be strong. I should stand up to my husband and tell him that I won't be silenced like this. But I don't. Is it because I'm not sure that I'm right and John's wrong? Or is it because I'm a coward?

"Come on, fella. What's the matter? What can we do to help?" John's trying for gentleness now, folding up like a concertina and squatting awkwardly down. Perhaps if he'd spoken softly from the start we might have got somewhere. Perhaps we still might. If John will just be patient. If John will sit down beside his son and let them both simply *be*, a companionable silence so Joel can creep out of his hermit-shell. This time. This time they'll get it. Joel's head is bowed, but I can tell he's listening. *Please, John. Give it one more minute. One more. Just wait. Just be patient. Just be.* On the screen, Joel's avatar stands still and slumped, meekly accepting the attack of the scorpion that will soon destroy it.

"Well, this is getting us nowhere." John's disappointment manifests itself as baffled anger. He picks up the headphones and snaps them effortlessly in two, then grabs the ruined controller. "But I can tell you now, we won't be buying another one of these, no matter how many times you ask Santa. And we're cancelling that bloody game subscription of yours until you pull your socks up and start taking school seriously. Do you understand?"

John is a gentle man; he's never hurt me or anyone. I've known this as long as I've known him. But when he stands over the hunched and cowering shape of our son, every solid inch of him ablaze with rage and frustration, I see that his gentleness might, in the right circumstances, be overcome.

"John. Please." I want to take his hand, but he's walking too fast. Instead I skitter in his wake, hobbled by my pretty, foolish shoes and the skirt I chose because it makes my waist slender and waify. The staff must be watching and judging us. *No wonder Joel has problems*, they must be thinking. *Look how he treats his wife. Look how she lets him. Poor Joel.* I want to do better, I want to help John build a better relationship with his son. I will do better. I'll find a way. "John, please, don't walk so fast, I need to talk to you."

"Let's get to the car before we start the post-mortem," John hisses, and flings the entrance door open.

"Be careful."

"What? In case I break it? This door? This door with reinforced glass?" John slams the door savagely shut again, pulling me out of the way as it rebounds from its frame. "This door is as tough as old boots. Now stop worrying about what people think and get in the car, will you? Please? Can we do that? And then go somewhere private and talk like adults? Please, love?"

I climb meekly into the car and sit quiet and still. The tyres squeal as he reverses out of the parking space and accelerates towards the gate, turning right across a gap in the traffic that I would dismiss as far too small. Ordinarily I would plead with him to slow down, be more careful, but not today. Today I stare steadily ahead out of the windscreen, and don't let myself flinch.

"Mrs Harper? It's Rachel from school." Rachel can convey

the essence of her whole message with the subtle inflections of her greeting. When the message is merely administrative, her opening words are *It's Rachel from school, don't worry, Joel's fine*. She hasn't said this so I know something's happened, but her calmness means the *something* is not a disaster, not something I haven't had to contend with before.

"Hi there."

"I'm afraid Joel's run away again. He's left the premises. He got upset during Maths, and when his teacher tried to talk to him he got quite distressed and ran out of the classroom. Mr Uxley did try to follow him but obviously he can't leave the other pupils unattended and Joel was running quite fast. It's only just happened, literally five minutes ago."

"Oh God, I'm so sorry, thanks for letting me know."

"What would you like us to do next? We can call the police for you? Or you can wait a little while and see if he turns up at home."

"I'll give him half an hour. He usually comes straight home." The shame of this being a *usually*, an incident whose unfolding I can predict with weary accuracy.

"Okay, that's fine. I'll make a note to say that you're aware and you'll be looking out for him. If there are any problems at all, if he doesn't turn up as expected, you know we're here to help. And of course don't hesitate to phone the police, they can take the report from you as well as from us."

"I'll bear that in mind. Thanks again."

"Now, because this has happened several times, we do need to call you in for another formal meeting to discuss where we go from here. Of course right now you'll just want to make sure Joel's safe, but if you could give the office a call tomorrow?"

"That's fine, I'll do that."

"And if we could ask that both yourself and your husband attend?"

My heart sinks. "Yes, that's fine." It's not fine. "I'll see what I can do."

Outside the car, the brown waters of the Humber roll swiftly past under a lemony autumn sky. The short drive hasn't given the car time to warm up and my hands and feet are cold. We sit side by side and watch the waves. I'm determined not to break the silence. I'm often determined to do things like this. I never succeed.

"Are you angry with me?" The frightened little-girl falter in my voice makes me ashamed, then glad. This is my secret strength. John can never be truly angry with me when I remind him that I'm weaker than him.

He brings my hand to his lips, pressing them hard against the knuckles. Then he gently opens up my fingers and spreads my palm across his mouth. I can't tell if he's kissing me, or begging me to keep him silent. We watch the river rolling and rolling, a ceaseless flow of water that gives the paradoxical impression of permanence. A man walking his dog glances greedily in through the window. I wonder what we look like to him. A courting couple, seeking somewhere quiet to talk, or secret lovers snatching a stolen half-hour. Surely we can't look like failing parents to a troubled boy who's being slowly torn apart between the two opposing poles of his parents. Surely no one would guess that.

"We have to be on the same side about this," John says at last. His voice is indistinct around my hand.

"We are on the same side."

"No, we're not. You keep undermining me. You don't tell me what's going on. You hide things from me. All that stuff that Elliott bloke said to us today, and I didn't know any of it! Because you hid it from me." He lets my hand fall. "Susannah, tell me the truth. Did you not tell me because you thought if I knew, I wouldn't love Joel any more?"

"No, of course it isn't. I just... I just..." I want John to interrupt me, to fill in the blanks for me, but he sits and waits instead. "I wanted to give Joel some space. Okay? To get himself back on track. I knew you'd be angry if you found out and I didn't want you to be angry with him—"

"Of course I'm angry with him! How can anyone not be? How are *you* not angry? God, I do my best, every day I try, but he's such a pain, he's such hard work, and he doesn't even love me back, not any more."

"That's not true! Joel *worships* you! He wants to make you happy, don't you see? He doesn't try in class because he's terrified of disappointing you. Every time you yell at him about his grades or tell him he's not working hard enough, he feels worse, and that's how it's spiralling, don't you see? It's you, John, I'm sorry but it's you, it's your... well, not your fault exactly, but you're the one who can change it. You need to be kinder to him. John, please listen to me, this is important."

"And I know you don't mean to, but you and Joel, you collude against me. You're like a little team all by yourselves. You don't need me any more, not really. If I disappeared and left you and Joel to yourselves, you'd be happier."

"That's not true."

"Yes, it is. It is true. It never used to be. Do you remember? We used to have each other's backs, always. We were on the same side. We knew that whatever happened, we'd always be okay, because we'd always have each other. Before Joel came we were fine, we were so happy. But since he came into our lives, everything's been worse, year after year after year."

"What are you saying?"

"God help me, Susannah, I'm saying sometimes I resent him. I resent my own bloody son. Because you love him more than me."

I don't know what to say. I can't tell him he's wrong, because we'd both know I was lying. Besides, isn't that how it's supposed to be? Isn't that how he feels too? Doesn't he love Joel more than he loves me?

"It's not my fault, Susannah," John says. "I know you think that but it's not true. Not entirely. Can't you see that?"

And so strong is John's will that for a treacherous moment I see myself and Joel through John's eyes. I see a son who needs discipline and support, not well-meant smothering. I see a mother who does everything she can to thwart her husband. I see a flawed but unbreakable alliance that acts at every turn to keep him from making any changes or doing any good. I see a man who loves me despite everything I've done to lessen that love. I see that to John himself, John is the hero of the story, and he's doing everything he can not to see me as the villain.

The sight terrifies me. John is wrong. But John is strong. And if we're not all very, very careful, John could end up tearing our little family apart.

"Sometimes," John whispers, "I wish—"

Oh God, no. Don't say it. If you say it I'll have to leave you. And I don't want to do that. I can't face it. I can't.

"I wish I could be more like you," John says, and lays his head against my breast and sobs.

I stroke his head and watch the river flow by and wonder if these are truly the words John meant to say.

Chapter Ten
Thursday 23rd November 2017

"So I was looking at your blog last night."

Jackie's eyes slide sideways at me over the top of her mug of hot chocolate. We're Christmas shopping in town, in a café called Heaven, taking refuge from the breathtaking cold that's sweeping down the country in one gargantuan Arctic sigh. I've never suited cold weather. It turns my nose pink and my skin dull, my hair frizzy and crisp and my eyes watery, and I do everything I can to avoid it. But Jackie comes alive in the cold, like a winter ermine.

"Must have taken ages to write."

"I… yes, I suppose it did really."

"The one about accepting that it's okay to, you know, keep going. Do nice stuff." As if her remaining child is a talisman, she lays one manicured hand on Georgie's fat belly as she slouches frownily in her scarlet travel-system, transfixed by a twirling blue star that hangs precariously from the ceiling, blown by the warm gusts of air from the heater. "You know, with everyone you've got left. I've been thinking about Christmas."

I stare steadily into my mug and breathe slowly and deeply. The lights that are everywhere now, blooming as if the cold has brought them into life, flash and flicker from every shiny surface, including the tears that tremble in the corners of my eyes. Christmas is the hardest, even harder than their birthdays.

"I mean, I'm hoping he might be back by then but—" In her face I see the shadow of what we both know is now the most likely outcome. "And it's this one's first as well. I had all these plans, you know? I wanted her first Christmas to be so special. And now... but I'm going to still do some nice things for Georgie. I decided last night. We'll still have an advent calendar. And a tree. And some little things for her."

I ruthlessly clamp down on the self-pitying whisper that tells me how lucky Jackie is to have someone to call forth the effort for. "That sounds really nice. I bet she'll love it."

"Ryan had this thing when I was pregnant with Georgie." Jackie presses her hand to her mouth for a moment. "He was afraid I wouldn't want him around any more cos I'd have this new life with Lee and the baby and he'd just be in the way. I think maybe that was why he was such a little shit all the last year, he was testing me, you know the way kids do, checking I'd still love him no matter what. So if there's any chance he's watching somehow, like if he comes back and looks at the house and he's not sure whether to come back or not, I don't want him thinking I'm making too much of a fuss, being all happy together without him. But at the same time—"

"I know."

"Yeah." Jackie gives me a wobbly smile. "I know you do. What are you going to do?"

"I think I'll go to my sister's. They usually ask me."

"Will you decorate your house?"

I think of the way my street has looked for the last five years. A string of pretty lights in trees and windows, and the single black cavity. "I might do. I'll see how I feel."

Jackie tears the top off a stick of sugar and pours it into her coffee.

"Can I tell you something? It might sound a bit creepy but it's not meant to."

"Okay..."

143

"It's like my Bible, that blog of yours. Whenever something happens to me and I get upset, I go online and have a look and there'll be some advice from you and it gets me through. I don't know what I'd have done without it. Talking to people that don't know what to say to me, how to cope with Christmas, cleaning up the house, the lot. You've saved my life."

I'm so pleased I can't speak.

"So do you mind if I give you some advice in return? Just to say thank you? And you won't get upset?"

I look at her warily.

"I just think you ought to start taking your own advice a bit more. I mean, you don't really follow all what you write about, do you?"

"Yes, I do."

"No, you don't. What was that thing you wrote, about needing to keep yourself strong and that means looking after yourself, letting yourself enjoy things?"

"I do, of course I do. Look at us right now, we've come out shopping, haven't we?"

"Only cos I rang you up this morning and begged you. If I didn't make you come out, you never would. Who else do you see besides me?"

I try not to show Jackie how much her words hurt. "I see my sister and her kids, I babysit for them at least once a week." Although I've been slack recently, preferring to cocoon in my own house with Jackie and Georgie, rather than force myself to confront the uncomplicated happiness of my sister's home.

"But that's just staying in someone *else's* house while *they* go out and have fun. What about something that's just for you? Like clothes. We've just been right round town and you haven't tried anything on. When did you last buy yourself something new?"

"I don't need anything."

"Look at your coat. The cuffs are fraying." I resist the

urge to fold my fingers over the ends of my sleeves. "Why not treat yourself a bit?"

"It was expensive. I like to get the wear."

"Okay, so how about your hair?" Jackie tugs gently at the fronds around my face. "You could try a new style."

"I like my hair this way, thank you very much."

"Look, I get it, okay? I do. You're trying to keep everything the same. So if, I mean, so *when* he comes back, he'll just slip back into his old life."

"It won't be the same because John won't be there."

"And that's another thing to think about. You're older than me but you're not exactly over the hill, are you? You've got a lot of life still to live."

"My life is fine just the way it is."

"No, it's not. It's lonely. You're lonely. I'm not being funny but I don't think you had a friend in the world before I turned up on your doorstep, did you?"

"Well, if you think I'm such a loser, what are you even doing with me?"

"Hey. Don't be like that." Jackie pats my arm. "I don't think you're a loser, when did I say that? I told you, that blog of yours, it helps me all the time, every day. I just want to pay that back, that's all."

"Anyway, who are you to tell me what to do? What have you done with your life that's so bloody marvellous? Had four kids with two different men. Or is it three different men? And lived off the state for years."

A dull red flush creeps up Jackie's neck.

"And you've got no idea what my life is like, okay? No idea at all. You've barely even started. Your boy's not been gone six months. Just you wait until it's been a year, and then two years, and then three years, and then five years, and Lee's left you and Georgie's growing up and you know that whatever you do, your life's only going to get worse from now on, okay? Just you wait until you've done that! And then you can tell me how I need to buy a new coat and get my hair done!"

Jackie's saying something but I'm too angry to listen. I stumble out of the café, indifferent to the avid stares of the other patrons. The wind slaps me around the face with a cold so intense I think my tears will freeze on my cheeks. I've left my gloves on the table but I can't go back for them.

Why did I screech at Jackie like that? I'm appalled at myself. I'm not fit to have friends. I can't be trusted with other people. From now on, I'll have to work even harder to keep myself small and tight and closed off. From now on I'll only speak to the people who love me and accept me exactly as I am. That way if I lose control again and start shouting, I know I can be forgiven. I fumble in my pocket for my phone and call Melanie. *Please answer. Please answer. Please answer.*

"Hi there." Melanie's voice is cool and guarded.

"Hi, it's me."

"Yes, I know." There's a nasty little silence and my heart skips a beat. Then, "Any news?"

"No. No news."

She normally says *I'm sorry*, but again there's a nasty little silence.

"So what are you all up to today? How are Thomas and Grace?"

"They're fine." Just that, no chatty news, no little stories of what Thomas asked at dinner the other day or what Grace did at playgroup. "And how are you?"

My heart hurts. I'm not used to Melanie being angry with me.

"I'm fine, I was just ringing for a chat."

"Susannah?" Melanie's voice is a little gentler. "Are you all right? Are you crying?"

"No, I'm fine, I'm really fine, I can tell you're busy, I'll call you later—"

"Where are you? Do you need me to come and get you?"

"No! No, I'm fine. I'm fine."

"You keep saying that, but you're obviously not." And at

last, the capitulation. "Do you want to come round here for a bit? Grace is at playgroup all day today, but we can have a chat?"

"Actually, is there any chance we could go out? You and me, I mean?"

"Um. It's not a great time. Well, no, hang on, I suppose if… I'll have to get Richard's mum to get Grace and Thomas, though. Um. No, the hell with it. Yes, why not, that sounds lovely. What do you want to do?"

"I want to get my hair cut."

"So what are we thinking today?" The hairdresser combs her fingers through my hair, smiling at me through the mirror. Her own hair swings around her face like a glossy dark curtain. The salon is busy and buzzy, offering beauty treatments as well as hair appointments, and Melanie sits with four other customers as she waits for her turn to be manicured. I have no idea how Melanie managed to get us both appointments here. Did she mention Joel, maybe even invent a poignant anniversary? Or were we just lucky that they happened to have the exact appointments we wanted even on such a busy afternoon?

"I felt like a change," I say. "Something a bit different. More modern."

"Maybe some of this length off?" The hairdresser folds my hair up under itself so I can see how I might look with my locks shorn shorter.

When Joel was little, he used to twirl strands of my hair around his fingers. I used to carry a tiny pair of scissors so I could cut myself free when he slept. "That sounds good."

She's still toying with my hair, folding it higher and higher. "If you wanted something really radical, you could try a pixie cut. That would look beautiful with your cheekbones. And it's so easy to take care of, just a bit of texturising and you're done for the day."

"No! No, not a pixie cut."

"Too drastic?" She smiles and lets the length fall again. "Maybe just to your shoulders, then."

"Yes, that sounds fine."

"And colour-wise?"

It meant a lot to Joel that our hair was the same colour. He used to love looking at childhood photos of himself and then of me, the illusion of a genetic connection so convincing even I could almost believe it. *You were always meant to be ours,* I used to tell him as we marvelled together at the resemblance between us. *It's just you had to grow somewhere else before you could come home to us.*

"Nothing too different, I want to stay blonde, I don't know really, I just looked in the mirror and thought it was time for a change."

"Some cooler tones would look really funky. See our Gemma over there?" She points to the pretty young junior sweeping the floor. Her hair is a soft silver-grey. "That sort of colour at the ends. And keep the warmer tones at the top. Take the length up to your shoulders, and some layers to add movement. What do you think?"

I have no real idea what this will look like, but I know it will be different, and when it's different, Jackie's words will lose their power because I will no longer be the woman I was this morning. From the seats by the magazines, Melanie nods reassuringly.

"That sounds great," I say.

Within minutes, I'm wondering what reckless insanity has led me here. The questions she asks me are normal, chatty questions, but for me it's like walking over broken glass. Do I have plans for tonight? No. Got any Christmas parties coming up? No. Am I working at the moment? No. Married? Seeing anyone special? No. And the hardest one: Do I have children? *No*, I say, despising myself, and then in a moment of brilliance I add the chirpy rider, *But my sister has two!* And instantly we're safe in the well-worn track of *All the best bits and none of the difficult bits* and *I bet you're their cool auntie, aren't you?* and *Are you looking forward to spoiling them for Christmas?* and *So lovely that you're so close with your sister.* I spool out the stories, performing my devoted-auntie routine for this kindly stranger (taking Grace to feed the ducks and Grace falling in, taking Thomas to an Adventure Park and coping with his terror of the dead-eyed perspex cow, buying them Moon Sand for Christmas and Melanie hoovering it out of the carpet for months afterwards), and then suddenly I'm being offered coffee and a magazine and the conversation is over.

Time passes. I turn the pages of my magazine, studying the winter party dresses as if I might actually buy one. I drink my coffee. Melanie is taken into the tiny sage-coloured side-room to have her nails soaked in warm water while she selects a shade of polish. My scalp tingles with chemicals. In the mirror I glimpse my head, covered with tinfoil packets. I look like an eccentric Christmas decoration. The last scrapings of dye sit incongruously blue and purple in their tubs. I've never understood how purple dye can make my hair golden. I wish I hadn't done any of this, but it's too late now.

"Mrs Harper?" It's Gemma, the junior with the ash-grey hair. "If you'd like to come over to the basins, it's time to rinse you out?" Her smile is nervous and I wonder how I must seem to her. A rich spoiled older woman with money to burn on an impulsive afternoon at the salon, someone of her mother's generation or perhaps even older, who she needs to keep sweet because I'm a paying customer. At my usual place they know everything about me. *That poor Mrs Harper whose son disappeared.* I can't decide if I prefer that, or sleek anonymity. I settle myself in the chair and feel the basin lap uncomfortably at the base of my neck.

"I'll just lift this up a bit for you?" She has that young girl's habit of turning every declarative into a question. The cold porcelain shifts position to become a little more supportive. "Is that better?"

149

"That's great, thanks."

"And I'll just get these last bits of hair out for you?" I lift my head and her fingers brush shyly against my neck. "There, I think that's all of it? Is this water all right for you or would you like it a little cooler?"

"It's fine."

I try not to wince as she strips the foils from my hair. This will all be worth it when I next see Jackie and show her my new hair, with its new length and new colour. No, that's not right. I can't see Jackie again ever. But it will still all be worth it. I'll have shown that I'm not a hypocrite and I really do practice what I preach and I'm living my life in the best way I can, despite everything. Who knew that a single haircut could mean so much? The foils are out now and all I can feel are warm water and cool shampoo and Gemma's hands, gentle but firm, massaging my scalp. This must be the first thing they teach on a hairdressing course: how to wash hair.

"Okay, I'm just going to put your conditioner on?"

What am I supposed to say in response? I give an awkward half-nod and mumble something under my breath. The kindly hands disappear for a moment and I hear faint plasticy sounds as she dispenses the conditioner. "Okay, Mrs Harper? If you're ready?"

The conditioner is cold, much colder than the shampoo, and it feels as if there's a lot of it. Perhaps this is because of the new colour. Perhaps they'll try and sell me some of it when I leave. Perhaps I'll buy some. It feels strange against my scalp, though, strange and heavy, and the scent is like barren soil turned over in a bleak garden in November. Is this what's supposed to be happening? Maybe I should say something. The water is turning cold, too, and the chill makes me shiver. I try to sit up but I'm weighed down by whatever she's put in my hair, as if it's full of concrete, and the basin must be filling too because I can feel water lapping against my ears. Is my hair caught in the drain? I try to sit up but then Gemma's hands are back on my scalp, and for a moment I feel relieved.

Then she grabs hold of my head and pushes, one single hard firm push, and the basin falls away beneath me and I'm suddenly drowning in cold water, held under by Gemma's strong slim hands. My eyes fly open in the panic but the water's too dirty for me to see through, it's brown and murky and I can already taste it in my mouth and my nose, it's thick with mud, the heavy brown mud that she put on my hair to weigh me down, and when I try to move my arms so I can push Gemma off and break through to the surface, I find I can't move them because they've already been caught and held by the sucking mud. She's pushing me down and down into it and it's got me, I'm going to drown in mud and water and there's nothing I can do. I'm dying. Right here in the hairdressers, I'm dying, coolly put to death by a young girl called Gemma with grey hair and a pretty face.

Maybe this is the right thing? Maybe if I'll die I'll see Joel again?

No. This can't be how it ends, I won't have it. I can't give up yet. I have to keep looking for him. I have to fight. I have to find out what all this means. I only have to last until Christmas Eve.

My lungs burning, my chest spasming, I make an almighty effort. I force my right arm free of the mud and push up through the thick water, trying to find something I can pull against to prise myself out. My body's fighting me, trying to make me take the breath of water that will kill me. My fingers find what feels like a handful of grass. I seize it and pull, one single strong pull, and I hear someone screaming but it doesn't matter because I'm pulling myself out, the water's growing clearer and I can see the light above me and as my lips break through the surface I take a single blessed gasping breath and flail my arms and another breath and I try to tread water and pray the water's deep enough that my feet won't touch the bottom so the mud won't grab me and pull me back down again.

But there is no water. There is no mud. There's only the

bright lights and stylish silver decorations and clean fruity scents of the salon, and a ring of frightened faces and a terrible hushed silence that's almost loud enough to drown out the oblivious chatter of the radio (*"Our phone-in subject today: does Christmas start too early these days? Give us a call with your thoughts…"*) and, just behind me, the whooping sobs of a young girl terrified beyond all reason.

"Mrs Harper? Mrs Harper?" It's the salon owner, patting gently at my shoulder. "Mrs Harper? Can you hear me?"

"She tried to drown me," I croak. "That girl. She put mud on my hair and she tried to —"

"I never! I never!" Gemma rushes forward from behind the basin, holding out her hands beseechingly. Her face is white and panicky. "I was just conditioning her hair and she suddenly started screaming and flailing about, I never tried to drown her!" A fellow customer tuts sympathetically and holds out her arms, and Gemma buries her face against the older woman's shoulder.

"Mrs Harper, I think you might have had something medical happen." The salon owner is speaking very slowly and clearly. "I want you to sit very quietly for me while I call an ambulance, all right? We need to let someone take a look at you. Can you do that for me?"

"I haven't had a stroke. I'm fine, I can talk fine, see? It was that girl, she tried to —"

"But I never touched her! I swear!" Gemma's frightened face, red now with crying, appears for a moment, then vanishes again. There's a small patch of crimson blooming on her scalp.

"Mrs Harper, I need you to just sit calmly, all right? The ambulance will be here soon… No, please, just sit quietly —"

I scrabble wildly round in my seat to look at the basin. It's shallow and empty. My hair is wet and silky, scented not with mud but with delicate floral conditioner. I swivel back round in my seat. The salon owner is on the phone. The circle of faces watches me, sympathetic but wary. I must look like a madwoman. Perhaps they're right.

All instinct now, I glance around the salon, little quick glances like jabs of a knife, working out my route. My coat? In the back. Never mind. Have to leave it. My bag? By the chair in front of the mirror. The door? Open. Here I go.

I leap from my chair, grab my handbag and race for the door. There are squeaks and squeals of alarm, but no one tries to stop me. Why would they? They probably all want me gone as much as I do. The cold clamps my wet head like iron and the air burns my lungs, but I don't have time to worry. There's someone chasing me after all, which means I have to keep running, keep running, keep running...

"Susannah!" A hand grabs my arm. I shake it off, but it grabs again. "Susannah!" A familiar voice. Melanie. "It's me! It's me. It's me. Stop."

I want to keep going but there's no point. I can beat Melanie over short distances because I'm taller, but anything more than a quick dash and she'll inevitably catch me. She's always had more stamina than I have. She clutches at my arm with fingers smudged with biscuit-coloured polish.

"Sorry about your manicure."

"Forget the manicure, I'm worried about *you*. What happened?"

"I don't know."

"I heard this awful noise, sort of like someone choking, then everyone started screaming, and when I came out I saw... You grabbed that girl's hair, Suze, you pulled out a clump by the roots."

I look down at my hand. My fingers are tangled with strands of grey hair.

"Now listen. They think you've had a stroke. Apparently it happens sometimes, something to do with the basin against the back of your neck. You need to calm down and come back with me and wait for the ambulance. Okay?"

I can't stay here. I can't wait for the ambulance and the questions and the hours in hospital. They'll look for a physical cause first, and when they find nothing they'll conclude there's something wrong inside my head, and they'll take me to a secure unit for assessment and observation, and that will be the start of a slow meticulous process that could take weeks or months or maybe only days, but it doesn't matter because I can't spend even days locked away from the world. I have to be at home for Christmas. I have to understand what the universe is trying to tell me. And that means I have to get out of here, quickly, before the ambulance comes.

"I'm sorry," I say again. "I'm so sorry. Give the kids my love. I'll call you later, all right?"

And before Melanie can grab me I leap past her, run the twenty feet and dive onto the bus that is about to pull away from its stop.

Life Without Hope:
Keeping the Feasts

If you've been bereaved, you'll already know how painful it is when the milestones of the year roll around. There are the private ones. (*This time last year we were on holiday, this was the last birthday although we didn't know it, a year ago today we first got the diagnosis, this was our last good day, this day the day we lost them, this the funeral.*) And there are the public ones, the ones where seemingly everyone else but you is having the perfect time with their perfect unbroken families, hunting Easter Eggs or trick-or-treating or getting ready for Christmas or whatever. It hurts. It all hurts. All of it.

With death we can think, *They wouldn't have wanted us to be miserable. Life has to go on.* Even if we feel guilty for eating the chocolate, lighting a pumpkin or putting up the tinsel, we can tell ourselves that this is part of moving on. If we're being watched, at least means there's someone still there *to* watch, which means there is life after we die, and we haven't really lost our loved ones at all.

But what about when they're simply missing?

For a long time, I was terrified of celebrating. I was afraid that if Joel came back and saw that I was having fun without him, he would think I didn't want him any more. So while everyone else's house was bright and happy with Hallowe'en lights, Christmas lights, Easter daffodils, football flags or anything else – while everyone else went to bonfires and carol concerts and festivals – I didn't dare do any of it. Just in case he was watching. Just in case.

Then six months after Joel disappeared, my sister's youngest child was born.

I'll be honest, her birth was bittersweet for me. She's Joel's cousin and she'll never meet him, she'll have no memories of him at all apart from maybe photographs. But when I looked at her face, I knew that I wanted to be more than Sad Auntie Susannah who never comes to birthday parties and won't take you on the rides at Hull Fair and doesn't celebrate Christmas.

So now, when it's time to celebrate, I celebrate with the loved ones I have left, with my sister, my brother-in-law, my nephew and my niece. And while sometimes I have to wipe away the tears, at least I'm there. Part of my family. Still living. Still loving.

Posted on 13th June 2015
Filed to: Coping Strategies
Tags: coping when a loved one is missing, missing people, support for families, Susannah Harper, Joel Harper

Chapter Eleven
Thursday 23rd November 2017

The bus is crowded, but I'm grateful for the body heat. I stumble down the aisle, trying not to mind or feel conspicuous as bags and fcct arc gathcrcd in and faccs starc in avid surprise. There's one seat left, next to a slim young girl with corn silk hair and heavy nylon lashes, who's absorbed in her phone. When I sit down, shivering and blue-fingered, my hair drips water onto her jeans. She sighs and turns away, but doesn't speak. The warmth of her young body is tempting, and I have to resist the urge to lean against her. The characters in the game she's playing all wear Christmas hats, and bright crumbs of electronic snow fall across the screen. I clench my jaw to stop my teeth chattering. After a few minutes, the window begins to mist up.

What just happened to me? I have no idea. I can't fight it, I can't resist it, I can't think or speak or do anything other than sit in dumb passive silence and endure, until the next thing happens to me and it's time to endure that too. This must be how animals feel when they're wrenched from their green field and jammed into a lorry with dozens of their companions, driven sightless and waterless across an unknown distance to a concrete bunker that smells of death. In my handbag, my phone flashes and shudders. *Melanie Mobile*, it says. *Melanie Mobile. Melanie Mobile. Melanie*

Mobile. I close my eyes and count to twenty, slow and steady. When I open them, I see a smaller message: *Melanie Mobile missed call*. Just as I begin to feel safe, another summons begins. *Melanie Mobile. Melanie Mobile. Melanie Mobile*. I stare at the screen in terror.

"You know you can just reject the call, right?" It's the girl in the seat next to me. She takes my phone from my bag and dabs at the fat red circle labelled *Decline*. "See? Just keep doing that and they'll get the message. And you can block the number if you want. And then all that'll happen when they call is it goes straight to voicemail. You don't even have to look at the messages or owt, it won't notify you. Is Melanie your ex or summat?"

I shake my head, not quite daring to meet her gaze. My phone starts ringing again. Once again my rescuer dabs at the screen.

"S'all right, I've got a mate who's a dyke, I don't mind. Lasses can be horrible sometimes, can't they? There was this one girl, Shell was only seeing her for three weeks and when they broke up she phoned her and phoned her and phoned her, all day and night, begging her to get back with her. She had to go to the coppers in the end, get her warned off." She puts a hand on my arm. "Get some help if you need it, yeah? Right, this is my stop."

She swings her strong young body past mine and strides off down the bus, followed by the approval of the rest of the passengers. We'll be the salty seasoning for many people's teatime chat tonight. *I was on the bus this morning and there was this poor woman, her hair was all wet like she'd just got out the bath and she hadn't even got her coat on, blue with cold she was. And her phone was ringing and ringing and ringing, it was her girlfriend apparently – yeah, her girlfriend, not her boyfriend, not that it matters these days – and there was this young lass sat next to her had to show her how to block the calls. Nice young lass, nice to see her looking out for someone like that.* Or perhaps *Not surprised it all went wrong, it's not natural, lasses with lasses, is it? Maybe now they'll both find themselves a decent fella instead.* It won't matter that none of this is true. The brief intersection of my day with theirs will be woven into the narrative of their lives, and I will be forever fixed as the mad gay woman who ran away from a bad relationship and got on the bus with wet hair and no coat on. *Melanie Mobile. Melanie Mobile. Melanie Mobile.* Five missed calls. Six.

She's not going to go away. I'll have to talk to her sooner or later, so why not sooner? Outside Hull Royal Infirmary's tall thin slab of windows, I get off the bus and stand in the slight shelter of the building's shadow. *Melanie Mobile. Melanie Mobile.* Here we go.

"Susannah? Is that you?"

"Of course it's me, it's my phone."

"Thank God. I was afraid you might be the police or something, I thought you might have got in an accident." Her voice breaks and I remember with something like pain that Melanie loves me. "Where are you? What are you doing?"

"I'm just in town."

"Is anyone with you?"

"No, of course not."

"I'm coming to get you. All right? And then we'll go to the hospital to get you checked over. So where are you?"

I could tell her I'm already at the hospital. I could even take her advice, go and join the queue in the Accident and Emergency department.

"I'm nowhere, I'm just in town, walking around, that's all."

"With wet hair? And no coat? You'll freeze."

I clamp my jaw to stop my teeth chattering.

"I'm fine. Why are you worrying about me? I'm an adult, I can look after myself."

"Why am I worrying?" Her laugh is slightly frightening. "You had some sort of fit in the hairdressers and attacked the girl washing your hair, and then you got on a random bus and

159

ran away from me! I wanted to go after you but I couldn't, I had to go back there and pay the bill and apologise, I had to tell them your whole history so they'd let it drop. And now you won't tell me where you are! Do you even believe I'm trying to help you? Are you even grateful?"

"Grateful?"

"Yes! Grateful! For cleaning up after you! Or do you think just one awful thing happening to you once gets you a free pass to treat everyone else like dirt for the rest of time?"

"How can you say that? One awful thing? Is that what Joel disappearing is to you? Just *one awful thing*, like a burglary or something? It's with me every single day, Melanie, every single bloody day I have to get up and face it—"

"I know that. And I am sorry, okay? I'm sorry I got to have my family and keep them, I'm sorry I got two children when you only got one, I'm sorry my husband hasn't left me, I'm sorry my son hasn't started bunking off school and messing around with drugs and I'm sorry I've turned out luckier than you. But my God, you punish me for that every day, don't you? And I let you. I do everything you ask, I take phone calls in the middle of the night, I have you round to ours whenever you want, even if all you want is to sit in a corner and brood while we all try and carry on as if everything's normal, my God, I even drop everything and cancel a trip out with Grace and her friends to go and see the reindeer, and phone round every bloody hairdresser in the area and get a bloody manicure I can't afford, just so you can get a haircut you didn't even stay for. I do all of that because I love you and I want to help you."

She's trying and failing not to cry. I wonder where she is. Perhaps a kindly stranger will come to her aid as well. I hope they won't. She deserves to be alone after what she said to me.

"But I can't keep doing it if you won't help yourself. There's something wrong with you, Susannah, and you need to get help. I'll come with you and see the doctor, or call me any time and I'll take you to the hospital, any time at all, okay? Because I love you. I love you more than you'll ever know. And saying all of this to you is killing me. But don't call for anything else. I can't talk to you until you're willing to look after yourself. I love you, okay? Call me when you're home."

And then there's only three little pips in my ear, and a long slow silence that stretches out like the long shafts of sunlight that stab suddenly through the clouds to light up the brilliant cold.

"Jesus, look at the state of you!" Jackie looks me up and down in horror. "Did you come all the way from home looking like that? What happened?"

"Please can I come in?" I think my knees might give way with the relief that Jackie is here, and appears to hold no grudge.

"Course you can, you daft lass. Why are you all wet?"

"I was at the hairdressers."

"And they left you like this? I hope you didn't pay 'em, the robbing bastards. And look at your hands, you're blue! Come on in and let's get you sorted."

She leads me in over the threshold. In the plastic carrier-bag behind the door I glimpse a small silvery tree, a long box holding a set of porcelain angels, a few skeins of tinsel that pour over the side like fat snakes. She didn't have them when I left her in the café. She must have carried on shopping after I left her. Patting and coaxing, she pushes me up the stairs and shoehorns me into a tiny bedroom, crammed tight with a cast-iron bed and a pair of matching wardrobes. Then she scoops up the slippery maroon throw from the base of the bed and wraps it round my shoulders. The gesture is so kind and automatic that I burst into noisy tears.

"Hey." Jackie sits beside me and pats my shoulder. "It's all right."

"I'm so sorry about this morning."

"God, you're not upset over that are you? That was nothing, forget about it."

"It's not just that. I had an argument with Melanie and something awful happened in the hairdressers and I don't know what's happening to me, I think I'm going mad."

"Right." Jackie's sharp, motherly firmness is exactly what I crave. "Shut up now, or you'll wake Georgie. Let's get you cleaned up and looking human. Then you can tell me what's going on."

I sit meek and childlike as two cotton pads are placed over my eyes and something cool and luxurious is smoothed onto my face. Deprived of sight, I become extra sensitive to the sounds and scents around me; the alcohol and cucumber notes of the cleansers, the click and squirt of the bottles, the faint hum of the radio from the room beneath us, the warmth of Jackie's fingers against my skin, the slow minty heaviness of her breathing. I wish I could lie against the pillow and relax completely, forget the perils and terrors and complexities of the day and simply sleep, sleep and sleep while my best and only friend takes care of me.

"Oi. Don't go to sleep on me." Jackie shakes my shoulder. "I'm getting the hairdryer out in a second, so don't get too comfy, all right?"

"I'm not going to sleep."

"Yes, you are." She fingers the ends of my hair. "Nice colour this. Bit long though. Were you getting it cut shorter? Want me to have a go at it?"

"No, don't worry, it's fine."

"It's all right, I got my City and Guilds years ago. I was going to be a hairdresser till I fell for our Jaden."

"I wasn't really sure about getting it cut anyway, I should probably leave it alone."

"Did you go because of what I said this morning? You don't want to take no notice of me, I've got no clue what I'm on about half the time. Right, let's get it dried and into some sort of shape." She hesitates. "Then how about I put you a

162

new face on? Get you glammed up a bit?"

I don't especially want to be made up by Jackie in her dramatic style, but the warmth of the hairdryer is so delicious, the peace of simply sitting meek and doll-like as she teases and smooths and straightens my hair, then fusses and pats and paints at my skin, is so compelling, that I give in to the comfort of letting her do as she pleases. After all, no one will have to see me. After all, I can't possibly look any worse than I looked on my way over here.

"Right," Jackie commands. "Take a look."

In the mirror is someone I don't quite recognise. She looks roughly like me, but more striking, more noticeable, and fiercer; someone you'd take notice of, but perhaps be cautious around too. Someone who might dance and drink and have sex. Someone who matters. Someone with a life.

"Better?"

Is it better? Or is it just different? I can't decide.

"Amazing," I say, and watch in the mirror as the strange woman's painted lips move in time with my own.

"So come down to the kitchen and I'll make us a cuppa. Then you can tell me what's been going on."

"I've been seeing things," I say. The thin porcelain of the mug is burning hot, but I press my hands close to it anyway, welcoming the fierce heat.

"What do you mean, seeing things? What sort of things?"

"Visions of... of drowning. Of being drowned. There's always someone there with me, someone watching while I... Sometimes they're holding me under. Sometimes they just push me into the water. It even happened at the hairdressers, for God's sake, she was washing my hair and I thought she was trying to drown me in the basin. And once I saw—"

"Yes?"

"I saw my husband," I admit, and bite hard on the inside of my cheek to keep the tears at bay. "He was angry with me. So angry I thought he was going to... But then he wasn't even

163

there! He wasn't even there. I think maybe they're telling me what happened to Joel. I think maybe he... perhaps he's... and maybe he's trying to tell me that   "

"Oh, love, no. No, no, no, don't say that. You don't know that, you don't." Jackie strokes my back gently. "He could still be alive. He could."

"I know he could. And that's why I'm so confused. Because I saw a fortune teller at Hull Fair and she told me he'd come back to me by Christmas and that must mean he's still alive, mustn't it? But then if he is, why do I keep seeing all this awful stuff about being drowned?" I take a scalding mouthful of tea. "Melanie – my sister, I mean – she thinks I'm going mad."

"Fucking hell," says Jackie, with sincere reverence. "I mean really. Just, fucking hell. You poor thing."

"I'm so scared. I don't know what's happening."

"Yes, you do, of course you do. It's the trauma, isn't it? It does things to our brains. Like soldiers. You've been in the trenches too long and it's all catching up with you."

"But what if it's real? What if Joel's really trying to get a message to me somehow?"

"Suze. Listen to me. Please." Jackie puts her mug down and takes hold of my shoulders. "There are no psychics. There are no ghosts. It's all bollocks. Whatever's happening to you, it's nothing to do with the other side trying to get in touch with us, and that rip-off merchant at the Fair can no more tell you when Joel's coming back than Georgie can. You know that. You told me and now I'm telling you. All right?"

"I know." I don't know if I believe her or not but it's easier to say I agree than to carry on arguing. "Thanks for listening."

"Do you think maybe you might want to talk to someone about it though? Like a doctor or someone?"

"No! Absolutely not."

"I'm not saying there's something wrong with you, but just to make sure."

"I don't need anyone to help. I can cope with it, I'm managing it. It's not hurting anyone but me anyway."

Jackie shakes her head. "You can't go on like this, running around town with wet hair and no coat on, scaring yourself stupid in your own home. You looked like a little ghost yourself when I opened the door. There's no shame in seeing someone for help."

"I can't. Don't you see? I mean, even if this is just all in my head. What if I remember something important? Something that might help find where Joel is? And what if the doctors make it stop?"

"But look, you can't—"

I hold up my hand for quiet. "I think I can hear Georgie."

"Do you really mean that? Or are you just trying to shut me up?"

"No, I really can, listen." Upstairs, we hear a loud thump, and then a joyful yelp. "See?"

Jackie sighs. "Give me two minutes."

When Jackie brings Georgie downstairs, she's bright-eyed and shrieky and stares at us with expectant eyes, waiting for us to produce something to entertain her. So we bundle her up in a stiff pink snowsuit and Jackie lends me a spare coat and gloves, and we lock up the house and take a walk through small streets and past old warehouses to West Park, Georgie bowling along in front of us. Within a few minutes, she's staring dreamily out at the world as it scrolls past her field of vision, sucking on her fingers and occasionally making a half-hearted swipe at the plastic rings Jackie's strung across the buggy.

The cold is bitter and unrelenting and the sky crammed with clouds, but the park is still astonishingly lovely. A bloom of ice crusts the shaded edge of the paddling pool and the leaves glow amber and brown. When we prise Georgie from her buggy she arches her strong straight back and reaches starfish hands towards the iron sky as if she's trying to grab handfuls of it to stuff into her mouth. In the aviary, the parrots huddle disconsolately at the back of their cage and ruffle up their feathers, and a lone wallaby leaves the safety of the huddle to venture across the paddock in small delicate hops, watching our hands to see if we have something for it to eat. Jackie holds out a handful of tissue and stealthily smushes Georgie's hand into the soft fur of its neck. Georgie shrieks in delight and the wallaby jumps back in surprise, the tissue dangling from its mouth as it leaps away.

"Poor wallaby," I say.

"Poor nothing. That's what it's here for. Paying its rent, aren't you, mate?" The wallaby lets the tissue fall to the ground and stares reproachfully at us with liquid black eyes. "Reckon they'll put them in Santa hats when it gets closer to Christmas? Let's sit down for a bit, these boots are killing me."

We sit down on the bench by the paddling pool and watch the runners, Georgie throwing herself from Jackie's arms to mine and then back again. I'm astonished by the strength she has. A man about my age, trim and greying and soaked with sweat, jogs past us. His eyes slide sideways towards us, pass over Jackie, snag on me. The rhythm of his feet slows a fraction. He smiles approvingly.

"He fancies you," Jackie says. Georgie lurches across towards me.

"No, he doesn't."

"Yeah, he does. Don't blame him, either. Your hair looks nice that colour. You look – God almighty, Georgie, you weigh a ton – you look years younger. Suits you."

Do I like being looked at this way by men? I'm not sure. There was something proprietorial in his gaze, as if I was a purchase in a shop or a painting in a gallery. He wasn't seeing me at all, not really; only the outer wrapping, newly painted and tinted in this season's colours. Georgie holds her arms out to me, and I brace myself for her enthusiastic bounce into my arms.

"Well, I'm not in the market for a date so it doesn't really matter."

"Why not? You're divorced, right? You're allowed to see other blokes." Georgie lurches back over to Jackie. Her right foot kicks me hard in the stomach. "Look, there's another one that's clocked you. See?"

Another runner, much younger this time with thick hair and a well-tended beard, but the same glance, the same assessment, the same feeling that I'm on display and being considered by someone who believes they have the right to choose or to reject, to admire or to deride, while I sit within my coat of paint and wait for their judgement. He must be twenty years younger than me but he still seems to approve of what he sees, as if the effort I (or more accurately, Jackie) has made with my appearance has been done for his benefit and he's happy to reward it with a little flirty smile. It doesn't seem to occur to him to wonder if I find him attractive in return.

Georgie throws herself towards me again. I take her on my lap and vary the game by turning her onto her back and scrubbling my hand in her middle. She yelps and folds around me like a clamshell. Do I want to spend time with a man who has only noticed me because other women have temporarily re-coloured my hair and skin and eyes and lips? What happened to finding a soulmate? Someone who's attracted to the person you are inside? But then again, what man in their right mind would be attracted to someone as damaged as me?

"You don't have to pick up some randomer in the park," Jackie says. "But don't you think it might do you good to have some fun? You're my mate, I don't like seeing you so lonely, it's not right. Susannah? Oi. Are you listening? Susannah?"

I can see Joel.

It's not Joel.

Except it is.

I've fallen victim to this illusion a million times. A glance across a crowded street, a face glimpsed from a bus, and for a moment it's *them*, just going about their business without a care in the world, and even though you know it's not them at all, you have to jostle through the crowd or jump off the bus and chase after them, until the illusion collapses and you realise that once again you're pursuing a stranger. I've done this and done it and done it, until at last I learned not to do it, to fight every instinct in my body and turn away and keep going about my day, and save myself the pain of once again swallowing down hope that's shattered like glass. Pain you can learn to live with; it's the unfulfilled hope that will kill you in the end.

But this is different. It really is Joel. It's really him.

He's taller and broader at the shoulders, still thin, but shaped like a man rather than a stretched-out boy. His hair has darkened by a few shades. His skin has cleared up and is shadowed with stubble. He's dressed in clothes I've never seen before. But it's him. I know it's him. Not because of the colour of his eyes, the shape of his mouth, the way he stands or the way his hands move. But because when he sees me looking, he speaks to me, and even though he's on the other side of the paddling pool and too far away for me to hear him, I watch the shape his lips make and hear the words chime like a bell in my head:

Help me, Mum. Help me. I need you. Can you hear me? I need you to come and get me.

And as I stand up, dazed and desperate, and pass Georgie over to Jackie without even realising what I'm doing, he turns and runs away.

I'm off like a hare out of a trap, running faster than I ever knew I could. Joel is fast, but I'm going to catch him, I have to. He needs me. He spoke to me. I'm going to reach him. The wallabies and the sheep hold up their innocent blank-eyed faces as we pass, first him, then me, separate but tethered by an invisible cord.

At the skate park I lose him. A girl in jeans and knee-pads and a helmet scoots up and down the half-pipe, flicking her board around at the top of the curve, over and over. When I gasp out my frantic question (*Did you see a young lad jeans and a green hoodie running past which way did he go?*) she looks at me warily as if I might be here to hurt her. I start to repeat the question, but then I see Joel disappearing behind a smooth concrete mound and I start running again, oblivious to the shrieks and curses of the skaters and runners and walkers whose paths I charge across, my lungs burning but my heart pounding a triumphant martial rhythm. I will be fast enough. I'm gaining on him. I'm strong enough to do this.

We're pounding down a wide concrete path lined with tall rusted shapes like aloe leaves, bent over at the tops and with street lights concealed in their peaks. My legs are turning weak but I can still see Joel, and that's all that matters; as long as I can still see him I have a chance. And then Joel turns round as if to check I'm still following and once again our eyes meet and he smiles and beckons me on.

I'm so happy I think my heart might burst out of my chest. My son is here. He's been alive all this time. I run down the path and feel as if I'm flying. He's still ahead of me, but the gap is closing, just another five strides and I'll be close enough to catch him.

"Will you stop running, you utter fucking nutter!"

Hands and hands and hands, grabbing at my arms and hair. I fight back wildly for a minute, but then my legs give up the battle to hold me upright and I crumple as if someone's cut my strings. Jackie is there, and one of the runners who was looking at me earlier. I have a sense of being enclosed, and I realise I'm sitting on a small patch of road between the bumpers of two cars. My leg aches fiercely. Absolutely everyone is staring at me.

"What's got into you? I had to leave Georgie with some woman, where is she, where's my baby—" Jackie is beside herself, barely able to speak. I spy a patch of scarlet and point wordlessly. Jackie swoops fiercely over the buggy and snatches Georgie out, clutching her like a talisman.

"Will she be all right now?" The runner is clearly desperate to get away, terrified of being made responsible for my fate.

"D'you want me to call the police?"

"No, she'll be all right now, I'll look after her, thanks for helping. You get off, we'll be all right here. I know what's wrong with her, don't worry."

I pull myself up, leaning against the bonnet of the car, and look wildly around for Joel. Where has he gone? Where is he where is he where is he? I can't see him anywhere. Jackie hauls me onto the pavement. The woman who brought Georgie disappears. The cars drive on, the drivers shaking their heads in disbelief. Only Jackie stays with me, clutching Georgie with one arm and grabbing onto me with the other.

"What happened?"

My left leg is starting to hurt and there's a smear of black dirt across my jeans. "I saw Joel."

"No, you didn't! We were just sat there talking, and then you suddenly handed Georgie over to me and stood up and took off like a maniac."

"But he was stood right across the paddling pool. He was there. I saw him." Jackie shakes her head. "I know, I know, but it *wasn't like that*. Okay? He saw me. He looked at me. He asked me to help him. Then he ran away. He was asking me to follow him, Jackie, I swear."

"There was no one there. Can you hear me? There was nobody stood there. You were following no one."

"But I saw him," I whisper. "I saw him."

"But he wasn't there. You saw him. But nobody else did. Look, you need to talk to someone about this. It's getting out of hand. It's more than you can handle by yourself."

"He was there," I repeat, and then Jackie's arms go around me and I feel her stagger under my weight and we sink to the pavement, Georgie protesting loudly as she gets caught somewhere in between, strangers tutting as they have to pass us, and Jackie strokes my hair and murmurs something into my neck and I know she's right, and this is more than we can handle by ourselves, and we need to talk to someone.

Chapter Twelve
Saturday 23rd November 2013

The house of the psychic is three-storeyed and sash-windowed, its creamy-yellow double front fringed with roses and terraced between two identical twins. The wreath of holly on the door is fat and luxurious, a single tasteful concession to the approaching season. *Where the money lives*; the phrase John likes to use when we drive through quiet exclusive streets like this one, or rather the phrase he liked to use in the time before Joel disappeared. These days we shy away from the possibilities of levity, cynicism, sarcasm, disparagement, as if they might scorch our flesh.

In my quest to find answers, John and I have driven much further than the ten miles or so that have taken us from our own quiet suburb to this exclusive street. We've visited pokey flats over takeaway restaurants, oddly business-like premises in bohemian commercial districts, over-embellished ex-council houses in neighbourhoods teetering precariously between gentrification and urban ruin; tumbledown cottages in small villages. This house is the first that we could almost certainly not afford ourselves. I like that. I like the implication of a success that's superior to our own. The man we're about to meet will be the right choice. This man has succeeded far beyond the rest, and therefore must – surely he must – be the diamond in the coal heap, the singular exception who can actually keep his promises. I reach for John's hand and offer him a quick bright smile, not too large because we don't do large smiles any more, but enough to let him know that I'm happy, that I have a good feeling about this one. And I do. I really do.

"We don't have to go in." John strokes my hand gently through the fur-lined leather glove. His own hand is bare, his coat unfastened, his head hatless. He's always been more resistant to the cold than I am.

"What? What are you talking about?"

"We don't have to do this. He's got our email address and our phone number but he hasn't got anything else, he's not going to chase us or anything. We can just walk back up the street and get in the car and go home."

"But why would we want to?" I'm genuinely baffled. "John, this guy's good, I've been asking around and everyone says he's great. He's worked with the police even, there was a case over in Manchester and he helped them find this woman—"

"Who did you hear that from?"

"I can't remember, someone online I think, but they had all the details, it was in the papers and everything."

"But you didn't hear it from the police?"

"Well, no, of course I didn't. I'm not going to ring up Manchester police force and ask, am I?" John says nothing. "Okay, why don't you wait in the car?"

"I'm not letting you walk into a strange man's house on your own."

"Are you just going to sit there and send out bad energy and ruin everything?"

"Bad energy." He laughs a little. "Susannah, that's not a real thing."

"Yes, it is, of course it is, you just don't call it *energy*, you call it *mood*. Bad moods can ruin parties and meetings, why wouldn't they ruin this too?"

"If it's a real thing then it should work whether I believe

172

or not. I can't make the lights go on and off just through my mood."

As it happens, I know John is wrong. There have been plenty of cases of poltergeists triggered by unhappy people in the house. Adolescents usually, whose families are suddenly plagued by an outbreak of power cuts, temperamental kitchen appliances, blown light bulbs and intermittent telephone connections. But I don't have time to argue now. Our appointment is for seven thirty, and it's already seven twenty-eight.

"If this is what you're going to be like, then you might as well not be here at all. I mean it John, you have to make the effort. You're not going to ruin this, are you? Not when it might actually work?"

For a moment, I think he's going to resist me, that he's actually going to insist that we leave.

"All right." His capitulation is both expected and surprising. Expected because I'm used to winning, surprising because we've both just remembered that me winning is not some sort of natural law. "I'll come in."

"And behave yourself?"

"I promise."

"And you'll join in properly?"

"I'll do my best, okay? I'll do my absolute best."

I'd be happier with another promise, but it's seven twenty-nine now and I don't want to make a bad impression, so I lead the way through the gate and up the path and onto the wide stone porch. The garden is higher than the street, the steps higher than the garden, creating an unpleasant feeling of vertigo as I lift the lion's-head knocker, careful not to scratch my gloves on the holly wreath. John hovers just behind me, as if he's waiting for me to fall.

"Mrs Harper?" The man who opens the door is perhaps in his early forties, neat and slick in his black jeans and black roll-neck and black goatee beard and rimless glasses that are just the right side of theatrical. He's not good-looking exactly

173

but the energy he exudes makes you feel that he is, like an actor or a stand-up comedian whose projected persona can temporarily seduce you into finding them the most exciting person on the planet. "I'm James O'Brien. James, obviously, not Mr O'Brien. Lovely to meet you, thank you for being so prompt. And Mr Harper?" He greets John with a respectful handshake, but his attention is focused on me, taking my coat and hanging it for me on the good wooden coat hanger that waits for it on the pegs on the deep-red wall.

In most houses a red hallway would be oppressive, maybe even vaginal, but this tall wide house with its tiled floor can take on the red colour and make it majestic, like the entrance to a beautiful old music hall. We're led into a room with a parquet floor where a small fire burns genteelly in the grate, and a spotted mirror in an old-gold frame shows us a dim startling glimpse of our faces. The walls bloom with outsized green roses that make me think of absinthe and arsenic. It feels both authentic and staged, a dreamy reminiscence of the glory days of spiritualism. It also feels dizzyingly expensive. I cautiously sit down on a green velvet chaise longue, feeling the wood shift slightly as John joins me. James O'Brien takes the spot on the sofa at ninety degrees to us. His body language is forward and open, in noticeable contrast to my own nervous neatness (feet together on the floor, hands folded in my lap) and John's disengagement (back against the back of the chaise longue, arms folded).

"So how are you feeling about tonight?" His smile is quick, white and reassuring. "I'm getting the impression you're a bit nervous, Mrs Harper? And Mr Harper, you're feeling somewhat sceptical about the whole thing?"

"Oh, you spotted that, did you," says John gloomily. I glance at him and he looks irritated, then ashamed of himself. "Sorry. But yes, to be honest, I am a bit sceptical."

"Understood. Understood. Are you happy to go ahead anyway? Or would you prefer to put this on hold for now? Give me a call in a week or two once you're really sure? Of course I'll refund your payment in the meantime."

This question takes both of us by surprise. John's eyebrows go up, his arms unfold, he leans forward, beginning to copy the shape James is making with his own body. Is this a good sign, or a bad one? What if John accepts James's invitation and gathers his coat from the hall and marches us back into the night? I don't know if I could bear that. If I'm not talking to James or someone like him, all I'll have left to keep me sane are my midnight walks and drives as I scour the city and the surrounding villages, looking for some faint trace of our son.

"Do a lot of your clients bail out at the last minute?" John asks after a moment's thought.

"Not a lot, but some. And that's all right. Sessions like this are an investment of time and emotion and the results are never guaranteed. I don't want anyone making that investment if they're not confident it's right for them."

Everything about this one is different. The house, so expensively tasteful. The man himself, well-groomed and well-kept, such a change from floaty batiks and fat torsos and copious silver jewellery. *Investment. Results. Confident. Right for them.* I feel a surge of hope. John pats my hand to get my attention.

"Susannah? It's up to you, love. I'll stay if you want to. If you're sure you're strong enough to go through this again."

"You've been to quite a few others," says James, with the faint tolerant smile that tells me everything I need to know about his opinions of those *others*.

"We have," I admit.

He doesn't say anything, just holds my gaze for a moment. He has one of the most expressively eloquent faces I've ever encountered. *I'm completely different to them*, he says to me without words. *But it's all right, you don't have to go through with this. There's no pressure. I don't need your money. You can see I'm doing fine for myself already. In fact, I might even ask you to leave in a minute. I don't want to put any pressure on you, because I'm just that good a person.*

"I'm sure," I say, before he can speak. "I'm definitely sure."

The moment where he considers my words is painful.

"All right, then," he says at last. "Then let's get started, shall we?"

There's a neat little mahogany table in the window and I wonder if perhaps we're going to sit round that, but instead James leads us back across the hall and into a chilly, bare-boarded space with blackout blinds pulled down to hide the windows, and a single bulb imprisoned in a cheap white paper shade that glows like a moon. In the centre, a square pine table is crowded around with four institutional-looking wooden chairs. The heavy glass jug filled with ice water, the stack of cheap thick tumblers, could have been stolen from the dinner halls of my childhood.

"No distractions," James says, that quick reassuring smile that tells me he's aware of my surprise and is prepared for it. "I know some people go in for scarves and rugs everywhere but I'd rather keep everything out in the open so you can see there's no enhancement going on." He gives John a quick little conspiratorial glance as he says this, nothing sly or subservient, just one man acknowledging to another that yes, there are some terrible charlatans in this world, and it's wise to protect yourself from them. "So, as I outlined to you on the phone, this is very much a preliminary session, all right? I'll be working mainly to establish the connection between us, and to start to get a feel for Joel himself. We may find something useful, but that's more likely to come in the later sessions, once we've established a good connection."

I can feel John's discomfort with this smooth casual segue into *later sessions* – I'd told him only one, it would just be the one – but I know he won't argue now. He promised to support me properly and with an open mind, and I know that's what he'll do.

"I understand," I say.

"And Mr Harper?"

John sighs and hesitates a moment, but then, thank God, he nods.

"Oh, I should probably say that there's absolutely no commitment to any future sessions. I never ask clients to commit to a second appointment, it's always down to you to say when you're ready to proceed. Does that make you feel a bit more comfortable, Mr Harper?" John has the decency to blush. "Good. Now, before we get started, would either of you like a glass of water?"

"No, thank you."

"Want to use the bathroom?"

"Oh. No, thanks."

"Mr Harper?"

John shakes his head silently.

"All right, then. If you'd both like to take a seat?"

I perch nervously in the smooth slippy seat of the little wooden chair. John takes the one to the right of me. James sits opposite. The room is very cold.

"So to start with, we're just going to spend some time concentrating on Joel, getting a feel for the kind of person he is." He places his hands on the table. "I'm just going to take your hands, and if I can ask you to join hands too and complete the circle to allow the flow of energy…" He says this completely matter-of-factly, as if he's asking us to turn on a light switch or show him where the fuse box is. "And now, if you can both think hard about your son, about a time when you were all together and you were really, really happy."

"Do we close our eyes?" John's voice is hoarse and nervous. This is a good sign, it has to be a good sign. It must mean he's seen something that's convinced him this is different.

"Whichever's more comfortable for you. The main thing is that you concentrate absolutely on remembering the times when you were happy and together with Joel." He glances at me. "And if you find that unlocks some emotions within

177

you, either happy ones or sad ones, that's absolutely not a problem, don't feel as if you have to hide anything or hold anything back. But please don't break the circle if you can possibly help it. All right?"

I'd thought I'd done rather a good job at hiding the tears that are already crouching in the back of my nose and throat. Unseen by James, John strokes the palm of my hand with the ball of his thumb.

Choosing a memory is like picking a rose from a bush full of thorns. If you want the sweetness, there's no avoiding the pain. Which should I choose? Which would have the most power? Sitting in the rocking chair at midnight with Joel drowsing half awake in my arms, gazing out at our familiar garden turned strange by moonlight, watching the small scurry of the hedgehog as it rushes over the lawn to the safety of the shadows? The tightness of Joel's fingers in my hair as he burst from the doorway of the playgroup and flung himself onto me? The clean damp scent of his sweat when we walked together in the park and fed the ducks, and he grew tired and I carried him home even though he was six years old and too heavy? Lying on our backs and watching the sunlight filter through the leaves of the apple tree?

Beside me, John takes a deep slow breath. I realise with a sharp stab of guilt that my happiest memories are of Joel and me alone. When I picture the three of us together what I mostly remember is anxiety, the careful delicate work of translating their meanings to each other without looking as if I'm interfering, endlessly modelling the behaviours I want to see from them both. *No, Daddy, I don't want you to push me on the swings, I want Mummy to push me! – Oh, Joel, sweetie, don't worry, Daddy won't push you higher than you want to go, all you have to do is tell him you're getting scared and he'll slow down, won't you John? And besides, Daddy's much stronger than me, he can push you for loads longer than I can... Or in a restaurant: Joel, Daddy only wants you to try his steak because it's yummy and he wants to share, okay? He's not trying to make you change your food, you can still have your chicken nuggets. In fact, why don't we all try each other's dinners? Why don't you give Daddy and me a bite of your chicken nuggets?*

"So I'm getting a picture of a little boy with blond hair, sitting in the sunshine. Somewhere in a garden? A back garden, with some sort of tree... a fruit tree... an apple tree. Mrs Harper, I'm thinking this is your memory, is that right?"

"Yes. Yes. That's me. That's what I was thinking of."

John's hand tenses slightly in mine.

"He loved the garden when he was little, didn't he? He looks very very happy in this memory. Oh, and he has some sort of toy with him as well. Some sort of toy animal? A plushy toy animal?"

James's voice is low and earnest now. I have to concentrate hard to hear him. I am acutely aware of the sound of my breath.

"Yes. Yes, he had, um—"

"That's all right, don't tell me, let the image come to me. I think he's holding a... a cat? No, that's not quite right... ah, okay, I've got it. It's a dog. A dog made out of patchwork scraps of fur. Does that sound familiar?"

My heart is trying to drive me from my seat. I want to leap up and spring around the room. James has seen Scrap-dog. He has seen Scrap-dog. No one has ever seen Scrap-dog before. This man is the real thing. I've finally found him.

"Remember not to break the connection," James says softly, and I force myself to keep still.

"So now I'm starting to get another image. This time you're somewhere with very big machines, lots of big machines. Um. Could you concentrate a little harder? I'm not quite seeing... ah, yes, some sort of vehicle. Trains, maybe? No, it's not trains, it's buses, although I think there might be some trains nearby? Somewhere very noisy. You're waiting for a bus, all three of you?"

I'm bewildered, but to my surprise John speaks.

"Yes. I was thinking of the first time we—"

"Ah-ah-ah, don't lead me, it's best if you let me just... feel my way into the image... ah, yes, I've got it now. It's the bus station. He's about four years old? It's a treat, I think, maybe a birthday? No, it's not a birthday, is it? Something significant, though."

I have no memory of this happening. How dreadful that this moment, which clearly meant so much to John, has tumbled through the leaky sieve of my brain and disappeared.

"Starting school," John murmurs.

"Of course it is. I could get that it was something important, some sort of milestone, but not the exact one... and you took him on the top deck, I think?"

"Yes. The top deck."

"I can feel how happy he was in this memory. How happy you all were. Thank you for sharing that with me."

From behind my closed eyelids, I see the light flicker.

"Nothing to worry about," James says. "Sometimes it happens when we make a particularly good connection, that's all. Or it could just be dodgy wiring." He hesitates, and clears his throat. "Now, I don't normally do this so early, but since we're doing some good work, I'd like to move forward in time, and I'd like, if you could, for you to concentrate on the last time you saw Joel." I try not to flinch. "I know that's going to be a difficult memory, so if you're not comfortable with going this far we can simply focus on building our connection using happier memories. You're in control, I'm just here to support you."

Why am I hesitating? He's found missing people before. People whose names were in the papers, although his connection to the cases is spoken of only in whispers, passed from one desperate mouth to another. He can have this memory if it helps. He can have all of them if it helps.

"Yes," I say. "That's fine. Let's do it."

"Mr Harper?"

"Yes. Yes. Right now." John's voice trembles. The light

flickers again. The room is very cold. I cling hard to the hands of the two men.

"So if you can just take yourselves back to that time… that morning when you last saw him…" James's voice is low and coaxing, like a hypnotist. "And I'm getting the very strong feeling that there was an argument, is that right? And he made some threats to run away. Okay, I can see him very clearly, he was still fair-haired, wasn't he, more like you in appearance, Mrs Harper. I can feel there was a lot of tension in the house that day, but also a lot of love. Try and hold onto the love. The love is what connects you to your son. Keep holding onto the love."

I concentrate on holding onto the love. It's not easy. There is something dark and frightening in the room with us now. I don't like the way this session is making me feel. The memories that come to me are not loving memories. I remember the fury that convulsed John's features into an entirely new shape, the savagery of his fists as he shook the bag of weed in Joel's face. I remember Joel's expression as he glanced back at me through the window. *Help me*. And I didn't. I didn't go after him. I chose to stay with my husband.

"Mrs Harper? Are you all right? I'm sensing this is very difficult for you, would you like to stop?"

"No. I want to keep going."

"All right then… so I'm with Joel. He's running down the street. He's got running away on his mind, but it's not a serious thought, it's got that teenage rage feeling to it. It's a fantasy, not a plan. He's going somewhere. I think he's going to school."

Hurry up, hurry up. We know all of this, everyone knows all of this.

"Okay, now I'm sensing a great deal of darkness. He's very unhappy. He's craving something, there's a very deep hunger. He's thinking about being very small, very very small, maybe even a baby. He's remembering a time when he was completely looked after and had no worries at all. There's something changing his perception now, things are getting quite fuzzy. It's possible he's been drinking, or maybe... I'm sorry to tell you this. Do you want me to carry on?"

"Yes." John's voice, low and passionate.

"Okay, there's another journey happening now. I think he must have left school. There's a great sense of movement, I don't think he's travelling on foot. I can hear shouting, there's a man with him who's very angry with him, someone he's afraid of, someone with authority over him. I'm... I'm getting the word *disgrace*, something about *what would your mother think*. He's growing very fuzzy now, very hard to keep hold of. I can sense water... it's very cold... he's somewhere near water, somewhere at the start of a journey, there's a very large ship that he wants to get onto but he's not sure if he can find a way. He's thinking about travelling, he has a very strong call to start this journey, but he's also afraid. He wants to take the first step but he's afraid."

"Is there anyone with him?" I don't want to interrupt the flow but I have to ask, I have to know.

"I think there's someone with him, someone he loves but who's also quite frightening, but this might just be a memory... no, I can't be sure. He's concentrating very hard on what's in his head rather than what's going on around him, and I'm... I'm afraid I'm getting tired now, I think we all are, I'm losing the connection." When I open my eyes for a second, his face is scrunched up tight and painful. "Mr Harper, if you could just rejoin hands I'll try and ... no, I can't, it's gone. I'm so sorry. If we try another time I may be able to find more."

It's not until James releases my hand that I realise he's gripped tightly enough to crush my rings into my flesh. I flex my fingers beneath the table, wondering if I'll have bruises later. I don't care. It's worth it. James looks pale but triumphant. Despite the clammy chill of our bare and comfortless surroundings, there's a gloss of sweat on his forehead. He reaches for the jug, pours some water, drains it in one long swallow.

"I'm sorry I lost him towards the end." He refills the water glass. "That was a very intense experience. Thank you for allowing me to share it. The strength of your memories of Joel were exceptionally strong. I think we've made some good progress, got some excellent insights that we can hopefully explore further some time." He gulps down more water. "I'm sorry, I'm being rude. Let me—" He pours two more glasses, offers one to me. I take it and sip hesitantly. I'm afraid I might spill it.

"Mr Harper?"

John isn't listening. Instead he's fumbling in his pocket. Surely he's not hunting for cash? We pay by bank transfer and we get a receipt. This isn't some grubby cash-in-hand enterprise. He's unfolding a sheet of paper, which he lays on the table like a loaded weapon.

"I wonder if you could take a look at this for me," John says.

James raises an eyebrow, but reaches for the paper anyway. I strain to read what he's looking at through the thin shadows cast by the ink as the light shines through. It looks like a screen-shot of a website. I can read the outsized title (*Shared Memories*) but the text beneath is a maddening small blur.

"If you wouldn't mind reading it out loud," John says. He's caught James's trick of disguising his commands as suggestions, that introduction of the unresolved *if* at the beginning of the sentence.

"The other night John and I were discussing our best memories of Joel. What surprised me the most was that we chose to remember him in such different ways. My favourite memories are domestic: giving him his bath, reading him his bedtime stories, snuggling under the blankets in his couch-fort, playing in the garden in the sunshine. John loves to remember the adventures we had: riding on the steam-trains up on the Yorkshire Moors, taking him for his first bus ride in last few weeks before he started school, paddling in the sea

and catching crabs on the beach at Hornsea. There was a beautiful comfort in sharing these memories—"

"That's enough. And now if you can just read the description at the bottom of the page..."

"Life Without Hope. A blog by the mother of a missing child. Mr Harper, I don't quite understand what point you're trying to make here."

"It's my wife's blog," John says grimly.

"I don't have a blog!"

"No, I know you don't. But he doesn't know that, he thinks this is your blog that you write and maintain. And if you google the name *Susannah Harper*, this comes up on the very first page." John's face is ugly with triumph, although I can't see what he's so happy about. What point has he proved here? What's he trying to tell us?

"Are you saying someone's keeping a blog and pretending to be me?"

"Mrs Harper, your husband's telling you he created it," says James with a sigh. "And he thinks I found it and harvested the content to create the experience we just had."

"He's a fraud, Susannah," says John. "Just the same as all the rest. Think about the *memories* he claimed to be picking up on. You playing with Joel in the garden. That was in the entry I just made him read out."

"But Scrap-dog, he saw Scrap-dog—"

"He *guessed* Scrap-dog, it's just cold-reading, they all do it. They feed you a bit of information and they look at the signals you give off and then they add a bit more information and look again, and before you know it they've guessed the colour of your underwear when you first met your husband. And that bus ride... did you wonder why you didn't remember it? I knew you wouldn't believe me unless I showed you proof, so here it is. There never was a first bus ride to celebrate Joel starting school. I made it up last week. And the only place *he* could have found it out is if he read this."

"Okay. I think I'm going to have to ask you to leave now. Mr Harper, it goes without saying that I'll refund your payment—"

"Keep it." John looks as if he wants to spit on the table. "Put it towards the new wiring. Merry Christmas. Come on, love."

My head feels as if it's about to float off my shoulders. I'm frozen to the chair. Which of the two men before me has betrayed me the most?

"Come on," John repeats.

If I keep still and stare at John for long enough, perhaps this will start to make sense.

"Mrs Harper." James kneels in front of me. "You're obviously very shocked by this. If you maybe take some time to think about what's just happened to you here? I can see you're feeling quite frightened. Is there someone I can call for you, to take you somewhere safe?"

"Shut your lying face. Get away from her. She's coming home with me."

"Your sister, maybe? I know she loves you very much—"

"I said, get away from my wife!"

And then I'm being lifted up, not dragged from my chair exactly but a feeling that's separated only from this by the inherent goodness of John's intentions, and I'm caught in his arms and we're tearing through the door and across the hall and out into the lamplit night. I think he'll put me down as soon as we're outside, but instead he carries me up the street towards the green-black land of the Westwood common where we left the car. It's not until we reach the ancient horse chestnut by the side of the road, and our car parked beneath it, that he lets me stand on my own.

Years ago, when I was hopelessly drunk among many other hopeless drunks at a party so raucous the police had been called, John carried me home. As the police knocked at the front door, he simply picked me up and carried me through the back, away from the unfolding chaos. I thought that as

185

soon as we were safely clear of the party's zone of influence he'd put me down and we'd look for a taxi, but instead he kept going, the whole three-mile walk, pausing sometimes to rest on garden walls or on green-painted benches that stared out across nearly empty roads to their identical twins on the other side. When we reached my parents' house he set me down on the doorstep, found my keys in my handbag and opened the door for me, kissed me gently on the mouth, then strode off again. I remember the sensation that enveloped me as he walked, the childhood feeling of helplessness and dependence. I remember having no fear whatsoever for his own safety. I remember thinking with drunken satisfaction, *My boyfriend is so strong, he could fight off anyone, even a bear, even an axe murderer.* I remember thinking, *This is it. The most romantic moment of my life.*

Now, years later, we stand beside our expensive car and watch each other's faces for signs of weakness and I think about my husband, my strong determined husband who could fight off a bear or even an axe murderer, and I think, *If it came to it, could I stop you from doing anything that you wanted to do?*

"I left our coats," says John. "I'm sorry. Get in the car and I'll put the heater on."

"Why did you do that? The blog and everything? Why come along tonight if you knew it wasn't true?"

"You wouldn't believe me any other way."

"But," I whisper, "but it felt real. It was real."

"I'm not saying he's not talented. I'm saying he's not *psychic*. He's just a very clever man who's very, very good at taking lots of little scraps of information and building them up into a convincing picture. And that's all he was going to do, love. Take our money and feed you little scraps for as long as he could get away with it. And I'm not having that. I love you."

"He saw Joel – he saw him going to water and boats – he saw him starting a journey – we have to follow that up, it might be something that will help find him—"

John thumps the roof of the car in despair.

"Well, of course he saw water and boats! We live in a bloody port city! What else was he going to see? If he's still alive then it's an image of him running away, and if he's... if... well, it could be that he drowned, or it could even be an image of the ferryman, couldn't it? You can do anything with a picture of boats and water. What? What?"

I feel as if I'm looking at a dual-image illusion. On the one hand, I can see that every word John says is true; the harvesting of images from my (John's) blog, the slow delicate feeling for bits of information that came together to form Scrap-dog, the infinite number of possible meanings for that final image of Joel. But when I concentrate on the darker side of the picture, I remember the words James spoke. Rapid motion; someone telling Joel he was a disgrace. Someone with him who he trusted. And water...

"Susannah. Please. Come back to me." John's hands on my shoulders. "You're going off into yourself again. You're leaving me behind. Please, stay here with me. Stay here. I need you to listen."

"I'm here. I'm with you."

"But you're not. You're not with me." There are tears pouring down John's cheeks. "I can't do this any more, Susannah."

"Can't do what?"

"I can't live like this. Look at the way we're living now, it's insane. You hardly speaking, going out every night to drive around the city looking for clues. Me running round behind your back creating fake blogs to prove something to you that should be obvious anyway. And you thinking I might have had something to do with—"

"No! No, I don't, I've never ever said that ever, not once."

"You don't need to say the words. I can see it in your face. You always did have the worst poker face in the world. And I can't do this any longer, love. I can't take you not believing in me. I can't do another Christmas like the last one. Neither of us can. I'll drive us home and then I'll sleep on the sofa tonight and tomorrow I'll be moving in with a mate for a while."

"You're leaving me?"

"I'll love you until I die."

"But you're still leaving?"

"I have to. I can't live with you and love you as much as I do, and know you don't trust me. I'm so sorry. I've tried so hard. But I just can't do it any more."

He doesn't want to do this, I can tell. He wants me to talk him out of it. If I said anything, anything at all, I could stop this from happening.

I take hold of the edges of my silk blouse, take a deep breath, and tear it open. I grab at the front of his shirt and rip off the buttons. The zipper of my beautiful long brown boots snaps off in my angry fingers and when I shuck off my jeans, I pull hard at the seam until they finally come apart into rags. The fastener of his chinos gives way beneath my assault.

On the back seat of the car, we bite and claw at each other. When he tries to kiss me, I slap his face, grab his penis so ruthlessly hard he yells with pain, and cram him inside me. I scratch hard at his back. When I come, I sink my teeth deep into his flesh, relishing the sudden salty pop as I break through the skin and into the wet redness beneath. He swears, pulls my hair, swears again and comes too, collapsing heavily across me so that my left buttock is painfully crushed against the seatbelt plugs. We lie there for several minutes, not caring that we're only a few feet from the road and can easily be seen. Perhaps I want to be seen. Perhaps I want to be shamed. A car passes by, slows down, flashes its lights and honks its horn in jeering solidarity.

This is how we say goodbye to our marriage.

Chapter Thirteen
Friday 1st December 2017

The little office that looks out from the front of my house like an eyrie is cold tonight. In the black-and-silver night, an owl hunches on the branch of the giant willow, feathers ruffled to trap as much warm air as possible against the creeping frost crusting the edges of the brown leaves in the roots of the privet hedges. Human beings are the only species who look forward to midwinter, teaching our young to count down the days until the heart of the frost, hanging lights and making feasts and showering them with gifts, showing them in every way we know that the time when the world turns black and cold is the best part of the year. It's cold, but I don't shut the curtains. Instead I make myself small inside my cardigan and tuck my feet up beneath me. I don't want to shut out the night. I want the companionship of these trees, that frost, even the owl with its fierce claws and pitiless predatory stare. I don't want to be on my own while I do the thing I should have done years ago. I've spent so long holding myself utterly still, like a years-long game of musical statues, believing that if I don't move, the truth can't catch me. Now it's time to move forward.

The first day of Advent. A day for opening doors and uncovering things hidden beneath.

I wake up my laptop. The room blooms with harsh

electrical blue. I open up a blank document and stare at it, and the words of my GCSE English teacher swim up towards me from the pool of the past: *Write something, anything, it doesn't matter. There's nothing more intimidating than a blank page.*

All right then. Let's start with a title:

What I know:

1. Joel went missing on 9th November, 2012. He ran away from school and was never seen again

2. On the morning he disappeared, he had a row with John about some pot John had found in his room

3. I wanted to go after Joel but John wouldn't let me. He said that something had to change and I was frightened because he looked so angry. The police do not know this

4. Before Joel came, John and I rarely argued. Once we had Joel, we argued a lot. Most of our arguments were about Joel. In fact, I think all of our arguments were about Joel

5. John tried so hard but he never understood Joel, never. He couldn't get him to settle when he was a baby. When they played together it usually ended in tears. Joel was frightened of John, but John never admitted that. I don't think he wanted to accept that he would have to change

6. John was jealous of Joel. He actually used those words, 'I'm jealous of my own son.' This was in the context of a row where John had been secretly checking my phone and monitoring my internet history

7. At the time I forgave this but now I come to write it out it looks so terrible. How could I let him do that to me? How could I keep living with a man who trusted me so little? Although in some ways John was right, I was doing things in secret, but they were all to help Joel. The police do not know that John did this

8. On the day Joel disappeared, there were several hours when John was simply 'driving around'. He stopped at a number of places where Joel has been found on previous occasions

when he's run away

9. Although he's not told me this in so many words, Nick believes the most likely explanation is that Joel is dead

10. Nick initially thought that John might have hurt Joel

11. I don't know for sure that Nick has ever stopped thinking that

12. The thing is, I don't think that. I never have. I've never believed that John would hurt Joel. I still don't believe it now. John is a good man. He loved Joel. He didn't understand him but he loved him and he would never, ever hurt him

13. But what if I'm wrong?

The eerie hooting of the owl provides the perfect counterpoint to the darkness that's blooming in my head.

Things that have happened recently:

1. I'm being haunted. I don't know what else to call it but a haunting. I'm being haunted by my own son

2. And also by my ex-husband

3. John is still alive, so the things I see can't only be visions of the dead. Does this mean Joel is somehow still alive? Is that even possible? And where has he been for all this time?

4. I know there are no ghosts, no psychics, no special powers. It has to be just something wrong in my head. Or maybe I'm remembering something somehow. But what?

5. Could I have seen Joel in the park yesterday?

6. Is he coming back to me after all?

Why am I doing this? It was supposed to be a summation of evidence. Instead I've got a few ancient bones gnawed naked years before, and a confession that could have me locked away in the madhouse. My cheeks burn with shame.

I should just delete the lot, but I can't bring myself to do it. Perhaps this will come in useful somehow, somewhere; perhaps I'll come back to it later and find new insight. I'll make it a folder to hide in, something dull and meaningless so no one will be tempted to peek. *Systems Manuals*, that sounds suitably anonymous.

I go to File Manager, only to discover there is already a folder with that name, which surprises me, because this is my personal filing area and everything in it is something I've created. So where did this come from? The folder contains a single document, also called *Systems Manuals*. How strange. I open it up.

The facts of what happened:

1. John and Joel didn't get on well
2. John was disappointed in Joel's school performance
3. John said that Joel had come between us
4. John told me *that very morning* that something had to change
5. Nick thought that John might have had something to do with it
6. John was driving around for hours after work
7. But when he did come home, he was just as worried about Joel as I was
8. I don't have any evidence that John did hurt Joel, but I do have evidence that he might have wanted to
9. I never told Nick about this. Even though he gave me lots of opportunities to
10. Is that because I knew it wasn't true? Or is it because I was afraid that it might be?
11. Would it have made any difference anyway? I don't know
12. This is all too hard, I'll come back to it later

The file's dated just over two years ago.

Who wrote this? It must have been me. Who else could it possibly have been? No one else comes in my house and uses my things. So why don't I remember creating it?

I don't like looking at it. It makes me feel as if there might be something wrong with me. If I've forgotten this, what else might have slipped my mind? I find another folder that shouldn't be there. *Programme Files*. Once again there's a single document, fourteen months old.

What I think might have happened

Joel left our house that morning, I know that for sure. He went to school and he registered, but then he walked out of his lesson and I didn't take the call from school because I was out for lunch with Melanie and my mobile was on silent in the bottom of my bag and oh God, what if I had? What if I had taken that call? No, I can't start this again, I need to concentrate.

John was jealous of Joel. He said that himself. He started acting as if he couldn't trust me, he was tracking my phone and Joel's phone to see where we were all the time. He said Joel was coming between us. Joel was struggling at school and John was not dealing well with that.

I lied to you, Nick, I'm sorry but I lied to you. I told you there were no problems in their relationship, but that wasn't right. Probably you're clever enough to know that anyway, and besides you never take anyone's word for anything, I know you'll have spoken to other people to find out what their relationship was like really.

But then, who would you have spoken to that wasn't me and that might have known how bad things got? Even Melanie and Richard never really knew, they knew John and Joel argued but I just told them that's how teenagers were and they accepted it. We didn't have any baby-group friends because when Joel was little he was all I wanted. We didn't socialise with his friends' parents because Joel didn't have those kinds of friendships.

Motive and means and opportunity. Those are the things you look for, aren't they? When people write crime stories they're about the motive, the motive drives everything, but you told me once that you start by looking for the people who could have done it, and most of the time the motive is either really simple or really trivial.

So really it shouldn't matter, should it, that I didn't tell you John told me exactly what his motive might have been? He might have had means and opportunity, but you never found any evidence. Murderers aren't professional criminals, almost no one does more than one. It's not something you can practice and get good at. But you didn't find anything. Nothing at all. So surely that means he didn't do it?

Because it wasn't him. It can't have been. John's a good man.

I don't know if I'll ever send this.

The taste of shock is sweet and metallic. Outside, the frost is reaching the dried brown hydrangea blooms. If I let go of the breath I've been holding, will it mist in the air before me? In the silence as I try to drag myself back together, I hear the faint thud of someone knocking against wood, as if a secret visitor is trying to ward off the ill-luck that stalks me.

I saw no one coming up the front path and it doesn't sound like the door anyway, but I go downstairs and check just to be sure. Only the cold waits outside, reaching for my flesh with eager fingers. The knocking continues. It's coming from the dining room. Someone's knocking on the table. That classic medium's trick to show the presence of spirits. Who's come into my house? Have they chosen the spot where John sat years ago, weeping as he held my hand and asked me if I believed I'd done harm to my son? And will they be seen, or unseen?

I throw open the door, but there's no one in the room but me. Just the slow steady knocking, sounding wetter now and more menacing. It's water, dripping steadily through the ceiling from the bathroom above and pooling on the table.

"Help," I wail, pointlessly because no one can hear me, no one can help me. I'm by myself in the house and this small domestic emergency is mine alone to cope with. Upstairs in the bathroom I find a cloud of steam, tiles sunk half an inch deep, the bath brimming with scalding water and the tap adding more and more and yet more to a tub that can hold not another single drop.

I must have done this, put the bath on to run and then forgotten it, just as I must have written those rambling records of my suspicions and then hidden them away behind dull innocuous names. But I can't remember. *What's happening to me?*

"Oh, please help me," I whisper as I turn off the tap. I wish John were still here. I wish we were still a team. He wouldn't be angry. He was never angry when I occasionally burned things or forgot things or broke them or left them in shops and had to go back for them. If he was here, we'd laugh together, and together we'd mop the tiles, drain the bath, run downstairs and dry off the table. I'd tell him how impressive it was that our hot water tank could create an entire bath's worth of hot water at one time, and he'd tell me he loved my optimism. Together we'd wait for the ceiling to dry. Together we'd buy paint to cover the water stains. And when we were old and creaky (old and creaky, but attractive enough to make it sweet and not repulsive that we still held hands in the street, still kissed in the moonlight, still pressed our bodies close together beneath the cool linen sheets), *Do you remember the night you ran the bath and forgot about it and it came through the ceiling* would be added to our store of sweetness, the secret sweetness that all couples in long successful marriages share, sustaining them through the short winter days before the final parting. As I stare at the mess and make my childish wish for things to be different, I realise I'm not picturing Joel anywhere in this story.

"Please help me," I whisper again.

The bath needs to be drained. The plug chain broke years ago. A small reminder of a long-ago bathtime when Joel held onto it to stand, and the chain snapped and his head dipped briefly beneath the water and I screamed in fear and John said Joel was only crying because I was frightening him, but I decided we were never having another chain on the plug in

195

case Joel did it again when my back was turned and hit his head hard enough to drown, and this is a bad memory but at least it's got Joel in it, at least it reminds me of how much we loved him, and that in spite of the agony of loss, our lives were better because he'd been in them.

But what if they weren't? What if Joel was a mistake? That was the thought that haunted John. I remember watching it grow in the dark behind his eyes. I take a deep breath and plunge my arm deep into the scalding water.

When water's hot enough to burn, there's a moment when your skin is fooled into thinking it's cold instead. In a minute the sensation will turn to fire, and I'll have to run my arm under the cold tap until my flesh freezes once more, and when I've finished torturing myself my mind will be clean and empty and I'll be able to forget all the thoughts I've hidden away like dead things. Where's the plug? The steam's making me blind. But how can it be steaming when it's so cold?

Then there's a hand reaching for mine and closing around my wrist. A big broad hand, much larger than mine, strong and dextrous. John's hand. I'd know it anywhere.

And then I feel the muscles flex and tense and he pulls hard and drags me down into the thick cold water, heavy and choking with the scent of mud. My ex-husband is trying to drown me.

So this is it, then. This is what's been waiting for me. I should struggle, but I don't think I can find the will. If I try to live, what will I come back to? An empty home. An empty bed. A vanished son. A head full of nightmares. What's the point? I'll just drown instead, let this hallucination take me, and when they (whoever *they* might be) find my swollen body, white and purple and coming apart in the slimy rank chill of the bathwater, they'll shake their heads and say, *well, perhaps...* and then feel guilty and stop themselves, but still they'll look at each other and know that they've shared the same thought: *Perhaps it was for the best.*

That's right. Don't struggle. Stay here. Forget everything. It's better this way. John is speaking to me inside my head. *Wait for me, my love. I'll come to you one day.*

And how about me? Where will I be when I'm dead? Somewhere peaceful and empty, waiting for John so we can be together once more, the way we were before Joel came and then went. John's married to someone else now but he still loves me best. I'll wait in that vast peaceful emptiness, and I'll watch over John and wait for him to come to me again, and as I wait I'll fill my days with remembrance. I'll remember his face when he saw me on our wedding day, as I floated down the aisle of the church in that ridiculous silk confection of a dress. I'll remember our honeymoon, the timeless blissful stretch of days when we lay in white sand and sunshine and retired each afternoon to fuck into oblivion and sleep in each other's arms. I'll remember kissing him in the church porch, confetti tumbling around us like rain, and the bells ringing in our ears.

There is a bell ringing, but it's not church bells. It's a telephone, shrilling wildly across the long inches that stretch from wherever I was to wherever I am, distorted by the water that fills my ears but still recognisable. There's still someone who wants me, then, someone who needs to speak to me, even if it's only someone trying to sell something unwanted to a stranger. Do I want to speak to them, when John's hand is clasped so firmly around my own, in such a perfect facsimile of love? I'd rather stay here and let fate take its course. The ringing stops and John's voice begins to speak instead; not his true voice but a recording, ostensibly left on my answerphone to fool and intimidate criminals (*Beware of the Man!*), but in fact, because I can't bear to let him go entirely. How easy death is when you simply give in and let it come to you. I thought I wanted to find out the truth, but this is what I want after all. To escape from everything by cutting myself off with a single watery breath.

And then, a boy's voice, high and panicky, not quite

settled into the register of manhood. Joel.

"Mum? Mummy? Are you there? Please don't leave me. I need you, please help me, I need you to come and get me. Please, Mum, please help me, I'm so sorry I ran away, I need you. Please help me, Mum. Mum? Can you hear me?"

I'm too far gone to feel any kind of emotion. What happens next is pure reflex, the electric twitch that drives the movement of a dead animal in a laboratory. My free hand stretches out behind me. I reach up, up, up until I find the smooth acrylic roll of the bath top. I push once, hard, with all the strength that's left in me. I feel my hand and arm come free from John's grip. The world whirls around me. My head makes it back into the air.

Crouched in a pool of water, I whoop and gasp and shudder. I want to sit on the floor and breathe and whimper and remind myself that I'm still alive, but the reflex won't let me. Instead I scrabble on hands and knees across the landing and slither down the stairs, headfirst because turning around would take time, and come to rest by the console table. I tug on the cable of the answerphone and haul it down into my lap like prey. The light is blinking.

This is the only thing, the one and only thing, with the power to call me back from the darkness. After all this time, I'm going to hear my son's voice. I stab at the button of the answerphone.

But the only thing that comes to me is the click and hiss and swoosh of a mobile phone moving through space, as if its owner has accidentally called me from inside their pocket.

I scrabble for the phone handset. It takes me a few tries to hit the right numbers in the right order: 1471. I was called today at ten thirty-nine hours. They do not have the caller's number to return the call.

I drop the phone on the floor beside the answerphone and put my hands up to my head so that I can hold myself and scream and tear uselessly at my hair to punish myself for not being quick enough. Before the madness takes over, I see that the broken chain of the plug is wrapped so tightly around my wrist and arm that the tiny silver beads are pressed into my flesh, and on the tender scalded skin of my forearm there is a flat livid print the size and shape of a hand.

Life Without Hope:
Parallel Lives

Today should have been my and John's wedding anniversary.

So many years! If we'd made it, by now I would have spent significantly longer as John's wife than as my own separate self. If we'd made it, I wonder what we would have done to celebrate? Perhaps we might have gone on holiday, just the two of us. Joel would have been eighteen, just finishing his A-levels, and probably more than happy for us to go away without him for a few days. But perhaps we would have preferred to bring him with us; perhaps he would have preferred to come along. The last holiday of his childhood.

Instead, we're spending it apart from each other. It's heartbreakingly sad, but I can't pretend to be surprised that our marriage didn't survive Joel's disappearance. We were so closely knit, the three of us. It would seem wrong for John and I to carry on together in the absence of the very best part of us.

I sometimes think about the theory of parallel universes. Perhaps somewhere there's another world where another John and Susannah are celebrating right now. Perhaps they (we?) are waking in a little hut with a grass roof, by a white beach lapped by a blue ocean. Perhaps we (they?) are on top of a mountain we've just climbed over a series of laborious days, me sandwiched between John and Joel as we pose for a picture. Or perhaps John couldn't get the time off and instead they're simply planning to go out for an expensive meal.

I could spend my time envying these parallel-universe couples. But I don't. Because if there are universes where the three of us are still together, there must also be many others where we were never together at all.

There must be worlds where John and I never met in that tangle of bodies on the dance floor. Worlds where he lost my phone number, or where he met someone he liked even more, and so he never called. Worlds where we didn't make up after arguments, or met other people, or just drifted apart over time.

There must be worlds where we never became parents to Joel.

There were so many ways it could have gone wrong for us. We might have balked at the courses we had to take, or become daunted by questions about coping with a child with additional needs or behavioural challenges, and decided adoption wasn't for us after all. A wrong word on a wrong piece of paper and we might have been passed over, and the astounding gift that was our son might have been given instead to another couple. And while I know in my head we would have loved any child we were lucky enough to adopt, just as fiercely as we loved Joel, my heart doesn't believe it. Joel was our son. He was perfect. Our time together was perfect. I wouldn't change a thing.

And if the price of that is that I will spend what should have been my wedding anniversary alone, at my computer, crying as I write… that's a price I'm more than willing to pay.

Posted on 26th April 2016
Filed to: Family Life
Tags: parenting journey, family life, marriage, divorce, missing people, support for families, Susannah Harper, Joel Harper

Chapter Fourteen
Friday 1st December 2017

The screaming and the rocking and the hurting myself have passed. Perhaps it helps that I'm already so hurt, my barely healed hand still pink and tender from the mirror, my leg still marked where the car made contact with me outside the park, and now a little chain of bruises around my wrist and that single, terrifying flat mark where John's hand reached out and held me in that tight, lover-like clasp beneath the water. I deserve all of these punishments, but I don't feel the urge to add more. I think this must mean I'm still sane. Only the very far gone would resort to hurting themselves when they've already been battered and injured as much as I have. Surely that's true.

"Hi, it's Susannah," I say into the silence of the hallway, testing to see how my voice sounds. I hardly recognise myself. I take a deep slow breath, hold it, let it go. "Hi. It's Susannah." That's better. Soon I'll be ready to talk to real people again. "Hi, it's me. Can I talk to you for a bit? Hello, it's just me." Yes. That will do. I glance at the handset on the floor beside me, but I don't feel ready to pick it up, not yet. The phone call from Joel might have saved me, but I don't think I can forgive the technology that so utterly failed to capture his voice. I stagger to my feet and make a shaky journey upstairs to where my mobile is. *See? I can walk. I'm doing fine.*

"Hello?" Melanie answers within two rings, but she sounds as if she's not sure who I am.

"Hi. It's just me. Um… I was wondering if I could talk to you for a bit, I'm having a bit of a bad night."

"Have you thought about what I said to you?"

When did we last speak? What did Melanie say to me? I remember standing outside the hospital with my hair wet and no coat on, trying not to shiver as the cold burrowed through my flesh to get at my bones. In the background, Richard murmurs something, nothing I can decode into speech, just a low bass rumble.

"You do remember, don't you? Susannah? The last time we talked?"

"Yes. I remember."

"Are you ready to get some help? Shall I come round and take you to the hospital?"

"I don't want to, I just… Something weird happened to me, that's all. I was running a bath and I forgot about it and all the water came down through the ceiling."

"That's exactly what I'm talking about! You're forgetting things, you're seeing things, you're acting completely unlike yourself. Please, let me come round and help you. I'll stay the night if you want and we can go to the GP in the morning and take it from there."

"I don't want to see the GP, I don't want to see anyone, I just want to talk for a bit." No reply, just a small whispering that's clearly not meant for me. "Melanie, can you hear me? Are you there? I said I just want to talk for a bit."

"No, shush, be quiet." She's talking to Richard, whose words I still can't interpret but whose tone is growing angrier. "She's my sister, okay? No, don't try and tell me what to do. Yes, I know what I said. Of course I'm going to stick to it. Look, just shush and let me talk to her, okay? Sorry, Suze, I'm with you now. I'll come round right now, shall I, and stay over? And then in the morning we'll see someone. Please. Let's get this sorted so we can all enjoy Christmas, yeah?"

"No, that's not what I want!" I sound childish and petulant even to myself. "I just want to talk to you. That's all I need, that's all I'm asking."

The silence is terrible.

"Are you still there?" I whisper.

"If you won't see the doctor then I can't help you." Melanie's voice is taut with pain. "I told you, Suze. I love you and as soon as you're ready for some proper medical help then I will drop everything and come and help you. But until then I can't talk to you. Okay? I love you. I love you so much and as soon as you—" Another interjection from Richard. "Yes, I'm winding it up, for fuck's sake, what do you want from me, this is my sister, okay? Call me when you're ready to get help. I love you. I love you. Please call me soon and say you're going to get some help. Oh, God, this is so hard, Richard, can you—"

And then I'm alone in the office staring at the bright bland colours of my phone screen. My sister has refused to talk to me. My sister thinks I'm mad. I'm alone.

Perhaps she's right. Perhaps I am mad. But how else would I be? How can Melanie understand, when she's never lost a child? We all think we can imagine but we can't. She was the wrong person to call. I need to call someone else instead. But who? Who else is there? Jackie. Jackie will understand.

A brief pause, as my phone sends out its little electronic signal. Will the owl hear it as it passes by? Does it disrupt the perfect silence of that cool gliding flight? I have no way of knowing. So much of the world is hidden from us. My phone rings, rings, rings in my ear. *Please, Jackie. Pick up the phone and talk to me. I need you.* But when I finally hear her voice, it's not her at all but simply the recorded greeting on her voicemail.

I dial again, hopeful and hungry for contact. Voicemail again. Do I dare to call a third time? As my finger hovers over the screen, her text message drops into my inbox: *So so sorry love I can't talk right now Georgie's sick will call you tomorrow ok? Take care sorry again J xxxx*

Jackie's lucky. She has others to keep her busy. We mourn our sons equally, but her life is less empty than mine. Her marriage will last or it won't and the statistics say it probably won't, but she'll always have her other children to stand between her and the screaming dark. Whereas I...

I'm being pathetic, but who's going to stop me or tell me to pull myself together? If John was still here... but no, I don't want John. Do I?

I hold my phone to my ear once more, and this time I know the call will be answered. It's a kind of hypocrisy to call him given what I've begun to suspect about him, but isn't this what investigators do? Perhaps he'll give himself away. One ring, two rings, three and then John's voice on the end of the phone, blurred and urgent with hope.

"Susannah? Is there any news?"

"No. No news."

A sigh then, of weariness or of relief or perhaps just of irritation. It doesn't matter. I have contact. I still exist.

"I just needed to hear your voice," I whisper.

"Hang on a minute." I hang, breathless, on the sounds that fill my ear. A rustle of fabric. The creak of wood. John's breathing, steady and slow. The faint change in sound as he moves to a different room. I've only been inside their house three times, but the brief forbidden peeks I've taken behind the closed doors of the upstairs rooms are burned into my brain. Does Nathalie know he's left their bed to talk to me? Does she mind? Of course she minds, how could she not; but she'll allow it, because she has everything and I have nothing. Nothing apart from her husband, who still comes to me whenever I call.

"Susannah? Are you still there?" John's question is folded securely inside a yawn, and I feel a twinge of guilt at waking him, but only a twinge.

"Yes, I'm here."

"So what's happening?"

He's answered my summons and now I have no idea what to say to him. "I... I just... I just needed to talk to you. Is that okay?"

"I thought maybe you'd heard something," he says. Is that reproach in his voice?

"No, nothing. It's just the weather, I think. I was thinking about Joel when he was a baby. Do you remember that first winter when we took him for a walk and we had him bundled up in three layers with his snowsuit on top? And he cried the whole time and we thought he was freezing, so we kept on piling on blankets?" I want John to join in with this memory, but there's only silence. "And when we got him home we took his snowsuit off and his little head was all sweaty and we realised he'd been crying because he was too hot? That was a good day."

"It was."

"He was our Winter's child, wasn't he, John? Our beautiful perfect Winter's child. We met him at the heart of winter and we knew straight away he was ours."

"Susannah, have you been drinking?"

"No, of course not."

"Are you sure? Because you don't sound quite like yourself."

This isn't what I want. I want John to join me in resurrecting the happiest days of our lives, to soothe me to sleep with the well-worn memories of those months when we were a perfect contented family of three. Why won't he do what I want?

"Susannah? Are you still there? Melanie called me yesterday."

This isn't right either. John and Melanie are connected only through me. They're not meant to speak to each other independently and without my knowledge. And what did they find to talk about?

"She's worried about you. She thinks you're, um, she thinks maybe you're having some problems with stress.

Something about the hairdressers?"

Melanie will have described exactly what happened at the hairdressers, but John being John, the good clinician, the gentle healer, is leaving me the space to explain the experience in my own words. I won't be a good patient. Instead I sit in stubborn silence and let the moment stretch out. How dare they talk about me behind my back?

"Okay, it's none of my business," John says at last. "But if you want to talk about it, I'm happy to listen. Oh, Lord, hang on a minute."

"What? What is it? What?" John isn't listening, he's concentrating on someone else. There's a clunk as he puts his phone down somewhere and then all I can hear is his voice murmuring, *It's all right, sweetheart, it's okay, just a nightmare, all right, Daddy's here. There's teddy, look. That's it... Back to sleep...* "Is everything all right? Is it Joel? Is he all right? Does he want me?"

"Susannah." The pain in John's voice tears at my heart. "That was Emily. Joel isn't with us any more. Remember? Susannah? Can you still hear me? Susannah?"

I can't bear this. It's too much. I need to matter to someone, to have their undivided attention for once, not just the little scraps left over from everyone else. I hang up. Then I sit and wait. He's going to call me back. He's going to call me back. He's going to call me back. He has to call me back. He always calls me back.

He's not going to call. Of course he's not going to call. He has his own new life to return to. His new daughter and his new wife in their new warm beds. Everyone's busy with their families but me. Everyone has someone to call them away from the desperate neediness of the neighbourhood madwoman, lost in fantasies of her vanished son. No wonder they don't want to talk to me. I wouldn't want to talk to me either. Who is there left?

"Susannah?"

"Nick. I'm sorry to call so late, there isn't any news. I just,

I needed to talk to someone and I know this isn't right, for me to call you like this, I just needed to hear your voice, all these things are happening to me and I keep seeing things and hearing things and I don't know what any of it means, I think I might be going mad, Nick, but what if I'm not? What if this is me remembering something really important?"

"It's all right. Where are you?"

"I know you can't just drop everything and turn out to see me, you've got a life too—"

"Never mind where I am, that doesn't matter. Where are you?"

"I'm at home."

"Are you alone?"

"Yes."

"Are you safe?"

"I—" I look at the tender boiled pink of my arm, the pale handprint, the chain of tiny bruises like a lover's tattoo. "I don't know. Something's happening to me. I don't know what it is but something's happening to me and I don't know what to do."

"All right. Sit tight. I'm coming round right now, give me twenty minutes."

He hangs up on my protestations. Tonight is not a night where I get to choose who talks to me and for how long.

Nonetheless, he's coming. Where is he starting from? I can't tell. I've seen the private lives of everyone else I've called tonight. I've spent time in their homes, I've met their partners and their children. In my hunger for human contact, my longing to escape into their own more satisfying worlds, I've glanced furtively into their medicine cabinets and crept like a thief into the rooms with the doors they kept closed. I know what their bedrooms look like. I've even laid my face against their pillows to catch the scent of their sleep. Only Nick remains a sweet mystery, a man in a good suit and expensive aftershave, with a sick wife I've never met and a house where I've never been. And yet he's coming to save me. How strange and how beautiful.

Now that I know he's coming, my aloneness becomes something to be cherished, the way a child will cherish the timeless limbo between the first of December and Christmas Day. Twenty minutes, he said. How far away is he? A few minutes of Googling takes me to a website that lets me draw a radius around my home. The driving will be urban and suburban, but it's late and the roads will be quiet; can he get as far as ten miles in the twenty minutes he's allowed himself? Perhaps not. Perhaps he's only five miles away. I zoom in and study the maze of streets in fascination. Which of these is Nick's home? Or perhaps he was at work after all, and he's only coming to me from the police station.

I leave the chilly little office and sit on the stairs to watch the front door. This is like being a teenager again, watching for the shadow in the glass that will announce the arrival of a boyfriend. It's late and my son is lost, and everyone else has abandoned me and the dining room ceiling is a watery mess, but there's a small dark spot of happiness in me. Nick is coming to help me. I matter enough for him to come when I call.

In the utter silence of the freezing night, I can hear every sound. The car slowing and stopping outside my house. The creak and click of the gate. Am I imagining it, or can I hear the crunch of his shoes on the frosty leaves that line the garden path? The shadow behind the stained glass looms almost as large as John's used to do.

He comes into my house in a cloud of cold, smelling of aftershave and clean frost. He's wearing the smart suit and very crisp white shirt that I associate with his working persona. In the living room, I tell him I'll make coffee for us both, but he surprises me by shaking his head and leading me gently but firmly to the sofa. Then he vanishes. I sit quietly, my feet on the floor, my hands in my lap, and wait to see what will happen next.

What happens next is that Nick appears with two steaming

mugs. He's taken off his jacket, which gives him the appearance of a man home from work. I fumble for coasters; he sits beside me, close but not intrusive. When he looks at me, I feel as if I'm made of glass.

"You found the coffee," I say, for something to say.

"I'm quite domesticated when I have to be. I think you have a water leak in your dining room, though."

"Yes, I know, it's a mess."

"I've mopped up a bit, put some towels down."

"Oh? Thank you. You didn't need to—"

"So," he says, with a quick friendly smile, "what's been going on?"

Those words, that smile, are all it takes to break me. My face crumples into ugliness and instead of the words I meant to speak – *Well, I've had some more strange experiences and I'm not sure what they mean* – the sound that comes out of me is a horrible mad-sounding howl. I want to throw myself into his arms and bury my face in his chest but I'm not quite far gone enough to do that, so instead I fold over onto my own lap and hide my face in my battered hands. What will he think of me now?

After a minute, there's a hand on my back and another reaching gently into the damp tangle of my face and my arms and my hair, unfolding me and turning my face towards his face.

"Let me help you," he says. "I want to help you."

"I don't know where to start."

"You said you'd been seeing and hearing things. Tell me about that."

So I tell him. I tell him everything, from the visit to the fortune-teller to the message I heard on the answerphone. I show him the bruises. I tell him about finding the files on my computer that I have no memory of creating. Then I take a deep breath, and I finally confess the secret I have been holding onto for so long: the way it was between John and Joel, the fears that haunt me sometimes in the long still silences of the night.

When I've finally finished he sits quietly for a minute. At some point in my long disconnected monologue he has taken my hand, I think to inspect the tiny chain of bruises and the tender pink texture of the skin, and that one astounding piece of evidence, the handprint. He places his hand over the shape of it, trying it out for size, then takes my other hand in his and gently, very gently, as if he's trying not to frighten me, he fits my fingers over the marks. They're a good match. But then, so were his.

"Does it matter that I didn't tell you at the time?" I ask at last. The words cling to my tongue and lips. I have to force them out.

"About John not getting on with Joel? No, it doesn't matter. I knew anyway. And besides, when it's a child we always have to look closely at the—" he stops, but not quickly enough. I'm already back there in that terrible little room with its closed door and harsh lights, the illusion of intimacy that grew despite the one-way mirror on the wall, the microphone on the table between us.

"Does this hurt?" he asks, resting his fingertips against my scalded skin.

"Not really. Not much. Well, a little bit."

"I don't think it's going to blister, but it's bigger than your hand. That means you should probably go to hospital."

"I'm afraid to go," I admit. "What if they think I'm going mad and lock me away?"

"They won't do that. Trust me, it's very hard to get people sectioned these days. More often than not you end up having to beg them just to take a look." He touches the bruises, the handprint, and smiles wryly. "Although they might ask you if I did this to you."

Of course he knows all about this. He lives with it on behalf of his wife, every day. No wonder he's so accepting of my own nonsensical experiences. No wonder he's so kind and gentle.

"I see a lot of people with mental health issues at work," he explains, as if he can guess what I'm thinking. "When they have a change of meds and it doesn't work out. Or when they just decide they're sick of feeling fat and half asleep and chuck them in the bin. Then they go to the other extreme and start climbing on buildings and ranting in shopping centres about the end of the world. Some shifts everyone we have in the cells belongs in hospital really."

"That must be hard," I say, because it's my turn to speak and this is how a conversation works, you take it in turns to speak and if you don't speak it becomes a silence, and while you're both together in that silence who knows what will happen?

"They're safer in the cells than on the streets. I'll admit it's not really what I joined the force to do. Locking up people who are ill, I mean."

"What did you want to do?"

"To help people who needed it."

"You do help people."

He touches the tiny purple bruises with his fingertips. "I couldn't help you."

"But you did help. You did your best, you looked for Joel, you did everything you could. You're still doing your best. You promised me you'd never stop looking. And you never have. Even when—" I can't finish the sentence, but we both hear the words. *Even when it's hopeless.* I want to make him feel better, happier, but instead he looks... Well, how does he look? What's the word for the expression on his face? I think I used to know but I forgot it long ago.

"Can I tell you something?" Nick says. His voice is so soft I have to lean closer to hear.

"Yes, of course."

"Do you know why I really wanted to find Joel?" When he hesitates and draws in a deep breath, I think of a diver on tiptoe, of the pause before the plunge. "I wanted..." His fingers come to rest on the fluttering pulse-point in my wrist.

"I wanted to be your hero. I can still remember how you looked when you opened the door. You were so beautiful and you'd been crying. And you... you looked at me. And all I wanted then... the thing I wanted more than anything else in this world... was to find your son and bring him home, and for you to look at me like I was your hero."

It's my turn to speak. I don't say anything, because this is not a conversation where the words matter. Instead I let my fingers creep up towards his face, touching the clipped edges of his hair, his rough stubbly cheek, the thin tight curve of his mouth. And he lets me. He lets me.

In the days before I married John, I was party to any number of kisses, but they had one thing in common: I always waited for the boy to kiss me. I wanted to be a good girl, and good girls were the object of desire, never the subject. But that was in the days before my good-girl life was taken from me. Who am I now? I am the woman who places her mouth over the mouth of a man who belongs to someone else.

His lips open. Our tongues meet. He tastes delicious. His hands are on my back. I tear at his shirt. I need to feel him against me. My skin is so hungry. All of me is so hungry.

I never thought I was the kind of woman who could do this.

It's hard to stop kissing him for long enough to drag him to his feet, but I manage it. When I lead him up the stairs towards the bedroom that used to be mine and John's, his hand is hot and dry. On the landing, I put my hand against his crotch and squeeze so I can feel how hard he is. His breathing is ragged. I wonder if his wife does this to him. I wonder if Nathalie does this to John. I feel no guilt and no shame.

In the bedroom, we strew our clothes across the floor. The room is cold, the sheets are cold, but it doesn't matter. We're creating our own heat. I should be shy, I should be worried about what he will think of my body once it's stripped naked and exposed, but I'm not. I'm only thinking about what I want. Nick with his clothes off is every bit as beautiful as

213

I've always imagined. It comes as a shock to me to realise that I have pictured this moment. Then I don't have time to be shocked any more because we're on the bed together, fitting ourselves into each other like a jigsaw puzzle, and in the moment before I stop thinking and concentrate only on taking from him what I need, greedy and demanding and forgetful, I think to myself, *At least I've got this. Whatever else happens after this, at least I've got this moment.*

Afterwards, when I've come and he's come and we've fallen apart again and we're lying beneath the duvet, drifting slowly back into our bodies, I feel Nick's wedding ring against my shoulder as he strokes it and I think again about his wife, who I have just stolen this moment from. I wonder if, when Nick leaves me, as he must inevitably do, I will feel guilty. I know so little about her, only her name and her illness, and the one quick glimpse of her face in the photograph Nick keeps in his wallet, a pretty face with dark hair and dark eyes. I know that she and Nick have no children. Once, in the days when I had everything, I would have pitied her. Now I'm the one with nothing, and if she's even aware of my existence, I'm sure she pities me.

I have stolen her husband for the night. When my elation passes, I should probably feel guilty. But I think that I won't.

Chapter Fifteen
Thursday 2nd December 2011

Our little household's simmering like a pot of soup. The surface looks calm enough, but watch for a while and you'll see the tension bubbling up and bursting on the surface. Do all households with a fourteen-year-old boy in them live like this? I don't know, because I've never dared to ask.

I've done a terrible thing. I've told a terrible lie. I've made sure the school won't contact John when Joel is in trouble.

It's terrifyingly easy, requiring only a few words and a few moments. My hand on the arm of the school secretary, a murmured confidence about stress at work, a doctor's recommendation that he avoids too much day-to-day worry. Would it be possible for all everyday communications to be directed to me? And of course, she says yes, because she's from another generation and it seems natural to her that the mother should be the alpha parent. Now, John lives in a fantasy world where there are no more phone calls, no more requests for meetings, and Joel has miraculously improved his attendance record and is beginning to turn a corner.

Of course, this illusion won't hold once his end-of-year report comes in. But in the meantime, it buys me the space I believe Joel and I need to work out his problems together, free of the terrible pressure of his father's disappointment.

Except that Joel isn't keeping up his side of the bargain. Things aren't getting better. They're getting worse. He's added a terrible new dimension to the secrets I'm keeping for him.

When I get the phone call, it feels no worse than any of those that have gone before and maybe even a little bit better. Joel's gone missing from PE, and while I know this is no more acceptable than missing any other lesson, my own residual hatred for the sights and smells and sounds of the gym (bouncing balls, squeaky shoes, shouted instructions too echoey to process, the derisory laughter of my classmates) makes me feel as if, for once, I don't need to worry too much. When he doesn't come straight home, the slow walk through crisp air and bare trees to find him feels like a stolen pleasure.

He's hiding beneath the willow tree, as I suspected he would be. He has a number of hiding places but this is his favourite, and even though the leaves are gone now, the bare golden fronds provide a surprising amount of camouflage. There's a notebook open beside him but his eyes are closed and there's a faint smile on his face, and he looks peaceful, so peaceful, as if he's climbed mountains and crossed oceans and searched the whole wide world over to find this, his own private belonging-place. I look at my lovely son, serene and still, all the anxious fretful energy drained out of him, no one teasing him, no one harassing him to complete tasks he can't see the point of or trying to make him into someone he's not, and I think, *If only he could always be this contented. Why can't everyone just leave him alone?*

I slide in through the curtain of branches and sit down quietly beside him. Sometimes when I find him here, the seductive herby scent of weed coils around us like a spell. But not today. I think this is a positive sign.

"Mum." He opens his eyes and smiles at me. "I'm so glad you're here."

"What are you up to, Joel Moel?"

"It's beautiful," he whispers.

"It's cold though. Don't you want to come home?"

"It's not cold, it's warm. Warm and beautiful and cosy. This is the nicest place in the whole world, Mum. I'm going to stay here for ever."

His eyes are especially blue today, the irises so bright they almost glow. Despite the greyness of the day and the shelter of the willow tree, his pupils are like pinpricks. It takes me a moment to realise what this means.

"Joel, tell me. What did you take? Come on, sweetie, talk to me. What did you take?"

He shakes his head, slow and dreamy. "Nothing. Nothing. Nothing. I'm just happy, that's all."

"Don't lie to me, I know you've taken something. What was it?"

"You don't need to worry, Mum, it's proper medicine." He yawns. "Just one dose and everything's all right for hours. Doctors give it to people all the time."

"What medicine? Tell me."

"Little green fairy," says Joel, and smiles foolishly. Beside him, a tiny brown bottle nestles in the litter of fallen leaves.

"Oh my God. Joel, no. No, no, no. You can't do this. I can live with the weed but not this."

"It's all right. They make it in a proper factory. All clean, proper standard. I know what I'm doing. It's medicine, it does me good. I wish I could feel like this always."

And the awful thing is, I can see what he means. Joel looks so happy. I can't remember the last time I saw him so happy. He looks as if this is how he was always meant to be.

"Listen to me. This is not medicine, this is hard drugs and it's dangerous. If school catch you, you'll end up suspended and maybe even expelled."

"Don't care. Don't like it there anyway. Just want to be at home with you."

"Well, I don't want you there if this is what you're going to do, okay?"

217

This seems to pierce the armour of chemicals. He looks at me with hurt in his face.

"Yes, I mean it! I really do! You can't do this, okay? You just can't." His eyes fill with tears. "Oh, please, don't cry, I'm sorry. I'm on your side, all right? You're my Joel Moel and I love you for ever. But you can't do this, my darling, you can't. You just... you can't. Stick to weed if you absolutely must, but not... not this. Promise me. Have you done this before?"

"No." He takes my hand and pats it. "First time. Promise promise."

Do I believe him?

"Thank God. Now you never will again. Will you?"

"Are you going to tell Dad?"

"Of course I am." Except I don't know how I'll ever manage it. How I can go home and say our son truanted from school to get high on methadone?

"Promise not to tell Dad," Joel says. "And I won't do this again. Promise. Swear. No more."

"We need to get you some help. Some counselling maybe."

"No. Don't need that. Won't take it again."

"Where did you get it? How did you find where to get it? How do I know you won't go back to the same place again as soon as my back's turned?"

"Just some bloke. Comes to school sometimes. Not often. Swapped him some games for a dose. He likes games so we swapped. Think the teachers know about him so he prob'ly won't be there again."

Should I believe this story like a fisherman's net, all raggedy holes held together with string? I don't know. I only know that he's my son, and he's in pain.

He reaches for my hand. "Mean it, Mum. M' useless but I'll do better."

"You're not useless."

"Finished letting you down now. Promise. But don't tell Dad. Scared of him when he's angry."

"Don't say that. He loves you."

There's a terrible lucidity in his face. "Does he?"

What can I say? He's my boy, and I love him unconditionally. But John may not feel the same.

"How was your day?"

John always asks this; sometimes as soon as he comes in through the door, sometimes only once we have fishbowl glasses of wine in our hands and the living room to ourselves. There's nothing different about tonight. Except that there is. There's something in his voice that I wasn't expecting to hear. Something that shouldn't be there.

"Fine," I say, trying to keep my own voice bright and unconcerned. It's not really working, any more than his faux-casual voice is working for me. We know each other too well to lie to each other. But we plough on anyway, like characters in a bad play.

"So what did you get up to? Anything much?"

"No, nothing special. I had a chat to Melanie earlier, they're thinking of going to France next summer."

"And did you go out at all?"

"No, not really."

"Not really? What's *not really*?"

"Oh, you know, just over the road to the shops. They've got their decorations up, maybe we should put ours up this weekend too. We could go out and buy some new ones together. Why are you asking, anyway? John? Is everything all right?"

When John doesn't speak, I know he knows that I've been hiding things from him, and that now he knows he's going to be angrier than I've ever seen him before. In a desperate attempt to stave off the impending battle, I plaster on a bright artificial smile and turn around to face him, only to find he's looking at me as if his heart's breaking.

"Susannah," he whispers. "Please don't lie to me any more. I can't stand it. It's killing me."

"I don't know what you're talking about—"

He holds up my phone. I feel as if my feet are sinking in to the carpet.

"I've been checking," he admits. "I'm sorry, I'm sorry, I know it's awful but I had to know. I knew you were lying to me about something and I guessed your passcode would be the same as your PIN number and it was."

"John."

"So I got into your phone and I turned on the location tracker and looked at where you've been going."

Desperation makes me brilliant.

"Oh! You mean when I go out for a walk in the afternoons sometimes? I just like the trees, that's all, they're beautiful at this time of year, when the leaves are off and there's that lovely nip in the air—"

"And then," says John, "I made Joel give me his phone. And I checked his too."

The light, airy lie dies on my lips.

"And I saw a pattern," he said. "Something that's happened three times since we went to that meeting. Joel's phone shows him leaving school, way before he's supposed to. Sometimes you go out to meet him, sometimes you just wait. But he comes home. And so do you."

My face is numb with shock and shame.

"And the day after," he continues, "Joel doesn't leave the house at all. Or if he does, it's only to go to the shop or something. And a couple of days after that, you go up to the school."

I don't know what to say. I want to sit down and take his hand and explain, but I can't think of a single thing I can say.

"I was going to phone the school and ask what's going on." John swipes savagely at the tears that linger on his cheeks. "But I didn't want to admit to them that my wife's been lying to me about our child. I was too ashamed. And besides, I can see what's happening. Joel's still truanting, isn't he? And you're covering up for him."

"It's not that," I say, which is absurd, because it's exactly that.

"Of course it's that! Stop acting like I'm stupid, because I'm not. I'm busy, and I leave a lot of the parenting stuff to you, but that is *not* that same as stupid, do you hear me? Now can we at least be honest with each other so we can sort this situation out!"

"This is exactly why I can't talk to you about it. You only get angry and shout. And that's not what Joel needs, you frighten him when you go after him like this."

"Do you think the performance he turned in last year was even faintly acceptable? Is that what you're saying? He needs someone to go after him. Do you want him to fail every exam they put him in for? Because that's what's going to happen. Or do you not believe what they said to us at that meeting?"

"They don't understand him. They put him under too much stress."

"According to you, nobody understands him but you. Do you ever stop to think you might be part of the problem? Every time you cover up for him, every time you make excuses and say it's going to be all right and he doesn't have to worry, what message do you think that gives him?"

I don't know anything about *messages*. I only know that when Joel looks at me with that frantic, desperate fear, as if he's drowning and only I can save him, I have to help him. What else can I do?

"I mean, it's not as if I'm not happy to get involved. I want to help, for God's sake! I'll sit with him every night and tutor him if that's what it takes, we can get some books and I'll coach him through it."

"No! You can't do that."

"Why not?"

Flashback to the awful scenes of Joel's primary years, the sobs and the pleading and the rages as John sat at the dining room table and tried, over and over, to force Joel to complete his small quantity of homework. I remember standing in the hallway and biting my own hand to stop myself from bursting in on them and snatching the papers away.

221

"Because he's afraid of you."

"I'm not bloody surprised! How can he not be afraid of me when you've built me up into this horrible boogeyman who can't be told the truth in case I get angry? What? What?"

I can't speak, because the words are too terrible to say. How can you tell your husband *He wants you to love him, but he's afraid of you?* How can you tell your husband, and *Sometimes I am too?*

"You shout at him when he gets things wrong."

"I do not!"

"Yes, you do, you shout at him when—"

"I shout at him for not trying. That's what I can't stand. The not trying. I want to help him, but I daren't even speak to him about this, do you know that? I'm frightened to speak to my own son." I go to put my arms around him, but John shakes me off. "And then I have to steal your phone and guess your password to even find out what's happening. How is this a marriage? Tell me that."

"I was trying to look after you!" This may or may not be true, but it at least sounds plausible, and it will do to shield me while I think of what to say next. "You get so stressed, you have enough to deal with at work. You don't need me bringing all Joel's problems to you as well. And it's getting sorted. He's getting better, he's turned a corner, he promised me he'd—"

"So how do you explain this? Is this you trying not to make me feel stressed?"

John is holding a handful of papers. I take them from him, my heart thumping. What will I see? The letters from the school? The correspondence with the welfare officer? The report from the consultant? The second report from a different, paid-for consultant, confirming that Joel does not have Asperger's syndrome, dyslexia, dyspraxia or any other form of identifiable learning disability, but that he does seem 'young for his age' and unduly anxious, especially about his relationship with his father? I force myself to look at the papers instead of John's face, and find I'm looking at a list of seemingly random scraps of information:

Searched for Lucca Princes Ave opening times
Searched for Da Gianni Princes Ave
Searched for book improving father son relationship
Searched for bus times Anlaby Road
Searched for navy maxi dress size 10
Searched for bad relationship father son
Searched for nude block heels size 6
Searched for risk factors father being violent to son
Searched for warning signs father dangerous to son
Searched for non-bio father killing son

The feeling of violation is instant and total, as if John's been spying on me getting dressed or using the bathroom, catching me in all the moments when I think I'm alone. It's so strong that it almost wipes out my shame.

I don't mean to whimper, but I can't stop myself. John is so big and so strong, and I'm not used to his anger being directed at me. The small hurt sound makes me despise myself, but it has the unintended effect of softening John, so that instead of standing tall and terrifying he puts his arm around me and leads me to the sofa. Hoping this means I've won him over, I try to kiss him, to melt against him, but he won't have it, he pushes me away, and I have to keep facing his eyes. His hurt, wounded, frightened eyes.

"Why are you looking for all this stuff?"

"I… It was just something I heard on the radio, nothing to do with you and Joel—"

"The truth. Please. At least be honest with me. Do you actually think I might hurt our son? Do you really think I don't love him as much because he's adopted?"

"Sometimes you get so angry. You expect such a lot of him."

"Expecting him to go to school and make an effort is a lot?

223

For God's sake it's only GCSEs, it's not exactly challenging stuff, is it? And I'm not expecting A* grades across the board, just on course for a respectable C in five or six subjects would do it!" His voice is rising again, the rage that I first glimpsed when Joel was small and that has grown along with our son, like a dark twin that lives inside the man I love.

"Please don't shout. Please don't. That's what scares me. I know you love Joel, I know you'd never hurt him—"

"Don't lie. If you knew that you wouldn't be googling all this stuff."

"I just… Sometimes I get worried."

"Susannah. We can't live like this."

"Don't say that." I want to hide my face in his shoulder but I'm not sure if he'll let me. "We have a good marriage. I love you, you're my husband and I love you."

"A good marriage? Okay, so here's what I see. You're sneaking around behind my back. You're lying to me and keeping secrets. Your search history tells me everything I need to know about what you think of me."

"That's not what I think of you, I was just worried, that's all, but I trust you, of course I do—"

"Look at what you're doing to me. Look at the man you're turning me into. I had to check your phone to find out what's really going on, for God's sake, I had to go into your computer when you were out and look at your search history. I don't want to be like that but what choice do I have? How am I supposed to be married to you if you don't trust me?" He rubs at his face and hair in bewilderment. "It feels like you're having an affair. Like I'm trying to catch you with him all the time, checking up on where you've been and when you've been there, then asking you questions to see if you'll tell me the truth. Only if you were having an affair, that might actually be easier because I could beg you to stop seeing him and we could work on things together. But you won't ever stop loving Joel more than me, will you? He's always going to come between us."

224

"All parents put their children first! That's how it's supposed to be!"

"Is that what you're doing? Putting him first? Or is it shutting me out? I mean, is this what you thought our lives were going to be like once we had a child? That you'd be in one corner with him, and I'd be in another corner by myself, and the two of you would be ganging up on me and keeping me out of everything?"

"You sound jealous."

"I am jealous. Okay? I am very, very jealous of my own son. He's ruining our relationship. Turning you against me. I don't know how much longer I can stand it. Something has to change or I don't know what I'm going to do. Do you understand?"

His voice is very low, very calm, but in that quiet and that calmness there's something that turns me cold. He reaches out his hands towards me. He puts them against my neck. Sometimes he does this as a way of drawing me close towards him for a kiss. Is that what he's doing now?

"Are you listening, love?" he repeats.

And then there's an explosion of sound and movement as Joel erupts into the room. He's wild-eyed and flailing, spitting insults and droplets, long skinny arms windmilling around. He looks insane. He looks furious. He looks terrified. He looks as if he might kill someone. It's not until he flings the slight weight of his wrath against John's immovable bulk and claws wildly at his hands that I can make sense of the words he's shouting. *Don't you hurt my mum don't you dare don't you fucking dare I'll kill you first, you bastard.*

I can't quite unravel what happens next because it all happens too fast for me to follow. Or maybe it's not the speed that confuses me but the awfulness, the horror of seeing your son attack your husband because he thought he was trying to kill you, and then your husband, in his turn, using his superior weight and strength to subdue his teenage son. I only know that within the space of a few seconds, John has

225

Joel pinned face down on the couch, one hand holding his wrists, one knee pressed against Joel's greenstick thighs, the other pressed against his slender back, while I stand uselessly in the corner with my hands over my mouth. I had no idea John knew how to do that.

"All right, then, fella." John's voice is quiet and comforting. "Take a deep breath. That's it for now, okay? Good lad." Joel doesn't speak, but John must sense some relaxing of tension within him because he lifts his knee off Joel's leg, then gradually releases his wrists. "Now, what was that about?"

"You were trying to strangle my mum."

John forces a laugh.

"Of course I wasn't! I was going to kiss her, okay? I was going to kiss her. That's all. Susannah, will you tell our daft-head son here that we were just kissing?"

You can hold a lifetime of silence in the fractional second between two breaths. When John looks at me, I know that if I let him down now, our marriage will end tonight.

"Of course we were just kissing. Joel Moel, how can you possibly think Dad was going to hurt me? When has he ever? Now come on, on your feet."

"And while you're here," says John, "maybe it's a good time to have a chat about—"

"No. Let's just all have some biscuits and a drink, okay? John, do you want tea? Joel, hot chocolate?" John frowns, but I don't care. I've done the right thing, I've backed him up when he really needed me to and now I get my reward, which is the freedom to overrule him. "We'll talk in the morning, all right? Right now we're all a bit upset. Aren't we?" My laugh is just right, light and indulgent but with the weight of authority that tells them I'm in charge now, and they're both silly little boys. My two silly little boys. My two silly little boys who wanted to kill each other. I want to ask Joel to come and give me a hand, but I look again at John's face and decide not to push my luck.

When I return to the living room with the tray, Joel and John are at opposite ends of the sofa, staring straight ahead, arms folded. But that's all right. I know how to fix this.

I wedge myself between them and turn on a quiz show. Then I take John's right hand and Joel's left and hold them, lightly and loosely, stroking each finger in turn. The tension between them gradually dissipates. When Joel finishes his hot chocolate and gets up to leave, the mood's lightened enough for John to murmur a brief *Night night, Joel Moel*, and for Joel to grunt something back that might be *Night, Dad*. We're past another crisis. I've kept them safe for another night. Tomorrow is always another day.

In bed, John reaches for me with an urgency and fervour I had forgotten could exist between us. Afterwards, drifting hazily on the slack tide of sleep, I wonder for a drowsy moment if he needed to re-assert his importance to me, by touching me in the only way that he is permitted but Joel is not.

Chapter Sixteen
Thursday 7th December 2017

"I need to see you," I whisper into my phone. The hushed tones and needy incantation of the secret lover.

"Why you whispering, soft lass? Hang on a minute—" Seashell sounds as Jackie cups her hand over the phone, and her voice, muffled but still comprehensible. "Fuck's sake, Lee, I'm on the phone to Susannah. Yeah, Susannah. No, she don't like Susie. Or Suze. Oh, just give over, will you?" Lee's replies are too distant for me to hear but I can guess from their cadence what they contain. He's mocking me for my perceived poshness, for coming from a richer part of town than he and Jackie, and for speaking with an accent that belongs to the East Riding rather than the city centre. Underneath all of this is a current of sexual predation. Lee knows that he is stronger than me and would relish the opportunity to prove it. The thought makes me shudder.

"Sorry about that." Jackie's back with me. "So what do you want to do?"

"I want you to come out with me."

"We going round town?"

"No... I want you to come to Beverley with me for the afternoon."

"What, shopping or something, you mean? It takes ages on the bus, do we have to? What's wrong with town?"

"Don't worry about the bus, I'll give you a lift. It's just I'm going to meet someone, and I wondered if you'd come with me."

"What sort of someone? Like a date?"

I remember Nick's skin against mine, the way he looked and felt and smelled and tasted and sounded. I want to do it again, what we had wasn't anything like enough, but I don't know if I dare to ask.

"No, it's not a date, it's... um—"

"Come on, you can tell me." Jackie's voice is tender and coaxing. "I won't laugh."

"I've found someone who can help. With... " I force myself to say it. "That day at the park. You remember? When I... when I—"

"Oh! Oh, okay. Well, that's really good. I'm pleased. Well done. God, really well done. I'm proud of you."

"So will you come with me?"

"How can I help?" His voice imbues this trite phrase with genuine meaning, as if he understands me to the core and really does want to help, as if helping is his true work and mission and the money that will change hands is simply a formal prelude to what really matters, as empty and meaningless as a handshake.

"I was wondering if I could book an appointment with you." My voice sounds hoarse and breathy, as if I'm trying to buy drugs or set up a meeting with my lover while a bystander listens idly in. "I've had some bad experiences and I think I need to talk to someone."

"Okay. Just give me a minute and I'll get my diary, and we'll take a look and see what we can work out."

A small reprieve as he disappears to find his diary. To stop myself from ending the call, I try to imagine what his diary might be like. A large red-bound book with luxurious gold custom lettering and thick creamy pages, perhaps, filled with exquisite lettering in old-fashioned blue ink.

"Hello? Thanks for waiting." I hear pages turning. "So… actually, forgive me for asking this, but I have the feeling we've maybe spoken before? Quite a long time ago?"

"I hope me mam's all right with Georgie." Jackie fumbles restlessly with her phone, flicking the screen on and off with deft touches of her fingers. Her nails, freshly painted with a new temperature-sensitive lacquer, are slowly turning a deeper pink in the warmth of my car. My heart thumps with excitement and guilt.

"Was she okay about taking her?"

"Okay-ish. She was going round to see her friend for lunch at the pub, but her friend's coming to her instead. I think they're getting M&S ready meals. God knows what Georgie'll make of it. I packed some jars but you know what nannas are like. Probably come back full of those foamy pink pig sweets. I'll just send her a text."

I watch enviously as she taps out the words on the screen. So many people who she matters to. So many people whose lives she's a part of. My envy makes me feel better about the deception I'm practising on her. If she has more than me, then it's okay for me to trick her into going along with what I want. She won't mind, not really, she's my friend after all, and friends forgive each other. Oh God, this has to be all right. It has to be.

"I thought we'd park on the Westwood," I say. Does my voice sound hoarse? "The car parks are going to be rammed."

"If you like. You sure we won't get stuck in the mud though? I know it's free parking but you want to be careful parking on grass, it happened to Lee once. Had to call the recovery truck to pull him out."

"It'll be fine, the ground's all frozen anyway. And it's not far to walk, his offices are nearby."

"No worries." Jackie shows me her feet, warmly encased in sheepskin. "I've got my shopping boots on."

The edge of the Westwood common is already busy with

dozens of other cars, waiting like dogs for their owners. I steer the car carefully between the frozen ruts of mud and park just beneath a signpost (*It is forbidden to park more than ten feet from the highway by order of the pasture masters*). "I just thought it might be a bit easier than queuing for a space for ages." When we climb out, the mud is crisp and frozen beneath our feet.

"God, what's wrong with you today?" Jackie looks at me shrewdly across the top of my car. The cold turns her breath white and pure. "You got something you want to tell me?"

I've thought through every part of my plan apart from this bit. Now I realise this is the only bit that matters.

"No. Well, no, not really."

"*Not really* means *Yes, but I'm too chicken to say it*. Look, is he not all right with me coming in with you? Cos I don't mind, I'll take myself into town for a bit while you go in if you want."

"No, it's not that, he'll be fine with you coming in too."

"So what is it then? What have you done? Is there something dodgy about this bloke, or what?" She stares at me for a minute. "Oh, for fuck's sake, no. No, no, no."

"What? I haven't said anything yet—"

"He's not a proper counsellor at all, is he?" Her face is as hard as iron, as pitiless as marble. "Jesus, Susannah, you have to be kidding me, you have *not* gone and booked us an appointment with a fucking psychic."

"I'm... um... My name's Susannah Harper."

A long silence beats out its slow pulses between us.

"I know it's been a long time," I whisper.

"Is your husband with you right now?"

The question catches me by surprise. "No, we split up, just after we... I'm here on my own, I live on my own. He wouldn't come with me."

"I gather you decided to keep going with the blog." His voice is carefully neutral, as if this is simply small talk rather than a reminder of our only dreadful meeting.

I close my eyes against the sharp sting of shame. *They're liars. They're frauds. They're leeches.* All those months and years of vitriol.

"I'll understand if you don't want to see me," I falter. "I know how it must look but I promise, I absolutely promise, I'm not looking for material. If you meet me, I promise I won't write about it afterwards. I'll sign anything you want promising I won't talk about it to anyone. I just—" the tears that shatter my voice are a curious blend of the natural and the manufactured. I'm trying to engage his sympathies, but there's something in them that's real and raw too.

"Please don't be angry with me," I beg. Jackie slams the car door and strides off down the road. "I just really need you to come with me, just this one thing, I promise you I won't ask you for anything else and there's no one else who can come with me—"

"Don't, okay? Just don't. No wonder you wouldn't tell me the bloke's name. Christ, I must be stupid." She walks down the road towards the town centre, head down, arms folded. I run after her. When I try to grab her arm, she shakes me off so violently I think for a moment she might hit me.

"Please, Jackie, just stop a minute and listen to me."

"Why would I want to do that?" Her voice pierces the clean quiet air. A slender elegant woman with a sleek bob of grey hair glances at us. Jackie gives her a challenging, wide-eyed stare. "Yeah? Can I help you, love? Want to come a bit closer so you can hear better? Nosey cow."

"Let me explain." I want to tell Jackie to keep her voice down but I know it won't do any good. She doesn't mind making a scene. "I'm sorry, I know I shouldn't have lied to you, that was a really shitty way to behave."

"D'you know, I think that's the first time I've heard you swear. You should do it more often."

"But I really need you to come with me. I can't do this

without you. And this was the only way I could think of to get you to come with me. I have to see him, Jackie. I absolutely have to. I just feel like he might be able to help."

"Oh, it's all about what you want, isn't it?" To my astonishment, there are tears in Jackie's eyes. "I'm just some add-on accessory to you, aren't I? Well, you're my fucking hero, all right? Heroine. Whatever. You and your blog, all that advice, all those *coping strategies.* You've been the only thing that's got me through this long. If it wasn't for you, I'd have been a raving headcase by now and Georgie'd be in fucking care. But I just kept thinking, *It's all right, Susannah can do it and so can you. She's stayed strong and she's got even less reason than you to keep going."* She takes a deep breath. "And now you want me to come with you and watch you make a bloody show of yourself with some robbing lying bastard who's just going to make up a pack of lies so you'll spunk over all your money? Not a chance. I can't watch that. You go and see him if you want, but don't come crying to me when it all goes pear-shaped. I'm walking into town and getting the bus back. See you later."

"No, you can't! Please. I can't do it by myself. You're right, it might all be rubbish. And that's why I need you, you see? Because you'll be able to tell if it's all nonsense." She shakes her head. "I'll pay, of course I'll pay, it won't cost you anything."

"I don't give a toss about the money, you stupid cow. You can't get everything you want just by throwing money around. Oh my God, please don't cry, Suze, I'm not trying to make you cry, I'm trying to look after you. You do know that, right? Come on, please don't, I'm sorry. You have got to be the softest person I know." From the shiny carapace of her handbag, she conjures a packet of tissues. "Here. Mop yourself up. For God's sake, come here and let me do it, you're wiping mascara everywhere."

As if I'm a child, I stand still and let her dab at me. For months and years, I've found my comfort in playing the part of the strong determined woman who has walked every inch of the hard road before her with bare, bleeding feet. Now Jackie is seeing the woman I really am. A hopeless contradictory mess, with nothing to offer anyone around her.

"Bet you haven't brought anything with you to touch up with, have you?" Jackie shakes her head. "Good job you're so gorgeous naturally. Right. So where does he live?"

"You're coming with me?"

"Can't let you go in on your own, can I. He'll have you for lunch."

"Oh, thank you. Thank you. You don't know what this means to me."

The complicated sadness in Jackie's face ought to break my heart, but I'm too high with triumphant relief to feel it.

"Yeah, well, you don't know what it means to me either, all right? And don't expect me to be nice to him either, I'm not going to play along with his stupid game just to keep things sweet. So let's just get this over with. Have we got far to walk?"

"It's that house there."

"That big one with the massive wreath of mistletoe on the door?" Jackie's high shrill laugh sounds almost natural enough to pass for cheerful scorn. "Done well for himself, hasn't he?"

"Mrs Harper." James O'Brien looks startled, as if we weren't meant to be here. My heart thumps. What if I've done all of this just to bring us here on the wrong day? "Um. Hello."

"It's the right time, isn't it? I've got the right time?"

"Yes. It's the right time. I just wasn't expecting—" he looks at Jackie. "Mrs Nelson, isn't it? I'm so sorry about your son."

"You told him about me? About my Ryan? You told him about my son?"

James shakes his head impatiently. "No, she didn't say anything, I promise, and I promise I'm not trying to show off. I just remember your face from the news."

Still he doesn't move aside, doesn't welcome us over the threshold. He holds out a hand to Jackie to shake, but she folds her arms stubbornly across her chest, her bright sharp gaze challenging him to call her out on her rudeness.

"You going to invite us in, then?" Jackie says at last. "Because it's brass monkeys out here, my hands are frozen. Or do we do it out here where the neighbours can get a good look?"

"I'm sorry. Come on in." Another moment's hesitation and we're over the doorstep, the teetering garden receding behind us as we reach the safe harbour of the hallway.

"Like a museum, this place, isn't it," Jackie says to my face and James's back as he leads us into the room I can't call anything other than the drawing room. I have to resist the urge to shush her. "Must be good money in making up shite to upset vulnerable people." She sits gingerly down on the velvet sofa. "Is this where it all happens, then? All the *magic*?"

"So." He sits forward, puts his hands together and rests his chin there for a moment, then straightens up, puts his hands on his knees. Moves again, this time to fold one leg across. Lets it drop again. It's like a pantomime of nervousness.

"You got fleas or something?" Jackie enquires sweetly.

"I'm actually wondering whether I ought to go ahead with this session after all." His fingers trill a little rhythm on the edge of his knees.

"Or worms. Me mam always used to say worms make you restless. You can get some stuff from the chemist, they won't judge you or nowt. You want to start washing your hands after you've been to the toilet though, or you'll just get them back again." When she sees me wince, she has the grace to look briefly ashamed of herself.

"It's all right," James says to Jackie. "I know you're not comfortable being here. You're a good friend, Mrs Nelson. I hope she appreciates how much it's costing you."

"It's not costing her anything, I said I'd pay—!"

"He's not talking about the money," says Jackie wearily. "All right, then, you got me, I think this is a load of bollocks and there's nothing you can say that's going to change my mind. I'm only here because you talked my soft mate here into believing you've got something worthwhile to tell her. But I'll tell you straight, I'm not falling for any of this crap and you'll be getting no business out of me, whatever rubbish you come out with. All right?"

"I understand."

"And if you're going to try and blame it not working on me, then you can forget that one and all."

"No, that won't be the problem." He looks at me carefully. "So…"

Jackie tuts and tosses her head impatiently. I want to take her hand for comfort but I'm afraid she'll push me away.

Someone gave you a prediction," James says at last. "Someone said something to you and now you think there's a chance your son is still alive. And ever since then…"

"I see things. People who aren't there. Places I'm not in. Or else people do things to me, only they're not really happening, because they can't be."

"Visions of water? Watery places?"

"Yes. Why? What does that mean?"

"It might not mean anything. It might just be the echo of what I saw for you the last time. Sometimes I plant things in people's minds that can reverberate for years. Or maybe—" he checks himself.

"Yes?"

"Maybe it means she needs to see the head doctor," says Jackie. "Susannah, please, I'm begging you. Come with me. Right now. This is messed up."

"Perhaps that might be best." No hint this time of the smooth financial advisor act he produced so flawlessly for John. This time he's all shadows and drama, torture and angst. He looks down at his hands for a minute, then up at me, a sad little-boy look from beneath his eyebrows, a perfect stage-

236

school facsimile of sorrow that is nonetheless convincing, because his skin looks tired and dry, as if he's slept badly, and there are dark circles beneath his eyes. "I can sit for you both if you want, but I need to warn you now that the results are likely to be confusing. If you'd prefer not to go ahead, you can leave right now and I'll refund the money to you straight away."

"Or," says Jackie, "you can do your little shitty act for us, and if Susannah's not happy with what she hears, you can refund her after. How about that?"

"I always refund if my client isn't happy." James stands up. "This way, please."

"Would either of you like some water?" Everything in the room is the same as it was the last time: the bare wooden floorboards, the school furniture, the lightbulb in its paper shade like a moon. Beside me, Jackie is breathing fast and shallow. I can feel the electric heat of her fear, threatening to scorch me if I get too close. "Would you like to use the bathroom first?"

"No, I'm fine."

"I will," says Jackie.

"It's the second door off the hallway."

James and I wait, suspended in time, mesmerised by the sound of Jackie's boots clicking against the tiles in the hallway, the opening and closing of the door.

"It's not too late." His words are startling in the stillness.

"What?"

"You don't have to do this. It's going to change everything. Not just for you, for your friend too. You should listen to her. That's why you brought her. Did you wonder why you felt so strongly you had to bring her with you? She was your way out. She was supposed to say no."

"She did say no," I admit. "But I—"

"—tricked her and bullied her and played on her loyalty to you. I know what you did, I can see it in your face. That wasn't supposed to happen. This is all your choice, you made all the decisions, but you can unmake them. There's still time."

"What do you know? What are you going to tell us?"

"I don't know, I never know until I start, but sometimes I get a feeling... this isn't going to make you happy, not either of you. Please. I'm begging you. Tell her you've come to your senses and you want to go home. It's what she wants to hear anyway."

A few weeks ago I would have done as he said. I used to be a good girl. I used to do what people told me. In the distance, I can hear the sound of water rushing against porcelain.

"You've still got time," he repeats. The door opens, then closes. Jackie's footsteps are getting closer.

"Is this part of the sales pitch? Increasing my commitment by telling me I can get out if I want to?"

"If you think I'm a charlatan then why are you here at all?"

"Because you said you'd refund me if I wasn't happy with the outcome," I say, and take my place at the table.

"If you could connect your hands to form a circle," says James. Jackie's hand in mine feels dry and feverish. She grips my fingers as if they're all that stands between her and drowning. "Now, Mrs Harper, if you could concentrate on a time with Joel when you were happy."

"What about me? What am I supposed to do? I never met him."

"If you could just try and lend Susannah your support... there's probably going to be some overspill, I'm afraid..."

Jackie's misery transmits itself into the skin of my hand like an electric pulse. I can tell from the way her breath hitches that she's already crying. It's hard to concentrate on my picture of Joel nestled small and tight in his cot, Scrap-dog tucked beneath his chin as outside the window, the creeping frost paints over the tiny pond with a thin film of ice like transparent paper. In the morning, I will take him down into the garden and show him a world transformed from dreary damp into crisp white beauty, and later we will make a cake and light a single candle. It is the night before Midwinter Day, and it is a whole year since Joel burst into our lives like a rocket.

"Midwinter," James says, with difficulty. "You're sledging, a very steep hill with a big house on the hill opposite. He falls off the side of the sledge and hits his head and cries, but when you say it's time to go home he begs to stay. And a cake, a cake with a single candle, and frost on the leaves outside… I'm sorry, this is jumbled because there are two of you, I can't tell if this is Ryan or Joel."

"I'm not leaving my mate alone with you. You'll do both of us or neither, you hear me?" I can hear the fear in Jackie's voice, and I realise something I should have known all along: she's not angry because she doesn't believe, she's frightened because she does. My unbelief was her shield, and without it, she's naked against the dark.

"He was a handful, wasn't he? But he loved you so much. You were the centre of his world."

Is he talking to me, or to Jackie? I have no way of knowing.

"Now, if you could please shift your concentration to the last time you saw your sons."

James's face is pale and sweaty and his hand is clammy. It's like holding hands with a frog, like touching an internal organ lifted out onto the cold autopsy table. I want to let go but I don't dare. To my right, Jackie's fingers clutch at me. The lights flicker. Jackie whimpers. I wait for James to reassure her, as he once reassured John and me.

"I'm so sorry," James whispers at last.

"What? What? What can you see?" Jackie's voice has the high rising intonation of hysteria. Another minute of this and she'll be screaming.

"Both your sons are dead. I'm so sorry. They both died on the day they disappeared."

All this time I've imagined that I have found a way to let

go of the treacherous yearning that whispers in my ear: *Maybe today, maybe today you'll see him. On the bus, in the park, walking between the trees and coming up the garden path.* I've watched as others have walked the same road, companions and comrades, even though we've never met. Each time I've watched one of these other stories resolve – nine times with the simple bleak announcement *the police have found a body*, only once with a wild unbearable joy so huge it was almost like pain, the words tumbling out as she gabbled out her story to the baby-bird reporters – *He's in Los Angeles he ran away because he was afraid to come out to us because of our church but his boyfriend finally convinced him to call, oh my God, I can't stop shaking* – I have felt a stab of envy. Death is the final dreadful solution to the riddle, but nonetheless it is a solution, and surely it's better to know than to live forever with the endless betrayal of *what if today* – ?

But I know now I've been deluding myself. I have never, ever let go of *what if today*. This moment here, in this cold room with my friend clinging to my right hand and a cold-skinned stranger holding my left, is the true death of hope.

"How did it happen?" I whisper. Beside me, Jackie has bent forward until her forehead is almost touching the table. She's making a slow wordless keening noise that cuts like glass. James looks at me bleakly.

"Mrs Harper, you already know. That's why you've come here today. To tell yourself the things you already know."

"No," Jackie moans, from within the walls of her own private hell. "No, no, no, this isn't true, it's not true, this isn't happening…"

"So who was it? Who was it that killed them? Was it the same person? Is that why we came into each other's lives? Is there a… a serial killer or something?"

"No. Two separate killers. They're hidden in darkness. One on land, hidden beneath trees. One in the water, near a boat that never moves. One was killed. Oh, God forgive me –"

He glances at Jackie, lost now and openly sobbing, her face

240

pressed against the old varnish of the table, and frees his hand from hers as if he can't bear the touch of her flesh against his any longer. "One was killed by his father... and one by his... by his mother."

Then Jackie scrabbles onto the table, clenches her fist into a ball and punches James brutally in the face.

"You," she hisses, "are a fucking liar, do you hear me? A fucking liar, and a shit-stirrer, and a nasty little freak. You don't know fucking nothing, you hear me? And if you ever say that again to anyone, especially the police, I will come round here and I will fucking kill you."

And in a quick series of movements she pulls me to my feet, shoves me ahead of her out of the room, runs to the front door and drags me through it, both of us stumbling and clinging to each other for balance as we flee through the garden filled with dead flowers, clattering clumsily up the street towards the safety of my car.

"Is he following us? Is he?" Jackie's breath comes in great gasps. "Is he coming after us?"

Why is she still here? I don't want her near me, not any more, not now that I know what she is. "No, he's not coming after us."

"Oh, fuck. Fuck me. That was... Oh fuck. Don't ever ask me to do that again. Not ever again. I swear to God. Not ever. Are you all right?" She pats my arm. I try not to shudder. "Hey, you know I don't believe it, right? He was just talking bollocks. Trying to make himself look important. Maybe even believes it himself, I don't know. But it's not true, not a fucking word of it, and I know that. All right? I know that and so do you."

How resilient she is. How quick to cover her tracks. No wonder Nick hasn't caught her out yet. But surely he will soon. I wish I'd listened to him. I wish I'd never let this woman get close to me.

"Are you listening to me? Susannah? Suze? Are you all right?"

Suddenly I'm very tired. I want this all to be over. I feel like sitting down on the pavement, so that's what I do. The concrete sucks the warmth greedily from my flesh, but I'll have to learn to live with that. From now on, the world will be a very cold place.

"What's the matter? Why are you looking at me like that? Get up off the floor, will you?"

"I believe him."

Jackie laughs shrilly. "You what? Course you don't, you dozy cow. You wouldn't hurt your boy, no mother would."

"I know I wouldn't."

For a minute her face turns blank and her eyes are dead and black. I wonder if this is how she looked when she killed Ryan. How did she do it? I expect I'll find out one day. Eventually Nick will catch her out.

"You utter bitch." She stares at me for a minute, as if considering whether to spit. "You make me sick. I hope you freeze to fucking death. And then rot in Hell when you get there."

I know she's leaving me because I can hear her footsteps getting fainter and further away, but I don't watch her leave. I sit quietly on the pavement, breathing in, breathing out, in and out, waiting for my strength to return so that I can decide what to do next, knowing as I do the identities of two murderers. For now it's enough to know that I will never see her again.

Life Without Hope:
How I got hooked on giving all my money to psychics

For the first few days after Joel disappeared, normality vanished. John and I both spent hours at the police station, being interviewed and giving information. We did interviews for news programmes and newspapers. We talked to everyone, every time they asked, going over the same things over and over; and we were glad to, because we knew that if we wanted to find our boy, this was the way to do it. We wanted everyone in the city to be looking for him. Everyone in the country. Everyone in the world.

Then as time went by and there was no news and no news and still no news, and the papers and the TV crews disappeared and the police investigation wound down and everyone else went on with their lives, I realised something terrible. I realised that this dreadful empty blank was our lives now. And somehow, we had to fill them.

John had his work. But I didn't have anything. And I was determined to do everything I could to find Joel.

So I started going to psychics.

I can still remember my first one. She was a nice middle-aged lady who lived in an attic flat in a beautiful old house and I found her in the phone book. She had a good opening patter, lots of talk about invoking *peace* and *light* and *kindly spirits*. She told me that Joel still loved me very much, that he always would, and that he wasn't in any pain and he wasn't unhappy. She said he was missing me. She said I would see him again one day. Then I asked her, *Is Joel alive or dead?* And she had no idea what to say. And I realised she was probably great at giving comfort to people whose loved ones were dead, but when it came to someone like me she was completely lost.

Now I know that's because she had no psychic gifts at all. None. Zero. She was just a nice old lady who knew how to talk to the bereaved. But before I left, she said something very clever that instantly convinced me of her talent, and that kept me hooked on psychics for an embarrassingly long time.

She said, *I'm so sorry I couldn't help you. My skill is mainly with those who have recently passed over. I think you need to find someone whose talents lie with finding the living.*

And that was it. That was all it took. Because I wanted to believe.

So I kept looking. I went to shows and I joined online forums and I just generally asked around. After a while, John found out what I was doing and he said it wasn't safe, going round to strange people's houses where nobody knew where I was, so he started coming with me. We went all over the country and spent so much money. I didn't mind about that part though. In fact, the more expensive they were, the more confident I felt. Surely no one would charge five hundred pounds for a half-hour session if they knew they were ripping people off?

(What I discovered later is that charging a lot of money is one of the tricks they use to get you to believe in them. The more we spend the more committed we feel. None of us want to think we've made a bad buying decision.)

We spent thousands. Maybe tens of thousands. And none of them, not one, was any help. Because psychics can't do what they promise. Their talent is to find out what you want to hear, and then say that to you for money. And it only works because we let it. I was eager to be ripped off. I let them do it. I *wanted* them to do it. Because I genuinely thought I was helping to find my son.

I thought psychics were like forensic instruments. I'd go in with a few scraps of information and a fat wad of money and they'd be able to find Joel. But in fact, they're like funhouse mirrors. They just reflect back at us whatever we bring into the room.

Posted on 24th November 2013
Filed to: Why All Psychics Are Frauds

Tags: psychic fraud, missing people, support for families, Susannah Harper, Joel Harper

Chapter Seventeen
Thursday 7th December 2017

At the edge of madness lies a curious invisibility. People slow their walk when they see me kneeling on the pavement, glancing at me cautiously from the edges of their vision; but no one stops, and no one speaks, and no one disturbs me. If I were sobbing, rocking, vomiting, if I were unconscious bleeding or bent over in pain, perhaps they'd stop and offer help. But I'm simply sitting, incongruous but seemingly at ease and not obviously wounded, and so they leave me to myself, hurrying obliviously towards the shops or back home again with a kind and gentle inattentiveness that I'm grateful for. Perhaps they think I've lost a ring and am searching for it in the gutter.

A man I think I can trust just told me that my friend killed her son. That wasn't all he said and I'll need to think about the rest eventually, but right now, I'm not ready. I've spent years pretending not to know, and although I know it's nearly time to face the truth, I'm not quite there yet. Instead I want to sit here on the footpath, and concentrate on the part I can bear to process.

It's the cold that gets me moving, creeping beneath the flimsy wrapping of my clothes to touch the skin beneath. When I try to stand, the cramp in my legs makes me whimper. I stagger back to my car and claw my way in, tearing a fingernail as I wrestle with the handle. I think I'll never be warm again. The thermometer on the dashboard reads six degrees below.

I turn on the engine and shiver in the dry sour warmth. On the back seat of the car, Jackie's scarf lies like a snake. I throw it out of the window. Will she be cold without it? Or does the terrible secret she has locked away in her heart keep her warm? The scarf is heavy sheepskin, buttery soft to the touch. It looks like a lost little animal, lying dead on the frozen puddle. But what if it's not dead? What if it moves? What if it reaches out for me?

When my fingers have unfrozen enough to grip the steering wheel, I reverse clumsily out onto the road and drive home. My driving is poor and more than one person throws their hands up in despair at my drunken steering, my slow reactions, my misjudged guesses about the behaviour of pedestrians. Normally this would have me cringing in shame. Today I don't care. I only want to be at home.

Home is cold. The boiler has gone out. I eventually manage to re-light it, but I wonder how well prepared it is for the coming winter. I should call an engineer and have it serviced, before winter takes too deep a hold. If my boiler failed me, how long would it take before I froze? And how long before someone noticed I was gone? Melanie has rejected me. John has a new life now. Jackie will never call me again. Who is there in this barren empty world who would care?

Standing in the silent chill of my kitchen, waiting for the kettle to boil so I can press a scalding hot-water bottle against my belly, the answer comes to me.

"Susannah?" Nick's voice is eager.

"I'm sorry to bother you."

"Don't be. Don't ever be. What do you need? Do you need help? Are you hurt?"

"Yes, I need help. I'm cold, Nick, I'm so cold. My boiler went out and my whole house is cold." I'm surprised by how breathless I sound. "I want you to come and make me warm."

He's with me in a few minutes, through my front gate and at my front door almost before the car engine is off. He's thrown on a heavy jacket over a worn grey T-shirt and jeans. I must have called him at home. Was his wife with him? And where does she think he is? I ought to care but I don't. Instead I pull his head down to mine so our mouths can fuse together. She has so much and I have so little and I am so cold, so cold and so lonely. All I'm asking is a little borrowed warmth. Are the starving judged when they steal a loaf of bread? Nick's breath is warm against my face and neck. The scent of his aftershave makes me want to bite him.

"I've dreamed about this." His words are like sweet poison in my ear, melting my bones and stealing my senses. "I've prayed for you to call. Do you know that? I've prayed for you to call and ask me to come to you."

His hands, his skin, his mouth. This is what I need. To be needed. To be craved. To be consumed. To be stripped. When I take his hand and show him where I want him to touch me, his moan of pleasure is almost too much to bear. The carpet is painfully rough beneath my back but his weight against me is so very tender, so very smooth. I would let him fuck me right here on the stairs if that's what he wants. Instead he lets me go and asks me to forgive him for being in such a rush, turning me round so he can kiss the tender places on my naked spine where the coarse wool has scratched my skin. He knows where my bedroom is, but he doesn't move until I take his hand and lead him, even though he's naked and needy and my compliance, my complicity, cannot be in any doubt.

In the bedroom, the chill of the cold sheets beneath me contrasts deliciously with the heat of our flesh. He mutters something in my ear, something about needing to slow down, to stop, that I've got him so nuts he'll never last a minute, not even a few seconds, and I claw at his back because I think a few seconds might just be all I need, but he pulls back, panting and wild-eyed, and stares at me, as greedily and openly as if I'm a sculpture or a photograph.

He's so dark, so lean, so skilled but still so hesitant, so forward and yet so reverent. I have never felt so powerful. I take his hand and guide it to the place where I want him to stroke me, and close my eyes and sink into the dark.

Afterwards, he dozes for a few minutes, and I watch the way his face changes in sleep. At work, he's closed and confident, his police officer persona sealed around him like a mask that covers his whole body. In my arms, he becomes someone else, someone softer and needier, wilder and more vulnerable. Now, while his soul wanders somewhere I will never reach, the body that remains behind has the look of a beautiful statue.

How will I tell him what I know? In his heart, he knows the truth already. He's tried to tell me, as much and as well as he can. Now I know too, but I can't tell him, because what will I say? How will I explain? He looks so beautiful asleep, all the tension smoothed out of his face, his eyes closed, that I'm almost tempted to try. I could lie beside him and trace letters on his back, letting him absorb my words through his skin. I could rest my mouth against the shell of his ear and whisper: *Jackie killed her son.*

As if my gaze has weight, is pressing gently against him, he wakes and smiles.

"Sorry. Late turn last night. Still catching up."

"Busy night?"

He looks at me warily, as if he's wondering whether to trust me. How strange that we can be as intimate as we are now, smelling and tasting of each other, our naked bodies twined together, and still he's unsure if he can trust me. Or perhaps it's not strange at all. Our ancestors variously believed that their king was appointed by God, that trial by combat would reveal the truth, that women's wombs could become detached and wander all over their bodies. Perhaps the belief in the deep and binding intimacy created by having sex is simply the delusion of our times.

"Quite busy," he says. "Can I kiss you again?"

"What are you working on? Can you tell me? Just a little bit?"

"Why do you want to know?"

"Because it's interesting."

"It's not interesting, it's boring. Lot of paperwork. Lot of cross-checking and asking the same questions over and over."

"So why do you do it if it's not interesting?"

"Because in the end, when you've done all the paperwork and the cross-checking and asking the same questions over and over... sometimes you get the bad guy. That's a good feeling."

"Are you close to getting a bad guy now?"

He shifts around a little in the bed so he can see my face more clearly. His instincts are razor-sharp. Or perhaps I'm just too easy to read. How else would James O'Brien have plucked my memories from me so effortlessly?

"Why are you asking?"

"I just... I suppose I just realised I don't really know you. Isn't that strange? I've known you for years and now we've gone to bed together and I still don't really know you."

"Susannah." He takes a lock of my hair and tugs it gently. "You're so beautiful, and I'm so crazy about you. But you're a terrible, terrible liar. What's really on your mind?"

"You know you warned me not to get too close to Jackie? Well, we had an argument today."

He keeps his face carefully still and neutral. "Did she hurt you?"

"No. Why would you ask that?"

"And are you going to patch things up with her?"

"No. I don't think we can. We can't be friends any more, it's over."

"I'm sorry. I know you liked her. But she wasn't good enough for you." He strokes my hair away from my face. "You're not like anyone else I know. You keep yourself locked away from everyone, like a glass princess in the centre of a maze, but when someone finally finds their way to the centre..." He laughs. "God, listen to me. I always was crap at English. I'm glad she's out of your life. If you can, keep her that way."

"She said you'd been asking her a lot of questions recently."

"We've had a couple of new bits of information, that's all. It's an ongoing investigation. They all have their ebbs and flows. If this doesn't pan out, we'll likely be back to weekly updates again for a while."

"Do you think she hurt Ryan?"

He picks up my hand and kisses my fingertips.

"We haven't ruled out any lines of enquiry."

"She thinks you suspect her."

"Does she? Sweetheart, I can't talk to you about this, you know I can't."

"Do you think I'm asking for her? That I'm going to tell her what you tell me?"

"It's not that, I swear. I trust you with my life. Christ, I *have* trusted you with my life. But I just... I can't."

He's not being completely honest with me, I can tell. But then, I'm not being completely honest with him either. In the yellow light of my bedside lamp, we lie and look at each other and consider the nature of trust.

"She's heartbroken," Nick says at last. "She's been in Hell since Ryan disappeared. But what you realise in my job is, sometimes the people who are the most upset are the ones who carry the most guilt." He strokes my hair. "I'm glad she's out of your life. I don't want her to hurt you. You've been through enough."

I think about Jackie's sharp clever little face. Her unexpected strength. It's rare for a mother to kill her own child. But it happens.

"So you really think she—"

"All I can tell you," he says, slowly, carefully, his eyes fixed on mine, "is that statistically speaking, the people most likely to hurt a child are the adults who have the responsibility to care for that child. That's not a trade secret, that's just the truth. Nine times out of ten, when a child or a young person comes to harm, that's where we find the perpetrator. In the home with them."

Before Judas pressed his lips against the cheek of his friend, there must have been a moment when he hesitated. The hesitation is the true moment of betrayal, because that's the moment when you acknowledge that, yes, what you're doing is wrong, you have doubts, you know that doing it will make you a bad person; and yet you're going to do it anyway, because the right price will buy you, and now you've been bought. My price is not silver coins but silver words and a shudder of deep-seated pleasure that's both profound and fleeting. I know this is wrong, because I'm hesitating. But I'm going to do it anyway.

"I think Jackie knows something about what happened to Ryan," I whisper. "More than she's said to you. That's what we argued about. I told her—"

"Yes?"

"I told her that I think she killed him."

The only sound in the room is our breathing and the ticking of the radiator as it warms.

"What makes you think that?" Nick asks at last.

"It's just a feeling I have."

"But what gave you that feeling? Was it something she said? Something she didn't say? Something you found, or saw her do maybe? You can tell me anything. Anything at all. I promise."

"I can't prove it. But I feel it." I put my hand on his chest so I can feel the throb of his heart. "And you feel it too. Don't you?"

"I can't say. Please don't ask me to say."

"Then tell me what you're thinking."

"I'm thinking," he says slowly, "that I am the luckiest bastard who ever walked this sorry earth. I'm thinking, how can this be happening? How can it be me here in this bed with you? I'm thinking that just you looking at me like that... that's probably enough to get me there." His eyes are huge with longing. "But I don't want to do that. I want to get you off first so I can watch your face, and then I want to be inside you when I come." His hand reaches out to me, trembles, pauses. "Is that all right with you? Can I please do that? What I just said? Can I please get you off first and then be inside you when I come?"

He looks so sad, so vulnerable and ashamed, and at the same time his hand against my leg is so dry and hot with longing, that there's nothing else I can do but kiss him, and all the things that come after kissing him, the touching and the stroking and the squeezing and the long slow unravelling. How long is it since I had sex twice in a couple of hours? Decades. How long for him? I'll never know.

Afterwards, he stands by the bed and stretches. This means our time is coming to an end. It's almost a relief. Such companionship, after such loneliness, has me stretched tight and painful, gorged to the point of sickness.

"Can I use your bathroom?"

"Of course. Just out on the landing."

I lie beneath the covers and savour the small sounds of his presence. The floorboards yielding to footsteps that aren't mine, the click of the light switch that I haven't touched, the running of the tap that I haven't turned. His sudden reappearance in the doorway of the bedroom makes my heart leap.

"Can you remember where I left my clothes?"

"They're somewhere in the hall. I think."

I hear the stairs creak, and the small sounds of clothes being gathered. "Fine copper I am. Can't even remember where I left my kit..." He dresses quickly, shyly, as if he's suddenly embarrassed about me seeing him. Should I offer him coffee? A sandwich? In his pocket, his mobile phone buzzes.

"Sorry," he mutters as he fumbles it out. I try to glimpse the name on the screen. Is it Bella, asserting her superior claim? Has she guessed his betrayal? Nick swipes the screen, raises his eyebrows in apology, and takes the call out onto the landing, a poor disguise since I can hear every word he says. *Hiya, mate, what's up? No problem. What? When? So where is it? And who was it found it? God, who'd have a dog, eh? And was it hidden, or... okay, yeah, got it. No, I know, they can't help themselves, it's just instinct, isn't it? Has it done much damage to the... Okay, well, let's hope. So who's attending from... okay, understood. Yeah, definitely the best. No, no problem, mate, I want to be there. Right. Got it. No. Yep. No. No, I agree, absolutely not, not until we've had someone take a look and confirm if it's a good match. Right. I'm on my way now, mate, see you there. Yeah, I know. Right, bye.*

Even if I was too stupid to understand what I've just overheard, I would be able to read it in Nick's expression when he comes back into the bedroom to kiss me goodbye. His face is closed and intent, his mind already elsewhere. This must be how soldiers look before they go to war, how hunters look before setting out across the plains.

"Is everything all right?"

He kisses me, hard and triumphant. "That was work. I have to go."

"You've found a body?"

"Yeah." He can't hide the excitement in his eyes. "Based on the description, it sounds like it could be a teenage boy."

My heart turns over in my chest. "Is it... it's not—"

"Oh my God, Susannah, sweetheart, no. I'm sorry, I'm sorry. No, it's not, it's not him, okay? I don't know for sure who it is but I promise, this is not Joel." He strokes the top of my head, then kisses me there, comforting and paternal. I can tell he's not sure, just as I am not sure, if the body not being Joel is good news or bad. "I have to go now, okay? Will you be all right?"

"Yes."

"I don't like leaving you on your own. I'll call your sister, shall I? Get her to come round?"

"No. We're not really speaking at the moment. Nothing serious," I add hastily. "It'll sort itself out. But just, no, don't call her."

"You'll be careful?"

"Yes."

"And call me if you need anything?"

How can I call him when I know the terrible work he's about to embark upon? "Yes, I'll call." Still he hesitates. "What? What is it?"

"Can I ask you to do something for me?"

"Yes, of course."

"Lock the door when I've gone," he says. "And don't call Jackie."

Chapter Eighteen
Friday 7th December 2012

When I leave the police station, I'm shivering as if I have a fever. The streets feel alien and oppressive and the trees stand watch like sentinels. The sensation is one of escape, but I know it's only an illusion. If the police want me back, all they have to do is to stretch out their hand and hook me back inside again. Perhaps they're only letting me go now so they can watch what I do when I think I'm not being watched. Is there someone discreetly trailing me? I look behind me a few times, but no one looks back at me with furtive innocence, and no one flinches back between parked cars or crams themselves into doorways, and no one's face grows gradually familiar. Is this because the person following me is too clever to be caught? Or is it because there's no one there at all?

I should wait at the station for John, but I can't bear to sit in that shiny-floored reception and watch the slow flow of people in and out. Instead I stand at the bus stop and let the shadows gather around me. The sky is heavy with rain that's only a few minutes away from becoming snow; another downward twitch of the thermometer and we'll be there, drowning in tumbling white. I wonder if it's obvious where I've been, if people recognise my face from the newspaper and television appeals. I hope not. I want it to be Joel's face that they remember. But even if that photograph of his tousled blond hair and anxious eyes has burned its way into their brain, what good will it do? A photo freezes us in time, and time has moved on. Even if they pass Joel on the street, see him getting on or off a bus or a train, entering or leaving a building, how will they ever connect the young grubby man with the rucksack on his back with the face of my lost boy? If he's still in the city, he'll be in the places where most people don't want to go, among the people we choose to look away from. The cold white light of the bus's interior drown out the anaemic watercolours of the winter sunset, and the bus driver has hung a boa of tinsel around his fat neck. I climb on board and take my seat among the silent crowd, staring blindly out at the Christmas lights that have begun to appear in the windows and on the walls of the houses we pass, each of us locked away in a bubble of solitude. How can it be so close to Christmas already, and Joel still not found?

At the interchange, the trains call to me as they always do, with their paradoxical promise of both order and adventure, the wildness of *elsewhere* corralled into a timetable, each journey into the unknown bound with iron rails. Did Joel hear them calling to him that afternoon? If I stand beneath the screen and stare for long enough, will I recognise the place he chose? Perhaps there will be a signal, a feeling, some jolt or twitch on the secret invisible connection that unites my heart with his. How will I tell the police that I know where he went? I'll have to invent some plausible-sounding lie. A conversation newly recalled, perhaps. *I just remembered that Joel told me once that if he was going to run away, he'd run to Nottingham/Penzance/Aberystwyth...* I'd like to think this will be enough to make them drop everything and tear off with sirens screaming but I know now it doesn't work like that. Instead they'll want to know when and where, what I said in reply, how long ago, and where did I say again? And why do I think he picked that place? I'll have to work out all the details first, and then maybe even take John into my confidence, to ensure my memorable day trips or family holidays don't take him by surprise.

I'll do this another day, another day when I have exhausted the possibilities of my own city. There are still places here I need to visit and re-visit, searching for the signal that I know is out there if only I can find it. Somewhere, if I look hard enough and often enough, there is something that will lead my back to my son. *Go home and try to rest*, they told me at the station, the way they always do, but I don't have time to rest. I have too much work to do. Four weeks gone, and I've begun to accept that Joel may not come back to me of his own free will, that it will take some special effort to wrench the universe into a shape that gives him back. I've not yet begun to accept that he may not come back at all.

In the time I spent in the police station, the world's grown darker. It takes me a long time to get home. It's much quicker by car, and I wonder if John might have beaten me home, but the house is like a tomb and the garage is empty. My feet hurt and I'm tired, but it doesn't matter. Nothing matters. I have to keep going. If I try hard enough, make enough sacrifices, the universe will relent and give me back my child. Before I leave the house, I scribble a note for John, just a few words so he knows I've been home and I'm not dead.

Gone out to look for Joel – S.

How often do people write notes for each other these days? So much simpler and more efficient to send a text. *Why would you leave me a note in a building I'm not even in yet, when you can just send me a text that I can read right where I am?* John asked me once, and for once John and Joel laughed together, and Joel hugged me and told me not to worry, I was still the best mum in the world and then later John kissed me and told me he loved me exactly as I was, old-fashioned notes and all. Will I ever have a moment like that again? (The answer is no, but I don't know that yet.) But there must still be a place for handwritten messages. If you were walking out on your marriage, perhaps. If you were running away.

Oh God, why didn't Joel leave us a note? Does this mean he must be…?

I can only escape this thought with action. I leave the house with the ordered frenzy of an overwound clockwork toy: hat, gloves, keys, phone, check the door and out of the front gate before my thoughts can catch up with me. The street is deserted, but nonetheless I feel breathless watchers staring out at me from the looming houses. I dart my eyes around trying to catch them, but find only my next-door neighbour standing tall and bent in his front bedroom window. When he sees me looking, he slowly raises one hand in greeting.

My need for movement takes me on the route Joel walked to school, on the days when he missed his bus or simply couldn't face the tight-packed proximity of his tormentors; a winding walk past houses and shops, and then a forbidden left-hand detour across the undulating folds of the common where travellers' horses raise their foals amid intermittent floods and hedges made alternately sweet and sharp with blackthorn. Today the hedgerows are bare and sullen, and the horses stand like passengers at a deserted railway station, staring out across over-grazed turf for a rescue that will not come. I stop to pet the soft pink nose of one benign-looking giant, only to jump back in shock when it lunges at me, all yellowy teeth and snapping jaws. Did Joel pass this way on the morning he disappeared? When I emerge on the other side of the common, the school looks just as it always has, grey and squat and stained with weather, its silence and emptiness rendering it threatening. A half-frozen rain has begun to fall, stinging my cheeks. I'd forgotten it was the weekend.

I can't bear to turn back, I have to keep going. So I walk past the school and take the path beside the wide dual carriageway instead, the heavy traffic muted by the broad avenues of trees that grow beside and in the centre. Growing up I took it for granted that our city, so endlessly reviled for its brutalist post-war concrete and bleak town centre, was nonetheless crossed and partitioned by these wide Parisian boulevards that each spring frothed with blossom and tender green leaves. It was John who first told me that the main roads into the city were built extra wide to accommodate tram-lines, and the green oases I loved so much were the grassed-over graves of a long-gone public transport network. *So what about the big wide verges at the side, then, why didn't they build houses there instead?* I demanded, and he laughed and said he didn't know, maybe someone in the Town Planning department just really loved trees.

When I'm grown up I'm going to live inside a willow tree. Joel, seven years old and holding tight to my hand as we walked slowly, slowly, slowly through the trees. We'd gone too far, as we always did. Soon he'd be too tired to go any further, and I'd have to carry him home even though he was years too big for me to manage.

You mean inside a tree? Like Robin Hood?

No. I mean under the leaves, like living in a tent. Look, Mummy. Joel parted the shimmering green curtain and led me inside. *See? It's lovely and quiet in here.* Joel always loved to be quiet, finding secret spots where he could hide and let the world unfold around him. Once, after a convincing performance for the school nurse won him a phone call home and a few hours' reprieve from lessons, we spent an afternoon together hidden in the shrubs of a traffic island where five roads meet.

My heart hammering, I thrust impetuously through golden leaves and half-bare branches.

There's no one there.

But then, there are many willow trees in this city.

I walk and walk and walk, until my feet are on fire and my throat is parched and my muscles are trembling. I couldn't even name the streets I walked down, led only by an intuition that is both seductive and faulty, for I've found no trace of where my son might have passed through, felt no inexplicable connection with one place over another. Joel's rucksack was not hidden beneath the trees or in the bushes I stared into, and I saw no glimpse of him slipping away behind a shuttered row of garages or quiet allotment shed. I know no more than when I started and yet the thought of giving up feels like a betrayal. It's only when I glimpse a row of houses that look faintly familiar, and realise I have walked in a huge circle that has led me close to my own front door, that I allow myself to stop. *There's always tonight*, I remind myself. *I'll wait until John's asleep and then go out in the car and search the city centre.*

John lies in wait behind the front door, opening it for me before I can even raise my key to the lock. I wonder if he'll be angry with me for leaving the police station without him, if he'll want to reproach me for the coldness of the note I left for him on the table. Instead he is brandishing a bacon sandwich, the crisp fat and salty meat oozing with brown sauce.

"No news," he says. The first words we always say these days.

No news. The first time I said those words I thought I'd swallowed glass. Now it's just one more part of our dreadful new routine for living together. "What's that?"

"You need to eat," he tells me. "No, don't tell me you're not hungry because I know that's not true. Come and sit down."

Another reminder that our lives have changed irrevocably. It's my role to lie in wait, ambushing my hungry boys with food the moment they cross the threshold. Is John letting me know that I'm falling down in my duties? Is he expecting me to carry on as if everything's normal? Is he reproaching me for my relentless focus on Joel? I take the sandwich and follow him to the dining room, where its identical twin waits for John. In the centre of the table, two cooling mugs of tea wait to be consumed.

"Have you been back long?" I'm wary of John despite how nice he's being to me. I feel strung up and tense, as if

I'm tiptoeing over a thin crust of a volcano. I feel as if I'm being softened up for some terrible unexpected blow.

"About half an hour."

"I'm sorry I wasn't here when you got back. I'd have come back sooner if I'd—"

"It doesn't matter. I saw your note. I knew you were out looking. I would have taken the car out to come and find you but I thought someone ought to be here, just in case."

Is he blaming me for leaving the house empty? Or is he sympathising with me, letting me know he understands my need to do something, even if that *something* is as pointless and stupid as looking beneath trees for clues? I don't dare say too much until I know how the land lies. It occurs to me that I've begun to be afraid of my husband.

He reaches out to me and I have to force myself not to flinch, but it's all right, he's only trying to take my hand so he can lead me to the chair he's pulled out for me, pushing me into the table as if I'm very small and young. I don't want to eat the sandwich but I can't help myself. My body is starving and exhausted and it needs fuel. My hand reaches out for the sandwich before I can stop myself. I'm scratched and dirty from all the rummaging I've done, but even the grey smudges that come off my skin and stain the pristine whiteness of the bread don't stop me. Sitting opposite each other, not speaking, not looking at each other, John and I devour our meal in hungry silence, slurping down sweet milky tea like animals at a trough.

"I needed that," I admit when my plate is clean. I have to remind myself not to lick at the slick of grease left on my plate.

"Me too." John reaches across the table and takes my hand. "I know it seems awful to be eating when Joel's... when—" his voice cracks and he has to swallow hard several times. "But if we're going to get through this, we need to look after each other." His fingers stroke mine. "We need to stick together. Don't we?"

My stomach clenches around its hastily swallowed contents. I look down at the table. The meaning of the sandwich, the mug of tea, the solicitude, suddenly becomes clear. It's a bribe.

"You were a while with the police," I say. I want to sound casual, but John knows me far too well for me to get away with it.

"They think I might have killed him," he says. John has no time for prevarication. He likes to have everything out in the open, very clean and precise. His touching honesty was one of the first things I loved about him. *I think you're lovely. I'd like to see you again. I think I'm falling in love with you. I love you. I want to marry you.*

"Oh, John, no! No, I'm sure that's not true, they can't possibly think—"

"Of course they do. That's their job. Assume nothing, believe no one, check everything. That's how they work. And right now they're checking whether I killed our son."

I can't think of a thing to say.

"There's this five-hour window," John continues. "That's what they call it. A five-hour window. I left the hospital at twenty past three. They know that because people saw me leave. I got home at half past eight. They know that because you saw me arrive. So there's these five hours I can't account for."

"But you must know what you were doing."

"Of course I—" he takes a breath, forces his voice to soften. "Of course I know what I was doing. I was driving around. Trying to unwind. I had three patients die on me. Three. I mean, I know why they died. But I was feeling bad. Really, really bad. And I was worried about Joel. So I bailed on a couple of meetings and left early and just... drove around. They know all of that, they could see where I'd been from my phone."

The process of enquiry is mysterious to me, but I know how this part works. My own phone showed me going for lunch with Melanie, coming home and staying there. Of course they don't rely on your phone (assume nothing, believe no one, check everything). I still remember them hammering away at the possibility that I left my phone behind and went out anyway. It's only thanks to my neighbour – my guardian angel – finally breaking his silence, saving me with that single mysterious message that I seem to have been taken off the list of people who might have hurt Joel. John is still speaking. I force myself to listen.

"And that's what they've been talking to you about?"

"Yes. Again. They keep going over and over the same ground, it's like torture. It must be a technique they teach them. Keep asking the same questions until you're about ready to die of boredom, and then slip in the one new thing they actually wanted to know so you're off guard."

I want to ask what the *new thing* was this time, but I don't dare.

"So where did you go that afternoon?" I ask, because I have to say something and I can't think of anything else to say.

"I went all over the city. Places where we've been happy mostly."

Back to places where Joel might have run to.

"But if you were driving the whole time, surely there's no way you could have—"

"But I wasn't. I parked up quite a few times. Got out. Went for a walk. Three or four times. Quiet spots they were, too, because those were the kind of spots Joel used to like—" He laughs. "I mean, if I was a police officer, I'd be taking a close look at me. You can't blame them for checking."

There's only one thing I want to say. Just one question that I want to ask. And I can't possibly ask it.

"Maybe you should have a solicitor with you. Are you allowed a solicitor?"

"Yes, of course I am, but I'm putting it off for as long as I can. The minute I get a solicitor involved they'll just be even more convinced I've got something to hide."

"They don't think you actually did it. They can't. They must know you would never—"

"They haven't arrested me yet, but that's not the same thing as thinking I haven't done it. They keep telling me I'm not a suspect. I don't know why because everything else they're saying and doing makes it bloody clear that I am."

"But you can't be a suspect, because Joel's not dead." This is the most important thing, the one thing no one must lose sight of. "He's just missing, they need to find him, they have to keep looking—"

"Susannah. Joel's been gone for a month now. There's no sign of him anywhere. He's not with his friends. He's not in a homeless shelter. He's not turned up on CCTV anywhere that they can find. He hasn't used his phone for anything, nothing at all, and the battery's long since run flat. I don't want this to be true, I'd give anything for it not to be true, but we've got to start getting ready for—"

"He's not dead. I'd know if he was dead. I'd know it. They can't stop looking!"

"They are still looking!" A flash of anger now and I flinch. John was often angry with Joel, but hardly ever with me. "Of course they're still bloody looking. But I think they're looking for his body now."

If I speak or move or breathe or do anything other than sit very still and quiet at this table, the world will crack in two.

"Anyway. The next time they ask to talk to me, I'm going to have to bite the bullet and take a solicitor in with me."

"But you said yourself that just makes it look like you might have—"

"I know, but this is starting to frighten me now. I have to get legal advice, it's gone on too long now. I need to protect myself."

We used to be so close it felt as if we were one person, but now we are splitting apart. Now I am me and John is John, and John requires protection, even though I myself do not. Perhaps I'm one of the people he must protect himself against.

"But what about the phone call? The phone call to the phone? The pay-as-you-go one? Surely that means there's someone else involved? They have to concentrate on finding the person who Joel called, they must know that's way more likely to be what happened than you... than you—"

"Oh, come on. You know who uses pay-as-you-go phones like that? Drug dealers. Joel might have gone off and bought drugs, but that doesn't mean I didn't... I mean, my God, if I found out about it somehow, it might even give me a reason to -" He hears the words he's saying and stops himself. "I'm just trying to think the way they think, okay? Maybe they think I found him getting high and I was so angry with him I—"

We used to be able to finish our sentences. We used to be able to look at each other.

"I just need you to know that I didn't," he says. "Okay? The next time they call me in I'm taking a solicitor with me, but that doesn't mean I've got anything to hide. I don't. I didn't do anything. I absolutely did not. I would never, ever, ever hurt our son." He waits for a moment. I think he must be waiting for me to speak. "You do believe me, don't you? You do know I wouldn't ever—?"

This is where I am supposed to say, *No, I know you wouldn't ever do that.* I am supposed to lean across the table and take his hand in mine. Perhaps I was even supposed to interrupt him before he even finished speaking. I wish I was with Nick instead, so I could look into his eyes and ask him the question I cannot ask my husband and see the truth in his eyes when he looks at me. I can be honest with Nick. But is Nick always honest with me?

"No," I say. "I know you wouldn't ever do that." I reach across the table and take his hand in mine.

We sit in the twilight of the dining room and hold hands and look at each other across the empty mugs, the empty plates.

Chapter Nineteen
Thursday 14th December 2017

Even the most desolate place can be transformed by the bright kiss of Christmas lights, and tonight my home town has made itself glorious. When I climb down from the bus and cross the plate-glass bustle of the station, I find its familiar concourse turned strange and lovely. Warm yellow lights twine around doorways and lamp posts, bright tinsel clings like ivy to the shopfronts and wraps around the bronze neck of the poet who strides, coat blowing, towards the trains. A clutch of chilly teenagers in thin coats and fingerless gloves – violins and violas and cellos, a sprinkling of wind and brass, and a single percussionist fluttering between drums and bells – are diligently playing carols beneath the green-black bloom of the naked Christmas fir tree.

Why is the tree bereft of its coat of lights and colour? Perhaps the money ran out. Or perhaps someone simply looked at the tree and thought, *Yes, that's all we need. What more do we need to remind us that even at the heart of winter, there is life?* I like the darkness of the tree as it towers over the children beneath it. I like the bleakness and the menace. I rummage in my pocket and drop a handful of coins into the open violin case that waits, hungry and innocent, on the outer edge of the music. I wonder where the teacher is. Surely they can't be here without an adult? The players look cold but intent, as if this is a duty they've imposed on themselves.

For a moment I'm watching Joel standing in the church, his face golden with candlelight, submerged in the ecstasy of self-forgetfulness. All the little faces of the children, so peachy and perfect, and three spaces from the end in the second row, my own little child, the anxiety smoothed from his face as he sang 'Once In Royal David's City' at the school carol concert. *I love singing in the choir*, he confided to me at bedtime, *because I can be as loud as I want and no one can really hear that it's me.* In the New Year John will accidentally steal all Joel's pleasure, by suggesting he might enjoy having private singing lessons, that he might even get good enough to be picked for a solo. But that's in the future. Right now, my son is singing and John and I sit misty-eyed beneath the Gothic curve of the church roof, holding hands. Tomorrow it will be time to light the candles in Joel's little cake and hold hands and exclaim, *Do you remember? Do you? Do you...?* But right now, we're happy.

I should be used to the sharp sting of memory by now, one cold hand caressing my face while the other drives the icicle through my heart, but there are some pains you never grow used to. I let the moment take me instead, tears gathering on my cheeks as I stand before the red-nosed, watery-eyed children, and listen to the music. Anyone watching will simply think I'm sentimental. Although probably no one's watching at all.

When the carol finishes, I smile and drop more coins into the violin case. I've come to town to be generous, after all. Jackie is lost to me, but I managed without her before and I'll manage again. It's time to pick up the threads of my own life, my real life, where my sister and her children will surely welcome me in for our usual bittersweet Christmas celebration.

True to her word, Melanie hasn't contacted me. Her impossible threat of medical care and psychological probing hangs between us like an iron sword. But today I will fill my arms with gifts and glitter and slip past the sword's sharp edges, winning my way to paradise like the heroine of a fairy tale. Grace's sweet muffin face will beam with delight, and she'll leap to her feet and clap her hands, wriggling like a puppy, calling out to me, *Auntie Susannah, Auntie Susannah!* And Thomas, shyer and gruffer, will nonetheless creep up behind me, slide his arms around my waist and squeeze tight, his head butting against my shoulder blades, his breath warm. I can win all of this for myself if I can only find the right gifts. Surely, somewhere in this multitude of booths, I'll find what I'm looking for. I leave the station and make my way to the frail glass artifice of the shopping centre next door.

Each shop briefly conjures paradise, with lights and bustle and music that sings of untold wonders within. I plunge eagerly through the doors, bewitched by flashes of colour and enticing shapes that are somehow never quite what I'm looking for. Something with pink and sparkle that instantly makes me think of Grace resolves itself into a cheap make-up set, tiny pots of lip-gloss sparsely scattered in a flimsy plastic casing. A fat paperback with dragons rampaging across the cover makes my heart beat faster, convinced I've found the perfect new world for Thomas to lose himself in; but when I look properly, it's only a notebook.

I scurry in and out of shops, endlessly dazzled by treasures that crumble when I look at them too closely. I sidle cautiously up to something that looks like a blush-pink angora jumper, willing it not to dissolve into acrylic, and reach out a hand towards it. From across the store, a shop assistant catches my eye and I wince, praying I don't look like a shoplifter, but she smiles and nods encouragingly, as if this is the proper way to approach the goods. *That's right*, she mouths to me, so clearly I can almost hear the words in my head. *Don't frighten them*. The wool beneath my fingers is so soft it's like petting something alive. Perhaps I should shop only from the corners of my eyes. For a moment I think I see Nick, but when I look it's only a security guard, reaching gallantly out to catch a hat and scarf set I've knocked to the floor as I fumble among a rainbow of knitwear.

"That's the way," he says to me, and as long as I'm not looking at him his voice is Nick's voice, and for a moment our hands touch and I let myself imagine that his fingers are Nick's fingers, and I think I might melt with desire right here in the shop. "Nice and slow. Take it easy."

"I'll be careful," I promise.

"I can help you if you'll let me. You know I want to help you, don't you?"

Is this an appropriate conversation for a security guard to be having with a customer? Perhaps my smile, warmed by my memories of Nick, invited more intimacy than I intended. Or perhaps I'm hearing things. The hat and scarf set is all wrong for what I wanted, the wrong shade of grey to suit Richard, the wrong sort of gloves, the wrong texture, everything all wrong, and for a moment the music comes to a stop and everyone in the shop turns to stare at me, their eyes black and accusing, their fingers ready to point and blame; but then a delicious scent of aftershave drifts across my path, spicy and musky and maddeningly sophisticated, and I'm drawn like a wolf scenting prey, and the music is light and beautiful once more, and the wrong hat and scarf are forgotten.

I wander dazedly from table to table, and then from shop to shop, so entranced that I barely notice the shock of the cold that greets me when I slip through the tall glass doors to the street outside. Above my head, the cool white stars on the lamp posts slip their moorings and dance a wild secret dance against the sky, unseen by the hordes of shopper who hurry, intent and eager, below. Perhaps I'm the only person in the whole world who can see what's happening above our heads. I want to stop and stare, but I know that if I do, the illusion will disappear. I can't be too greedy. I need to be satisfied with mere sips of wonder. On the war memorial, the men have laid down their arms and stand with their arms around each others' shoulders, drinking in turn from a stone cup that passes from hand to hand. The traffic lights halt the stream of vehicles so we can pour across the road like water.

How beautiful my city is, at this hour and in this season and in this perfect violet half-light. *It's so grey and ugly*, visitors love to tell us, staring at us in triumphant accusation, as if our grandparents and great-grandparents chose the nights of bright fires and wailing sirens and the cold refinement of the radio announcer's voice declaring that *Further air raids were carried out on a north-east town*. But today, there's no ugliness, only the beautiful contrast of our city's concrete scars, nestled close to their surviving Victorian gems. My heart, frail and frozen as it is, lifts at the sight. I reach out and caress the yellow bricks of the wall, imagining I feel it heave a sigh of satisfaction at my touch.

Then someone tugs gently on my sleeve, and in the moment before I turn my face fully towards her and see her face resolve into the kind plain ordinariness of an older woman wrapped in layers of fleece and wool, I see the wise tricksy face of the fortune-teller.

"That young lad," she says. "Over there, look. He wants to talk to you."

"What? What young lad?"

"He knows you. Look."

I follow her pointing finger. My breath catches in my throat. He's only there for a second, but he's unmistakeable, his appearance validated by someone who can have no way of knowing what this means, who she's just pointed out to me. Joel's gaze meets mine, briefly, shyly. And then, before I can spoil it by staring too long, he's gone, slipping through the doors of the bookshop.

My impulse is to tear through the crowd like a savage, bludgeoning people out of my way, but I've learned better by now. I need to be slow and careful, not look too closely. I let the tide of people carry me, wandering slowly in through the doorway and pausing by the table that waits, strewn with blues and greens and enticing gold swirls, to lure me into a purchase. I know where Joel will be, but I won't frighten him by coming too close too quickly. Instead I flit discreetly from section to section, navigating Christmas Bestsellers, Staff Recommendations, Christmas Gifts for Young Adults, Christmas Gifts for Children, mounting the stairs and drifting past book bags and bunting, through Local History, Travel and Mind Body Spirit. Each shelf cries out to me in longing, begging me to moor up for a while and browse their wares, but I resist the urge. I need to stay firm and safe in this world, not get lost in another.

The Horror section's empty. For a moment, I waver. I was so sure I'd find him here. But no, there he is, disappearing around the corner and towards the stairs. He's restless, shy, afraid of being caught. But if I give him time, he'll let me catch him. I'm careful to keep several people between us as I follow him.

"Susannah." Nick is with me again, this time in the form of a man in a thick puffy crimson jacket. "Be careful."

I'm being careful, I think, half resentful at the implication that I might not know how to approach my own son. But there's no time to stop and talk, because Joel's already through the door and turning left, and I have to follow him.

Above the orange glow of the sodium lights, the violet sky has turned ultramarine and the breeze is trying to flay the flesh from my bones. I don't care, I have all I need to keep me warm. Joel's walking more slowly now, pausing often to look in shop windows, and I begin to close the gap, holding my breath in case I frighten him away. If he shows any sign of flight, I'll drop back again. But instead, he turns his head and for a breathtaking moment we make eye contact and he sees me, he *sees* me, and then he smiles, as if this is all he has ever wanted, and although the next minute he's moving again, I know we're on the same side, that this is simply him feeling his way back into my company again. I've waited more than five years. I can wait a little longer.

Where are we going? Ahead of us, three huge blue glass

ships shimmer in the stylised waves that float on the curve of concrete above the old Co-op building. Perhaps this is a clue to where Joel has been. Signing on with a boat and letting the ocean take him wherever it will. Is this still possible in an age of passports and paperwork? The boats rock treacherously in their blue glass ocean, and I wonder if he was ever seasick. I hope not. I can't bear to think of him alone and cold, with no kind hand to soothe him as his stomach roiled and turned. Perhaps he hid inside a lifeboat and never came to shore.

On we walk, past cheap brick buildings thrown hastily up in the aftermath of victory, and into the small part left untouched by the Luftwaffe; the art gallery, the city hall, the strange curved triangle of the old dock offices that houses the Maritime Museum. In the centre, a dead queen stands frowningly on a pedestal and stares out towards the water. I'm glad her back is towards me, this woman who birthed and raised nine children while simultaneously heading an empire. I can't imagine she'd approve of me.

Where is Joel leading me? When he was small he loved to lose himself among the small connecting rooms of the museum, hurrying past the snarling polar bear and the mannequins standing in the Inuit canoe to stand tranced and blissful amongst the wails and whistles of the room filled with whale bones. But it's late and the doors are locked. We must be going somewhere else instead.

And sure enough, there he goes, the hood of his coat fluttering as he hurries down the side of the museum towards Queen's Gardens. I hurry eagerly after him, so eagerly that I almost step out in front of a tall red bus, crammed with Christmas shoppers, tilting precariously around the curve of the road that half encircles the Rose Bowl Fountain. A man grabs my arm and pulls me gently back, shaking his head indulgently. The bus half halts, then sets off again. From behind the steamed windows, I hear the strains of perfectly harmonised carols. How beautiful. The passengers are singing as they ride.

"Susannah." It's Nick again, or rather Nick's voice, whispering to me in the private places inside my head. "Please be careful. Don't go any further. Stay with me."

"I'm fine, I can cross the road by myself." Did I speak out loud or only to myself? I can't be sure. This isn't good. I need to concentrate or I'll lose myself as well as Joel. Has he gone already? No. He's sitting on the edge of the fountain's wide stone bowl, and now as our eyes meet once more he smiles, that small shy heartbreaking smile that creeps out at me from beneath his lowered eyelids, and he holds out a hand towards me, beckoning me closer.

Before I can cross, another bus comes, tearing along so fast I think it will surely tip over as it rounds the curve. The breeze of its passage tugs at my clothes and tries to pull me off the curb, which seems suddenly like the edge of a precipice. What is the driver thinking? The passengers must be terrified.

Joel has taken off his trainers and rolled up his jeans. For a moment he balances on the edge of the stone basin, rocking slightly for balance. Then with a light little leap he's in the water, laughing and holding his hands out to catch the spot-lit spray that tumbles from the raised central bowl. He looks so happy, so happy and so free, as if every worry he has ever had has been washed away. I want to join him. The buses keep coming, one after another after another, but I'm determined. I watch my moment, waiting and waiting, counting seconds and fractions of seconds in my head, estimating just how small a gap I can cram myself through. Finally I thrust myself recklessly into the dark dieselly space between two buses, ignoring the screech of brakes and the horrified cries of warning, and then for a moment I'm stranded in a patch of tarmac between two walls of traffic. Then I find another too-small gap to hurl myself into, and I'm on the other side of the road, and nothing but a few yards of sandstone pavement lies between me and my son.

He's still dancing in the water, chuckling to himself as the spray wets his hair. For a moment I wonder how he can bear its chill against his tender skin. But as I get closer to the fountain, the air grows warmer, as if the water is lit by the hot summer sun and not simply a floodlight installed deep within the stonework. I want to be in the water with Joel, dancing by his side. Later can come the questions and the explanations, the long slow unravelling of the mystery of these last years, but now all I want is to get into the fountain, and bask in the warmth of Joel. Does he understand this? Of course he does. He's happy, nodding encouragingly as I tug at the zippers of my boots. *I'm so sorry*, he mouths. *I love you, Mum. It's just so beautiful.*

So long since I could hold my son. So long since I could stroke his face. I put my hand on the edge of the stone basin. His hand comes towards mine.

"Susannah. Please don't. Please. Please listen to me. You don't have to do this."

Someone else's hand on me now. Someone else's breath warming my cheek. I want to push them away but I can't, because it's Nick. Nick, who rescued me. Nick, who brought me back to life with the touch of his skin. Nick, who wants to be my hero. But why would I need a hero now?

"That's it. Please look at me. Look at me. Please. So I know you're listening to me. Please look at me."

I shake my head stubbornly. If I turn away from Joel, will I ever see him again? He's stopped dancing in the water and is watching me reproachfully. He's disappointed.

"I have to go. Let me go."

"No. Please. Stay with me. Please. Just a little bit longer. Just look at me for a minute."

"But I can see Joel. If I look away he'll disappear again—"

"Susannah, there's no one there. You're staring at empty water. Please listen to me. Let me get you back to safety and we can talk. Please, love. Don't leave me like this."

It's the word *love* that does it, the slippage from professional coaxing to raw need that calls me back towards him, this man who I do not love, who does not love me, but who has held me while I wept, and shared my bed, and risked everything he has to do so. I sigh, and turn to look at him. He's startlingly close to me, his mouth near enough to kiss, and his face so hungry with longing that for a second I think I might do just that. But it's so cold suddenly, so cold, and my muscles are cramped and painful and my hand is clutched tight around something that I know instinctively I mustn't let go of. I can still hear water, but instead of the delicate golden plash of the fountain it's the drag and suck of the thick cold river, and where the hell am I? How did I get here? And what is Nick doing beside me? I whimper in confusion, and try not to panic.

"It's all right." Nick's trying to sound calm but I can hear the fear in his voice. "Keep still. Don't worry. I'm going to get you out of here."

"But where am I, what's happened, where are we? How did I get here?"

"You're on Drypool Bridge. It's all right. You were walking up and down the bridge, what they call *acting strangely*. Then when we all turned up you climbed over the parapet. You've been here for about an hour now."

I risk a brief dizzying glance upwards at cold ironwork, blue with paint and glinting with frost. The river terrifies me, I've never liked the way it looks. I can't have climbed over here to get closer to it. There must be a mistake.

"And... did you... how are you—"

"Don't worry, it's all right, I promise. We're going to get you out of here safely, but we're going to have to go really, really slowly. All right?"

"I can't move. I can't. I'll fall."

"You can move and you won't fall. But don't do anything yet."

"I can't even move my hand. My fingers are stuck. I'm stuck. My legs hurt."

"That's just the cramp, because you've been still for so long. I know it hurts but just try to bear it a few minutes longer. All right? They're going to send down some clips and a harness so we can get you up safely. Just sit tight a few minutes longer. No need to move, no need to do anything at all, just keep on being brave for a little while longer while I make you safe again. Can you do that for me, love?"

He's eerily good at this. Is this something they learn in training? Or has he had to do this for Bella, in the deepest days of her madness? All I know is that despite everything, despite the freezing iron, the shivering in my flesh, the proximity of the water, I feel safe and protected. Nick is here and he is going to look after me and somehow, I will be all right. If I close my eyes, will I see the fountain again? Will I see Joel's spectre, enticing me into the cold waters below? I don't dare to look.

"I don't know how I got here," I whimper. "I can't remember how I got here. I think I must have been dreaming."

"It's all right." His hand creeps across the ironwork to mine. "I'm here. I'll look after you."

And then there's a slow confusion of lights and voices and ropes and somehow, somehow I am persuaded to let go my frozen grip of the ironwork and I'm lifted into space and onto the tarmac, and there's an ambulance and some nice people in green uniforms and a blanket and some talk of assessment and I start to panic because I don't want to be taken to hospital, I just have to hold on another few days and Joel will come back to me. But then Nick is talking, explaining my history and the time of year and that I'm already getting help and he'll make sure I get home safely and that there's someone with me and that my doctor's called in the morning, and thank the Lord for the overstretched NHS, God bless the shortage of staff and the shortage of mental health beds, they're going to let me go, they're going to let me go, they're actually going to let me go. I'm bundled tenderly into Nick's car and the chaos is all shut away behind the door of the car and we're moving smoothly through the streets, and there's music in the background to cover the silence and my mind contains only small physical truths: that my legs are stiff, that my entire body is cold and cramped, that the seat I sit in is soft and comforting, that Nick's profile against the window is beautiful and his aftershave smells delicious.

"I'm so sorry," I say when we're clear of the city centre and cruising out towards the suburbs.

His smile is quick and generous. "Don't be."

"I don't even know how I got there, I didn't mean to... I mean, I wasn't trying to, you know, do anything stupid—"

"Hey." He takes his hand off the gearstick and rests it gently, shyly on my wrist for a moment. "There's nowhere else I'd rather be, nothing else I'd rather do, than come and help you when you need me. Okay? That's what I want to do more than anything else in the world."

The warmth of his car is so comforting that I find myself dozing. In the dream, Nick parks his car outside my house and comes round to open the passenger door for me, guiding me out with his hands and arms as if I'm very drunk or very old or very ill. The front door's locked and for a minute I panic, but then I reach into my coat pocket and there are my keys, as if I've conjured them simply by wishing. We go in through the front door and Nick tells me to sit quietly while he goes and runs a bath so I can warm up. Sitting on the sofa, waiting like a child for Nick to come and take me on to the next thing that will happen, it comes to me that this isn't a dream; I'm simply so tired and confused that it feels like one. When he undresses me in the bedroom, he touches me only as much as he absolutely has to in order to remove my clothing. I'd forgotten there could be such reverence in the world. As I sink blissfully into the bathtub, he soaks a sponge and gently washes my shoulders.

"Would you like to get in with me?" The warm water trickling across my skin makes me think of his fingers, the butterfly brush of his skin against mine, as if I'm infinitely fragile and might shatter in his hands if handled too roughly. "I can make room."

"I'd love to. But I won't." He reaches for the luxurious

shower crème Melanie bought for me last Christmas, untouched in its beautiful bottle. In all the nights that have passed since, I have never had an occasion worthy of its unbottling. Its scent is complex and seductive, enough to make us both swoon. "This is all for you."

And that's how it goes, this slow dreamy gentle encounter between a woman who is surely half mad and a man who must have lost sight of all reason, risking everything he has simply to be here, with me, washing my back in a candlelit bathroom. From what hidden place in my home has he conjured the gigantic softness of the towel that wraps around me like fleece around a shorn lamb? Where did he learn to brush the knots from my hair, beginning with the ends and working his way up to the roots, until my whole scalp's alive with pleasure and my skin tingles with longing and all I can think is how much I want him to stroke and smooth me all over? When he takes the towel from me and lies beside me on the bed, his clothes shed like water, the slow smooth surety of his touch is enough to drive me into a frenzy. But instead I wait, disciplining myself to be as still and quiet and careful as he is, letting the moment unfold like the dark petals of a flower. I nearly died tonight. If it brings me an hour like this, almost-death may be a price worth paying.

It's only afterwards, when Nick sprawls against the pillow, his hand resting gently against my hip, both of us drenched in a clean fresh sweat that dries quickly in the warm air, that it comes to me how strange it is, that Nick should be aroused to such reckless passion by me, that he should risk his whole life for me, as damaged and as ordinary as I am. After a while, it comes to me that perhaps this is the secret. Perhaps it's the damage that's been done to me, and all the possibilities of rescue it implies, that makes me so irresistible to Nick. I lie beside my lover and think of Bella, my twin sister and my rival, and I wonder if Nick has some kind of fetish that draws him into the lives of broken women, and if perhaps the more broken I become, the more Nick will like me.

Life Without Hope:
Moving On When You Can't Move On

Here's something I've learned about moving on: in a lot of ways, I can't. I won't ever be able to stop wanting things to be the way they were *before*, when Joel was still with me and my life was happy. That's never going to stop.

And so for a long time, I didn't dare to move on from that moment when I realised he was missing. Not in big ways, not in small ways. I didn't dare stop buying thick-sliced white bread or full-fat milk every week, even though the only person in the house who ate and drank them wasn't there any more. I kept his toothbrush in the mug by the sink. I kept all his clothes. I didn't dare move anything around in the house. When the kettle broke and I had to buy a new one, I cried because I couldn't find one the same as the one I was replacing.

And I didn't dare do anything for myself. If I thought it might help me, I didn't do it. Didn't take the tablets the doctor gave me. Only sat down when my legs gave way. Only ate when I was almost fainting with hunger. Only slept when I couldn't fight it any longer. Never bought anything that was just for me. Because if I started looking after myself in even the smallest way, that would mean accepting that this was how it was from now on, and I was going to make a new life without Joel in it.

That's the hardest bit. The very hardest bit. And I'll be honest, living like this nearly killed me.

Here's how I finally learned to accept that I needed to care for myself. I remember when Joel was a baby, and how everyone would tell me, *Remember, you can't look after your baby if you don't look after yourself.* (Of course I did a rotten job at actually doing this, the same way all parents do, and I ended up on my knees with exhaustion and stir-crazy from spending too long shut up in the house with a baby, but thanks to all the nagging and advice, I did a slightly less rotten job than I would have done if no one had said it to me.) And gradually, I came to understand that if I was going to have the strength to last until Joel was found, I needed to look after myself.

So I started to do small things that were just for me. A hot crusty roll with my soup. A mug of fresh coffee. A walk in the sunshine.

And when the guilt strikes – when suddenly I'm trapped in that hamster wheel of *What am I doing, how dare I be happy when my son is still lost?* – I remind myself I'm not forgetting him. I'm looking after myself, so that I can be ready.

Because I do believe in my heart that one day, somehow, my lost boy will be found. And whether my task on that day is to welcome him home and start to rebuild our lives, or to say my final farewell (God it kills me just writing those words, but I know it's a possibility). I will need to be strong. I will need to be well. I will need to be ready.

Posted on 24th November 2013
Filed to: Coping With Missing Loved Ones
Tags: missing people, coping strategies, support for families,
Susannah Harper, Joel Harper

Chapter Twenty
Tuesday 19th December 2017

Two days until Midwinter will be here. The date sings in my blood, every cell in my body alive with memory. Two days until Midwinter. I should be getting ready to celebrate, I should be buying small gifts and perhaps one large one. Two days until. I should be making a cake and covering it with candles. Two days.

What can I do? I'm filled with purposeless energy. I wander from room to room as if I'm a hundred years old and lost in my own home, picking up belongings and putting them down again in places where they shouldn't be: my keys taken from the hook by the door and abandoned on the floor of the hallway, the clock from the mantelpiece balanced carefully on the side of the bath, a pair of shoes displayed like ornaments on the windowsill. What can I do?

Lonely for light and colour, I turn on the television, but the dramas and intrigues of the people who live behind the glass screen are too complex to focus on. The news, then. Surely I must be able to follow the news, with its simple three-minute storylines and careful presentation of the facts. I turn over and find myself staring at a slowly panning shot of a small house in a row of other small houses, maddeningly familiar although I can't remember how or why I might know it.

It takes me a moment to process what I'm seeing, to make

sense of the faces that loom out at me. My friend Jackie, her husband, Lee, my lover, Nick. What are they doing on the television? The answer comes in a blink of darkness, my hand reaching for the remote control in denial of what I know to be the truth: that my friend killed her own son. Nick must have arrested her this morning. Does he feel like a hero now?

I'm cold; cold despite the relentless dry heat that beats out from the walls. The thermostat is set at twenty-five degrees. I'll have to turn it down soon, or else shiver through a penurious January. In the kitchen, I find my gloves arranged neatly on the cold cooker top. If I put the oven on to bake something that will add extra warmth. Perhaps I should bring cushions and blankets from my bedroom and retreat to the kitchen and live here for the winter. Why not? I would have heat and light, food and water. I could wash in the sink, create some sort of arrangement with buckets and holes. I could use my waste to fertilise my garden while it slept, and wake up in the spring to a profusion of daffodils. The image hovers tantalisingly in my head, but I can't make myself believe in it. I will not live in my kitchen. I will not grow daffodils. There will never be another spring.

Now I'm back in the hallway, holding my gloves in one hand and my keys in the other. I have my coat on. I must be going somewhere. There must be something I need to do. Where could it be? Nick told me to be careful. Does this count as careful? Perhaps I'm going to see Jackie.

No. I'm not going to see Jackie. I'm not going to see Jackie ever again. Jackie is lost now. She's been lost for long weeks, for months perhaps, perhaps even for years. How long does it take for a parent to wander off the rough, straight, difficult path of *I will love and protect you no matter what*, into the darkness of the woods where no one will see or know the things you do to them? When did she first begin to hate Ryan and to wish him dead? And when did John first begin to...

This is it, the thought I've been patiently stalking through all the rooms and doorways of my house. I leap forward as if it's a physical thing, something I have to catch and hold and tear at. The movement is so huge that it takes me out through my front door, down the front path and into my car in a single seamless motion that feels like water flowing through a lock gate. Then it's gone again, slipping through my fingers and melting back into the dark. There was something I had to do. Somewhere I had to go. I was going somewhere.

I'm going somewhere. Am I going to John? I'm sure John was in it somehow. I put the car in gear, pull carefully away from the kerb. My thin ancient neighbour, watching from his front window, raises his hand like a benediction. He sees everything that happens in this quiet stretch of street. He must have seen Nick come to me, seen him hurry up the path with the special eagerness of a man coming to the woman he craves. Does he judge me? I like to think that he does not.

John's new house in its quiet suburban cul-de-sac is as discreet and secret as a lunatic asylum, tall and solid behind its high privet hedge and the prima-donna magnolia tree, dancing solo in the front garden. Two days before Midwinter, the tree should be a bare skeleton, but John and Nathalie have festooned it with cold white lights that blink and shimmer in the silence. They look elegant but unwelcoming. Christmas should be red and green, spilled blood and returning fertility, not this deathly celebration of the freezing sterile whiteness that's swallowing the world. I park in the curve of the cul-de-sac, the back of my car half across next door's drive (he won't like it and if he sees me will come out to complain, but the driveway is long and I know that if I watch my rear-view mirror for the flicker of his front door opening, I'll have time to start the engine and leave before he can reach me). I sit with my hands in my lap and make myself still and small, and I wait and I watch and I hope.

The front of the house sleeps in darkness. They must be in the cosy back sitting room, where a profusion of throws smother the sofas and their daughter can tumble and snuggle and suck her thumb in peace. Perhaps she's asleep there. Perhaps John and Nathalie are smiling at each other over their daughter's head. Perhaps their hands reach out to each other beneath the once-fashionable pelt of imitation wolfskin; perhaps they share a stealthy lingering kiss, a promise of further warmth to come when Emily's curled like a snail beneath her sugar-pink duvet and the night is all theirs. Midwinter is the best time to conceive new human life. The thought comes to me again that there was something I had to...

Behind the brilliant glowing branches of the barren magnolia, the front room blooms into life. I can see Nathalie, her bobbed brown hair heavy around her rosy face as she takes a moment to gaze out at the lights. The curtains are flowery and chintzy and cheerful, an incongruous country-cottage choice in this stern faux-Victorian suburb; nothing I would have ever chosen. Did John marry Nathalie because she is so unlike me to look at? Did he breathe a sigh of relief when their first child was a daughter? And will he ever dare to roll that particular set of dice again, and risk the Fates presenting him, once more, with a son?

Does she know I'm watching her?

I could sit here for hours, gorging myself on secret knowledge, but I know I won't be able to. When Nathalie comes to draw the curtains, she looks out for a few moments, perhaps thirty seconds at the most. She has a small child in the house. Her time is in demand. Remembering how that felt – to be needed so much and so endlessly – makes me ache with envy.

Dreaming in her window, Nathalie suddenly grows still, drawing up and into herself, peering suspiciously out into the dark. The bonnet of my car must be poking out. I hastily start the engine and reverse out of sight, trespassing onto her neighbour's drive so I can turn the car around and drive around the vast clump of trees and make my escape in their shadow. Nathalie might suspect I've been here again, but she won't know, not for sure, and as long as she's not sure she won't give me away. There will be no phone call from John tomorrow morning, heavy with casual enquiry, checking to see if I'm all right. The night is still mine. I'm still free. Where shall I go?

"Please. This isn't appropriate. You can't do this."

"This is important to me."

"Yes, I can see that."

"I've come here for your help, that's all. I need you to help me. That's all I want. Please, won't you do that for me? I'll pay. You know I'll pay."

James O'Brien's black shirt is silky and smooth beneath the mulberry velvet jacket with the black lapels. Above the shirt, his face is a little pale, a little sweaty, his hair lank and slightly oily. I must have caught him at a bad time. Like me, he's beginning to unravel a little. But that doesn't matter. We don't need to look good to do what we need to do. The tip of his tongue darts out, then disappears.

"Okay, so how about if we go into my drawing room and I make you a drink? Something to warm you up, it's a cold night. Some coffee maybe? Or brandy, I have brandy. Would you like some brandy?" His long pale hand rests tentatively on my forearm for a moment. I try not to shiver as he touches me, but I can't quite suppress it, and he lets his hand fall again.

"No. No, thank you. No brandy. I just want to go straight to the... to the... um... the reading."

"Mrs Harper, I can see you really need help. It's just I wasn't expecting you. If you could come back to see me when I've had time to prepare? Shall I go and get my diary? And we can look through it together and find a good time?"

"I know this isn't how you like to work, but if I can just make you understand how important this is —"

"I promise, I really do understand. I absolutely do. I know how difficult this time of year is for you." He pauses for a moment in the way I've come to associate with an imminent revelation. "It was Midwinter, wasn't it? The day you became a mother."

"Yes. But it's not that."

"I'm sorry, I shouldn't have assumed—"

"My friend," I whisper, hating myself for the way my lip trembles. Hating myself because I forgot and called her *my friend*. "Jackie. The one who was with me the last time. She was arrested this morning. I saw it on the news."

"Oh my God." His pale face becomes even whiter, a sickly green sheen washing over him as if he is a fainting Victorian lady. I wish I had some smelling-salts. He's no good to me if he's not awake.

"So you see, I have to talk to you. I have to be sure. You said, one by their mother and one by their father."

"Susannah, please, I'm sorry for what I said. I should never have... I honestly don't know why I... I'll be honest, it frightened me, I don't even know where those words came from. I can give you guidance, but what I see isn't always reliable."

"But it was true. It came true. Jackie was arrested. And that means my husband – my ex-husband, I mean – John... I have to know what he did, I have to—"

"All right." He takes a deep breath, then gives me a brilliant, confident smile. "All right, I understand now. I do. I want to help you. Do you understand, Susannah? I want to help you. And I will."

"Oh, thank you, thank you—"

"The only thing is... the thing is, I've already got someone booked in for this evening. Someone in desperate need. She called me a few days ago. She's very, very distressed, she urgently needs my help. And she's not strong. Not like you. You're so strong, that's one of the first things I noticed about you, do you remember? Your strength. So maybe you could just find it in you to be strong once again. Come back tomorrow. We'll meet tomorrow. And we'll get to the bottom of this."

He's so convincing that I'm almost deceived. What it is that gives him away? The way his eyes hold mine for a fraction of a second too long, perhaps; the way his hair hangs a little limp and a little untidy, whereas I've only ever seen him immaculate and fresh. He's lying, but it's a polite lie. A butler lie. That's what John used to call it. *We'd love to, but we've already got something on with Susannah's sister and her husband. Really sorry I can't stay longer, I've got a meeting to get to. Mr O'Brien can't make that appointment with you today, he has someone else with him.* The correct thing to do is to accept what we're told, to hand in our card and retreat politely down the steps, understanding that our business will have to wait for another day.

"There isn't another client," I say. "You're lying to me. Aren't you?"

"Of course I'm not—"

"No, you are. I know you are. Please don't lie to me, please, I've always been honest with you."

"You're very perceptive."

"Thank you."

We stand, irresolute, in the hallway, and study each other carefully. I have no way of making him do what I want, no way at all. He doesn't want my friendship. He doesn't want my body. He doesn't even seem to want my money. All I can do is hope that he'll pity me enough to help me.

"Please," I repeat. I inch closer towards him, and just as he did to me before, I lay my hand on his arm. It's such a clumsy attempt to build rapport that I can't see how it can work. But to my amazement, when he moves away from me, he takes me towards the door that leads to the bare little room with its schoolroom table and the single lightbulb that hangs over it like an omen.

"So what do we do? Do we hold hands again?"

James and I sit as close as lovers over the table. I can see the faint grey-black pinpricks of stubble creeping into the outlines of his neat goatee beard, the lines at the corners of his eyes. I try not to mind that he in return will be able to see every pore, every wrinkle, every patch of dryness burned into my skin by the unforgiving cold. I must look like what I am, a shrivelled up woman whose life has turned to dust.

"Before we start, do you mind if I just leave you in here? Just for a minute?"

"Why?"

"I've got something I need to see to in the kitchen, I just need a minute and then I can give you my full attention, all right? If you'll just wait here, I'll get everything put to rights and then I'll be all yours. All right?"

The clock in the hallway said it's almost half past seven. His explanation is perfectly reasonable. So why am I hesitating?

"Susannah? Do you mind if I go to the kitchen and turn off the gas under the saucepans? Just so I can make sure the house doesn't burn down around us? And then I can help you. Just wait here and give me a couple of minutes and I'll go and turn off everything in the kitchen and then I can help you. Does that sound okay?"

He's very clever, very persuasive, but there's something not quite right about this. He wants to get away from me. He doesn't want me here. He's lying about the kitchen. There's nothing in danger of burning. He's planning an escape of some sort. Like John, who left me and ran away to find someone else to live with, another house to share with her, another child to raise. Everyone in my life runs away from me, one way or another.

"I think you're lying about the kitchen," I say. "I'm sorry, I know this sounds rude, but I do. You're lying, just like you were lying about the client. You're trying to make an excuse to get away from me. So no, you can't go to the kitchen, and you can't go to the toilet, and you can't get a glass of water for either of us. I need you to stay right here with me. Please," I add, remembering that I have no real power here, that he's younger than me and presumably stronger than me and I can't actually compel him to stay here.

"No, I promise I'm not—" he shakes his head. "Oh God, all right, all right, I'm sorry. Yes, you're right. I'm lying. Do you understand why?"

I look closely at his face.

"You're afraid," I say, wonderingly. "You're afraid. But why?"

"Yes. You're right. I'm afraid. I am very, very frightened, Susannah, and I don't know if I can work effectively when I'm frightened. I'm so sorry, I really am. I want to help you, I want to give you what you need, but I just don't think I can."

"I've got faith."

"To make the connection I have to open myself up, be completely ready for whatever might come. And I can't do that when I'm afraid. Fear is like a barrier, do you understand? It's a barrier in my mind and as long as it's there I can't let my guard down."

"Then don't try to make a connection. Don't try. Just tell me what you saw last time. Talk to me about that. Start with Jackie. Tell me about what she did, why she did it, and then maybe I can start to understand about—"

"I can't. I don't know anything about why she did it. I can only tell you what I saw. I'm so sorry. Please don't hurt me."

"What? Of course I won't hurt you, how could I? Just do your best." I try to take his hands but he won't have it. "Tell me what you saw about Joel. And… and John."

"Susannah, please, I want to help you, but I don't think I'm the right person. If you have suspicions about your husband—"

"Ex-husband." The words sound sharper than I intended.

"Of course, I'm so sorry. Ex-husband. Your ex-husband. But if you have suspicions about him, you need to talk to the police. They can help you far more than I can."

"They thought it was him. That's what they thought when Joel disappeared. They questioned him for hours, over and over. They couldn't find anything, he wouldn't say anything, so in the end they had to let him go. But they were right, weren't they? It was him all along."

"Susannah, do you understand that nothing I can tell you will help you with the police? They won't listen to evidence that comes from a psychic."

"That's a lie!" My hand slaps the table, so hard it makes us both jump. Why did I do that? I didn't mean to do that. "Everyone says you've worked with the police, that's what I heard, that's why I first came to you. They must listen sometimes." My hand stings and tingles. I have to stop myself from cradling it for comfort.

"Okay, sometimes I've worked with the police. *Occasionally*. And never officially. And only when they call me in. They have to come to me. I never go to them. Because ninety per cent of police officers – maybe even ninety-nine per cent – don't want to listen to me, you see? They think I'm a con artist. Maybe they're right. Maybe I can't really do it. I don't know. Sometimes I wonder myself."

"But you were right about Jackie, weren't you? You said she'd killed Ryan and she did."

"Please. I'm frightened. I'm frightened and I need you to let me go."

"I'm not making you sit here. You could leave this room right now if you wanted to. You're here because you want to help me. You're a good person, I know you are. And I need you. I can't find the truth on my own. I need you to help me. So help me. Talk to me about what you've seen."

"That first time. When you came with your husband. I could see how bad things had been for you, all three of you, even before Joel disappeared. There were arguments, weren't there? And drugs. Joel took drugs, didn't he? That first time I made contact, when he was so foggy and lost... he was high on something." His face is dreamy now, as if even the memory is enough to send him soaring. "It reminded him of his childhood and it was such a beautiful feeling. He was so serene. He wanted to stay like that for ever…"

"Yes. Yes. That's right. He was in trouble. He didn't sell them or anything, but he took them." Even now it hurts to admit this. I have to bite my lip hard to keep the tears inside. "I tried to stop him. I tried to help him."

"I know you did." His voice is very gentle. "You're a kind person. You wouldn't want him to be hurt. You wouldn't want anyone to be hurt. "

"Never mind about me. Keep going. Tell me what happened next. Tell me what else you saw."

"Susannah, you already know the truth. You see it sometimes, don't you? It hides in the shadows, but every now and then you see a glimpse."

"Keep talking. You said… what did you say? A boat. Water. The smell of mud coming off the river." Am I describing his visions or my own? It's all merging into one. I'm forgetting where the boundaries are.

"You don't need me to tell you! You know this! I can see it in your face. You've had visions… experiences…"

"How do you know about?" I shake my head. It doesn't matter. "Yes. That's what's been happening."

"You've been wondering if you've been imagining it all, haven't you? But you're not. This is a message. Something you need to know."

My throat is too dry for me to swallow. I clutch at the edge of the table. His eyes are wide and frightened.

"Please, Susannah, I'm so scared. Just tell me what you want. You want me to talk to you about what you've seen? Describe it to you? So you know you're not imagining it all?"

I nod.

"All right. You've seen—" he swallows. "You've seen what I've seen. Water. Mud. Drowning. Strong hands. Your husband, full of rage because of his son. You've heard Joel's voice calling out for you. Begging you to help. But you didn't hear him. You were far away…"

"Yes. Yes. All of that. What does it mean?"

292

"You know what it means. You've always known. You just don't want to see. Please, can we stop this now? Can't you let me go?"

"How did he do it? How did my husband kill our son? How? Tell me! Tell me!"

"Please. I'm so scared. Please make this stop. You can make it stop, Susannah, you're in control. It's your choice. Please let me go."

"I need you to help me. Tell me where I can find the proof of what he did."

"There isn't any proof." His eyes close and his head rolls a little, as if I've shaken him hard by the shoulders. "There isn't any proof. It was all lost. It drowned with him. It all drowned in the mud."

"Don't say that. I don't want it to be lost, maybe I did once but I don't any more. I'm ready to find out. I want to know the truth. I want to help Joel. I couldn't help him before but I can do this for him, I can prove what happened to him and make sure John pays for what he did. Just tell me what I can do! There must be a way to prove it, there must, there's always something left behind, always."

"Please. I've done all I can. Please be kind now and let me go. There's so much kindness in you, Susannah. So many terrible things have happened, but you can make it stop. Let the kindness win. Let me go."

"You keep saying that! How am I stopping you?"

He doesn't speak. He tries very hard to hold my gaze. But he can't prevent the brief flick of his eyes as he glances down at my right hand that rests on my lap beneath the table. In the cold pitiless light of the bulb in its paper-moon shade, I see that there's a knife there.

"What? That's not mine." But it is mine. It's the carving knife from the butcher's block in my kitchen. "It's not dangerous, I promise I'm not dangerous." But I'm clutching the knife so tightly my knuckles are white, and the point is towards his belly. "I wouldn't hurt you." But there's a smear of blood on the blade and his face is white and sweaty with pain. "I don't even remember bringing that in with me." But now I remember a brief scuffle at the doorway, a moment when he wanted to keep me out and I wanted to be let in, and somewhere in that scuffle I might have... just to make my point... just to make sure he really understood... just for a moment.

"Please." James's voice, the velvet turned harsh and raggedy now. Pleading for his life. "I know you're a good person. Terrible things have happened to you, you've lived through so much darkness, but you can choose to do the right thing. I won't say anything to the police, I promise, I swear. Not ever. This will all be between us, our secret, always. Just let me go and this can all be over."

"This won't ever be over." I push my chair back and stand up. My hand aches from gripping the knife so tightly for so long. I want to leave it behind, but I don't dare. I'm in enough trouble, James already has enough to take a decent shot at ruining me, but if I leave the knife behind, I'll surely be finished. "This is my life now. And it won't ever stop until I've made John pay for what he did to Joel."

When I get out of my car and stand in the pinky-orange glow of the street lamp outside my house, I find the north wind has blown down from the Arctic and hung every barren branch with a garland of frost. The moonlight blazes bright from the cloudless sky and catches the ice crystals as they dance in the air. The sight is so beautiful it hurts my heart.

I go upstairs. I undress. I put on a thin silky nightgown. Then I walk down to the apple tree. If I stand here long enough perhaps I will become a frost creature, dusted with the same fragile perfection that has turned all the dead things in my garden so beautiful. I would like to die like this, to become a woman of cold air and frozen water, and when someone reaches out a curious hand to touch me, I would like to melt away into nothingness beneath the warmth of their fingers. A woman made of air and water can have no past and no future, no will and no memories. A woman made of air and water could not hold a knife to a man's belly and compel him into prophecy. I want very much to become a woman of air and water. Perhaps if I stand here for long enough I will find a way to do it. In the breathless quiet that comes with profound cold and deep night, I hear the squeal of my front gate opening, and then a slow faint shuffle as someone creeps down the side of the house.

My neighbour, like me, is unsuitably dressed for the weather; his thin grey pyjamas inadequately shrouded beneath a heavy blue towelling dressing gown, his feet creeping along the path like snails in the thin shells of his slippers. He's holding a bottle of milk. I think perhaps he must be the last person I know who has their milk delivered. Where is he going? Has he finally slipped over the edge from eccentricity to frank dementia, and become one of the lost wandering souls who roam restlessly in search of long-vanished places and phantoms who slip from their grasp? Should I try to guide him back into his house?

He's coming towards me. Perhaps he's come seeking companionship. Perhaps the milk bottle is a way of starting a conversation, in which he might propose the sharing of a midnight cup of tea. Perhaps this will be the moment when he finally crosses my threshold.

His hand is brown and speckled, the veins thick and ropey. His voice is rusty from disuse.

"Too cold," he whispers to me, shaking his head. "Too cold. You'll freeze."

"I'm fine," I whisper back. What I mean is, *I don't mind dying*.

"No," he says. "Not yet. There's something you need to do."

Chapter Twenty-One
Sunday 21st December 1997

"Come and sit down." John's hands press on my shoulders, firm and kindly. "You're going to wear yourself out before we even start."

I sit down obediently beside him, then stand up again. John laughs and shakes his head.

"I just want to check my lipstick, that's all. Do I look all right?"

"Susannah. Love. You look beautiful. You always look beautiful. But nobody will care about your lipstick."

"Do you think I'm overdressed? Do I look too dressed up? I don't want them to think—"

"Stop worrying! They won't think anything, they won't be interested in what you're wearing, I promise." He stands behind me and puts his arms around my waist. "Apart from me. But I'm always interested. Hey, don't cry. What's the matter?"

"I'm so sorry we have to do this. I'm so sorry I couldn't have our baby for us."

"What are you talking about? Joel's going to be our baby, you know that."

"And you're sure you don't mind that I couldn't—?"

"First of all," John says firmly, "it wasn't *you* that couldn't, it was *us*. We're unexplained, remember? So it's just as likely to be me that couldn't."

"But—"

"And," John continues, "I am not disappointed. This is not second best. Okay? This isn't us being unlucky, this is us being lucky. We're going to meet our son in an hour, and that makes it the best day there'll ever be for either of us." He looks at me through the mirror. "Unless you're having doubts."

"No! God no, no doubts at all. Just seeing the photos was… oh my God, we're going to meet him, aren't we? This is really going to happen. We're really going to be parents."

"And it's Midwinter Day," says John. "He's our Midwinter gift. The Winter's child."

"Our child. Our Winter's child." I can hardly believe it's true. "Oh, John—"

He takes my hand and kisses it.

Before we leave the house, I stop to take a deep breath. Although he won't come home with us today, we are going to meet our son for the first time, so this is the last time in our lives when we will be just the two of us. I want to remember this moment for ever.

Joel's foster carer greets us at the door. She's older than me, dowdier, softer, her greying hair pulled carelessly back in a scrunchie, dressed in ancient jeans and a stripey top that would only look flattering on a taller, skinnier woman. Her face is tired. Her smile is bright. She looks like a mother. As far as this little boy-child knows, she is his mother, and I'm a raw idiot recruit, standing in my stupid clothes and my ludicrous shoes and pretending I can take the place of this magnificent battle-scarred warrior. I feel sick.

"Susannah? I'm Lynne." Her smile's warm and real. She is on my side. She's going to make me a mother. I can still hardly believe it. To my shame, I burst into tears. Lynne laughs and pats my arm.

"It's all right, it's an emotional day. Come on in and meet

him. He's unsettled at the moment."

"Will we be able to hold him?" John's question startles me. I'd almost forgotten he was there.

"Of course you will. Come on in and meet him."

As soon as we get into the house, I hear it: the high piercing shriek that stabs at your ears, more intense than any I've heard before. We were warned to expect it, we've been shown videos, but nothing could prepare you. It sounds as if something's being killed. Lynne bundles into the living room ahead of us, reaches into the trembling Moses basket and scoops out a small shrieking scrap like a piglet in a onesie.

"All right, little man," she says, tucking him expertly underneath his chin. The change in his cry is immediate; it continues, but lessens. "All right. Come on now, Joel, we've got someone for you to meet. This is your mum and dad."

"Oh God," says John, reverently. "That's our son. That's our son." His hands reach out. "Can I hold him?"

In John's hands, Joel looks even tinier. His cries wind back up to their highest pitch. John lays Joel against his shoulder and pats his little back. To my eyes, he looks too rough. I want to snatch Joel from his arms and hold him myself. I would do it better, more gently. Lynne watches John with a crooked smile on her face. I see the glint of tears in her eyes.

"He's not due his dose for two hours, but he doesn't know that, poor love. He's down to one a day now. He'll be completely off the meds by the end of this week, so you won't have to worry about it when he comes home."

Joel's shrieks of horror are unabated. His back is arched and rigid, as if he's trying to throw himself out of John's arms. I can see the panic in my husband's face. He presses Joel hard against his shoulder, trying to force him to relax. I think he might break him.

"Can I please take him for a minute?" In my attempt to avoid any hint that I'm criticising John, I end up sounding like a child asking for a sweet. John surrenders our son with reluctance, hovering close to me so he can peer into the rageful little face. I fight the urge to turn my back.

I have a child. I'm holding our son in my arms. I've dreamed this moment so many times, and now it's here.

In so many ways, this is nothing like my imaginings. Joel's come to me not from the safe cocoon of my own body, but as the tragic fallout of a young woman's hopeless and helpless addiction, itself borne out of the kind of misery we all wish we could close our eyes to. So many other paths could have led him elsewhere. To the arms of his mother, who was desperate to hold onto her baby and for a few weeks seemed to be doing so well, until she failed to turn up to treatment and was discovered lying, apparently asleep, on a bare mattress. To the homes of any of the other adopters. Even – my hands tighten around him as I think it – to his own death, gone before he ever drew breath. But instead he's coming to me. To me. To me. He's going to be all mine.

Joel's shrieks hurt my ears and my heart, but I endure them gladly. I snuggle him under my chin the way Lynne did, feel a fractional relaxation in his steely little body. The shrieking continues, but at a slightly lesser intensity.

"Good work," says Lynne. "I'll make us a cuppa, shall I? How do you both like it? Milk? Sugar? Right, back in a few minutes."

And for the first time, John and I are alone with our son.

We sit beside each other on the sofa, cheeks flushed, hearts banging. I'd imagined a reverent inspection of perfect little fingers and ears like seashells. Instead, we have a red-faced screamer who, apparently, hates us. I don't care. I love him, instantly. He didn't grow in my body, but he's my son. John takes him back from me, jiggles him against his shoulder again, stands up and walks around the room.

Joel doesn't like that, I think. *He wants to be quiet and calm. To be held still. To feel safe.* I have to force myself to stay sitting down, counting down the seconds until I can legitimately take Joel back and return him to his spot under my chin, thus inducing the slightly lesser degree of shrieking that is what seems to pass for contentment.

"Well, you're a little shouter, aren't you?" John says. "You were smiling in your picture, but you're not going to smile for me today, are you? Quite right too. Who wants to smile at my ugly mug, hmm?" He kisses Joel's forehead. I hope John's bristles don't prick his tender skin. Sometimes the withdrawal makes them extra sensitive to pain.

I watch the clock, willing myself to wait at least three more minutes before snatching Joel back. The cups of tea are taking for ever. Lynne must be giving us some time alone. Two minutes left. John swaps Joel to the other shoulder, jiggles Joel a bit harder. One minute. *Stop jiggling him,* I think. *Be gentle. You need to be gentle.*

"Here." John sits down beside me and passes Joel over. "It's all right, love, I don't mind. You have him for a bit. I'll have years and years to cuddle him."

John can't bear to see me wanting something and not give it to me. I'm so lucky. I've always been lucky and now here I am, lucky again, receiving an almost-impossible gift. No known biological father who could assert his genetic primacy and steal Joel away. No birth mother to send yearly photographs and letters to. No living relatives to swoop in and snatch him from us. Our son will come home before he's even three months old. Joel will be weaned off the Oramorph and we'll get him through the shock of being taken, once again, from the woman he thought was his mother, and he'll learn to love us.

Lynne reappears with a tray, liberally covered with three mugs of tea, a large plate of biscuits and a bottle of formula. Is that why Joel's crying? Is he hungry? Why didn't I think of that? I'll have to do better in future. I reach for the bottle, then glance at Lynne for permission.

"You go ahead," she says. "I've written down his feeding schedule for you. He's on quite a lot of small feeds because he's a bit of a titch still and he doesn't always feed very well. I usually change him before his bottle, just so he's not in a wet bum if he goes to sleep. All the stuff's in that storage box over there."

"Can I see the schedule? What milk is he on? And what size and brand of nappies?" John takes out the folded list of questions we worked on together. I'm so glad he's here to ask them, working out the theory of looking after Joel so I can snatch this first precious opportunity to actually do something for my son. The poppers of the suit come open to reveal his belly, and I kiss its impossible perfect softness, not minding that he flails wildly at my head with furious feet and crumpled fists. His nappy is damp but not soiled. I take a wipe from the packet and clean him. Halfway through he pees, a startling clear arc that shoots up like a fountain and splashes onto his face and suit. I wipe him down, bundle him out of his wet onesie and take the spare one from Lynne as she laughs sympathetically.

"If you keep a muslin cloth handy, you can drop it on as soon as he starts peeing. Don't worry! All baby boys do it. It's the cold air."

I already know this; I've spent enough time haunting parenting forums. I should have been prepared. Now my son has to wait even longer for his milk. I work as fast as I can, feeling spaghetti arms into sleeves, trying to pin his trembling legs into place. Then I snatch the bottle and retreat to the sofa and coax the teat into Joel's wide, furious red mouth.

This is where he should fall into blissful, miraculous, greedy silence. I've seen this done so many times before, with bottles and breasts and even dummies. But Joel doesn't drink. His mouth refuses to clamp shut, and the few drops of formula that land on his tongue only seem to enrage him more.

I nudge the teat gently against the roof of his mouth, trying to activate his suckle reflex. His mouth closes and he swallows a few gulps of milk. Then he chokes, gasps and starts screaming again. I refuse to give up. I nudge again at the roof of his mouth, marvelling at the strength of his gums as he gnashes at the bottle. Another few gulps, and then back to screaming; but in the moment before Joel's mouth opens, his navy-blue eyes meet mine and we look at each other and I know he understands that from now on, we're in this together.

From the corner of my eye I see John silently cleaning up the mess we left – bagging the nappy, mopping the pee, spraying and wiping down the change-mat, asking Lynne where to store the sodden onesie – but I can't find time to be grateful. I sit Joel up a little and keep trying, watching with awe and delight as gradually, gradually, the volume in the bottle begins to fall. Joel's still furious with the world, but at least now he's not starving.

"Well done," says Lynne. "He's taken a good amount there. You've obviously got the knack."

Her words make my heart glow. I sit Joel up in my arms and rub his back with a slow, circular motion to bring up his wind.

"Pass him here," says John, holding out his arms.

I hope my reluctance isn't visible. When I let Joel go, my arms feel ridiculously light and empty.

"Come on, fella." John folds Joel forward over his forearm. "Let's see what we can get out of you." His big hand pats firmly at Joel's back. *Not too rough!* I think. Joel lurches to one side; John catches him. *Don't let him fall!* John's so strong, but still so very gentle. It's one of the things I love the most about him. John presses hard between Joel's shoulder blades. *Oh, that's too hard! He's so tiny. Don't break him.* Between two screams, Joel produces an almighty comic belch. We all laugh. John looks pleased.

"Any more where that came from?" John keeps patting, keeps rubbing. Is that all right? Is there any more to come? How do we know when to stop? And surely he's being too rough? I glance at Lynne but she's clearing up the untouched mugs of tea. I want so much to tell John that I know best, but I don't. We've known Joel for precisely the same amount of time. We've read the same file, wept shamelessly over the same background information. I can't claim any sort of superior knowledge.

Except that just for a moment, Joel looked at me, and I knew we were on the same side, and he was trusting me to take care of him.

Even as I think this, Joel produces another tremendous burp, followed by a plume of curdled milk. John laughs and reaches over Joel's head for a muslin cloth. *Don't squash him! Don't hurt him! He's so tiny!* Lynne comes back in, sees what he's doing, and laughs.

"I see he christened you," she says, and pats Joel's fluffy little head. "Good work, mister."

Joel, of course, keeps screaming. I can't tell if there's any change in the intensity or not. I ache to take him back and tuck him into the place where he belongs, the safe spot under my chin where he can feel wrapped in warmth and comfort. I make myself wait two more endless minutes before I finally crack and reach my arms out. John goes upstairs to the bathroom. I stand in the bay window, swaying slowly backwards and forwards, murmuring into Joel's scalp, hoping he'll find peace.

"He'll be much better in a couple of weeks," Lynne says. "This is his worst time because he's waiting for his dose. But two more days and he'll be off the medication, and a week after that his system should be clear and he'll be much happier."

"I don't mind."

"I know. They get into your hearts even when they're yelling like banshees, don't they?"

"I feel like I'm stealing your baby," I blurt out.

"No. Not at all. He's your baby. I've just been looking after him for you. Don't worry. You'll be his mum, and John will be his dad. It works even if they come home when they're two or three or four, so just think how much easier it's going to be with Joel. Hey, listen to that."

Beneath my chin, Joel hiccups, sighs and then falls silent.

The sudden peace is deafening. John clatters down the stairs and I pray he won't wake Joel. When he sees Joel asleep, he looks at me in awe, then creeps over to inspect him.

"So you can stop shouting when you want to," he says, chuckling. "That's good to know." One finger reaches out to touch the perfect bow of Joel's mouth.

"Don't wake him, don't wake him—"

John sighs, and lets his hand fall. In infinitely small increments, I make my way to the sofa and sit down. John sits beside me, and together we admire our sleeping son for eleven silent minutes before he wakes with a start, and begins screaming again.

Despite the screaming, we stay two more hours, taking it in turns to hold, rock, pat and nuzzle our son, only leaving when Lynne's teenage children come home from their last day at school, laden with cards and a term's worth of work, and bringing with them three friends, so suddenly we're outnumbered by the younger generation. As the clock ticks round to six o'clock, Lynne goes to the kitchen and comes back with an amber glass bottle and a dropper.

"Poor little mite," she says, and the fierce tenderness in her face as she takes Joel from me makes me feel once more as if I am stealing her child. "This is what you want, isn't it? I'm sorry. I'm sorry. Things will get much better for you once this stuff's out of your life, I promise."

"We'll see ourselves out," says John firmly. "Thanks so much for, well, everything."

"My pleasure. See you again tomorrow morning. Bring your travel system, you can take him out for a walk if you feel up to it. Come on, then, little man, let's get this into you."

She holds the dropper carefully over Joel's yearning mouth. We close the door and creep out of the house like burglars.

We get into the car and sit in silence, dizzied by the experience of meeting our son. I can smell Joel on my skin and on my clothes. I can feel the weight of him in my arms, the exact shape of his body against mine. This is what motherhood feels like. I want more. I want to go back to Lynne's house and beat down the door.

"Blimey," says John at last, and scratches at the stiff milky stain on his jeans. "Fake it till you feel it, hey?"

I look at him blankly. The last three and a half hours have been the most beautiful and fulfilling of my life. I'm not faking anything. I am genuinely, completely, utterly besotted with our child.

"We'll figure it out," John says, and pats my leg. "Well, I suppose we'd better get home. Get some rest before Round Two begins."

As the car pulls away from the curb, I'm transfixed by the final image I have of Joel; lying in the arms of a strange woman, his mouth open like a baby bird, waiting for the Oramorph his little body craves to be dripped gently onto his tongue. I think how strange and sad it is that it should be this, and not milk or warmth or cuddles, that should be his first and most intense experience of need satisfied. I wonder if the sensation reminds him of the days and nights he spent swimming in the toxic chemical soup of his birth mother's womb, and if the gradual disappearance of this first and most needful comfort from his little life feels like the slow withdrawal of maternal love.

Chapter Twenty-Two
Sunday 24th December 2017

When Nick's car pulls up outside my house, he's greeted with a festival of lights. As eager as he is, he still lingers in my frozen garden. The dried-out heads of the hydrangeas have bloomed again with a blue-white glow that flickers off the strands and slivers of silver hanging from the stems, and the path is lined with tiny bulbs like snowdrops. From behind the blue velvet curtains of the front room, I savour the sight of this beautiful forbidden man who I've lured to my side with a few words on an electronic screen. I wanted holly for my doorway, but the shops were bare of it and I lacked the courage to steal what I wanted from the trees, so instead I've added even more lights, framing the doorway so that Nick, waiting for me to greet him, is almost literally dazzled. When he sees me properly, he has to stop and stare for a moment.

"Wow," he manages at last.

"Do you like it?"

"You look—" he shakes his head in amazement. "Can I kiss you? I don't want to spoil anything."

So the long hours at my dressing table were worth it; the careful patient work with brushes and lotions and blenders and creams has not gone to waste. For tonight, I've brushed the dust from my make-up box and used every half-forgotten trick I once knew to make myself young and dewy again, concealing wrinkles and shadows, painting on the lines and shapes and shades that will make my eyes larger, my lips softer, my cheeks plump and ripe. In sunlight, I would look overdone and over-coloured, but by the cold white lights of winter, among the silver tinsel and white-painted glass globes, I look perfect.

There's more. I've soaked my hair in a long luxurious drink of moisturiser, dried it soft and sleek and then smoothed each strand further between hot ceramic plates; piled it high and soft and luscious, studded it with crystals that invite only the most delicate of touches, the most reverent of caresses. And then there's my frock, my foolish frivolous crushable fragile blush-coloured frock, lovely enough to be married in, bought with money I don't have from a shop I have never been to before. I'm remote and polished and dazzling, something to look at but not to touch. I look delicately beautiful but also slightly mad. Exactly the type Nick craves. The last time we were together he fell on me like a starving dog. This time I see the same hunger but also a reverence, a desire to admire from a distance and perhaps show me to other men. *See what I have? See what's mine? But don't look too long or I'll have to kill you.* I lead him into the front room, where a fat green bottle slumbers within a silver bucket.

"Happy Christmas," I say, and give him a tall crystal glass that shimmers with bubbles.

He raises the glass, hesitates, takes a single delicate sip. "I have to drive afterwards."

"It's only champagne. It won't get you drunk. It only makes you happy."

His eyes meet mine. "I'm already happy."

And for this moment, I'm happy too. Not the sunflower joy that blooms in the summer of our lives when our children are young and our husbands faithful, but the deep velvet black of the Christmas rose that blossoms in spite of the darkness, lovely and transgressive and poisonous to touch. I clink my glass against Nick's and let the champagne take me, bubbles dissolving in my bloodstream. Nick's fumbling in his pocket, taking out a square flat package that shimmers with ribbon and silver paper.

"I wanted to give you this," he says. "I hope you don't mind. It seems a bit presumptuous but I saw it and I just couldn't resist—"

A gift for me, from my lover. The first gift for... How long has it been? Too long. Chosen by someone who sees me as an object of desire. I want to keep it just as it is, all its meaning and secret potential wrapped tightly in glimmering silver paper. I also want to tear the paper off like a savage and see what's hidden inside. When I look at Nick, I see him looking at me and wrestling with the same impulse.

I tug delicately at the ribbon, catching it between my fingers as it tumbles. I unfold the paper from around the turquoise box, pry open the lid with a manicured fingernail. Inside, a diamond glows cold and fiery from its intricate prison of silver, suspended on a chain of tiny links like manacles.

"Oh!" My breath catches. "Oh! This is... It's so lovely... You didn't have to—"

"I couldn't resist. I saw it and all I could think about was how lovely it would look on you. I thought of you up in your bedroom, picking up your phone and telling me I could come to see you, wearing just that necklace. I could picture it so clearly—"

And on the strength of that brief moment of desire, of a need so intense it was like sickness, he took his credit card and spent – how much? Hundreds? A thousand? More? – on this necklace, the price of fulfilling his fantasy. If I was his wife, I'd have to laugh and frown and shake my head and ask how much it cost, steer the perilous course between finding out the truth and spoiling his surprise, between keeping control of our finances and making him feel less of a man. I'd have to think ahead to a lean three months of fried eggs for dinner and nights in watching movies on the sofa while we cleared the balance from our credit card. But I'm his mistress, and mistresses are creatures of pure cold fantasy. *Up in your bedroom, wearing just that necklace*. All that money, simply so he could speak these words to me and pray that I'll one day repay him by making his dream come true.

His fingers brush against my neck as he fastens the clasp. He's so filled with need and greediness that for a moment I think I might melt. Shall I let myself become flesh again? Shall I abandon my plans for the evening, take down my hair, shimmy out of my dress and give him what he wants? Beyond my reflection in the window, the path is white with frost. There's still something I need to do.

"Is everything all right?"

"Everything's wonderful."

"You were staring out of the window."

"I was looking at my reflection," I tell him. "At my present. It looks beautiful."

"Only because you're beautiful." Nick's words vibrate against my neck. He's kissing me, gently but firmly, and all my skin is on fire with his touch. It would be so easy.

I force myself to break away from his searching mouth.

"I have a present for you too," I say.

He watches me as I go to the heavy oak sideboard. When I kneel to open the door, the zip of my dress grazes against my spine. I wish it was Nick's fingertips instead. It's hard to stay balanced on my tall silver shoes.

My gift for Nick is packed in a tall square box, wrapped in green-and-scarlet paper and tied with a red velvet ribbon, like an illustration from a children's story. He takes his time, just as I did, savouring the slow unwrapping that I know he is reimagining as another, more urgent, unwrapping to follow. Inside, the box is packed with scarlet tissue.

What is he hoping for? What sort of gift do women like me give to their lovers? An outfit that fulfils a sinful fantasy perhaps, or a wicked little toy for consenting adults only. A reminder that we, our own selves, are all the gift we'll ever be able to offer. He plunges his hand inside. I hold my breath and watch the subtle movement of the muscles of his wrist. A moment later and he's holding Scrap-dog.

I'm ready with my explanation, but I can tell he doesn't need it. I've seen Nick in many moods and wearing many different skins, but the one constant truth of his nature is that he is always, always a good copper. He knows exactly what he has in his hands.

"Where did you get this?"

"Do you remember the day I cut my hand? You asked me to tell you if anything else happened, and I said I would, but I didn't quite dare, I didn't trust you. But now I do. I found Scrap-dog, Nick. I found him in Joel's room. He came back to me. And so did something else."

"Tell me."

"I know now what happened to Joel."

Nick's fingers tighten around Scrap-dog's neck. His eyes are bright.

"You've remembered something?"

Could you call it that? Is that what's been going on? Survivors of conflict frequently find themselves back in the battlefield, their lives torn apart not by phantoms but by the ghosts hiding in their own nervous systems. "Yes. I've remembered something. Something important. You were right, Nick. You were right all along."

"About... about..." I can see the name *John* hovering on his lips, but he swallows it back down, forcing himself to take his time. He knows how fragile my remembering may turn out to be. "Okay. Okay. I understand. Tell me, my love, and we'll take it from there. I'll do everything I can to help you, you know that. Just tell me what you've remembered."

I've felt this way before, felt the way Judas must have felt in the moment before that kiss. I've been caught once already in that moment of hesitation, forced to confront the wrong that I'm about to do. But I wasn't wrong last time, and I'm not wrong this time either. I've already given Nick the gift of

310

Jackie. Now it's time to give him my husband. This is what I have been hiding from all these years. But now I'm finally ready to face it. Why should I hold back?

"I need to show you," I say. "Is that all right? Will you come with me so I can show you?"

I wonder if he might be irritated by my impulse, but Nick is not like John, who loved me best when I was whole and sane and capable. Nick loves my scars, my damage and my fragility, and Nick is more than willing to guide me into the passenger seat of his car, saving the hem of my dress from soiling, pointing out the puddle of ice that might spill me from my feet. He helps me with my seatbelt as if I'm a child. When he turns up the heat to keep the chill from my bare shoulders, I sense he would like to have a blanket to wrap me in.

"So where are we going?" he asks.

He wants to know our destination, but I can't see that far ahead. Our route only reveals itself in fragments, like sudden gleams of moonlight between trees at midnight. So I sit with Scrap-dog on my knee and I say to him, "Follow the road round and then turn right," and then "Keep going straight," and "Still straight", and "Left here", flashes of insight that come to me unbidden. Nick accepts my directions in rapt silence, driving as carefully and gently as if I'm made of glass.

The town centre, its offices closed but still intermittently hectic with party-goers and last-minute shoppers, is a patchwork of brilliant revelry and eerie darkness, lit from above by the unending relentless glow of the Christmas lights. Why are all these people still here? Don't they feel for the workers who have to plaster on a smile and twine tinsel in their hair and serve up cashmere scarves and sticky drinks and embossed boxes of scent? Don't they feel the slightest twinge of guilt when they tell these men and women to "Smile, love, it's Christmas"? I'm glad to stop in the dark streets by the law courts, where all activities are suspended until well into the New Year. At my imperious direction, Nick parks the car.

"Now we have to walk," I say.

"Where are we going?"

I don't know. I only know we're getting closer. "You'll see when we get there."

"Is it far? I don't want you to hurt your feet. Those heels—"

"Then I'll take my shoes off."

"But the cold—"

"I'll be all right."

"Susannah." Nick takes my hand gently. "Are you sure about this?"

"Of course I'm sure."

"Are we going to find anything... anything that might upset you? Because if we are, you can just tell me where we're going and I'll go there alone. You don't have to come with me."

He thinks I'm going to show him Joel's body, but it was all lost in the mud. I know that now. All I can do is show him where it happened, and how it happened, and hope that this will be enough to break John open like a nut so he'll finally confess what he did. This is the best I can do for my son, and how little and pitiful that *best* is. Would it have been any different if I'd let myself see the truth earlier? Surely not. What the mud swallows, it holds onto forever. I have to believe this is true.

"I'm coming with you," I tell him.

The sound of Christmas Eve waxes and wanes. A pack of males who would want to be called *men* rather than *boys* reel past in a cloud of beer fumes and curses and laughter. The sight of me, shivering and bare-shouldered in my formal dress, clutching a worn cuddly toy, induces a frightening, predatory pause – they jostle to a halt, look me up and down, lick their lips, consider Nick's capabilities as a protector – but then some hidden impulse is transmitted between them and they lurch off again into the night, laughing as they pass around their assessment. *Too fucking old. Her tits weren't bad though. Nah, they'd hang to her fucking knees when you got her kit off. Come on, let's get some more fucking drinks in and find some proper lasses, eh?* Nick winces, but I don't care. What does any of it matter? There are more important things to think about. I take Nick's hand and we slip between tall shadows and down onto the wharves, where a fishing boat, scarred from its long battle with the ocean and the Icelanders, has found anchor in the river where she can lie and dream of past glories. The smell of the water rolls towards us like mist. When I turn my face towards the sky, I feel the silent flutter of snowflakes falling against my cheeks. How perfect. We're going to have a white Christmas. Joel always loved the snow.

"It was here," I say. My voice is no more than a croak.

"What happened?"

"It was John. He was angry with Joel. Disappointed. He'd wanted so much for his son, and Joel was failing him in every way. So he found him. And he took him. And he drowned him."

The warmth of my breath hangs in the air for a moment, then blows away.

"How do you know?" Nick takes my hands between his and holds them gently, as if he's afraid of frightening me into silence. "Susannah, love, I believe you, but how do you *know*?"

"Because of Jackie," I say.

"Because of *Jackie*? I don't understand."

"We went to a medium, and he saw it, and it all came true," I say. I must sound mad, but I don't care. "Jackie and I went together, and he saw both of our boys, dead. He said, *One on land, hidden beneath trees, and one in the water, near a boat that never moves.* He said, *One was killed by his father, and one was killed by his mother.* And it came true, didn't it? That's why you arrested her."

"No, love. That's not true."

313

The snow is like feathers, like petals, like kisses. If I stand still for too long I'll be covered over.

"Yes. I'm right. It's true. I saw on the news. It was on the news. I saw the pictures, it said you'd arrested someone, you'd got her in custody. I saw their house, their house was on the news. You found Ryan's body."

"We did, love. But it wasn't Jackie. It was Lee. His stepfather."

One was killed by his father. And one was killed by his...

And then, just as the gypsy woman promised, Joel comes back to me.

I'm at home. My house is clean and peaceful. I have eaten a nice lunch with my sister. There are small chores I should be undertaking – laundry, dusting, the folding of clothes – but I'm replete with food and too lazy to move. Instead, I sit in my nicely decorated living room and think about what I might add to make it even more beautiful. New cushions for the sofa and matching curtains. A different clock for the mantelpiece. Flowers for the table. Beside me, my handbag begins to vibrate.

I reach for my phone, but of course it's switched off, I switched it off so I could enjoy my lunch with Melanie uninterrupted. What I can hear is my other phone, the cheap pay-as-you-go mobile that I bought months ago and have kept hidden in a dozen secret places ever since.

I'm putting a new number in your phone, I said to Joel. *You're the only one who'll have the number. So if you ever need to call me and for Dad not to know about it...* His blue eyes wide and startled, as if I'd grown a new face. *Don't ever tell anyone, okay? It's just our secret.* And it has been just our secret, called with increasing and terrifying frequency over the weeks and months as my son's life grown darker and more confusing. His voice is slow and slurry.

"Mummy? Mum? Are you there? Please don't leave me, I need you, please help me, I need you to come and get me.

Please, Mum, please help me, I'm so sorry I ran away, I need you. Please help me, Mum. Mum? Can you hear me?"

The gentle selfish pleasure of my afternoon is over. I have to get back to my real life, where I keep my son safe from his father, so he can have the space to overcome his demons and heal his wounds and become the boy I know, I *know*, he truly is inside.

Keeping this secret requires certain precautions. I go to the coat cupboard and take out an ugly green fleece whose malevolent cut adds instant pounds to my body. I wipe off my lipstick, take out my earrings, unpin my hair and brush it limp and flat. I replace my pretty dress with faded jeans, my pretty heels with ugly elastic-sided black boots. I take out my real phone – my official phone – and lay it on the table. I leave my house by the back door and scuttle furtively down the narrow passageway. My neighbour, who has not yet forced himself to overcome his horror of the back bedroom where his daughter lived and died, does not see me. Even angels are blind sometimes. I take the bus into town and walk, walk, walk from the bus station to the place where my son waits for me.

He's by the river, tucked away behind the broken doorway of a semi-derelict building that must have been a warehouse. We're moments from the heart of the city, but despite the hum and rumble of the endless freight lorries making their way up to the ferry, we're alone here, alone in a way that can only happen in a city, where no one knows anyone and no one watches if you choose to slip away, quiet and careful, beneath the branches of a hanging willow tree. Or into the bushes at the centre of a roundabout. Or behind the doorway of an old warehouse by the river. Joel's always had a talent for finding places to hide.

"Joel." I stroke his face. He is incoherent with whatever he's taken, jaw slack, eyes rolling, skin sweaty, hands soft and useless. "Sweetie. It's Mummy. I'm here. I'm here." His eyes peel open and he smiles blissfully at me for a moment, then lapses back into the embrace of the chemicals that sing within him.

"Joel. Come on. We need to get you home."

"Don't wan' go home. Wanna stay here. Stay here w' me, Mum. S'beautiful."

"Sweetie, we can't." I try to lift him, but it's like trying to lift a sack of flour. He's never been this bad before, never. Panic licks at my heart. In my head, a clock is ticking, counting down the moments until John will come home. What has Joel taken? How long will it last? Is there any chance of Joel being even semi-presentable by the time John walks through the door? "We need to get you sorted out. Dad's coming home in a few hours. You want to be home for him, don't you?"

"No. Dun' want to see Dad. M'scared of Dad."

"Don't say that. Dad loves you."

Joel waves his forefinger slowly in front of my face. His eyes crease with laughter. "Then why you always trying a keep me safe from'm?"

My heart feels cold.

"He wants me t'b' different. But you love me just'z I am, don't you?" Joel's smile is as sweet and melting as when it was a baby. It's a terrible thing to see it appear on the face of this limp ravaged body slumped across my lap. "You love me just'z I am. S's why I love you best. You dun make me be anyone 'cept than who I am…"

"But this isn't who you are, sweetie."

"Yes 'tis. S'how I feel happiest. When'm high… 'n' you're here w'me… I know't dun't matter, c's you love me anyway. Thas wh' makes me happier'n anything inna whole world." He sighs and takes my hand, tucking it away like a treasure beneath his chin. "Dun't ever wan' go back to rest'v world, Mum. Less you'n'me stay here."

"We can't. This can't go on. It can't, we can't keep living like this. Joel, you're getting worse. You have to have some help."

"No, Mum. You're helping. Y' come'n get me. Y'll always

look aft' me. Keep'a whole world away." He yawns. "Night night."

"No." I shake him. "Not night night. Time to wake up. Come on, get up. On your feet."

"I can't. 'M not well. Can't go school today."

"We're not going to school, we're going home. Come on. Stand up. Stand up. Up!"

Somehow I wrestle him to his feet. He sways heavily and leans against the wall. I glance around apprehensively, afraid of being seen, afraid John has a network of spies who watch me. But there's no one else here. No curious faces glancing out of windows. No fellow wanderers taking in the murky river air. We might be alone in a desert.

"That's better. Now we have to walk. Okay? Walk. We're going home. You hear me? Move your feet." He takes a few shuffling steps. "That's it. That's it. Keep doing that."

A few reluctant steps and we've made it out of the warehouse. Then he folds at the knees and like that he's down again, rocking and swaying at the edge of the wharf, and nothing I can do will persuade him to his feet. How am I going to get him home? How?

"Joel." I can feel the tears pouring down my cheeks. "Sweetie. This can't go on. This isn't a life. Not for any of us."

"Mum, I'm scared." He clutches at me. "My head hurts. All'v me hurts. I dun't want to go school. Wanna stay here."

Whose fault is this, this sickness that hides inside my son? Can I blame the woman, scarcely more than a child herself, who carried him in her belly? The foster carer who dropped Oramorph into his yearning, toothless mouth? The doctors who prescribed it? Is it John's fault? Or is it mine?

"Make it stop," Joel begs me. "You c'n do anything, Mum. Know you can. Make it all stop."

Here's how my life will go: I'll hide Joel's addictions for as long as I can, until one day they spill into the open and John sees everything, all the secrets I've kept and all the lies I've told. John will leave me. Joel will stay. I'll have my son,

317

to cosset and care for, to feed and clothe and nurture with everything he desires, for as long as his body can hold out. He'll grow older and taller, but he will never leave me. My nest will never be empty. It will be just Joel and me, for ever and ever. Once, becoming a mother was all I dreamed of.

Or I could do something else. I could make it all stop. I could take away his pain.

I kneel beside my son. I hesitate. I press my lips against Joel's face.

"I love you," I say.

And then I push him hard over the edge of the wharf and let the river take him, drowning out all thought and feeling, filling his eyes and ears and lungs with the oblivion he craves. The sinking is slow and peaceful. His eyes are open. His hands are still. No one sees us. I watch him as he leaves me.

Afterwards I stand and stare sightlessly out across the water and wait to feel something. I'm waiting to be overwhelmed by a guilt so huge that it will fling me into the water after him. But instead the feeling, when it comes, is one of a strange and terrible relief. I've passed the test. I've done what my son asked. I've kept him safe from everything he's afraid of. He'll never have to go back to school. He'll never have to face his father. I've made it all stop. I have not failed him.

Behind the door of the warehouse, I find Joel's rucksack. At the bottom is Scrap-dog. Joel always took him everywhere. The rucksack needs to follow him into the water. But what about Scrap-dog? Do I keep him? Or send him on with Joel, as grave goods? I stare into the river that has swallowed my son and think, *I need to decide soon. I have to get the next bus home. Joel will be home from school soon. I need to make him a sandwich.*

The waters of memory should not close so easily over what I did to Joel. But the truth is that they do. It shouldn't be this easy to get away with killing someone. But the truth is that it is.

318

"Susannah. Love. Look at me. Talk to me." Nick is shaking me gently by the shoulders, trying to get my attention. "Please. You're frightening me now. What's happening to you?"

I think I should be paying attention to this man. He used to matter to me, I remember that. I remember the feel of his hands on my body, his mouth against mine. I remember an expensive gift. I remember the gleam in the gypsy woman's eye as she laughed at me in a painted wooden caravan filled with china and crystal. *He'll come back to you, my love,* she tells me, *and now the snow's falling on Christmas Eve and here he is, see? Do you see how your son's coming to meet you? And now you'll never be apart again.* Something disturbs the surface of the mud.

"Look," I say. "Can you see that?"

"See what?"

"Out there."

"Susannah, there's nothing there. Just water and mud."

"No. I can see him. He's coming for me. He's come back to me. She told me he would, and he has."

The man by my side is talking to me, but I can't understand what he's saying, he's not important any more. His job was to help me find Joel, and that's what he's done. Now I can forget him.

Joel is struggling up out of the mud, his movements slow and jerky like an old film. His gaze is fixed on my face. His face is coated with mud and I can't read his expression, but his eyes are as blue as they ever were. Is he angry with me? Or does he forgive me? Perhaps he's even grateful? When he finally stands on the glossy brown surface, his feet leave no imprints.

"I love you," I say.

"I love you too," says the man at my side, his voice sick and wretched. "Susannah, do you hear me? I love you. Come away from the edge. Please don't do this. Please stay."

"I have a present for you," I say to Joel.

Beneath the mud, Joel's face moves, but I can't say whether it's a smile or a snarl. It doesn't matter. He's my son, and he's come back to me, and now we will never be apart again. His hands reach out towards me. He wants me to join him.

Holding Scrap-dog, I walk off the edge of the wharf to greet him, off the wharf and into the mud.

Life Without Hope:
Am I still a mother?

Am I still a mother?

I ask myself this question every day. I still don't know what the answer is. It should be the simplest thing in the world, but when I meet someone new and they ask me about myself, the question always comes up – *Do you have children?* – and I freeze. Am I still a mother? Do I still have a child? Do I say, *I had a son, I didn't give birth to him but he was my son, and he went missing when he was fifteen and I don't know if he's alive or dead?* Or do I lie and say, *No, no children, how about you?*

There's no simple answer. No way to get round the fact that it hurts to deny my son's existence, or to explain my life to a near-stranger and live with what happens next. A mother whose child has died may stop us in our tracks, but on some level we understand that this is simply one of the many ways in which the universe is cruel. But a mother whose child is missing – perhaps run away, perhaps driven out by something dreadful at home – invites judgement. On their faces, I see all the questions they don't quite dare to ask. *Was he unhappy? Were you too strict? Were you unloving? Abusive? What did you do to him to make him run?*

So, yes. Sometimes I lie and say I have no children, because I'm weak and I don't know how to face the pain it causes. But when I feel strong enough, I tell the truth. Yes. I had a son once. *His name was Joel. I loved him so much. I love him still. And I hope one day I'll see him again.*

Posted on 24th December 2017
Filed to: Miscellaneous
Tags: missing people, support for families, Susannah Harper, Joel Harper

Acknowledgements

As always, the first and biggest thank you belongs to the amazing team at Legend Press, and especially to my lovely editor, Lauren Parsons. I'm proud every day to be a Legend author, and glad every day for the support you give my writing.

A special thank you to my very dear friend Krista Wood, for being my on-the-spot personal consultant on police procedure. Any remaining mistakes are my own.

Thank you to Louise Beech, Vicky Foster, Michelle Dee, Linda Harrison, Julie Corbett and all the other amazing Women of Words, for teaching me to stand tall, breathe deep and stop hiding behind the mic stand.

Thank you to my family – and most especially my mum, Judy May, who made damn sure my brother and I fell as deeply in love with Hull Fair as anyone could.

Thank you to my children, Becky and Ben. One day soon, either I'll write a book you can read, or you'll be old enough to read the books I've written. In the meantime, please read this, and know how very much I love you.

Most of all, thank you to my husband, Tony. You make it all possible.

We hope you enjoyed Cassandra's novel. If you did, and
would like to read more, there are three
other novels available.
Here's the first chapter of the fantastic debut,
The Summer We All Ran Away.

chapter one (now)

This Thursday, in the middle of August, had been the most
terrible, apocalyptic day of Davey's nineteen years on earth.
Getting drunk seemed the only possible response.

Slouched hopelessly on the grey-white steps of Trafalgar
Square, his rucksack between his knees, he forced the vodka
down his throat. Was it supposed to taste like this? Or were
his mother and stepfather storing oven cleaner in the drinks
cabinet for secret reasons of their own? He imagined it
burning through his stomach and intestines, fizzing gently,
creating thick yellow fumes. Stubbornly, he took another
swill, and wondered if he might go blind.

Of course, if he did, then maybe he wouldn't have to—

"All right there, mate?" said a companionable voice.

Davey squinted up through dust and sunshine to the
policeman who stood, sweating amiably, by the steps.

"Bit early to be drinking, isn't it? Not even lunchtime
yet."

Years of public school training smoothed over his terror.

"Er yes, sir. Sorry, sir." His words slightly blurred by
alcohol.

The policeman nodded wisely.

"Good." His gaze took in the clean hands, the good jeans,
the bottle of Stoli. The rucksack. The dark hair capping the
young, weary face. The bloom of fresh bruises, one on the

jawline, one high on the cheekbone. The crust of blood at the hairline. "You've been in the wars."

Davey flushed. The policeman sat down beside him.

"Need any help? Got trouble with them at home?"

Davey wondered what incarnation of *them* the policeman was picturing. An alcoholic mother. An unemployed father with a drug habit. A violent girlfriend.

"I'm f-fine," he said. His stammer peeking out from beneath its stone. Would the policeman read anything into it? "But, erm, th-thanks."

The policeman looked thoughtfully at the rucksack.

"Running away's bloody hard, you know. You might think it solves everything, but it mostly makes it worse."

"I'm n-n-n-not erm—" Davey suddenly discovered he was a terrible liar, even to strangers. "How—"

The policeman gave him a penetrating stare.

"Look, you're not causing any aggro, so I'll leave you alone if you want. But you'd do better to sort it. If you're getting hit, we'll help, but you have to ask. All right?"

Horrified, Davey stood up. The ground rocked treacherously beneath his feet.

"Where are you going?" The policeman had hold of his elbow, his grip firm and impersonal.

"Train station," said Davey, indistinctly.

"Yeah? Where you headed?"

Over the policeman's shoulder, a paper bag danced in the breeze. West Cornwall Pasty Company.

"Cornwall," said Davey, after a slight pause. "I'm g-g-going to visit my aunt."

"Your aunt in Cornwall? What's her name?"

"Dorothy," said Davey, desperate. "My Aunt Dorothy. I'm g-g-going to stay with her for a bit. G-g-get my head together. You know?"

"You've got money for the ticket?"

Just let me go.

"Yes, yes, plenty." Davey showed his wallet. "See?"

"You sure there isn't anything you want to tell me? 'Cos they'll do it again, you know. They always do."

"Not if I'm n-n-not there," said Davey, and grabbed his rucksack.

"All right, son," said the policeman, resigned. "Off you go. Good luck."

A blink, and he was on the Tube. How had he got here? He remembered a barrier, a platform, a ticket machine, a handful of change, but couldn't string them together into a coherent narrative. But he was going to Cornwall. Guided by a paper bag. Well, why not? He had to go somewhere. His contempt for himself had his stepfather's voice. *Only cowards run away, real men stick around and sort it out.* He drowned it with vodka, and felt a giant wave of collective disapproval break over his head.

Above his head, the adverts were moving. A girl on a poster winked at him. She was pretty and confident, and had saved up to one hundred and fifty pounds on her car insurance because she was a lady driver. Davey's stepfather had tried to force him into driving lessons, but so far he'd managed to resist. Two panels down, a man dressed as Nelson had also saved money on his car insurance. Was that because he was an Admiral? The parrot's gaze was knowing and sly.

The lines of the Tube map made him feel sick. Lying on the floor was a newspaper, open to the showbiz pages. An iconic British actress had walked off a film set because her husband was sleeping with the actress playing her daughter; a battered California starlet had wrecked her car and checked into rehab. Their faces stared accusingly up at him, as if these events were his fault. Regurgitated vodka crept up his throat. Was he going to be sick? He picked up the newspaper in anticipation. The woman next to him edged away.

Another blink, and he stood at the foot of an escalator. The platform swayed beneath his feet. If he was on a ship, would the ground feel stable? Was this why sailors drank? The handrail's speed was treacherously slower than the escalator and he had to keep letting go and grabbing on again, convinced each time that he would fall backwards into the chaos below. Staggering off the top step, he fell into a man in a suit.

"Jesus Christ, just *fuck off*, will you?" he snarled. Davey clung to the man's shoulder, trying to re-orient himself. "Let go of me or I'll fucking deck you." His expensive aftershave was like a scented cloud. "Are you drunk? Police, police, I've got a lunatic here, police!" A privileged voice, used to be being obeyed.

"No, I'm sorry, I'm *sorry*—" Davey let go and stumbled away. The crowd parted, then refused to re-form around him, leaving him for the policemen to find. He began to run, realised how stupid this was, forced himself to stop again. High-vis jackets over black uniforms appeared at the bottom of the escalator. The crowd rustled with excitement.

"I haven't got fucking time for this," said the man in the suit, and gave Davey a spiteful shove. "Piss off, you disgusting little shit." He straightened his jacket and marched away.

As if his departure proved that Davey was not, after all, a lunatic or a terrorist, everyone returned to their business. The police arrived, looked around, saw nothing, swore, began to ask questions. A woman with henna-red hair pointed them in the direction of the man who had called them.

Reprieved, Davey crept along the wall of the tunnel. His forehead was dewy with sweat. Was it against the law to throw up at a Tube station? He began following a woman with a large suitcase, hoping she would lead him to the railway.

They crossed a huge white concourse, Davey's stomach clenching, the woman's sensible low heels clicking. Would more vodka settle his nausea? The phrase *hair of the dog* floated across his mind, but the thought of hairy dogs – stinking and drooling and wet – made him gag. The woman with the suitcase was climbing some steps now. Where was she going?

Clinging to the rail for support, he broke through the surface to open air.

Another blink, the smell of diesel, everyone with suitcases, whistles shrieking like birds. Was this the train station? A giant board filled with letters and numbers. Just when he'd got a fix on them, the display refreshed and he had to start all over again. Fast-food smells coiled around his nostrils. Gulping desperately, he found the gents, scrabbling in his pocket for change to get through the turnstile.

The steel toilet bowl looked dirtier than ceramic, even though it was probably more hygienic. The vodka tasted even worse coming back up than it had done going down.

By the basins, he took another deep swig from the bottle to cleanse his palate, aware of the basic stupidity of the action, but reluctant to disobey the stern signs over the taps: NOT DRINKING WATER.

"Where are you travelling to?"

A ticket-selling woman behind a glass screen, her voice coming to him via an intercom. There was a slight delay between the movements of her mouth and the arrival of the words.

Buy ticket. Get on train. Run.

"Cornwall," said Davey.

"Which station?"

"W-w-w—" His stammer loving the vodka. Was this why he'd never really liked to drink? "Which ones are there?"

"Information centre's over there," she said wearily. "Come back when you've chosen."

Davey found a touch-screen kiosk, but you could only operate it if you already knew where you wanted to go. Behind him, a woman sighed and said loudly, "You can't work it because you're *drunk*—" and Davey, ashamed, slunk away to a row of chairs. The carpet's pattern looked like germs swarming. He wondered if he was going to be sick again.

After a few minutes, the man next to him left. On his chair was a tourist leaflet.

A spreading ripple of movement and rearrangement, everyone sitting up, paying attention. Davey opened his eyes. Strangers opposite him; stranger beside him. Wide glass windows. The sensation of speed. He was on a train. Which train? A huge ogre squeezing his way towards him.

"Tickets, please." The guard was enormously tall and fat, barely able to fit between the seats. Why had he chosen a job he was so obviously not designed for? Or had he been thin when he got it, then gradually grown into his present size?

"Ticket," repeated the ogre, holding out his hand. Davey groped desperately back through the blankness of sleep. Did he have a ticket? Could he have got on the train without one? He remembered the ticket office, he remembered queueing, he remembered not knowing where he wanted to go. He found his wallet; there was a lot less money in it than he remembered. The other passengers watched with interest.

Panicking now, Davey began to rummage through his rucksack. On the very top was a bottle of Glenfiddich whisky, half empty. Had he drunk that? He remembered vodka, not whisky. Then something flickered in his brain, just a couple of neurons mindlessly firing up, and he reached into his jacket pocket and found a rectangle of cardboard.

Together, they inspected it dubiously.

"Railcard," said the guard at last.

Davey rummaged some more, found a holder with a laminated card. He held it out and waited miserably for the guard to pronounce his fate. The guard looked at it for a long time.

"So you're old enough to be drinking," he said. "I was going to confiscate that bottle, son. If you give me any trouble, I'll have you put off the train."

"Okay," Davey agreed meekly.

The guard was looking at the bruises.

"Change at Truro."

The carriage contained nothing but staring eyes. Davey slumped down into his jacket. Outside, the world unspooled like a roll of film.

"Where are you headed?"

The woman next to him was speaking. Davey, head reeling from the inch of Glenfiddich he'd gulped down in the toilet, tried to focus on his ticket. Where *was* he going? Was this still the train with the fat guard? Alcohol had turned his memory into a swamp; no clues on the surface, hideous monsters lurking below.

You've made a complete mess of your life.

It's for your own good.

I'm trying to help you.

He shivered, and stared downwards. The letters on his ticket flickered and danced and refused to turn into words.

"Can I see?" She took his ticket from him. "You need to change at the next station."

"Thank you."

"No problem."

He studied her in shy glimpses. She reminded him of Giles's mother. Small and soft, fair wispy hair. The train was slowing.

"Okay," she said briskly. "This is me. And you. Up you get." She chivvied him out of his seat, handed him his ticket, saw him off the train.

"Thanks," he mumbled again, not daring to meet her eyes. He was terrified of needing help or asking for anything. Since he was three years old, *getting in the way* had been the unforgiveable crime.

"I've got a son your age," she said vaguely, and he stared at her in astonishment.

"Are you Giles's mum?" he called out as she disappeared across the platform; but she was already gone.

A sudden jerking stop, a sign right outside the window. Another platform to negotiate. His rucksack caught in the closing doors. The stillness of the ground was too much, and he was painfully, shamefully sick in a bin. He could hear the sound of judgement being passed, and blood singing in his ears. As he straightened up, he heard seagulls.

He stood in a steep street, a finger of tarmac leading straight down to the quayside. There were no barriers. How good would it feel to ride a skateboard down, down, down and off into the oily water? Did he have a skateboard?

He rummaged hopefully in the rucksack, but was distracted by the Glenfiddich. His mouth tasted like a drained pond. As he unscrewed the cap, he suddenly remembered the terror of stealing it, less than twelve hours ago.

On the other side of the harbour, a rose-coloured house stood by itself. In a high window, a tiny light hung like a red star.

A worm of memory wriggled at the back of his sodden brain.

"Steady there," said a man, helping Davey aboard the boat. Dazed and mystified, whisky swimming in his blood, Davey sat down on an iron park bench screwed tight to the wooden deck.

Where was he going now? On the quay was a shelter with walls of cool, cream-coloured concrete. He would have liked to rest his hot cheek against the wall and close his eyes, but instead he was on a rickety ferry that smelled of diesel fumes and sweaty humanity, going - somewhere. No one else shared his bench. Did he now look so wild and unkempt that nobody dared sit next to him?

He realised he was starving, and looked in his rucksack again. Why on earth had he ignored the contents of the fridge and cupboards, but packed six pairs of black socks, a battered photograph album, a stolen newspaper and *Alice in Wonderland*? How could that have seemed like a good idea?

You're a total fuck-up from start to finish.
I don't know why I even bother any more.

The seagulls sounded like crying children. He was crying too, no tears, just a contortion of his face and a keening sound that escaped in gulps and bursts. The sea spray had the approximate taste of tears but with more complex afternotes, like a good wine.

The boat sat alarmingly low in the water. Was it safe? Were there people who checked these things? The man in the wheelhouse smoked a cigarette and stared across the water. His expression reminded Davey of long-distance lorry drivers at service stations; a professional surrounded by amateurs, inhabiting a different world.

The bump and scrape of wood against stone, ropes thrown and tied up. The same man who had helped him onto the boat now helped him off again. Davey marvelled at the un-self-conscious way he touched Davey's hand and elbow. At school, physical contact was governed by unbreakable rules. Shoulders and upper arms were all right, as long as you slapped hard. Legs were for kicking. Heads were for capturing in a headlock and thumping. Penises, bizarrely, were acceptable, in certain situations. Hands and forearms were too close to holding hands, therefore a shortcut to social death. He tried to remember the last time he'd been touched gently by someone who wasn't his mother, and remembered a nurse bandaging his arm one night in casualty. "How did this happen?" she'd asked him, and when he'd stammered out something about a broken glass, she'd smiled cynically and shaken her head. He still had a jagged, silvery line to remind him.

He was exhausted, but something in him was forcing him on. He climbed a steep, narrow street – barely wide enough for a single car – and opened the whisky bottle, now nearly empty. A woman walking her dog glanced at him in disgust. He tried to apologise, but his mouth was too dry. The double yellow lines were like those on the floor of the hospital, guiding bewildered patients around the labyrinth.

I've got to get up high.

He was clammy with sweat and his head and his legs were agony. The sun had filled the harbour with molten gold. He could smell himself, a vile blend of vomit, sweat and alcohol; but he could also smell the coconut of the gorse bushes.

Stumbling into the hedge, his hand slipped between the greenery and found granite. It was a dry stone wall, covered with plants. How long did that even take to happen? He'd seen dry stone walls in Yorkshire; the most they could manage was a bit of lichen, which the Geography master had told them grew by about one centimetre a century. The wall they'd crouched behind to smoke was six hundred years old. Dreamily, he dug his fingers into the wall and began to climb.

At the top was another gorse bush. He flung himself recklessly over, relying on his clothes to protect him, getting scratched as he tumbled down the other side. Then he was behind the wall, looking across a vast expanse of scrubby moorland towards a pink-walled house that stood alone on a ridge. His head cleared and he thought, *Yes! That's where I was going, that house, that light—*

He was desperately thirsty. He hadn't pissed for hours, he wasn't sure if he even could, every drop of water had been leached out of him. If he died right now, he wouldn't rot, he'd desiccate, just a sack of leather with clothes on. Stopping to rest, he put his hand down on a sheep's skull. It was oddly beautiful, clean and white, the huge ridged yellow teeth fallen from the sockets. He held it for a while, then put it carefully in his rucksack.

Instead of getting closer, the house merely got bigger, disclosing a whole private landscape surrounding it. He thought of the word *grounds*, and then the word *acres*. The sun was almost out of the picture now, and his body had achieved the clever but uncomfortable trick of being both sweaty and freezing. He wondered what else was out here with him in the twilight, and made his feet move faster.

Surrounding the rosy house was a rosy wall. It was high and smooth, and even if he wasn't starving, dehydrated and drunk, he'd never climb it. Still, it almost felt like enough, to have got this far, to have made this strange, difficult journey to another place, another world, another life. Keeping his hand against it, he began to skirt the perimeter of the grounds.

Why had it been built so high and so strong when the house was already so isolated? Periodically, the house hid behind trees, but the wall was his faithful companion, guiding him onwards and onwards. The dew began to settle, and he knelt and licked unashamedly at a clump of grass.

Then he was suddenly clinging to a tall pillar. Its identical twin was perhaps twenty feet away. Between them, a gravel driveway shot through with primroses led to a wide wooden door with a deep, tiled porch before it.

Oh, thought Davey, blinking. *Oh. Yes. That's what, that's where I was going, that's exactly where I was thinking of - my God, I made it, I actually made it—*

He journeyed up the driveway on his hands and knees, barely conscious of the stones bruising his hands. His entire self was focused on the doorway, which he thought perhaps he had seen in a book, or a dream, or a photograph; it looked welcoming and familiar, planted long ago in a secret part of his heart, and waiting for all of the nineteen years of his life for him to arrive.

The porch floor was inlaid with black-and-white tiles in a diamond pattern. He lay down with his head on his rucksack and ran his fingers over them. He didn't want to knock on the door and present whoever lived here with his stinking, drink-sodden, disgusting self, but to his weary bewilderment the door was moving, light was spilling out, and someone with cool hands was kneeling beside him and touching his face gently.

"Good Lord," said a woman's voice from somewhere above

him. He tried to focus, and saw a pale face with a generous mouth, large brown eyes and soft, mousy brown hair looking down at him. "Where did you come from? And what happened to you?" Davey tried to open his mouth to explain. "No, shush, it's okay. You're safe. Let's get you inside."

"Who is it?" asked a girl's voice from somewhere beyond the doorway.

"No idea. Can you stand up, sweetheart?" Davey tried, but the strength was gone from his legs. "Not to worry. Priss, can you get Tom, please? I need some help."

The shadow of someone else looming over him, a brief, interested pause, then footsteps passed by, crunched on the gravel, receded. Davey closed his eyes and abandoned himself to the bliss of that hand on his forehead, not stroking, not moving, just lightly resting there, like a kiss or a promise; like a balm or a blessing.

"What's going on?" A man's voice, anxious, ready for a fight.

"It's fine, Tom, no need to panic. We just, well, we seem to have this boy."

"What boy? Who is *that?*"

"Let's just get him in, shall we?"

"Well, if you're sure—"

The hand left his forehead, and then someone who smelled of fresh air and wood shavings gathered him up in his arms, staggering a little as he stood up.

"Are you going to make Tom bring him in the *house?*" A girl's voice, Liverpudlian and incredulous.

"Why not?"

"He could be fuckin' anybody."

"Obviously he's *somebody.* But you can't just leave people out on doorsteps, it's not fair."

"Well, put him in the outhouse at least! He might be a psycho or a junkie or—"

"Shush, Priss." The voice sounded amused.

"You're too good to be true, you are."

"Be nice," the man's voice commanded.

"I don't need to be nice. You and Kate have got *nice* covered. I'm bein' fuckin' sensible."

"God always takes care of drunks and little children," said the woman. "Stop being horrible and bring up a jug of water. Can you hear me, I wonder, whoever you are? Don't worry. You're safe now."